THE PILLAR OF DOMINANCE

BY

VALYA BOUTENKO

COVER ILLUATRATION BY JONAS AKERLUND

Printed in the U.S.A
First edition, March 2016

At Tree Castle Books we hope to produce books that will warm the hearts of our
readers, and spark thier imaginations.

CONTENTS

PART ONE

ONE
Accepted - 1

TWO
The Girl at the Market - 6

THREE
The Witch of Apple Grove - 11

FOUR
The Tournament - 17

FIVE
The Last and Final Prophecy - 37

SIX
Aleafia's Request - 43

SEVEN
The Pillar of Dominance - 48

PART TWO

ONE
The Love Letter - 60

TWO
Salvador the Hero - 69

THREE
The Peculiar Delusions of Patient #338 - 86

FOUR
The Stranger - 94

FIVE
Oatmeal - 100

SIX
Crolackrolite - 105

SEVEN
The First Lesson - 110

EIGHT
Windore - 119

NINE
Sparks - 125

TEN
Session Number 4 - 129

ELEVEN
A Meeting of Wanderers - 137

TWELVE
The Map - 143

THIRTEEN
Wooffen's Curse - 158

FOURTEEN
Augden City - 162

FIFTEEN
Captured - 167

SIXTEEN
The Brute - 177

SEVENTEEN
Inside the Fortress - 182

EIGHTEEN
Escape from Augend City - 200

NINETEEN
Battle in the Clearing - 222

TWENTY
Phantom in the Woods - 234

TWENTY ONE
Warren's Life - 236

TWENTY TWO
Wolf - 242

TWENTEY THREE
The Sacrifice - 248

TWENTY FOUR
Return of the Twin Princes - 266

TWENTY FIVE
On the Road Again - 269

TWENTY SIX
The Unexpected Visitor - 277

About the Author - 286

THE PILLAR OF DOMINANCE

BY

VALYA BOUTENKO

TREE CASTLE BOOKS

PART ONE - ACCEPTED

It was a pleasant summer morning. A drowsy breeze wound gently through the air, in no hurry at all to get where it was going. An old man was busy tending his rose garden, his white hair gleaming like snow against his faded purple robes. The garden surrounded a small, three-story mansion, the front of which was lined with several rows of arching windows. Winking in the sunlight, the diamond-shaped windowpanes showed off their beveled edges. A swimming pool fed by a deep freshwater spring, shimmered in a light blue spot to one side of the building, and the garden's blooming flowers, fruit trees, and greenery perfumed the air with their sweet aromas.

A post man pausing on the outside of the stout rout iron fence that lined the perimeter of the castle scowled, as he glanced though a thick pack of envelopes in his hand. A red envelope sealed with brown wax stood out from the rest.

"You've filled that boy's head with dangerous dreams," said the postman.

"What is a head for if not to be filled with dreams?" replied the old man, and glanced at a small sundial attached to his wrist by a leather strap. The pointer on the face of the dial followed the direction of the sun without needing to be adjusted. "Any moment now…" he mumbled to himself, holding his wrist at a better angle to the light.

"But can he be entrusted with such a severe responsibility?" asked the postman, his overgrown eyebrows furrowing together to form a deep worried wrinkle on his brow.

"He is by far the most gifted student I have ever trained," said the wizard.

The postman shifted his weight uncomfortably and said, "Never mind the fate of the world, think about the boy for a moment. He has little chance to succeed, you *know* that! You are likely sending him to his death!"

The wizard's face remained neutral.

"Even if he survives," continued the postman, "he will be left with a sense of disappointment that will break his spirit and undermine his confidence for the rest of his life. Is that what you want?" The letter shook in his outstretched hand. "Pull him out of the competition before it is too late!"

"How little you know of the human spirit," began the old wizard, taking the scarlet envelope.

"He is just too young and inexperienced to qualify," argued the postman, his hand moving quickly down in a sharp chopping motion as if to repudiate the wizards argument once and for all.

"You underestimate him," said the wizard.

At this moment, a screaming young man in pale blue striped pajamas was powerfully projected out of a third story window and hurled into the swimming pool with a giant splash. The postman and the wizard followed the flying youth with their eyes, their noses drawing two identical arches in the air.

"The launch bed gets him up on time every morning without fail," explained the wizard with a grin.

"Your student grows more arrogant each day," said the mailman, determined to persuade the old wizard. "And you are doing nothing to address this. When he is finally humbled, it will be at a grave price indeed."

"You mistake confidence for arrogance," said the wizard. "True, Wendell is aware of his talents, and that he shows great promise, but his ambition is not the enemy, for without it, where would he find the motivation to accomplish all the great things he must do?"

"Ambition becomes an enemy when it oversteps integrity," challenged the mailman.

"I have chosen Wendell as the least likely young person to be corrupted by his developing powers," explained the wizard. "Besides, who is to say that denying ourselves the fulfillment of our most benevolent dreams is not overstepping integrity in itself?" He tugged at his beard and looked with lively hazel eyes at his worried companion.

The corners of his mouth slumping in a frown, the postman griped, "I am concerned that you do not see the dangers we face if he does not succeed."

"Failure is but a wise old teacher, strict and compelling, not a hungry tiger lurking in the bushes."

"And what will we do if he should fail?"

Glancing at the red envelope in his hand, the old man said, "a warrior from another region will go in his place, it wont be the end of the world."

"It just might be," growled the postman. "Though I cannot bring myself to approve of Wendell, I shudder to think what could happen should they send someone else in his place. A stranger on the journey— it is unthinkable, even worse than your untrained-hotheaded-teenage-halfwit."

"I quite agree," said the wizard. He opened the letter and broke into a smile as his eyes moved across the lines.

"Before it is too late," said the postman, fidgeting anxiously, "I urge you to choose another student, someone older and more qualified."

"I have no other students," the wizard responded, still engrossed in the letter. "Wendell is the last of his kind."

The postman swallowed hard and glaring at the wizard asked, "How many years of training does he have?"

"Four," said the wizard.

"Four!?" the postman exclaimed, "I thought ten was the minimum required before he can wear the robes."

"I believe he is ready," replied the wizard, "besides, there wasn't time for the traditional schooling."

"We've got to do *something*, if you let him go like this…" The postman exhaled sharply, frustrated with the old man's lack of concern. "Because you are my friend, I'm warning you, little good will come of this."

"A little good is better than none at all," smiled the wizard.

The postman huffed, and turned to leave.

"Wait, take some roses before you go," said the wizard, handing him a bundle of brilliant red blooms, "They smell sweeter than honey."

The postman accepted the gift reluctantly.

At that moment a soaking wet youth exploded from the ancient oak door of the castle and raced barefoot down the steps at breakneck speed. His tan skin and sun-streaked hair suggested a love of the outdoors. A strong jaw line indicated an inherent stubbornness. Although disheveled, he was a handsome young man, with a bright open face and a cleft in one cheek that had formed from frequent smiling. He looked upon the world with an uncommon candor, being too optimistic to believe in hierarchy, and too naive to know shyness.

As the youth ran down the path, the round paper lanterns tastefully hung on either side, burst into flames as he passed, leaving singed skeletons in their place.

"Master Loriander, the letter!" shouted the youth breathlessly, "What does it say?"

"Why don't you find out for yourself?" suggested the old man, handing him the letter.

The boy tore it from his master's hand and eagerly soaked up the text with his eyes. One of his eyes was brown, and the other blue.

"I'm in," he whispered and glanced up at his teacher. "I'm in!" he yelled, punching the sky with his fist. In his other hand, the letter burst into flames, and for a moment, the three of them watched the ashes drift away in the breeze.

"Wendell, you must learn to control your powers," said the old wizard disapprovingly.

Too overwhelmed by the news, the boy didn't seem to hear him.

The postman aggressively dropped his hand to his side in frustration, turning the bouquet of roses upside down, and letting the flowers smash against his thigh. Several battered petals tore free and fell to the ground leaving crimson spots on the stone path beneath him. "I shall see you at the tournament," he said unhappily and turned to leave.

"See you then," called the wizard after him politely.

"This is the happiest day of my life!" shouted Wendell. "I have to tell Prince Airyallen."

"No, there is no time for that, you need to study," the old wizard urged, suppressing a smile that twitched at the edge of his lips, but Wendell tore from the garden, passing the disgruntled mailman and turning onto the main street.

For a moment the old wizard felt a twinge of regret for having taken Wendell to so many of the Kings counsel meetings, and introducing him to the royal family, for although Wendell had become fast friends with the prince, it was not the young wizard's place to socialize with royalty. Even if someday Wendell would serve the prince as Loriander himself served the King, Wendell's inability to understand social boundaries could someday lead to dangers the youth could not foretell. Shaking these melancholy thoughts from his head, and remembering the remarkable news of the morning, the old wizard went back to work in his garden.

THE GIRL AT THE MARKET

Wendell sprinted through the commotion of the main street, ignoring the surprised glances of the townspeople. His wet blond hair bounced against his forehead as his legs carried him effortlessly forward through the crowd. The cobbled street was lined with vendors selling and trading goods of many kinds. There were fine ceramic dishes, weavings of silk and wool, magic infused armor and gadgets, alongside endless booths of freshly prepared foods. Delicious smells wafted through the boulevard in mouthwatering torrents. Running past a pastry table, Wendell grabbed an apple tart and without slowing his pace, took an enormous bite.

"Hey!" yelled the baker. "I know where you live, wizard scum!"

Wendell laughed and increased his speed, happily stuffing what remained of the pastry in his mouth and licking some yellow cream from his fingertips. Wendell sprinted in the direction of the castle. Glancing behind to see if he was being followed by guards, he suddenly bumped into an obstacle. With a jolt, he looked before him at a young woman whom he had nearly thrown to the ground.

"Watch out!" she said, her face hidden behind a curtain of red curls. Apples rolled on the ground in every direction. She knelt to collect them into a silver pail.

"I'm sorry, I didn't see you," mumbled Wendell apologetically as he stooped to help her. He could not recall ever noticing her at the market before. She wore a white dress that seemed light as air and gave her every movement a sense of effortlessness. Apple blossom petals were tangled magnificently in her hair. Wendell went to reach for an apple, when suddenly she tucked a lock of hair behind her ear and he caught a glimpse of her face. She was strikingly lovely, with an exquisite composition of features. Her large eyes were uncommonly bright and clear. Wendell bent down lower craning his neck trying to get a better look of her face. She remained entirely unaware of his attempts to steal a second glance at her. Picking up the last apples, she finally straightened and looked up at him for the first time. Wendell slowly mirrored her movement, paralyzed by her beauty. He handed her the only apple he was able to pick up, and she broke into a gorgeous smile.

"What is your name?" asked Wendell.

"Why do you want to know?" she responded, lifting one elegantly arched eyebrow a fraction above the other.

A group of guards charged toward them from the busy street below. The angry pastry maker was among them.

"If you do not tell me I will suffer the rest of my life seeking a name worthy of such beauty."

"Seize the thief!" yelled the baker.

The guards grabbed the boy and violently bound his hands behind his back with a length of coarse rope.

"I do not give my name to thieves and criminals," said the girl.

"You are so lovely," Wendell went on, unable to tear his eyes from the girl, "I don't even mind going to prison to have met you."

The young woman laughed softly, but the baker silenced her with a glance.

"First day at the market and already she is mixing with the wrong crowd," he grumbled, "should have left you in the orchard."

A guard shoved Wendell in the direction of the prison and the boy, complying with the unspoken command, regretfully moved as he was directed. They had moved away several paces when one of the guards grabbed Wendell by the shoulder and peered at his face.

"Hey, ain't you that wizard kid who's gonna compete in the tournament?" he asked, sizing him up with a skeptical glance.

"Yeah, why?" asked Wendell.

"You're just so young…" the guard trailed off, "…and scrawny, even for a wizard." He felt Wendell's bicep. Wendell yanked his arm away. Although quite tall for his age, Wendell indeed felt small compared to the guard, whose thick chest barely fit inside his tunic. The rope binding Wendell's wrists began to slowly untie itself behind his back.

"Not everyone was born to look like a horse," said Wendell, watching the blood rush to the guard's face. The man immediately took a swing at Wendell, just as the youth ducked between the two guards and made a wild dash for freedom. The guards leaped after him. They grabbed him before he had time to pick up any speed, firmly clasping his wrists. The enlivened rope attacked the larger guard, snaking up his leg and winding itself around his chest and throat. The guard struggled to pull it free, wrestling it off of himself. He sliced through it with a knife and the rope went limp. He threw it on the ground. The two pieces played dead for a moment, and then slowly inched away.

"Lets put the *iron* shackles on this conniving little twerp," said the large guard to his companion. Wendell was roughly handcuffed. He winced as the bracelets were tightened extra tight around his wrists. Wendell was escorted into the prison and locked inside a damp cell. The youth plunked himself down on a pile of rotting straw in the corner and put his hands behind his head. Looking up at the dirty ceiling, all he could see was the face of the girl at the market. When he pictured her eyes, he felt a tearing sensation in his chest that made it difficult to breathe. There was something so sincere, so intense about her. He relived the moment she had first looked up at him again and again, wanting to drown in that gaze of hers, and never surface.

An hour later, a prison guard notified Wendell that he had a visitor. Wendell rose and brushed himself off. Prince Airyallen hurried down the prison hallway to Wendell's cell and grabbed the bars with both hands. He was a broad shouldered youth, easily the more handsome of the two. He wore a gold and blue riding uniform. The bridge of his nose had a slight diamond shape, giving him an appearance of honor his character did not yet reflect. A head of thick raven curls gave his figure a look of nobleness that was at this point more inherited than earned.

"What, again?" groaned the prince. "Wendell, you're killing me." He smacked the palm of his hand against his forehead in a gesture of mock fatigue. "Still in your pajamas and already in prison?" he scoffed, observing Wendell's damp sleepwear. "Do you enjoy the breakfast here, or what?"

Wendell laughed. "It's hard for me to manage my appearance after so many years of being homeless on the streets."

Prince Airyallen turned to the guard. "Release him at once!" he commanded.

"Your majesty," muttered the guard with a low bow, and began nervously fumbling with his keys.

"So?" asked the prince, looking eagerly at Wendell.

"So?" shrugged the boy in return, unsure what he was being asked. The guard opened the gate and let Wendell out.

"Did you get the letter? What did it say?" asked the prince.

"Oh! The letter!" nodded Wendell, remembering the acceptance letter. "Yes! I'm in!" he said with renewed excitement. "I was on my way to tell you."

Overjoyed, Prince Airyallen clapped his friend on the back.

"You must win the Determination Tournament, Wendell," he said. "There's no one else I would rather have by my side on the Day of the Dominance."

Wendell beamed at him.

"How did you end up in prison anyway?" asked the prince curiously, as they made their way toward the exit. Two guards opened the double doors for them to pass through.

"I ran into a girl," said Wendell sheepishly.

"A girl?" asked Prince Airyallen with a laugh.

"You should have seen her…" Wendell trailed off, his eyes glazing over. They stepped out onto the street, leaving the thick marble columns of the prison behind them.

"I never knew you were such a lady's man," teased the prince, poking him in the ribs with his elbow.

"She was so beautiful," said Wendell numbly.

"Are you in love with her?" laughed the prince.

"Maybe," said Wendell seriously.

Prince Airyallen pushed out his lower lip and nodded, weighing the intensity of Wendell's words and rarity with which he spoke in this manner.

"So what's her name?" asked the prince with an evil smile.

"I don't know," replied Wendell, "she wouldn't tell me."

"How are you supposed to find her if you don't even know her name?" asked the Prince.

"Oh I'll find her," said Wendell. "Perhaps I will just think of the most beautiful name I have ever heard and assume it to be hers."

"Yuck," said the prince. "Romance does not suit you in the least, my friend."

They passed the pastry table and the baker shot Wendell a nasty look, obviously displeased with his quick release. Wendell snapped his fingers.

"That's right, I think she works in an apple orchard somewhere."

"How long will this postpone your training do you think?" asked prince Airyallen sarcastically.

"Not any longer than your sour attitude," said Wendell, flying up the path to his master's mansion.

The prince followed close behind. "You are the only person who can speak to me that way without being beheaded," he said with a laugh.

THE APPLE ORCHARD

Wendell was weary after a long day of training. As the date of the Determination Tournament grew nearer, his studies had become increasingly demanding. Incantations reverberated through his tired head like the flopping contents of a fisherman's net. He snuck out the side door and into the gardens. Glancing in through the window, he saw his master inside with his back to the window, resting in his rocking chair. The old man gently rocked forward and back as he smoked his pipe and poured over a thick volume. Biting his bottom lip, Wendell tiptoed from the yard.

The old wizard glanced up from his text in time to see the boy's tiptoeing reflection distorted in a glass of water before him. He snorted and went back to his book.

Delighted with his escape, Wendell rushed through town until he came upon a dirt road leading away from the center of the city. He pulled out an old map and studied the twenty-seven sites circled on the parchment before continuing. Twenty-six of the sites had already been crossed out. He climbed the steep path for a long while until it opened up onto a wide road.

In the distance, he saw an old woman in black robes gathering a barrel full of firewood. Wendell wiped the sweat from his brow with his sleeve and moved on. As he approached, he could see that the poor woman's clothes were heavily worn. He remembered all to well what it felt like to have such tattered clothes, and he felt a strong desire to help her in any way he could. The old woman's back was hunched and her steps slow with age.

"Hello," said Wendell from afar, not wanting to frighten her,

"Can I help you with that?"

The woman glanced stiffly back at him over her shoulder. She was even older than he had guessed, and her face was heavily creased with wrinkles.

"Be on your way young man. This is no place to wander," she grumbled, her voice dry and crackly like aged paper. She knelt down, struggling to pick up the leather straps of the now filled barrel.

"Please, let me help you," said Wendell, easily shouldering the heavy barrel. "Where do you want this?" he asked.

"At the top of that hill in my cottage," said the woman, indicating to a small structure not far away. She squinted one eye at Wendell, and he felt as though she could see right through him. Wendell walked in the direction of the cottage. He stepped carefully to avoid slipping on the rocky trail.

"You move like a sick cow," said the old woman following behind, "Are you ill or injured?"

"Neither, I am troubled," replied Wendell.

"Over what?" crackled the old woman.

"I am looking for a girl who works in an apple orchard."

"And?" prodded the woman sternly.

"There are twenty-seven apple orchards in the city, and I have been to nearly each one seeking her. I fear I will never find her."

Not far ahead, a squat little cottage came into view. It had cracked stucco walls and a sunken straw roof.

"There is another apple orchard over yonder," said the old woman. "Just there," she said, pointing a crooked finger toward a small cleft in the hillside, "on the sunny side of that rise lives the woman you seek."

Wendell smiled at the news, relieved to be reassured at last.

They had reached the cottage, and Wendell carefully slid the heavy barrel off of his shoulders and set it down by the narrow porch. He panted, catching his breath from the short, but strenuous trek.

The old woman hesitated. "Though I would not suggest you going there, since I can foresee that meeting her will make you terribly unhappy for the rest of your very long life."

"You have the sight?" asked Wendell with wonder.

She did not reply.

"I don't care what the future holds, I must see her again."

"Very well," said the old woman darkly.

"Thank you," said Wendell, bowing slightly in gratitude for the guidance. He turned toward the direction she had indicated and continued on his way. As he departed, the old woman sighed heavily behind him.

Wendell soon discovered a trail leading in the direction he was aimed and he quickened his pace in the fading light. He soon came upon a small valley tucked into the side of the hill. It was nearly invisible from down below. The hill seemed to sink slightly in this one area just enough to contain a small apple orchard. Wendell couldn't believe his eyes. The trees before him were mature but had remained small in size and were so short they barely went past his shoulders. Apples hung densely from the slender branches. The fragrant fruits were rather small, but perfectly shaped with blushing rosy sides. Ever in bloom, and ever bearing, the dwarf orchard was breathtaking to behold. The setting sun drenched the valley in golden light. There, in the midst of the trees was the girl from the marketplace. She was lovely as ever. Her long red hair was pulled back into a loose bun at the back of her neck. The hem of her violet dress teased in the wind. Sensing his eyes, she turned and looked at him.

"Wendell," she called, her voice like music. She moved toward him, fighting back a smile. He met her halfway.

"You found me," she said.

"How do you know who I am?" asked Wendell.

"You are the wizard boy who steals my father's apple tarts at the market."

"Your father is the baker?" exclaimed Wendell.

She laughed, and tossed him an apple. Catching it, Wendell broke the apple into two pieces and bit into one of the halves with a loud crunch. He closed his eyes, savoring the delicious flavor.

"This explains why I only steal tarts from your father," he exclaimed, before taking another bite.

"Apples are ancient things," said the girl, thoughtfully gazing into her pail where several apples lay glowing brightly, reflected in silver. "They are not true to seed, meaning that every apple seed will grow a different kind of apple. Most apples grown from seed taste rather sour and bitter, but every once in a great while there is a rare exception. The variety you are eating this evening grew from an accidental seedling one thousand years ago."

"If you believe in accidents," interjected Wendell as they strolled slowly through the orchard.

"The flavor of this apple was discovered by a hungry beggar," she went on, "and was soon renowned as the best apple in all the land. But an apple tree only lives for fifty years. In order to preserve this one variety, gardeners carefully took cuttings from the original tree and grafted them onto other trees, thereby cloning the original apple tree and prolonging its life."

Wendell listened with interest, immensely enjoying the sound of her voice.

"It is for this reason," she continued, "that you are eating an apple tonight that is identical to the very first of its kind, and was in fact grown by a branch of the very same tree that was discovered one thousand years ago."

"What would If gardeners were to stop grafting apple trees?" asked Wendell.

"Within fifty years, all varieties of apples known to man would be lost forever," she answered.

"That would be a great loss," said Wendell.

She looked at him from beneath long curving eyelashes.

"Tell me, why have you come?" she asked

"I had to learn your name," he replied.

"If I tell you, will you then leave?"

"Not if you want me to stay."

She paused contemplating his reply. He came around to face her.

"So what is your name?"

"Is it true you will compete in the tournament?" she asked, changing the subject, and moving around him.

"It is."

"Are you the only wizard in the competition?" She moved ahead without turning around.

"Yes," said Wendell taking several quick steps to catch up to her.

"Are you the youngest member as well?" she asked.

"I am, although there is a warrior from the Gator region who is only a couple of years older than me. Wendell made a face. "Are you worried about me? I'm eighteen, and that's plenty old enough," he said, not without some pride.

"Some people don't believe you are ready."

Wendell waved her statement away. "Let them say what they want." He stopped and she also paused beside him. "I could win it you know," he hesitated and then added, "I could win it for you." He blushed slightly with these words.

"I want you to lose it for me," she said mischievously.

"Consider it lost then," said Wendell casually.

"You would lose it for me?"

"I would do anything for you."

She broke into a smile.

"I think you might have a bit of a crush," she teased.

"So what if I do?" replied Wendell, looking deeply into her eyes and taking a step closer to her.

She laughed and moved away.

"Wendell, help me pick some apples."

Wendell plucked an apple and immediately took a bite out of it.

"How can you resist eating these?" he asked.

"I can't," she said biting into one as well. She looked at him through the branches of a short tree between them with clear, intense eyes.

"I can get you a seat in the king's balcony for the tournament if you like," he offered.

Her lovely face was conflicted for a moment.

"Aleafia, time for supper!" called a woman's voice from across the field. The girl turned her head in the direction of a hut at the foot of the valley.

"I have to go," she said, suddenly flustered. "Oh no, I have not filled the pail!" she said sadly, casting down her eyes toward the nearly empty pail in her hands.

"Aleafia!" whispered Wendell, beaming now that at last, he had learned her name. His palms aglow, he flicked his wrist in a twisting motion. At once, apples began to spin themselves free from the branches around them. They sailed though the air landing softly into the silver pail. Aleafia breathlessly marveled at their dance, but Wendell only had eyes for her., Aleafia beamed at him and ran toward the cottage, the small pail filled with apples swinging in her hands. Wendell waited for her to glance around her shoulder one last time before heading in the direction of his own home.

THE TOURNAMENT

Wendell awoke with a start as his bed sunk several feet sharply into the floor. He rubbed the sleep from his eyes with one hand. The window panels had already moved apart on the ceiling. He hopped out of bed just in time for the launch bed to jab sharply toward the open skylights on its thick coiling springs. Wendell's stomach was in knots.

"I didn't hear a splash," called the muffled voice of Master Loriander from the kitchen below.

"There isn't going to be one," shouted Wendell back, throwing on some clothes and thundering down the stairs.

"I'm impressed—" yelled the old wizard. "Now come have breakfast," he finished quietly upon seeing Wendell appear in the doorway.

"I don't think I can stomach anything."

"How about a nutritious green salad?"

"I don't want to puke green muck in front of everyone," muttered Wendell, plopping down on a stool and sticking out his feet. His leather lace-up boots thumped down the stairs after him and began stuffing themselves aggressively onto his exposed feet. Wendell folded his arms, jerking erratically as he endured the attack. He winced as the laces tied themselves snugly around his ankles.

The old wizard observed his student for a moment.

"I have something for you," he said, handing Wendell a black velvet bag tied about with a silver ribbon.

Unaccustomed to gifts, Wendell briefly held the bag in both hands as if the package itself was precious enough. Wendell carefully loosened the ribbon and peered inside.

"They are beautiful!" he exclaimed, pulling out a set of new purple robes.

"Today, you are a wizard," said Master Loriander. "Put on these garments and wear them proudly. As the last of our kind, you are burdened with more worldly problems than any one man should have to carry. Yet this is your destiny. Let the colors of these robes signify that you are a friend to all those who are in need of help, and a foe to those whose actions detriment this world."

"Thank you master," said Wendell, placing one hand over his heart and bowing slightly.

"Come now, we have a tournament to win," said the old wizard, briskly heading to the door.

Wendell threw on his new robes right over his clothes and followed his master. The old man walked out onto the street and raised his hand. One of the passing carriages stopped immediately. The carriage was drawn by two impressively large reptiles. The creatures had darting uncompassionate eyes, with splotchy yellow irises expanding and contracting around inky slivers for pupils. Their elongated leathery snouts were filled with several rows of gleaming teeth. They snapped their jaws, briefly revealing the soft meaty insides of their giant mouths. Wendell shuddered. It was difficult for him to avoid thinking about ending up in one of those mouths some day. He climbed into the open coach and took a seat opposite his master. It was a sleek wooden carriage with comfortable cushioned seats. Each reptile was strapped into a thick emerald-studded, leather harness that held a rider and was attached to the coach by a strong timber dowel. Their riders were dressed in black and green close-fitting robes. Watching the gator riders proudly astride their trained reptiles had always instilled a deep sense of respect in Wendell. The reptiles ran in a sweeping serpentine pattern, the tips of their scaly tails completing each motion as every step surged through their bodies like a wave of energy. The riders easily contained the wild power of their reptiles by pulling on long silver reins made from unbreakable steel. Gator riders, or "Gators" as they eventually came to be known, were famous not only for taming the most unruly of beasts, but also designing a deadly style of evasive combat for which there was no match within the seven regions. It was said that facing a Gator in combat was like fighting a ghost.

The carriage approached the castle. Seven sandstone towers reached into the sky before them. Ivy climbed the smooth walls and archways like living green flames. Hundreds of aquamarine windows gleamed in the morning light and blue flags flapped festively in the wind. An arena large enough to seat several thousand people had been constructed for the tournament in the middle of the main square.

As his master thanked and paid the Gators, Wendell leapt from the carriage, marveling at the colossal arena. Wendell thought of the battle ahead. He felt nervous and clenched his hands into fists to keep them from trembling.

"Come along, Wendell," said the old wizard.

Wendell followed his master through the entrance and down a curving side hallway. As his eyes adjusted to the dim light, Wendell could make out rooms built beneath the scaffolding of the arena. The old wizard led him down the corridor until he came to a thick metal door with a rusty knocker attached to its dull surface. His master paused, putting his hand on Wendell's shoulder and bending down slightly toward his pupil.

"From this point on, you must go on alone." He spoke softly to ensure that only Wendell could hear. "I cannot help you once you are in the arena. Your training is all you have to rely on. I believe that it will be enough."

Wendell nodded solemnly. "You have already made me proud by coming this far," whispered his master, "Try not to get killed, and don't use more fire than you can put out. I will find you when it is over." With these final words the old wizard used the knocker to rap loudly on the door.

"Who goes there?" asked a gruff voice from within.

"It is I, Master Loriander Ragendar. I bring you the last wizard of the Amethyst Era, the descendent of Delominar the Great to compete in the challenge."

The door opened a crack, and a stout guard with a bulbous nose peeked his head out. He eyed Wendell up and down suspiciously. "Send 'em in," he rasped, pushing the door open.

With a final squeeze on the shoulder, the old wizard ushered his student through the entrance. Wendell stepped through. The guard quickly closed the door behind him and turned the lock.

"It's not like the olden days," he muttered, "In these passive times, this old beauty doesn't get used like she did in the olden days." He touched the rusty wall of the building lovingly.

Wendell looked around. He was in a cluttered dusty room. Milky framed mirrors lined the walls. Moth-eaten furniture was strewn illogically throughout the space. The rumpled floorboards, and the blackened candle chandelier, were but the vague suggestions of a once glamorous interior. Six other warriors inhabited the tight room, one from every region. Several of them glanced up as Wendell entered the room. There was the Gator in his early twenties sitting on the dressing table with his legs hanging off the end and his arms folded. He had raven-black hair, sharp green eyes, and was clad in the traditional black and green silk robes of his region. In the gator tradition, he went into battle unarmed, carrying only a small silver shield and a thin dagger attached to his boot.

Next to the Gator stood a large grizzly man leaning against the wall. He had a thick blond beard and blue eyes. The muscles on his shoulders rippled in thick ropes when he moved. The sheathed sword at his side revealed that he was a swordsman from the Coalsmith region. The blond man conversed quietly with a Hexitore chemist, who was a sturdy man of forty with a thick belt of potions attached to his waist. The many bottles tinkled and chimed as they clicked together, some of them bubbling or foaming. The chemist's flowing yellow robes gleamed against his dark skin.   A huge Stealthalore Phelenium from the Diamondell region paced back and forth across the room. The cat-like creature was massive, and it sported a shaggy grey coat and long flowing whiskers. The Phelenium's long fur echoed the smooth motions of his enormous body. His chest was covered in spiked armor that seamlessly moved with his silent prowling movements. His blue irises pulsed, expanding and contracting rapidly as he looked about with a hypnotic gaze.

A warrior dressed in the woodsy style of the Finklefoot region practiced his aim in the corner of the room on an old dress manikin, which had a line of arrows running down its midline. The Finklefoot warrior was slender and agile in his brown leather uniform. One of his hands was engulfed by an impressively crafted glove. It was made out of a thin metal, and yet was flexible allowing for the full motion of his armored hand with which he handled his falcon. The bird itself sat on a nearby coat hanger intently following its master's every move with tiny jerking motions of its head.

The fighter from the Citrulene region sat in a faded plushy chair deep in meditation. His eyes were rolled back into his head revealing the whites of his eyeballs as he mumbled a monotone chant. An extra eye on his forehead indicated the highest possible rank of priesthood. The simple turquoise robes draped around him were tied at his waist by a red tasseled belt holding a whip that wrapped around him in several tight loops.

Wendell gaped at the meditating monk, transfixed by his peculiarity, when suddenly, the third eye on the man's forehead snapped wide open and stared back at him. Wendell jumped.

"It's okay," laughed the Gator, "He cannot see you, that eye can only perceive what is beyond the material."

Slightly shaken, Wendell leaned against the dresser next to the Gator.

"Nervous yet?" asked the green-eyed man with a smile.

"About what?" asked Wendell weakly, and they both burst out laughing.

"My name is Galator," said the Gator. Wendell introduced himself in return, briefly clasping forearms with the young warrior. "To die in battle is considered the highest honor in the Gator region," said Galator, "I am honored to face death alongside you, wizard." His eyes shone brightly with an intense alertness.

Although their years were similar, Wendell knew Galator had much more experience and training, yet he was surprised that the Gator lacked any hint or inflection of superiority in his tone. Wendell was grateful for this, and felt inspired by the steady courage of his new friend.

Trumpets blared outside announcing the arrival of the king.

"Spectators and citizens," boomed the King's regal voice from up above the rafters, "We welcome you to the first Determination Tournament in all of Windifera. The winner of the tournament will accompany my son, Prince Airyallen Amadeus Miramar, of the Sapphire Kingdom on the perilous journey to the Pillar of Dominance as was decided by the high council of the Seven regions." The audience cheered. "As you well know," continued the King, "the Blue Sapphire era soon comes to a close. She has been named the most peaceful time in our history, and shall therefore be repeated for another millennium!"

The crowd hooted and cheered. "Let the tournament begin!" called out the King, and the crowd went wild with applause. Drummers thumped an anticipatory march on their instruments.

Down below, the stout guard eagerly pressed his ear to the door. "It's time!" he hissed, his eyes bulging with excitement. He unlocked the door and pulled it open. Shocked that everything was happening so fast, Wendell followed the other warriors out of the waiting room.

One by one the contestants were announced and welcomed into the arena. As each of them jogged into the ring, they showed off one of their skills.

"Beastador Willdenwild, of the Colesmith region," called out the voice of an announcer.

A giant stone was wheeled into the arena. Six guards with difficulty shoved the granite block off their cart. Beastador drew his sword and ran into the ring toward the stone. With a yell, he struck the block, splitting it into two even halves. Sparks bounced off his glowing blade as the stone halves fell to either side of him. The audience erupted in a roar of approval.

"Kaolin Hopindiffer, a chemist from the Hexitore region," shouted the announcer.

Kaolin Hopindiffer vanished himself momentarily in a blast of yellow smoke before reappearing as two copies of himself and bowing to the raving crowd.

On his turn, Theodor Madderlin of the Finklefoot region threw his falcon in the air. The bird soared into the sky and dropped an apple. Theodor shot an arrow toward a target on the opposite side of the arena and skewered the apple to the heart of the center mark.

Galator the Gator preformed an impressive series of acrobatics, and the giant cat bellowed a glass-shattering roar, shredding the ground with its mighty paws. The Citrulene Monk used his whip to stir a small tornado into life and whirled it around the dusty arena to the delight of the spectators.

Wendell was last. As he entered the stadium, he was momentarily blinded by the brightness of daylight. Most of the audience cheered, but there were patches of people who booed. Not everyone believed he was worthy of representing his region. Wendell moved toward the center, tripping over his purple robes. The densely filled arena seemed to spin around him. He felt disoriented. The crowd grew quieter, sensing his confusion. He searched wildly for Aleafia. At last he found her seated in the King's balcony next to the prince. Wendell was intensely glad to see her. Overwhelmed that she had come, he felt himself losing control of his powers. There was a whistling sound, and suddenly, an explosion of fireworks exploded above him. He punched his fist into the sky, and more fireworks thundered into life, trailing downwards in golden shimmering showers that shone brightly even in the light of day. The audience sighed. Aleafia reached out and grabbed one of the glowing embers. Wendell silently willed it to never burn out. Smiling, Aleafia attached it to her necklace, unburned by the magic fire.

"On my mark!" commanded the King. The contestants gathered in the center of the ring with their backs to each other.

"Open the gates!" ordered the King.

One giant gate was rolled open before every contestant. An army of fifty men charged at Beastador Willdenwild, armed with bows, blades, and spears. Snakes oozed out of the pit before Kaolin Hopindiffer, the Hexitor Chemist, one of them the length of a small tree and twice the thickness of a man. Three trolls and a Cyclops lunged toward the monk, who pulled his whip from his belt and held it at the ready. A bone-chilling howl pierced the air, and a werewolf bolted out of the gate before the giant cat of Diamondell. Theodor Madderlin threw his falcon into the sky, pelting a squad of green-skinned, slimy goblins with a torrent of arrows. Half a dozen hungry reptiles raced toward Galator the Gator. The young man held his ground anticipating the attack.

Wendell's gate remained vacant. Quickly surveying the chaos around him, Wendell peered again into the depths of the murky chamber before him.

"Watch out!" cried Galator, and threw his shield at an angle toward Wendell's chest. It spun through the air just in time to catch an arrow aimed at Wendell's heart. Wendell searched the field for the source of the stray arrow, but in the mill of combat it was impossible to tell where it had come from. The silver disk hit the ground, Wendell rolled toward it. Grabbing it, he yanked out the arrow and threw the shield back to his friend.

Galator seized it just in time to block the first set of teeth snapping at his shoulder. In one nimble movement the young Gator flipped himself astride one of the massive reptiles surrounding him. The beast bucked and thrashed beneath him, twisting its head up and back snapping at its rider. The remaining reptiles drew closer, each seeking an angle at which to tear off a better piece of the Gator Rider.

Wendell clenched the arrow in his fist. Shaken by his near death experience, he strained his eyes at the darkness within his gate. Something large pawed the ground and snorted in the shadows, when suddenly, a rhinosaur pounded from its hideout. Roughly the size of a small building, the muscular beast had a gray leathery hide with streaks of blue and yellow across its back. Its three-toed hooves showed off impressive hooked talons in the front. Powerful jaws hid a mouthful of dagger-like teeth. It moved with the lumbering motion of a giant boulder, unstoppably plowing ahead. Bellowing a deep nasally scream, it ran at Wendell with its head bent downwards. In this position, all seven of the giant horns growing down the length of its nose were pointed toward Wendell.

Wendell outstretched one arm and pulled the other one back, pinching the arrow between his index and middle fingers. Concentrating his energy into his hands, he began manifesting a curved longbow. The grooves between his clenched fingers radiated golden light-rays as the weapon unfolded, expanding and lengthening from where his hand held the invisible handle. The rhinosaur raced toward the boy, its blood-red eyes unblinking and focused on its victim. It was seconds away from impact. Before his bow was fully formed, Wendell took aim. The moment he felt the wood solidify, he pulled back the string and released.

The arrow was true, zipping effortlessly toward its mark. It smashed against the monster's forehead, splintering into a hundred pieces. The rhinosaur barreled on without even flinching. The young wizard lunged to the side and tumbled away, barely missing the creature's terrible piercing horns and stomping feet. The creature thumped past him, unable to stop its own heavy momentum. It slowed, preparing to turn around. Keeping the rhinosaur in his line of sight Wendell quickly surveyed the arena.

Unconscious men lay strewn about in a circular pattern around Beastador Willdenwild. A platoon of at least fifteen new soldiers fell on him all together, finally forcing him down on one knee. With a roar, he rose to standing again, projecting all of them off at once.

The monk had his whip wrapped around the neck of the Cyclops, and was making the trolls dizzy darting between them while tugging the Cyclops to the ground. The giant cat and werewolf were locked in brutal combat, their bodies intertwined as they wrestled in the dirt. Theodor Madderlin fenced off the goblins with a thin, spear-like blade while his falcon retrieved his spent arrows, pulling them from the limbs of wounded goblins. Covered in dust, Galator rolled with the reptile as it struggled to free itself from his grasp.

Eight different Kaolin Hopindiffers hacked at the twisting snakes at their feet with identical gleaming swords, when all of a sudden, seven of them vanished like smoke, leaving only one. The giant serpent had coiled itself around the remaining Kaolin Hopindiffer, squeezing the life from the yellow-robed man. His belt of potions had been crushed by the thick rings of the snake's body and the multi-colored liquids spilled over the glossy black scales of the serpent. The snake opened its enormous fanged mouth above the man's balding head. Kaolin forced his strong arms out between the coils and grabbed the great serpent's neck just below the head. His face was contorted in exertion as he fought for his life.

Wendell shifted his feet in the dirt conjuring a difficult spell. The palms of his hands began to glow brightly. The rhinosaur had turned around and was galloping back in his direction, picking up speed for a second attempt to skewer the wizard.

"Veroven-ovendell!" shouted Wendell, and Kaolin Hopindiffer instantly crashed onto the ground, as the great serpent encircling him transformed into a thick, lifeless rope. Kaolin breathed, his sweating, swollen face regaining some of its previous vigor. The other snakes around him were also turning into ropes. They coiled and twisted, as if resisting the transformation. The fleet of enlivened ropes then slithered across the arena binding the legs and wrists of attackers along their way. The audience cheered.

Wendell faced the rhinosaur once more. The stubborn beast seemed determined to end the boy's life. Wendell looked at the charging animal. It was a rare creature. He did not want to kill it but he had to find a way to stop it. He reached for its will with his own, mentally forcing his way through the creature's resistance, and absorbing its rage into his own body. He trembled with concentration. Beads of sweat formed on his forehead and slid down his temples. The rhinosaur showed no sign of slowing. Wendell projected his hands toward it, his fingers contorted with the effort of channeling energy from one vessel to another. The distance was rapidly closing between them.

"What is he doing?" asked a man standing up in the suddenly quiet audience. "Get out of there!" he called, putting his palms around his mouth.

A wave of red energy erupted from the advancing beast, and whooshed into Wendell's chest, absorbing into his body like smoke. The boy stepped back, concaving his shoulders as if hit by an invisible blow. The rhinosaur skidded to a halt just seconds from impact, digging its claws deeply into the ground. The creature's irises had turned from red to blue. Wendell patted one of its horns, and raised his hand to the audience. The spectators went wild with applause. The rhinosaur nuzzled against him, nearly knocking Wendell to the ground. The audience laughed with pleasure. Wendell whispered something in the beast's ear, and it peacefully trotted from the arena back into the gate from which it had come from. The door slid closed behind its vanishing grey rump. Wendell's gate was the first to close. The crowd cheered wildly, delighting in his success. Only Wendell's teacher, seated up in the King's balcony alongside the royal family, furrowed his brow in concern.

Uplifted by his triumph, Wendell looked around. He heard a laugh coming from Galator's direction. Glancing toward the Gator, he could see that the young man had bound the snout of a reptile he was wrestling firmly shut with a length of overly willing rope.

Beastadore Willdenwild was still in the midst of battle, forcing what remained of the unbound, still conscious soldiers back into his gate with terrifying blows of his sword. Kaolin Hopindiffer was throwing the rope off of himself, one thick coil at a time. The Citrulene monk had hypnotized one of the trolls to turn on the other, and he repeatedly clubbed his companion with a blank expression on his face, compelling him to move back inside the gate. The monk pulled his whip from around the neck of the Cyclops. The creature inhaled a raspy breath, and also scampered toward the dark pit behind him. The monk landed a final lashing on his rear, sending him hopping into the darkness.

The giant cat of Diamondell held the wrist of a hunched man in its mouth and was leading him from the arena. The man wore a scrap of ragged fabric around his waist, and was heavily scarred but showed no signs of flesh wounds. The cat on the other hand, was nursing a painful-looking limp and was bleeding from several nasty slashes in its striped hide. His spiked armor was covered in scratches and teeth marks.

Theodor Madderlin was swarming with goblins. They leapt onto him, biting at his arms and legs. He slashed at them in a desperate frenzy as they scratched at his eyes and neck with dark-green little claws. He threw down one, and three more leaped onto him. The man was covered in short pairs of bleeding scratches that had ripped through his clothes. The sleeves of his tunic were shredded. His flacon helplessly pecked at the goblins attacking his master. Both Wendell and the monk ran to his aid.

"Leave me!" shouted Theodor Madderlin falling to his knees. "I will not accept help!"

"The ability to accept help marks the wisest of men, for few great feats are accomplished alone," replied the monk, cracking his whip. The goblins hissed and pulled back from their victim. He lashed out at them again, cracking his whip like thunder. The goblins screeched and raced away behind the closing gate. The ground was stained heavily with their green blood. Theodor Madderlin moaned, collapsing in the dust.

"Rest, you are safe now," rumbled the monk. The crowd cheered loudly at the rescue.

Wendell looked at the monk. The man was the true embodiment of honor, standing tall, his robes billowing in the wind. "Excellent work," said Wendell with admiration, "What name do you go by?" he asked, unable to recall hearing anyone address the monk.

"My given name has been erased by what I have become," replied the turquoise clad man turning to the boy, his face hardening as he did so.

"And what have you become?" asked Wendell.

"Empty," said the Monk. His eyes closed and his third eye flicked open. He raised his whip. The audience watched in disbelief, as the Monk lifted his hand and landed a heavy blow on the young wizard. Wendell knelt and blocked with his wrist. The whip wrapped around his forearm, cutting deeply into his flesh. The monk yanked on the whip, tugging Wendell to the ground. Pulling his weapon free, the monk immediately took aim and struck once more. Wendell rolled away from the strike, and leapt to his feet. The Monk's whip lashed out like lightning once more, leaving a deep bleeding gash on Wendell's shoulder. The young wizard felt an unexpected surge of rage course through him alongside the burst of pain. Wendell's palms began to glow. The light pouring from his hands had a tint of red. He took a firm stance.

"Wendell!" cried Galator, grabbing the boy by the wrist. The light went out of Wendell's palms.

Several warriors ran to Wendell's side, including Galator, Beastadore Willdenwild, Kaolin Hopindiffer, and the cat of Diamondell.

Kaolin put himself between Wendell and his attacker, bravely shielding the boy with his own body.

"He is a danger to us all!" spoke the Monk firmly.

Beastadore lunged at the Monk with his sword drawn. The Monk lashed at him. With one even cut, Beastadore sliced through the whip, rendering it useless. Galator nimbly sprung himself beside the Monk and snatched what remained of the weapon from his hand.

Now unarmed, the Monk threw himself toward Wendell. "He must be stopped!" yelled the Monk.

Beastadore and Galator restrained him, firmly grabbing hold of his arms on either side. The Monk resisted them as if possessed. He seemed to have inhuman strength in his determination to reach Wendell. A troop of guards came onto the arena to take him away.

"What is with him?" mused Kaolin, watching the Monk struggle to break free, still focused on getting to Wendell. Suddenly, the third eye on the Monk's forehead closed and his body went limp. The guards picked him up and took his unconscious body from the arena. Kaolin followed them off. He had not succeeded in his challenge.

The audience buzzed. Beastadore, Galator, the cat of Diamondell, and Wendell faced the King and bowed low. The King rose from his throne.

"You have done well," he said. His noble voice carried easily across the arena. "Each of you has bravely accomplished the task you were assigned. Now you must face one final feat. I fear not all of you will survive this last remaining battle, and so, I ask those of you who do not wish to continue to leave now."

The warriors held their ground, looking solemnly up toward the royal balcony. The giant cat breathed a quick sniff. It was keeping most of its weight off of one of its hind paws.

Wendell glanced at Aleafia, seated up on the balcony. She looked tense. Her lips were pressed tightly together.

"He who is able to defeat the beast shall be named victor," announced the King. "For one great warrior may walk with ease, through lands where armies fell!" The spectators cheered. "Release it!" commanded the King with a wave of his hand. The stadium erupted in applause.

On the opposite side of the arena, three of the smaller gates had been locked together forming a much larger door. It swung open on giant rusty hinges. The four warriors faced the gate, squared their shoulders, and drew their weapons. Beastadore took a few practice strikes, slicing the air with his shining blade. Galator peeled a thin webbing from around his shield, revealing a razor-sharp edge.

All was quiet for a moment. There was a slight draft, as if the air itself was being sucked into the dark pit before them. It pulled at Wendell's hair, and he swept it back from his eyes just in time to see the first burst of fire erupting toward them. The thick torrent of flames came at them in a molten white-hot blaze.

"Stay low!" yelled Beastadore, as they dove away from the flames. A black dragon emerged from the darkness. It swiped its scaly, armored tail and bared its teeth, hissing a stern warning. The audience gasped. The monster was thick with bands of muscles contracting beneath its hide. Its scales gleamed and crackled when it moved. The dragon's long neck held a fearsome reptilian head with narrow eyes and two rows of sharp spikes running down its back. Its underbelly glowed bright orange.

Wendell watched it, wide eyed, as it spread its leathery wings, appearing even larger, and bellowed a teeth-clenching roar. It flapped its boney wings and took to flight. The dragon inhaled deeply and blasted a river of flames before itself as it circled the arena, singeing the ground and forcing the warriors into the center. The cat of Diamondell barely escaped being burned, slinking away from the fire just in time. The warriors huddled together with their backs to one another.

"That thing is intelligent!" exclaimed Beastadore. "I should like to cut off its head!"

"If you do, it will sprout two more!" warned Galator. "The only way to kill it is to spear it through the heart."

"Then that is what I will do!" yelled Beastadore, and with those words he charged at the dragon with his weapon drawn. The monster exhaled a spout of flames in his direction. Beastadore blocked himself behind his shield just before the flames engulfed him. The intensity of the fire striking his shield was so powerful, that it pushed his feet backwards through the sand even though Beastadore leaned into his shield and dug his strong feet into the ground with all his might.

Wendell projected his energy toward Beastadore, cooling the

portion of the shield he was holding so that it would not burn him.

"Galator," rushed Wendell, "how do you tame a reptile?"

"You must break its will," replied the Gator, taking aim, and throwing his disk sideways.

"How?" demanded Wendell.

"You have to make it surrender." The disk ripped through one of the creature's black wings, and the dragon fell with a screech to the ground, retracting its wings in pain. Beastadore ran toward them discarding his shield, which was now a red-hot melted mass of metal except for the place where Wendell had cooled it.

Galator looked at Wendell and the cat. "Distract it," he said to them, "Beastadore, and I will take him down together." The two of them departed, moving quickly along the side of the arena toward the furious creature.

Wendell laid a hand on the back of the giant cat beside him. He cast a simple healing spell over the great feline to knit together the open wounds and repair injured bones. His palms glowed a warm yellow light as the magic moved through Wendell and into the beast's body. The cat looked up at him gratefully.

"We must draw its attention away from them," said Wendell. The cat nodded and with a snarl, leapt forward toward the dragon with restored energy. The giant cat clawed the ground and roared, opening an invitation for battle.

Now wounded and earthbound, the dragon eyed Beastadore and Galator suspiciously. It inhaled. Wendell could predict what would happen to his friends if he didn't manage to get the creature's attention. He felt a surge of adrenalin. His palms brightly aglow, he hurled a fireball at the dragon. The ball of flame whizzed past the dragon's nose. The dragon looked at Wendell, momentarily confused.

"That's it," whispered Wendell, and threw another. This time the gob of fire landed on the dragon's wing, scorching a dark spot next to the cut from Galator's ring. The dragon screamed in rage, and threw itself toward the boy. The cat of Diamondell met the dragon before it could reach Wendell and leapt onto the dragon's thick neck, sinking in its razor teeth and claws. The dragon bellowed a scream and wildly shook its head, flinging off the attacker. The cat twisted in mid air and landed effortlessly on its paws, disturbing a shallow cloud of dust into life around its elegant striped body.

Blue blood poured from the puncture in the dragon's neck, and it viciously blasted a surge of flames toward the cat. The cat leaped out of the way, as the dragon followed it with its fiery breath. Wendell forced his energy into his hands. Straining with effort, he projected an invisible shield around the Diamondell warrior. The fire bent around the cat but did not burn him. Noticing this, the dragon snarled angrily and turned once again to the young wizard.

Beastadore had positioned himself slightly behind the dragon. He locked his fingers together. Galator was a few paces away from him. The Gator ran and leaped onto Beastadore's interlaced fingers with one foot. Beastadore threw him high into the air. Galator flipped in the sky and landed on the Dragon's back. He loosened a length of chain at his hip. Wendell focused on shielding his friends from the fire. Galator threw the chain around the dragon's neck, catching the loose end as it swung around. He fastened the ends together, forming a necklace around the dragon's neck. He un-sheathed the small dagger from his boot. Taking a firm hold of the silver linked chain with one hand, Galator leaped from the dragon's back and swung himself around the trunk of its massive neck with his blade exposed.

It looked like victory was near, but just before Galator could stab his dagger into the dragon's heart, the beast reared up onto its hind-quarters. It thrashed around forcefully, refusing to surrender. Galator was thrown from the chain around its collar. Wendell moved one hand through the air palm upwards, bringing his friend safely to the ground and breaking his fall. Meanwhile, the fire-spewing dragon picked up the cat warrior with a taloned paw and threw him against the wall of the arena. The cat collapsed and did not rise. The dragon leaped over Beastadore toward the wizard boy, whom he had realized was the real source of his troubles.

Wendell turned to face the King's balcony.

"Aleafia!" he yelled, "Do you still want me to lose?"

"No! Win you idiot—win!" screamed Aleafia, rising from her seat to clasp the railing with both hands.

"Are you sure that's what you want?" yelled Wendell.

"Yes! Oh! Win already!" shouted Aleafia.

Wendell shrugged and spun around to face the charging creature once more.

Prince Ariellen looked at Aleafia's lovely worried face. "What a show off," he groaned.

Wendell stepped forward. The dragon snarled at him, its charcoal body radiating heat. Instead of fear, Wendell was overcome with a sudden rage. He could not remember ever experiencing so much anger before. He allowed the feeling to course through him like venom. He shifted methodically in the sand, his palms once more glowing a strange red color instead of the usual golden light. Rusty orange flames erupted from his hands and ripped toward the dragon. The dragon replied in kind. Fire whipped through the air in giant sweeping coils as the two fire-wielders fought, smashing rivers of fire against each other. They were equally matched. Wendell enjoyed unleashing his powers with reckless abandon. He was more powerful than even he had suspected. But the dragon was clever. It slowly advanced, pushing the boy against the side of the arena. His heart pounding in his ears, Wendell projected a thin veil before himself as a shield from the flames that curled around him. The walls behind him caught fire and the flames were getting out of control. Several of the observers seated in that area had to quickly move to avoid being burned. Seeing his victim was cornered, the dragon leaped onto the young wizard. Wendell rolled between its legs and rose to standing behind it. The dragon swiped its tail, attempting to strike the wizard. Wendell ducked and tail whooshed over his head as the dragon wheeled around. Again and again, Wendell hit the dragon with blinding blasts of fire. Wendell ground his teeth together and projected all the energy he could muster into the streams of flame producing from his palms. He wrapped a coil of fire around the dragon's neck, and tightened it like a living, fiery leash. The dragon violently shook its head, fighting the constricting collar. The young wizard focused his energy around the beast. Wendell felt his powers wavering, and he pushed a fresh surge of energy forward with all his might. He was losing his focus. Projecting what remained of his energy, Wendell numbly fell to his knees as he forced a gigantic cage to manifest itself around the dragon. He felt his strength pulling from his chest through his arms as if his blood was quickly draining from his body.

In the light of day, the materializing bars gleamed bright silver. As soon as the metal was solid, the dragon snapped its mouth shut and shrunk back into a corner of the cage. It cried a heart-wrenching sob. The audience erupted in applause. Wendell looked about the smoldering arena, and raised his hands in the sky. The volume of the applause grew to a deafening roar.

A stretcher was brought out for the cat of Diamondell. Beastadore and Galator took their places beside Wendell as he faced the King's balcony.

The King rose. "I hereby proclaim, Wendell Odelious Bloomer, descendent of Delominar the Great, as Winner of the Determination Tournament!" announced the King. The audience thundered their approval.

"You have proven yourself worthy of the honorable, and dangerous journey to the Pillar of Dominance," said the King. Cheers erupted once more from the crowd. "Within twelve days, when the location of the pillar reveals itself," he continued, "Prince Airyallen Amadeus Miramar, accompanied by Master Loriander Ragendar, as well as our new victor, shall travel to the new location of the energy vortex to place the blue sapphire on the pillar and renew our era!"

People leaped from their chairs. Hats were thrown in the air. The spectators were delighted with the outcome of the battle they had witnessed. They poured into the arena. The caged dragon shrunk away from anyone who approached it, unable to challenge even the Gator riders who slid the cage onto several sets of wheels in order to pull it away. A large number of reptiles were harnessed together to tug the massive cage through the opening of the large gate.

Wendell was swarmed by a mob of congratulating people. Beastadore slapped Wendell on the back in a cheerful farewell gesture.

"Well done," he said, "You have made your region proud."

Galator gripped Wendell's hand before departing. "How did you guess its will was in its freedom?" he asked.

Wendell shrugged. "I just thought about myself and where I source my own powers."

"If ever you should be in need of aid, I would be honored to fight alongside you once more," said Galator, and with a wave, leaped onto a passing Gator carriage.

Wendell's master approached him smiling broadly.

"I have never been so proud of a student as I am on this day," boasted Master Loriander merrily to the swarm of admirers. "You have surpassed my highest expectations." He took hold of the boy's hand and lifted it into the air. Cheers erupted all around them, followed by whistles and hoots. Wendell smiled and glanced up at the now nearly vacant balcony above. His master followed his gaze.

"Go ahead," Loriander whispered, "I will distract them." There was an explosion of music, as a band struck an enticing array of chords. Everyone looked to the source of the sounds only to find a hoard of instruments magically playing themselves, and floating through the crowd. Delighted squawks and gasps broke out among the people. Wendell ducked down and crept through the mob. He raced up the stairs to the King's balcony and stepped through the blue velvet curtains. Prince Airyallen was leaning on the railing.

"Your Highness," said Wendell with an excited grin and a comical bow. "I am honored to accompany you to the Pillar of Dominance."

The prince looked away. His jaw was set. "So I hear," he muttered under his breath.

But Wendell didn't catch the snide remark, nor the icy tone of Prince Airyallen's voice, for his attention had turned to Aleafia. She sat on a fancy stuffed chair wearing a pink and blue dress as light as flower petals. The fabric was sleek against slender form, and laced up in the back with a silver cord. She reached out her hand. Wendell brought it to his lips.

"My lady," he said, looking up at her.

She fanned herself with a lace trimmed collapsible fan, the ember glowing on her necklace. Suddenly, she stepped closer and pulled him in for an embrace. Wendell closed his eyes, deeply enjoying the contact. Inhaling her perfume, and holding her close, he wrapped a loose strand of her hair around his finger behind her back.

"Dine with me tonight?"

She pulled away and whacked him with the fan. "You could have been killed!" she cried. "You brought me here for what? So I could watch you face your death?" Her eyes were filling with tears. She hit his tan, blood streaked shoulder weakly with her fist. "How could you do that to me? Don't you know I care about you?"

Wendell slipped his arm around her waist, smiling tenderly. "Let me make it up to you." He pulled back the entrance drapes and escorted her from the stadium.

The prince remained on the balcony. He gripped the railing so hard his knuckles turned white and his fingernails left crescent shaped dents in the gold-painted wood.

THE LAST AND FINAL PROPHECY

Wendell awoke the next morning feeling quite ill. The celebrating of the night before was like nothing he had ever experienced. He looked at the clock. It was late in the afternoon. He groaned. His master was sure to reprimand him for his excessive partying. He pulled on some clothes, his head still swimming with illogical spinning flashes of the night before. He saw a long table laden with food, someone mumbling a drunken toast, Aleafia dancing with him, her eyes shy and happy. He saw her bidding him good night, and then more music and feasting.

Wendell glanced in the mirror. His hair resembled a bird's nest. He smoothed it with one hand. Not certain that he had made an improvement in his appearance, he snorted at his reflection and hurried down the stairs.

His master was seated in his rocking chair, smoking a pipe and looking out the window. Wendell cleared his throat. The old wizard made no response. Wendell walked over to his master's desk. Usually tidy, it was in disarray, littered with scraps of parchment.

"Do you want me to finish these incomplete hexes?" asked Wendell, indicating the bits of parchment scattered on the table. He hoped to soften his teacher's temper with a generous dose of helpfulness, but the old wizard waved him away, only grunting a vague reply. The old man stared out across the garden with an unseeing gaze, exhaling a puff of smoke. Wendell came beside him.

"What troubles you master?" he asked.

"Hum?" responded the old man, absently looking up before

returning to the window. "I am puzzled," he said, leaning his cheek on his fist. "The Seer of Apple Grove has given the King her last and final prophecy."

"Her last?" asked Wendell. "Is she going to die?"

"She passed this morning," said the old wizard. "She was the last of the Great Seers."

Wendell took a seat near his master, recalling his brief and only encounter with the Seer on the day he had sought out Aleafia in the orchard.

"And what of the prophecy?" he asked.

"She spoke of the chosen one," replied his master. "A boy who would set things right, born to the seventy-fourth son of the sapphire dynasty—fifty generations from now." He put a heavy emphasis on the last part of the sentence to convey the vastness of that span of time.

"Set things right from what?" asked Wendell.

"That is what troubles me most," answered the old wizard grimly. "I am concerned that we may have wearisome competition for the dominance." He looked at Wendell. "Whatever happens, we must make absolute certain that no one gets to the pillar before us. For if someone does, the results may be devastating for this world." The old wizard was serious. "You must take your training more seriously."

"But I do—" began Wendell.

"This is not like the tournament," said the wizard sternly. "Go and train with the prince."

"Physical combat is not my forte," replied Wendell.

"Then it must become your forte!" shouted the wizard, slamming his palms against the arms of his chair. "Now go!"

Wendell reluctantly headed for the door. He had come to dread his training sessions with the prince. Once outside, he felt significantly less burdened. The outdoors often had this effect on him. Something about the open space seemed more like home to Wendell than the rigid dwellings of man. The evening light was warm on the back of his neck. As he walked down the street, people waved to him. Overnight, he had become a hero and it seemed as if everyone in the city was suddenly his friend. Vendors refused pay for food. Booths he ordinarily bought goods from became suddenly busier with customers.

"Shh! Here he comes! Act normal!" Wendell caught the tail end of a whisper just before rounding a corner. Squaring his shoulders, and taking on a somber, noble expression, he stepped around the bend with a confident stride. A cluster of girls working at a vegetable booth had quickly composed themselves, stealing quick glances in his direction. He was pleased to note that all of them had previously ignored him, and were now desperate for his attention. Wendell smiled at them, making them erupt in a fit of giggles.

"He looked at me! Did you see?" pined one of them as he walked past.

It was still light when Wendell reached the castle, but the day was heading toward evening. The guards by the carved double doors nodded courteously and let Wendell into the castle. Wendell walked through the lavishly decorated halls, his footsteps echoing quietly against the marble walls. The gold trim shone along the towering ceiling, framing the vast murals painted on the plaster high above. A fountain gurgled in the center of the main hall. Cascading white curtains and suits of historic armor adorned the walls. Wendell passed a line of portraits depicting the royal families of previous generations. The last painting in the series was a family tree. Some of the branches remained blank and untitled, awaiting the names of those who had not yet been born.

Wendell continued on into the training courtyard. Prince Airyallen was already warming up. He was clad in his practice armor.

"What kept you?" he asked, handing Wendell his uniform.

Wendell half-heartedly pulled it over himself and began buttoning the padded jacket.

"I was delayed talking with my master about the last prophecy."

"Excuses, excuses," mocked the prince.

The trainer rubbed chalk on Wendell's hands.

"Do not be late again," said the prince, tossing Wendell a sword, hilt first. Prince Airyallen unsheathed his own blade.

"Begin," commanded the trainer, standing back to watch.

The prince was first to attack. He swung his weapon through the air and landed a hard blow on Wendell's sword. Wendell blocked just in time. The young wizard shoved his weight against his blade, pushing the prince away. Quickly regaining his balance, the prince attacked once more, this time hitting Wendell with three quick blows from alternating angles. Wendell blocked, feeling each strike ricochet through the bones in his arms.

"That's it, lean into it Wendell," coached the combat master, mimicking their movements with his body.

Wendell came at the prince with a series of slashes followed by a sharp jab forward. Prince Airyallen deflected the attacks easily, turning Wendell's last strike against him by weaving away, making the wizard momentarily lose his balance when his blade swooshed through the air instead of making an impact. Taking advantage of his opponent's position, the prince came down hard, landing strike after strike on his friend.

"How are you so good at this again?" asked Wendell, struggling to fight him off.

"I told you, I practiced hard in my past life, and it transferred over," laughed the prince.

The prince landed another hard blow and let his blade slide down to the hilt of Wendell's sword. They pressed against each other, but the prince was stronger. He shoved Wendell back. The wizard dropped his weapon and fell backwards onto his hands. Prince Airyallen kicked Wendell's weapon away, and stabbed at the boy. Wendell rolled just in time to miss being speared.

"What are you doing?" asked Wendell in shock, rolling back over onto his back and raising his palms in front of his face in a sign of surrender.

"Break," commanded the trainer, helping Wendell up. The boys strode over to the resting corner for a short break.

"What is with you?" asked Wendell, sheathing his sword. "You are not yourself tonight."

"I just want you to be ready."

"I think there's something you're not telling me," said Wendell, picking up a jeweled goblet of water.

The prince sighed. "I think I'm in love," he said.

"You? In love?" snorted Wendell. He leaned on the table with one hand. The tablecloth instantly burst into flames around his fingertips.

"Yes," said Prince Airyallen irritably. "You can be in love, why can't I?"

"Fair enough," said Wendell, empting his goblet on the fire, and awkwardly patting out the flames. The wet fabric now had a large, black-rimmed, smoldering hole in its silky golden surface.

"Anyway," sighed the prince, "I don't know how to woo her." He sank into a stuffed velvet chair.

"What do you mean?" laughed Wendell.

The prince made a face, "I've never had this problem before," he said, "but she is being..." he trailed off, curving his upper lip, "difficult." He concluded. "None of the stuff that usually works is having an effect. She is as impervious to flattery as a shield is to arrows. I don't know what to do. Yet the more she pushes me away, the more I desire her. It's like I'm under some kind of ill-cast spell." He slouched against the back of his chair, his crown sliding down onto his forehead. It was a slender silver ring, with a series of short pointed peaks in the front. The tallest center point was set with a blue sapphire gem.

"A woman is nothing like a shield," said Wendell.

The prince groaned in frustration, flexing the muscles of his hands discontentedly. "I know, but I want to impress her! What should I tell her?" he demanded.

"Be as much yourself as you have the courage to be," replied Wendell.

"And what if she doesn't like who I am?" he retorted, angry like a child denied a fancy toy.

"She will either like you, or she won't," said Wendell. "At least if you are yourself from the beginning, you won't have to keep pretending to be someone else just to keep her affections."

"I find that difficult advice to heed," snorted the prince, "I never feel like myself around her. Besides, *I* don't like me, why should *she?*"

The trainer paced impatiently in the courtyard.

"You're a prince, everyone likes you," said Wendell.

Prince Airyallen smiled guiltlessly.

"So you think I should use the prince card, ay?"

"It can't hurt," shrugged Wendell, and turned away, heading back to the training field. Prince Airyallen stared darkly at his friend's retreating back. Wendell felt the burn of his eyes and glanced back at him over his shoulder.

"Are you coming, or what?" asked Wendell.

ALEAFIA'S REQUEST

Wendell collapsed on the couch. It was late afternoon and the mansion felt hot and stuffy. After days of endless study, he felt physically and mentally exhausted.

"Try it again," said his master.

"I'm tired," replied Wendell. "Let's take this up tomorrow."

"No!" insisted his master. "You must learn it today."

"Why?" resisted Wendell.

"Because tomorrow, you will be learning to freeze an opponent amidst action."

Wendell sighed.

"Acrilla-mikerdova," he said. A nearly inaudible whisper emanated from a rolled up scroll on the short table before him.

"Again," commanded the old Wizard.

"How is this useful again?" asked Wendell.

"You can use this spell to extract critical information from a book, scroll, or even another person's mind without them even noticing. You do not always have the time or the opportunity to ask questions, or copy a precious text."

Wendell grimaced. The rigorous training was wearing on him.

"Acrilla-mikerdova!" he yelled angrily.

"*Those who won't ask, shall never see, what truths bewitch the tongue's last plea,*" whispered the scroll, the words loosely formed in ghostly cursive letters as they were uttered before shattering into tiny grains of disappearing sand.

"Good, now keeping that intensity, pronounce it a little bit softer," said the old wizard. "If you are extracting a message from a map in the hand of a sleeping general, you don't want his entire army to hear you."

"What does that even mean?" asked Wendell indicating to the scroll on the table.

"It means that a dying man's final wish is what is most telling about the contents of his heart regardless of how he lived his life."

Wendell wondered what his last request would be. It was difficult to sort out what he would ask for if he could only ask for one last thing. He had recently faced his death in the arena, but he still didn't know what he wanted.

There was a knock on the door. The two of them looked at each other, and then snapped their heads toward the entrance just seconds before the door burst open and Prince Airyallen rushed into the room.

"It's time!" he shouted.

Goose bumps spread across Wendell's body, making the tiny hairs on his arms stand on end. He rose.

"Now?" he asked in shock.

"Yes!" said the prince. He looked feverish, his blue eyes sparkling.

"So the location has appeared on the map?" inquired the old wizard.

Prince Airyallen nodded fervently.

"Then the day of the Dominance has arrived!" the old wizard exclaimed.

"Yes!" cried the prince. He clapped Wendell on the shoulder. "Are you ready for this?" he asked.

"I am always ready for an adventure," said Wendell with a grin.

"Where is the new site of the pillar?" asked Master Loriander with immense concern in his voice.

"It is nearby!" replied Prince Airyallen with eagerness. "That is what is most extraordinary. The Pillar is located right in the midst of the Monsonett Mountains, no more than a two day's trek from here."

"Oh!" cried the old wizard sinking down in a chair, closing his eyes and placing a hand over his heart. "Then we have a good chance of reaching it first." He sat forward abruptly, "We must waste no time." The two boys nodded in agreement.

"We leave at once," said Master Loriander firmly.

Wendell rushed to the door.

"Where are you going?" asked the old wizard sternly.

"I just have to say goodbye to someone," called Wendell over his shoulder. Glancing back, Wendell briefly caught a smile lingering on prince Airyallen's lips. Wendell pulled open the door and bounded down the front steps before anyone could stop him. He rushed quickly through town, heading for the apple orchard on the hill. His head was bowed low, ignoring the eyes of strangers as he contemplated what he would say. He was passing the market when suddenly, he saw her. She was helping her father at the bakery stand, her red hair dangling down her back in two thick braids. Wendell's heart skipped a beat.

"Aleafia!" he said, smiling openly and approaching the stand. "I was just looking for you."

She returned the smile from behind the counter.

"Father, I'll be right back," she called to the baker, who nodded, shooting Wendell a dark look.

Aleafia walked around the bread-laden table. Wendell helped her down the few steps. Her apron was dusted with flour. The ember from his fireworks at the tournament still burned on her necklace. She touched it, seeing him looking at it.

"You are so beautiful," said Wendell.

She laughed and pulled away, releasing his hand. He followed her.

A bouquet of wild flowers picked itself up and drifted toward Aleafia from a nearby flower stand. The ribbon untied itself and twisted through the air alongside the free-floating blossoms trailing behind the girl. The stems of the flowers began to weave themselves together with the ribbon forming a wreath. Once complete, the ring of blooms landed gently on Aleafia's head. Reaching up a slender hand, she touched the burgundy bow in the back of her crown, exploring its shape with her fingertips. She beamed at Wendell, whose palms were glowing. The flower vender shook his head at the young wizard with an understanding smile.

The pair soon turned down a narrow cobbled alleyway, away

from the main street. Small shops and cafes were built into the sides of the towering stone walls. Long overflowing flowerpots ran the length of the tiny street up above their heads. Wendell and Aleafia slowed their pace.

"I have some news," said Wendell, pausing in the middle of the alley to face her. "The Day of the Dominance has arrived, and the new location of the pillar has revealed itself on the Seers' Map of Diamondell!" Wendell rushed with excitement. "We leave for the pillar immediately!" Aleafia looked happy, but unsurprised. Wendell beamed at her. "Aleafia." He was overwhelmed. Leaning toward her, he placed one hand on the wall beside her. "I've come to tell you that…" he trailed off. "That I—"

"I know." She said.

"You do?" asked Wendell looking deep into her eyes.

"Prince Airyallen told me."

"He told you!" exploded Wendell in disbelief. He ran his fingers through his hair and looked away, blushing slightly. "How could he? Why would he tell you?"

Aleafia laughed. "He told me you were leaving to find the pillar tonight, because I'm engaged," she answered. "He said there ought to be no more secrets between us."

Wendell was suddenly unable to breathe. "What?" he asked, scanning her face uncertainly, the smile fading from his lips. He was confused.

Aleafia clasped her hands with excitement. "I know, it's so sudden, it surprised me also when it happened," she bantered happily.

"To whom?" Asked Wendell numbly.

"To the prince, of course!" smiled Aleafia. "That's what I've been trying to tell you."

"No," whispered Wendell, willing it to be untrue, as the pieces began fitting together in his head against his will.

"Yes!" cried Aleafia merrily.

Wendell felt ill. He stepped back, reeling as he listened to Aleafia explain how it all had happened. The prince had been courting her since the day she sat next to him at the tournament.

"Do you love him?" interrupted Wendell.

"Well, I don't know—"

"DO YOU LOVE HIM?" he demanded.

"Yes," said Aleafia simply. The sincerity was apparent in her voice.

Wendell looked away.

"Promise me you'll protect him," she said.

"Do not ask this of me," said Wendell, the muscles clenching in his jaw.

"Promise me," said Aleafia, touching the side of his face. Her voice was sweet as honey. He could smell the flowers in her hair.

Wendell looked at her. "I promise," he replied, his voice breaking on the last syllable.

THE PILLAR OF DOMINANCE

It was a cold, chilly morning. The sky was still dark. Wendell shuddered in his armor. He was unaccustomed to the restrictions of the metal plates. His head still swam with Aleafia's words. "*To the prince of course... that's what I've been trying to tell you!*" Not more than a few hours had passed since they parted, yet he felt as though she had been torn from his life forever, cut from his heart with a poisoned blade. She was never to be with him. She had chosen someone else. How could he not have seen it coming? He braced himself for a life without Aleafia, a life without her eyes, her voice, her presence, her affection. He would have to find someone else to love, but there was only one Aleafia! A shadow of his dream of her still lived within him, fluttering his heart like a wounded bird. He had wanted to be with her forever. How differently it was all turning out. Tears came to his eyes, and several of them to fall silently down his face before he brushed them away. Wendell placed one ironclad boot inside the triangular metal ring dangling from the saddle of his steed, and pulled his heavy body up onto the leather seat. His master and the prince were already seated on their horses, waiting inside the royal stable by the entrance. Small parcels of provisions were tied securely to their saddles. The horses shifted their weight beneath them, sniffing the air with their velvet noses. A tube dangled at the old wizard's hip containing a drawn copy of The Seers' Map of Diamondell, marking the location of the pillar. Wendell walked his horse up alongside his master. The old man nodded to his apprentice.

"Glad you could make it after all," said Prince Airyallen sarcastically, indicating Wendell's lateness.

Wendell did not reply. The prince smirked. Master Loriander

lifted a silver eyebrow at the exchange.

Trumpets blared outside, announcing the appearance of the King and Queen on the castle balcony. Wendell could hear the noise of the massive audience that had gathered outside in the main square. He imagined the thousands of upturned faces eagerly awaiting the news.

"The rumors are true!" He heard the King's voice call across the square. "The day of the Dominance has arrived, and the location of the pillar is known!" The audience exploded with cheers. "We have the advantage of being closer to the Pillar of Dominance than any of our competition. Utilizing this advantage, we shall send our three chosen warriors underway within this very hour." Applause erupted enthusiastically. "Long live the sapphire Kingdom!" shouted the King over the noise, and the cheers doubled in volume. Music thundered from the royal orchestra as the stable gates were drawn open before the three riders. Wendell urged his horse forward alongside his companions. The crowd parted before them, forming a path for them to pass, and they charged forward through the square. Rose petals were tossed at the passing riders. The prince waved to the spectators enjoying the attention, but Wendell was grim. He avoided people's eyes, focusing instead on the cobbles below. He wound his fingers into his horse's mane, and patted its neck as if it were his only friend. Citizens of the Sapphire Kingdom stood waving along the roadsides all the way to the outskirts of town. At last, the riders raced through a stone archway that marked the outer limits of the city. A vast grassy plane stretched out before them, on the other side of which towered the Monsonett Mountains. They galloped toward the mountain range riding side by side, their horses kicking up swirling clouds of dust behind them.

"Gentlemen," said Master Loriander, "might I suggest a truce just for the duration of the quest?"

Wendell tapped his horse's neck, urging it to move faster, and he shot ahead of his companions.

They rode for several hours until they arrived at the foot of the mountains, which rose steeply into the sky from the valley floor. The three riders dismounted and led their horses to the stream meandering at the base of the mountains. A stable master met them and took over the care of the horses, providing fresh grass and clover for the sweating, tired beasts. The horses were immensely happy to see the stable master, nuzzling against him, and nibbling on his clothes affectionately. They followed him without need of reins. He held open a small bag of oats for one of the horses. The metallic jingle of coins issued quietly from the bag. Master Loriander glanced up at him in alarm.

Taking large impatient steps, Wendell and the prince obliviously shouldered their packs and headed up the winding path. The old wizard pulled out a retractable walking stick from within his robes. He snapped it open and threw the stable master a stern look. The other man cast down his eyes. Without a word the wizard followed the two young men up the path, leaving the stable master to stand awkwardly in the field. The man absently patted the neck of one of the tired stallions, more to comfort himself than the horse. His face wore the unmistakable expression of shame.

The sparsely forested mountain inclined sharply and was largely comprised of lose boulders. A narrow path had been trampled into the stones. The boulders shifted around underfoot and quietly threatened to become a pummeling rockslide at any moment. The trail climbed the sides of the mountain in innumerable switchbacks, streaking across the steep slope in zigzagging angled stripes. The boys marched in silence. Wendell kept his distance from the prince, staying several paces behind him. He pretended to not compete for first place, yet remained just a few strides away every time Prince Airyallen looked back. The prince was determined to lose him. He sped up to an unsustainable pace, pushing forward with the force of will alone. The hours wore on. As the sun rose in the sky, so did the temperature. They did not pause for so much as a drink of water, much less a moment of rest to recover their aching muscles. Wendell felt his back become gradually soaked with sweat, the fabric of his tunic sticking unpleasantly to his back underneath his armor. The muscles in his thighs and calves began to scream with each step upwards and his knees, unaccustomed to such abuse, buckled with increasing frequency. As the boys gained altitude, the danger of tripping and falling to their deaths below became more and more of a risk. Wendell had already made the mistake of looking down once, and he mentally resolved to never do so again. In places, the path had been washed out by rain. The boys fearlessly leaped over these patches suppressing any physical expression of their elevated heart rates. Lose pebbles collected in the center groove of the trail, making it easy to twist an ankle. At midday, Wendell began to worry that they had left his master behind. Finally, he spoke up.

"We should wait for Master Loriander," he said. The prince did not respond and continued to climb, leaning slightly harder into his stride. Wendell followed him reluctantly. Several minutes passed before he spoke up again. "I really think we should slow down and let him catch up to us."

Prince Airyallen paused with a snort and glanced at him around his shoulder, finally allowing Wendell to catch up to him.

"Are you afraid?" he asked with a sneer. "You need an old man for protection?"

It was at that precise moment that Wendell intuitively outstretched one hand, and caught a large, gray stone that had been speeding toward the prince's head. He had stopped it only inches from his temple. The two boys froze, looking at each other wide-eyed. Prince Airyallen drew his sword. Wendell's palms began to glow, infusing the stone in his hand with energy. The stone began to quickly change color.

"Find the map!" commanded a man's voice, as a gang of blue-clad soldiers leaped out from behind the trees and boulders with their weapon's drawn.

"They are from my own Kingdom!" exclaimed Prince Airyallen in shock. The soldiers came at them from all sides. Wendell and the prince were outnumbered ten to one. The prince's blade met the steel of an assassin with a piercing clang. The fighter had a serrated blade, and he used the grooves in the steel to try to disarm the prince. The prince was forced back from the repeated blows until he rubbed shoulders with Wendell. Wendell threw the now orange glowing stone in his hand toward a cluster of men charging at him from the opposite direction. It exploded in midair, cracking like thunder and expanding into an incinerating ball of fire. The noise of the explosion sent a cascade of boulders spilling down the mountain like a bowl of upturned beads, thundering downwards in a deadly waterfall. The soldiers momentarily diverted their energy from attacking them, to avoid the rockslide. A tree caught fire from Wendell's explosive, and crackled as the hungry flames consumed the oils in its leaves. The fire quickly spread onto several other trees around them. Wendell blasted a wave of energy toward the swordsman attacking the prince, and the man flew backwards, but was quickly replaced by several fresh fighters. Wendell and the prince were surrounded. The circle of soldiers closed in.

"Duck!" said Wendell. The prince quickly knelt on one knee. Wendell flicked his hand at the wrist, and a shower of small boulders leaped from the side of the slope and rained down onto the soldiers. Several of them were taken by surprise by the unexpected blows, and they tumbled down the side of the steep slope, chased by boulders that mercilessly crashed against their bodies. The renegades advanced in spite of Wendell's efforts to detour them. One of them, a man in his late forties, stood to the side of the action, whispering to a pair of stones in his hand. He was obviously a trained wizard.

"Look out!" cried the prince, grabbing Wendell by the forearm and dragging him behind himself. The rocks in the path near their feet had begun to magnetically bind themselves together. Before their eyes, the gray and brown boulders began linking together in clusters, taking the shape of a giant man. The rock giant moved toward them even as it was forming. The oblong boulders crackled up its legs in rivers, building onto the thick torso as it advanced. The head and arms had barely manifested when it stumbled toward them swinging a massive club at their heads. The boys backed away. The traitors of the Sapphire Kingdom stood behind them, pointing their mismatched swords at their backs.

A single heavy boulder positioned itself on the shoulders of the boulder giant as the head. It whooshed its club through the air at chest height. The prince jumped over, and Wendell ducked under the blow. The young wizard threw a blast of energy at the monster, hacking off its arm. The arm immediately grew back twice as thick as before. The hunched stone-clops sucked up more rocks through one of its legs. They rattled up its body. The stone fingers of its new hand closed, forming a giant fist. The fist wound up and flew at the prince in a mighty punch. The prince rolled away from the strike, sending the stone-clops flying over the path and down the side of the mountain. The rocks disassembled in mid air, raining down like giant hail. A second stone giant immediately leapt out of the side of the slope beside the prince, forming from the sedentary stones just as before. Its form was identical to the first, only comprised of differently shaped boulders. It stomped toward them, its thick back hunched over its blind, lumpy face. The prince swiped through its knees with his sword, trying to undercut it. Instead of breaking, the giant's legs thickened and grew before their very eyes, making the giant taller and stronger than ever. It swung at the boys with long heavy arms, aiming to pin them to the ground. Dodging the blows, the prince fell backwards onto the ground. He looked up as the stone giant lifted a bouldered foot to crush him. Flexing his fingers, Wendell reached a hand out, and then quickly closed his fingers and pulled his arm back into his body, conjuring a retrieval spell. The prince slid across the ground toward Wendell as if dragged by a ghost. The stone giant thundered his foot down, stomping the ground where the prince had been only seconds before.

"Warfuuna-muffuldoff!" shouted the voice of the old wizard. Suddenly, everything became still. The blue clad soldiers had frozen in their positions. The stone-clops was paralyzed in mid strike. Even the fire in the trees had taken the shape of a bright orange scarf that was quickly fading to gray. Wendell helped the prince up. They dusted themselves off as Master Loriander approached them. His lips were tight.

"From now on, we stay together!" he said sternly, and marched past them up the path ahead.

The boys looked at each other, and then silently followed him. They continued their climb throughout the night, summiting only at sunrise. When Wendell finally reached the top of the mountain, he paused to take in the view. The valley spreading out below was breathtaking to behold. Rivers weaved through green patchwork fields under the blushing rosy sky. The Sapphire City was nestled peacefully at the heart of the valley like a crown jewel. The air was so fresh it made Wendell's eyes water. He breathed in the scent of the old growth forest down below. The landscape was so dear and familiar, every inch of it filled with memories. A small rodent scurried past Wendell's boot.

"Warfuuna-muffuldoff," he said, and the mouse froze, slowly turning to stone. The prince grinned at Wendell's bit of magic, but the old wizard huffed disapprovingly, and turned to face the east.

"It's not far now," he said, examining the map. "Come along," he called to the boys, who rose with difficulty and dragging their feet, followed behind him.

They set off walking along the crest of the mountain range amidst a thin forest of altitude-shortened trees. They trod along the crest for several miles. Pine needles littered the rich dark soil of the forest floor, softening their footsteps and crunching pleasantly underfoot. At last, they came to a small clearing that broke off into a cliff ledge on the left hand side. There, in the slope of the mountain, gaping at the base of a giant rock was the entrance of a short, dark cave.

Master Loriander leaned on his staff. Wendell swallowed hard and threw down his pack. Staring at the jagged rip in the granite wall, Prince Airyallen followed suit, coming up beside the two wizards. The three of them peered into the black hole. A barely detectible hum issued from within the gap as the wind passed across the cavity in irregular bursts.

"I will guard the entrance," said Master Loriander, handing Wendell his walking stick. The prince ducked into the cave, and was immediately engulfed by the darkness. Wendell glanced nervously at his master.

"Be quick," said the old man quietly, urging him on with a slight jerk of his chin, before turning away from the cave entrance and scanning the horizon with watchful, ancient eyes.

Wendell went in after the prince, submerging himself into the inky mouth of the cave. It was much larger inside than it had seemed from the outside, and the arching ceiling was lost in the murky spaciousness. He could hear the prince moving around somewhere up ahead. As Wendell stepped away from the entrance his eyes struggled to adjust to the lack of light. The cool sandy floor of the cave absorbed his weight in an unsettling fashion, as though at any moment it might swallow him up. The thud of each step echoed quietly against the damp walls.

"Light the torch," muttered the prince. Wendell squeezed the walking stick in his hand, and the small purple orb attached at the top began to glow brightly, casting a cool violet light onto the path ahead. As the boys followed the winding passageway toward the heart of the mountain, their shadows arched across the walls and onto the ceiling above them like giant contorted monsters. At one end of the tunnel, a pinhole of light appeared. They quickened their pace, instinctively wanting to leave this place. The light flickered in and out of view as they moved forward. It grew colder. A damp icy breeze chilled their armor and sunk through their robes to bite at their skin with frosty teeth. Wendell locked his jaw tightly to keep his teeth from chattering.

They progressed through the cave toward the spot of light up ahead, their footsteps thudding lightly in the sand.

"Congratulations," whispered Wendell.

"On what?" asked Prince Airyallen.

"On your engagement," said Wendell. "I can't believe you didn't tell me you proposed to her!" Wendell finished, the resentment apparent in his voice.

"Seriously, it's no big deal," said the prince. The source of light up ahead was only a few paces away now.

"Anyway," said Wendell, "I realize that we are like brothers, and it is you she loves, not me. So I have decided to overstep my anger and—"

"Aleafia is so desperate to marry me, she would do anything," interrupted Prince Airyallen with a laugh. "She's practically eating out of my hand."

Wendell felt a strong irritation rising in his chest, and he wrestled it down with difficulty. "I urge you not to speak of her this way," he muttered sternly. The prince only smirked in reply.

At that moment they came upon a small chamber, whereupon the path ended. In the center of the cavern was a small stone pillar, no more than four feet high. It was carved from a piece of crumbling sandstone. A single beam of concentrated light fell onto the heart of the pillar from above forming a perfectly round spot of blinding light at the center.

"That's it?" asked Wendell in disbelief. "It's so..." he trailed off searching for the right word, "simple," he finished.

"She is so naïve," continued the prince, not taking his eyes off his friend. "She believes everything I say."

Wendell ground his teeth, this time not from the cold.

"Let's finish what we came here for," grumbled Wendell.

"And she doesn't even know that my marriage has already been arranged with someone else," sighed Prince Airyallen casually.

Wendell lunged at him. They fell to the ground wrestling in the sand.

"You spoiled ignorant ass!" yelled Wendell. "You hurt people you don't even know for entertainment. You make me sick." He threw a punch that was instantly deflected by the prince who pinned his arm and tried to break it at the elbow. Wendell screamed and twisted away just in time to save his arm.

Outside the cave, Master Loriander heard the faint echoes of the boys' angry voices, and he nervously glanced behind himself at the black hollow.

"And you are a show off!" shouted the prince. "You use magic to win people over. I have always hated you for that." He threw himself at the wizard, punching him painfully in the ribs. Before the second blow could land, Wendell blasted the prince against the cavern wall slightly harder than he had intended.

"You are just jealous of my abilities! I have powers you could never dream of. You, with all your noble blood and mountains of money!"

Prince Airyallen recovered quickly, and drew his sword. Unarmed, Wendell took a firm stance. The prince advanced, swinging his weapon in trained deadly cuts. Wendell dodged blow after blow, backing away slowly, his palms beginning to glow.

"You are nothing more than a homeless gutter rat," spat the prince. "A good for nothing beggar boy."

Shaking with rage, Wendell projected his hands toward the prince's throat.

"You would be there still, sitting in your own filth if it wasn't for that old—" The prince broke off in shock when he felt his necklace jerk violently on his neck. The chain broke and the blue sapphire shot through the air, landing into Wendell's outstretched hand. Wendell closed his fingers around it tightly. Prince Airyallen looked suddenly lost, as if he understood that the quarrel had gone too far. Wendell smiled, sensing his victory. He clutched the stone in his fist, overcome with malice for his former friend.

Wendell felt the rage of the rhinosaur still churning within him, trapped in the vessel of his own body. The stone clasped in the boy's pale fingers began to rapidly change color as if infused with the young wizard's rage and hatred.

"No!" shouted the prince helplessly, as Wendell blasted him away with another invisible blow and shoved the now blood-red gem onto the pillar underneath the beam of light. The prince hit the stone wall with a sickening smack and fell to the ground in a heap. There was an explosion of crimson light that shook the small cave like an earthquake. Wendell shielded his eyes from the blinding flash with his forearm. He fell to his knees. Everything went dark. Panicking, Wendell looked around for his master's staff. It lay in the sand nearby, glowing dimly. Grabbing it, Wendell aimed the light in the direction of prince Airyallen's body. He threw down the staff and scooped up the unconscious prince, throwing his limp body over his shoulder and ran from the cave down the dark passageway. There was another quake, and the room containing the pillar caved in with large dusty boulders behind him. Wendell ran as fast as his legs would carry him, feeling the cave wall with one hand. The mountain seemed to be collapsing in on itself. Choking with dust and the effort of carrying the prince's body, Wendell finally stumbled outside. His master was busy casting a complex spell. The old man shifted around in the sand, muttering incantations under his breath.

"What are you doing?" asked the youth, setting the prince down on the soil which had turned a lifeless rusty red. Upon seeing the color of the dirt, Wendell looked around. The giant trees were disintegrating before his very eyes, as the red energy spread across the land in a decimating explosion radiating from where he stood.

"I am protecting the Sapphire Kingdom, sealing it inside a dome to keep it safe from your handiwork," answered his master unevenly.

In the distance, a transparent bubble appeared over the Sapphire City. From these heights, it looked no bigger than a thimble. As the red desert spread across the land like a fatal disease, the small patch of living soil inside the dome was the only spot of green that remained of the once beautiful vista.

"Master, I—" Wendell began, but the old man interrupted him.

"You have sentenced us all to a lifetime of misery and despair in exchange for your momentary revenge," shouted Master Loriander shaking in anger. His gnarled fingers flexed in anguish as he turned to the boy. "You have forsaken the only world that is your home."

"But—" mumbled Wendell, in terror of what he had done.

"Silence!" shouted the wizard, "You must learn, at any cost, the lessons I have failed to teach you!" The palms of his hands began to glow a brilliant yellow light.

"No!" cried Wendell, shielding his face with his hands.

The old wizard forcibly uttered an incantation the boy had never heard, in a language long forgotten. There was a blinding blast of light, followed by a ringing silence.

"What have you done to me?" asked Wendell, feeling no different, but knowing something had changed. He looked at his mentor questioningly.

"I am your master no more," said the old wizard. "Let time be your teacher now." With these words he un-strapped the sundial from his wrist and threw it to the ground beside the boy. The wizard turned his back on his student. With difficulty, he carefully picked up the prince and began the long descent down the mountain.

"Wait!" cried Wendell. "You don't understand." He fell to his knees as he watched his teacher's retreating form become suddenly blurry from tears. "This can't be happening," he whispered, his strength abandoning his limbs. In a sudden burst of rage, he blasted a ball of fire toward a nearby stump. It exploded, sending blazing woodchips cascading into the air like fireworks. Wendell felt a sudden burning sensation in the palm of his hand. Overcome with frustration and pain, he sucked in a hissing breath through clenched teeth. A tiny black stone fell from the palm of his hand and landed in the red dust beneath his feet. Wendell picked it up, examining its perfectly round, flawless form. Without a moment's thought, he hurled it down the slope, instantly regretting that decision. Wendell contorted with pain. He felt as though his very soul was being ripped from his body against its will. He cried out. Crows from the nearby trees took flight at the sound.

A good distance away, the wizard paused upon hearing the noise, and was momentarily overcome with grief for the boy. The old man pressed his lips together and quickened his pace.

Wendell squirmed in the soil, paralyzed by an invisible fire that consumed every inch of his body. He struggled to breathe, knowing for certain that death was near, waiting in the shadows for its kill. He dragged himself through the dirt, intuitively moving in the direction he had thrown the stone. As he drew closer to it, he felt a slight sense of relief. Uncertain, but hopeful that he had found the cure, Wendell pushed his body toward the stone. He found he was able to move better as he drew nearer to it. The boy searched for it in the dry leaves for what seemed like an eternity. Finally, his fingers found the round object in the dirt. The moment it was near him, the pain vanished without a trace. Feeling normal again after what he had just been through brought with it a relief that briefly took his consciousness. When he came to, Wendell looked at the dusty bead in his hand and felt a sinking sensation in his chest that was deeper than bones.

PART TWO - THE LOVE LETTER

The history teacher held a ruler up to the chalkboard and drew a thin white line. "There have been many different eras," he said. "Back and back they go, long before recording systems were even developed." He waved a chubby hand away from himself as if to suggest the many eons of time that had elapsed. "Today we will discuss the four most recent, and therefore most pertinent millenniums. The Diamond Era was the time of the great clairvoyant seers," he explained, drawing a vertical dash through the line at one end. "The last diamond has been lost to us and so the clairvoyant era is never to repeat again, although it was a time of great progress in the evolutionary consciousness of man."

Two teenaged boys watched him from behind identical desks, but the pair of them could not have been more different. One was a slender, dark-haired youth with introspective auburn eyes. His features were soft and almost childlike, having not yet matured into the face of the man he would become. His long hair was bound in the back by a thin leather cord. He was dressed in a loose fitting black tunic and brown leather trousers. He watched with interest, leaning forward over his desk, resting his head on his elbows.

The second was a robust young man, tall and broad. He sat with his arms folded across his chest, leaning back in his chair. His blond hair gleamed like straw as it spilled down the back of his neck. The chair seemed uncomfortably small for him. His face contained every feature suggestive of strong character; a well-defined jaw, a chiseled nose, slanted cheeks, and a large forehead. He wore a billowing white shirt with full sleeves that were fitted in the cuffs. His large blue eyes had the glazed look of poorly disguised suffering.

"Next was the Amethyst Era," went on the historian, pushing his spectacles up on his nose and drawing another dash ten inches away from the first. "It was a time of wizardry and magic, where any person could acquire powers with which they could rule the world. Naturally, it was a time of immense bloodshed and destruction."

"Any person?" asked the dark haired boy.

"Yes, Warren," replied the teacher, "Magic was equally accessible to anyone who chose to study it."

The blond youth spastically changed positions more and more frequently, impatiently tapping his fingers on his desk.

"Does anyone study magic now?" asked Warren.

The historian laughed.

"Oh no, not for a very long time."

"Why not?" asked Warren.

"If you keep interrupting, we'll never make it through the lesson," replied the historian, returning to the chalkboard.

"Yeah, stop interrupting," said the blond boy.

Ignoring the remark, the historian continued. "The Amethyst era was followed, as you well know, by the Sapphire Era." He marked a third dash on the timeline. "It was named the most peaceful time in all of recorded history on Windifera."

The blond boy was in mid-yawn when the teacher turned around and glared at him. The historian cleared his throat before going on. "It was decided by the Seven regions that the Sapphire era would be repeated, but an evil wizard betrayed the Kingdom, placing a stone of his own creation on the pillar. It remains unknown what stone he used, but as you can see," he gestured out the window to the landscape beyond the dome, "it was infused with a powerful negative magic."

The two students looked out through the glass at the rusty lifeless mountains looming in the distance on the other side of the red desert. The blond boy puffed out his cheeks and slowly exhaled looking up at the ceiling.

"Salvador!" cried the exasperated tutor. "Pay attention! This concerns you more than anyone!"

Salvador looked unhappy. "*This concerns you more than anyone,*" he mouthed silently behind the teacher's back. Warren pressed a hand to his mouth to keep from laughing.

"At last, a new era is just around the corner," said the historian triumphantly. He drew a final dash and turned to face his students. "Our world has been ruled by the destructive red energy for nearly a thousand years, but the Red Era will soon end, and you, Salvador the savior, are destined to restore the balance as was prophesized by the final dying vision of the last descendent of the Great Seers of Diamondell!" The historian turned around, out of breath with excitement.

Salvador puffed out his chest and took on a noble expression. Warren laughed, breaking Salvador's concentration and making him crack up as well.

"No, like this!" cried Salvador in hysterics, composing himself long enough to pooch out his eyes and flare his nostrils before dissolving in another fit of laughter. The historian pursed his lips. He took off his cap, ran his fingers through his silver hair, and then pulled it back on again.

"Warren," he said stiffly, "your mother will be very displeased when she hears of this."

"What did I do?" asked Warren dejectedly. He snorted priggishly, unable to contain himself as Salvador continued posing.

"Another delightful hour, your Highnesses," said the tutor with a scowl, "another meaningful hour of studious labor." He stuffed his books in his bag, and moved to the door. The handle turned and the door opened before he was able to reach it. The Queen stepped into the classroom, her golden gown trailing behind her and her crown sparkling. He bowed to her. The boys quickly acquired serious faces.

"Master Ozren Zeffeldrick," she said pleasantly, "how was the lesson?"

The historian hesitated. "Err, most excellent." He mumbled, and hurried through the door.

The Queen frowned at the guilty-looking boys.

"Go and apologize for whatever it is you've done," she said. "Mistreating an elder is a cruelness unworthy of princes."

The boys rose and reluctantly headed after their teacher.

"Warren," said the Queen. The dark haired boy paused in the doorway. "Your father said that you spent all night writing a love letter?"

Warren nodded.

"Is there a lady on your heart?" she asked kindly.

"No," replied Warren, "it wasn't for me."

"Oh? For who then?" asked the Queen.

"Salvador the hero," replied Warren, jabbing a thumb behind his shoulder.

The queen put her arm around his shoulder and drew him in for a gentle squeeze.

"It seems he's not the only hero winning the hearts of the ladies," she smiled.

"I don't care if he's the hero. Why does everyone think I'm jealous of him?" asked Warren defensively.

"Because they imagine they would be in your place," sighed the Queen.

"Well I'm not," said Warren.

"And that," replied his mother, "is why I know you are good for this world in no lesser way than your brother."

He looked up at her.

"There are warriors, and there are poets," she said. "I am lucky enough to have one of each."

"We would have made a perfect man had we been born as one person instead of two," said Warren.

"I would have it no other way than the way it is," said the Queen "Having two sons is twice as wonderful as having just one."

Salvador rushed back into the room.

"Warren, I need to talk to you in— eh, private," he said, with a sideways glance at his mother.

"Did you apologize?" she asked.

"What? Yeah," replied Salvador.

"Did he look relieved?"

"I'm sure he *felt* relieved regardless of how he looked," answered Salvador with a wink at Warren.

The Queen rolled her eyes. "I expect you in the dining room

in no more than twenty minutes," she said on her way out the door. As soon as her footsteps quieted, Salvador grabbed hold of Warren's arm.

"Well?" he asked eagerly, "Do you have it?"

Warren pulled out an envelope from within his robes and handed it over. Salvador took it, breathlessly reading the address.

"I'm pretty sure that will do it," said Warren.

"Great," said Salvador, opening the window. He put out his arm and cooed loudly, rolling the r's in the back of his throat. A dove appeared with a ribbon attached to one of its talons and landed on his hand. Salvador pulled it inside and hastily fastened the letter to the dove's leg. The bird lethargically endured the jolts of this careless procedure, sporadically lifting its wings to keep its balance.

"Wait, don't you want to read it first?" asked Warren with concern.

Salvador tossed the dove into the sky, and snapped the window shut as it flapped off.

"What for?" he asked, "I know you did your best." He patted Warren on the shoulder.

"No, I mean if she talks to you about the letter, what are you going to say?"

"You worry too much little brother," said Salvador with a smile.

"Stop calling me that. I'm only two minutes and twenty-four seconds younger than you," said Warren.

"Which sill makes you the youngest," laughed Salvador, ruffling his bother's hair on his way to the door. Warren looked irritated.

"Last one down is rotten lizard puke!" yelled Salvador as he ran across the room, swung around the doorway, and thundered down the stairs, leaving Warren to stand alone in the empty classroom.

"Hey, wait up!" called Warren, chasing after him. He rushed down the stairs and ran through the hall toward the dining room. When he arrived, he found that lunch had already been served. The King sat at the head of the long table with the Queen and Salvador on either side of him. Salvador poured himself a bowl of soup and piled a small mountain of salad on his plate. Warren took a seat next to him.

"It displeases me to hear that the two of you are not taking your studies seriously," said the King as Warren picked up a platter of steamed veggies.

"Dad," groaned Salvador "can't a man eat in peace?"

"You're not a man until you learn to think intelligently for yourself," said the King, smearing some butter on a piece of toast. "What, you think it is your age that makes you a man? Or perhaps you believe it is your size?" The King lifted an eyebrow eyeing Salvador's heaping plate, "Or maybe your appetite?"

Salvador threw him a reproachful glance.

"The privileges of being a prince come with a responsibility to the people whose well-being depends on you," said the King, helping himself to a baked yam. "The duty of cultivating and sustaining the prosperity of a Kingdom is a difficult task, but it does not have to be an unpleasant one. There is, after all, nothing more rewarding than seeing something thrive under your care."

"If I wanted to be lectured, I would have stayed in the classroom," complained Salvador.

"Because of that last statement," calmly replied the King, "you will stay in the classroom for three extra hours today, writing me an essay on why poorly educated rulers are often greedy and hungry for acclaim at the expense of their people." He sliced the yam into orange rings with his knife, "And you had better be convincing," he added.

Salvador smacked his forehead and groaned.

"Make that four hours."

Salvador grunted miserably.

"Five," said the King and bit into his slice of toast.

"Now then," said the Queen interrupting the squabble, "can we just have a nice meal together?" Everyone was quiet for a moment concentrating on their food. The King took a date from a shallow dish on the table and took a bite. "Ah, the Amber Onex date," he said, "It is the second sweetest date on the planet."

"Which is the first?" asked the Queen.

"Why that would be a date with you," replied the King placing his hand over hers. The Queen melted into a smile, and beamed him a look of utmost adoration.

Salvador sniffed, and stuffed a piece of broccoli into his mouth. Warren smiled at his parents and dished himself a ladleful of mushroom soup. A servant approached the dining table. He notified Salvador that a letter had arrived for him. Salvador nearly dropped his utensils. He stabbed six pieces of asparagus onto his fork and with difficulty managed to fit all of them into his mouth. Following suit, Warren quickly vacuumed up the hill of peas on his plate and stuffed two giant pieces of steamed zucchini behind each cheek. Quickly scarfing up the last bit of food and slurping down soup, the boys hastily excused themselves and tore upstairs to Salvador's room.

"Animals," said the Queen gesturing to the state of the table after they had left. "We've raised animals."

The King chuckled.

The boys hurried up the spiral staircase leading to their bedrooms. They lived in two identical towers, which were known as the "twin towers." Built in the exact same fashion, they differed only in their interior design. Salvador's room was extravagant. He had insisted that no less than seven suits of armor (one from each region) be placed around the perimeter of his living quarters. The metal suits gleamed in the daylight that poured in from a strip of windows wrapping around the waist of the tower. Blue velvet curtains draped across the ring of windows as well as Salvador's four-post bed in heavy swaths of fabric. An enormous gold-framed portrait of his favorite legendary hero, Beastadore Willdenwild, hung over his dresser. The paint had cracked and flaked with age, but according to Salvador, this only made it look cooler. Luxurious pieces of stuffed furniture were placed stylishly within the room, some against the walls, and others freestanding. The letter rested on his bedside table on a silver tray.

Salvador tore it open and unfolded the piece of paper within. He paled.

"What does it say?" asked Warren.

"What did you write?" demanded Salvador.

"Let me see it," said Warren taking the sheet of paper. The letter consisted of only one word, "*Yes.*"

Warren looked at his brother apologetically.

"What did you write in that letter?" demanded Salvador grabbing the front of his brother's tunic.

"Well at least she didn't say no!" said Warren in his defense.

"Warren, if you don't tell me right this minute—" began Salvador.

"Okay, I get it," said Warren, wrestling free. "I told her she had pretty eyes, and stuff, women like that sort of thing." He bit his lip.

"And?" urged Salvador.

"And, I—uh, sort of told her that I—I mean *you*, can't bear to exist another moment without her and that you live only to hear her confirm that she too feels the same way and is willing to meet with you at sunset on the far side of the lake to hear in person your vows of true love."

"You didn't," whispered Salvador blankly.

Warren inhaled through clenched teeth, making the arteries stand out on his neck in cords. "I told you to read it," he said in guilty anxiety.

"What am I gonna do?" howled Salvador, grabbing his head with his hands.

"There is only one thing to do, meet with her and tell her everything."

"Everything?" asked Salvador. "I'm not sure I understand what everything even is." He frowned, "and if I did, what's the use anyway? We can never be together, she is not even of noble blood." Salvador breathed heavily in aggravation, sinking down on the sofa with one hand over his eyes.

Warren took a seat next to him.

"King Airyallen Amadeus Miramar married Aleafia Goodlin, even though his marriage was prearranged at birth to someone else, and Aleafia was a commoner," he said.

"Yeah, but he was a great king."

"You'll be a great King some day," argued Warren. Salvador repressed a smile, enjoying the drama of the situation too much to allow Warren's compliment to comfort him.

"The predecessors won't hear of my courting a city girl," said Salvador.

"Father wants you to be a man? So do the right thing and follow your heart!" cried Warren.

"You're right!" said Salvador, standing up. "Oh, but there's the matter of that essay I sort of have to write for father…" He looked at Warren with pleading eyes.

"I'll take care of it, just go before you're late!" said Warren.

"Thanks little brother," said Salvador, and hurried from the room.

Warren sighed, pulled out a stack of blank paper, and headed up to the study room in the north tower.

SALVADOR THE HERO

The next morning at breakfast, the King praised Salvador's essay. He went on and on about the thoughtfulness and clarity of the concepts as well as the effective use of verbiage and illustrative metaphors.

"In fact, it was everything I had hoped it would be," he said with a smile. Salvador looked pleased with himself. Warren listened with interest as he ate a bowl of applesauce.

"The only thing that would have made it better is if you had written it yourself," said the King. Salvador froze. He gaped wide-eyed at his father, a spoonful of oatmeal half way to his mouth. The King slapped down that morning's newspaper on the table before him. On the front page was a caricature of Salvador kissing some frilly young woman.

"Stupid paparazzi!" grumbled Salvador, eyeing the sketch.

"Salvador, this is politically unacceptable behavior," said the Queen.

"Oh big deal!" shouted Salvador. "I kissed a girl! I'm sixteen!" He shoved his chair away from the table, making the dishes clink together. "I'm tired of living in this prison." He rose aggressively, and stormed off.

The royal family ate in silence for a moment.

"It was a very good essay," said the King to Warren with a wink.

Warren smiled and quietly excused himself from the table. He followed the direction Salvador had taken. He searched for his brother in the study and in his bedroom but his twin was nowhere to be found. Finally, Warren went to the stables. Salvador's horse was missing. Warren walked around to the neighboring stall. A magnificent black stallion whinnied, and swung its head greeting the boy. Warren produced an apple from his pocket and held it out to the animal. The horse happily chomped it up in one juicy bite.

"Moonlight, have you seen my brother?" asked Warren patting its nose. He pulled a saddle from a peg on the wall and placed it over his horse, fastening the straps around its body. Warren opened the gate of the stall and led the horse out before pulling himself up into the saddle. Moonlight broke into a gallop, delighted to be outside the stable. Warren directed him toward a small forest up head, enjoying the rolling rhythm of Moonlight's hooves striking the grass below. Warren loved to ride. He felt a slight breeze scoop inside his shirt, and he urged his horse faster, racing across the field. The new day sparkled against the dome above. The clear, half circle of glass capped the entire Kingdom in a giant arching bubble that spanned a circumference of several miles. The dome protected the city from the harsh conditions outside, where the lifeless red desert spread out as far as the eye could see. Outside the palace walls, a small patch of the forest that had originally surrounded the city during the Sapphire Era was left standing within the dome for the enjoyment of the villagers and the royal family. Warren slowed his horse to a walking pace upon reaching the cluster of trees. He rode through the thin wisp of forestry to the lake that had been dug out on the other side. The blue circle of water was still and serene. Salvador sat by the water's edge. Warren dismounted, letting his horse graze alongside his brother's white stallion.

"Its not fair," said Salvador, as Warren sat down on the sand next to him. "I didn't choose to be born the chosen one. Now I have to live by the rules they make up for me."

"It stinks," agreed Warren.

Salvador picked up a stone and skipped it all the way across the lake. The flat rock bounced against the water, leaving a trail of expanding ripples behind it as it sped away, landing in the grass on the other side.

"At least it's not forever," said Warren. "Eventually the Day of the Dominance will arrive, and when you return from your quest, no one will ever tell you what to do again."

"Yeah, but who knows when that will be," sighed Salvador.

Warren laid back, resting on his elbows.

"So how did it go last night?" he asked with a smirk.

Salvador curved his bottom lip in disgust.

"She's not my type."

"That bad?" asked Warren.

Salvador laughed.

"It was pretty bad. She was after me like a hungry cobra after reading your letter." He made a cutesy face, clasped his hands together, and batted his eyelids. "Oh Salvador, is it true you think my lips are like rose petals?" he screeched in an awful falsetto.

"Perhaps I overdid it," said Warren thoughtfully.

"Perhaps I ought to teach you a lesson," snorted Salvador, lunging at him.

Warren leaped away and ran to his horse. "You'll have to catch me first," he laughed, and quickly mounted. He urged Moonlight into a gallop and raced away around the lake. Salvador was right behind him.

They spent the day riding in the fields at the edge of the dome, only returning home after dark.

"Just think," said Warren, approaching the stables, "some day we will have all those mountains to ride in, and more!" He gestured to the red desert beyond the dome.

"Yeah, and we won't have to stay in these puny little gardens anymore. We'll have real adventures," said Salvador. "In new places."

"Places we've never seen before," added Warren.

"We could visit the seven regions," said Salvador.

"I can hardly wait!" said Warren, "I mean, right now, even our *outside* is inside the dome, but not forever, and that's what makes it bearable," said Warren.

"Yeah," sighed Salvador. He was quiet for a moment. "You think I'm really cut out for this hero stuff?"

"Oh come on, of course you are, you're the chosen one aren't you?" said Warren. "If anyone can do it, it's you."

"I guess you're right," Salvador smiled.

They made their way to the stables. After feeding and watering their horses, they headed back to the castle. The blue tinted windows glowed a warm green with the flickering of candle chandeliers within.

Red cheeked and hungry, the brothers came into the main hall from the front entrance, laughing and bantering.

"Your Highnesses, the King requests your immediate presence," said a guard, opening the door for them. Salvador grimaced. Warren gave him a commiserating look. Accompanied by several guards, they walked through the main hall into the counsel room. The King and Queen both rose from their thrones upon seeing them. Their movement was echoed by dozens of counsel members, who also rose and remained standing.

"At last, my sons," said the King, pulling both of them into an embrace.

"Father, I apologize—" began Salvador.

"There is no need, I quite understand."

"You do?" asked Salvador. "Then why did you request to see us?"

The King paused, looking at his two sons. "It's time," he said. The Queen fought back a sob. Warren felt his stomach drop.

"What?" breathed Salvador.

"Now?" said Warren and Salvador at the same time. The twins looked at each other in shock.

"The location of the new pillar has revealed itself on the Seers' Map of Diamondell, come look!" said the King. They gathered around an ancient piece of parchment stretched out beneath a glass case on the King's table. There was a spot of fresh green ink amidst the faded red outlines of the Seven Regions.

"My goodness," whispered the Queen.

"*The Wanderers' Mountains*," Salvador read the inscription below the fresh ink. "That's more than two hundred miles away!" he exclaimed.

"That is why you must leave at dawn," said the King. "And," he added, "you must go alone." Salvador looked up at him. His father continued. "The mistake King Airyallen made was to trust another with such a vital mission when the only one a man can trust is himself. We will not make that mistake again. That is why, my son, you must go alone on this dangerous journey." Salvador nodded.

Warren swallowed. His mouth felt dry.

"We must make the final preparations," said the King, turning to his group of advisors. "Collect what relics remain of the Amethyst era."

Two men in pointed silk hats rose, and departed, moving quickly to the exit. "Prepare the city for the departure of the prince," commanded the King. Six other members of the council moved to fulfill this task. The King turned to the master huntsman. "Pack a light parcel of necessary provisions." The huntsmen wasted no time, quickly moving to the door. "Find me the fastest horse," ordered the King to the stable master. The woman nodded and followed the others out.

"What can I do?" asked Warren.

His father smiled. "Go to bed and get some sleep," he said.

"I want to help," said Warren.

"You need your rest."

"No I don't."

"Sweetheart," said the Queen, "everything is being taken care of. Please try to get some sleep."

"I won't, I can't," said Warren. "I want to stay with Salvador." He stepped closer to his brother.

"So be it," said the King.

All night they poured over the map, plotting the shortest route to the pillar. A copy of the map was drawn for Salvador to take with him. The group of advisors discussed the potential dangers in hushed voices.

"The Wanderer's Mountains are a labyrinth," warned a grisly-looking warrior with an eye patch. He was an old man, with several deep scars in his left cheek. "He will need more than a compass to navigate those traitorous lands. Many a man has lost his mind in that ghostly place."

The King turned to Salvador, "If ever you are lost, try to match the land features to the markings visible on the map."

Salvador studied the Seers' Map intently, as if memorizing it. They labored late into the night, planning and going over potential problems and obstacles. Finally, the King pulled Salvador aside to go over some features of the city that were known to him alone. Warren watched the two of them huddled in the corner. Salvador was listening intently, trying hard to remember everything.

An hour before dawn, a group of maids came to collect the boys and prepare them for the ceremony. Warren resisted leaving Salvador's side. Seeing this, the head maid positioned her large body between Warren and Salvador, separating the two boys.

"This may be the last time I get to see my twin brother," said Warren, accidently betraying his worst fear. He attempted to push past the head maid, but she grabbed a firm hold of his collar.

"Prince Warren, I would advise you to comply, unless you enjoy compromising the respect of your father by looking as you do," she said.

Warren glanced at his father, aghast to be spoken to in this manner. His father nodded in agreement with the maid. Warren realized with a jolt that his hair contained bits of hay, and he still smelled like horse.

"Your highness, we must ready you for the ceremony at once!" cried a second maid. Warren pulled free. He fixed his collar with dignity before reluctantly following the maids from the council room.

Once in the dressing room, the maids attacked him with brushes, combs, and garments.

"Sit!" commanded the head maid.

Warren did as he was instructed and the women proceeded to force a pair of white tights onto his legs. His pony tail was untied, and hot hair curlers were wound into his chestnut hair.

"Up!" said the maid.

Warren stood and lifted his arms like a small child. A billowing silk shirt was pulled over his head.

"We shall dress you in your finest," chatted the head maid in a baby voice, pouting out her lips as she undid the silver buttons of a blue waistcoat. The fabric was shot with tiny silver threads. Warren sighed. He had always disliked this costume, though it did match the style of the times, and was among the finest in the court. After ramming his legs into the knee-length trousers, held open by three different pairs of hands, and slipping on a velvet overcoat, Warren glanced in the mirror. A slender, feminine-looking youth stared back at him with stormy brown eyes and tight lips. He was dressed in a blue silk shirt with puffy matching pumpkin pants and a shimmering vest. Thick winding curls lay heavy around his face. One of the maids placed a frilly white cravat around his neck. Warren glared at her, but remained silent, knowing all protests were useless. His only consolation was a small dagger on a gem-studded belt that hung low on his hip.

There was a noise outside the door. Salvador popped his head into the dressing room. "Are you done preening yet, princess? You are about to miss the only important ceremony of your life," he said.

"I'm coming!" Warren shouted. "Where are my shoes?" he demanded of the maids. Shoes were immediately placed before him. Warren felt his heart sink. Two large bows decorated the toes of each sparkling high-heeled shoe. Grabbing the heels, he stuffed his feet inside them on his way out the door. The double doors of the great hall had not yet been opened. Musicians were playing a forlorn departing tune. Salvador appeared from the direction of the fountain. He was now wearing a dazzling suit of magnificent armor. A hooded velvet cape draped over his broad shoulders and spilled behind him in a dense blue trail. A sudden pang of jealousy swept through Warren's chest like a burst of wind, and he quickly reasoned it away.

"Here goes nothing," said Salvador with a smile.

Warren almost cried. The two of them moved in the direction of the royal balcony side by side. Servants removed their hats as they moved past them. Together, the brothers ascended the long staircase. Warren tried to keep his heels from clicking loudly on the wide steps and echoing across the spacious hall.

"So the day has arrived when we must say goodbye little brother."

"It has come so much sooner than I thought," said Warren, tears welling in his eyes. "Swear to me that you will return?"

"I will do my best," said Salvador, "but just in case, take care of mom and dad for me, okay?"

Warren nodded, unable to speak.

The King and Queen were already waiting when they arrived. It was a chilly morning, the frost had not yet melted from the branches of the trees below. Trumpets announced the arrival of the royal family, and the four of them stepped out before the crowd gathered in the main square. Warren had never seen so many people before. Even servants and peasants were mixed into the audience along with the nobles. The faces of the citizens were thin and pale, their clothes tattered rags. Several hundred people had gathered in a giant ring around a marble statue at the heart of the square. Warren had seen the sculpture up close countless times. It was a carving of a young woman. She sat gracefully on a large boulder with her head slanted to one side, a faint smile lingering peacefully on her delicate lips. One hand lifted to her face, was holding a sphere with a clear gem set at its center. Her hair cascaded down her shoulders in immovable white spirals. The fabric of her robes was crafted so well that the stone visually captured the true weightlessness of cloth. The slight translucency of the white marble gave it a luminous quality even in the blue light of the early morning. Slanted letters looped the words "The Seer" on the base of the statue's platform. The Seer was the legendary heroine of many children's stories. She was said to be a powerful clairvoyant, hidden from time itself in a secret place, and prophesized to return in a time of great need. Storybooks depicted her as sleeping in a hidden chamber, or looking down from an infinitely tall tower. Long ago, the people had hoped for her return, but centuries of hard times had convinced them that she would never come. Warren had always been mesmerized by how lifelike the sculpture of The Seer was. More than once he had caught himself expecting the stone girl to come to life. Warren held his breath, wondering if now, drenched in the rosy light of dawn, and looking almost human, the girl would at last magically come to life, but much to his dismay she remained perfectly still. The square was silent as the townspeople turned their undivided attention to the King.

"The long awaited Day of the Dominance is upon us at last!" announced the King, his crown glinting gloriously around his head. The audience thundered their applause and whooped shouts of joy. Warren had a whooshing sensation in the pit of his stomach and felt his knees go weak.

The King waited until the townspeople quieted before going on.

"The Seers' Map of Diamondell has revealed the new site of the Pillar of Dominance," continued the King. "On this morning, my eldest son, Prince Salvador Theodorin Miramar, chosen by birth for this quest, will set out to fulfill the prophecy and restore the power of the blue Kingdom!" The King triumphantly lifted his arms to the sky. The crowd cheered wildly. People tossed their hats into the air along with flowers, and ribbons. The King turned to Salvador. The audience quieted respectfully.

"Salvador, you must reach the new location of the pillar as soon as possible," he said, his voice echoing across the square, "and place our blue sapphire gem on the Pillar of Dominance before another's stone determines the dominant energy field of our planet for the next thousand years."

A servant approached the royal family carrying a sparkling silver box. The King placed a hand on one of Salvador's massive shoulders.

"My son, do you accept the great honor of this quest?"

Salvador knelt before him on one knee. "I accept, Father," he responded confidently.

"Do you vow to protect and fight for the people of the Sapphire Kingdom?"

"I do!" Salvador shouted passionately.

"Even if you must sacrifice yourself to do so?" asked the King.

"Yes," said Salvador fervently.

Hastily brushing a tear from his cheek, the King opened the box, and pulled out a shimmering necklace. An enormous blue jewel dangled from the blindingly glittering chain. Holding it up for all to admire, the King slowly placed it around Salvador's neck.

"Then we place our trust in you," he called out across the courtyard to the townspeople. The crowd went wild, roaring with shouts of support and admiration.

"We place our trust in you! We place our trust in you!" chanted the people.

"Long live Prince Salvador the champion, our last and final hope!" called someone from the crowd.

"Long live prince Salvador! Long live prince Salvador!" cheered the citizens at a deafening volume.

Salvador rose and drew his mighty sword, lifting the magnificent hilt high into the air. His face was serious and his jaw line determined.

"You have not misplaced your trust!" he shouted, "I will restore the Blue Empire!"

The crowd exploded with several more passionate bursts of cheering and applause, after which musicians pulled out their instruments, striking cords with jubilant fingers, and the streets dissolved into rivers of dancing and singing people unwilling to return to their homes and duties, overwhelmed by the events of the morning.

The royal family was escorted from the balcony back inside the palace. The guards closed the doors behind them.

Warren trembled with pride for his brother.

"Hooray!" he yelled, leaping weakly into the air. A guard clapped him merrily on the back, making Warren lurch forward, but the prince didn't mind, for on this day, everyone was equal.

"Is it hard living in the shadow of so great a man?" asked the guard. His cheeks glowed pink with excitement.

"No, it's inspiring," said Warren, breaking into a smile, and rushing to keep up with his family. They moved slowly down the stairs, stretching the time they had left together. The King held his wife's hand. As they entered the main hall, the double doors were opened before the royal family. A brown stallion was brought forth for Salvador. The stable master led him to the prince's side. A large lumpy pack of provisions had been securely fastened behind the saddle. Salvador climbed nimbly astride the horse and walked it in the direction of the Glass Gateway, through which he would exit, but could not return. Warren felt his lips tremble as he fought back tears. As Salvador urged his horse forward, the crowd parted, clearing a path for him to pass. Many people pressed handkerchiefs to tearful eyes.

A little boy, trailing after his mother in the crowd, bounced on his tiptoes and shouted, "I'm Prince Salvador the hero!" He waved a toy sword above his head. Murmurs of laughter erupted from the surrounding people. Warren grinned so wide it made his cheeks hurt, and felt his eyes get watery. The royal family followed Salvador as he rode to the gateway. Each stride brought Salvador closer to the desolate world outside the dome. The King and Queen walked solemnly behind their son. Warren trailed after them, struggling with heavy emotions.

He dared not look away from his brother, for fear of missing a single precious moment with him. The villagers accompanied the royal family all the way to the overgrown archway etched into the smooth surface of the dome. By the look of it, much of the ivy had recently been cleared away. Warren knew the only way he would ever see his brother again was if Salvador was successful in his quest or somehow managed to survive. The dome would dissolve with the next era. Hopefully it would be the era Salvador had set. What unknown dangers lay outside awaiting him, Warren could only guess. One thing he knew for certain was that Salvador would have some terrifying competition racing him to the Pillar of Dominance. History had warned of the bloody crimes some were capable of to get to the pillar first. Entire armies had fallen, attempting to win the dominance.

Salvador paused by the gate. He turned his stallion to face his parents and the hundreds of villagers behind them. He raised his hands in a final farewell. Mournful sighs and gasps escaped his spectators.

"I'll wait for you!" moaned the voice of a young woman from somewhere in the crowd.

The King reached up and clasped hands with the prince. "I am proud of you, my son," he said. "And I am confident of your victory!"

The Queen tenderly held Salvador's other hand.

"Let this day be remembered not as a sad day," she said, "but as the beginning of a new era. A peaceful abundant era, brought forth by our brave and fearless son!"

The people cheered.

"Farewell!" called Salvador.

A shadow of emotion momentarily contorted his handsome face, and he quickly turned toward the gateway. Salvador kicked his horse into a gallop. The horse charged toward the glass wall. Upon impact, the massive glass seemed to turn to liquid for a brief moment, and then sealed behind Salvador forever. They watched his distorted retreating form through the dome in silence until it vanished on the horizon. Warren stepped forward and touched the solid glass wall in utter bewilderment.

"Come along now, son," said the Queen, gently pulling him

away.

A feast awaited them upon their return to the palace. Many dishes were laden with foods that were rarely eaten due to the scarcity of food. Sweet drinks, fresh fruits, roasted root vegetables, and fragrant salads decorated the tables. Blessings were given and toasts were made, but Warren was not hungry. He picked at his food, unable to stomach more than a few bites. The celebrations went on late into the night. At last, he was permitted to leave the table and head off to bed.

Worn out from the activity of the day, Warren entered his bedroom feeling thoroughly exhausted. One quarter of the circular room was a library of new and old books. The orderly bookshelves lined the walls from the floor to the ceiling. A sliding ladder attached to the middle shelf by a silver rail, enabled Warren to easily reach any book he desired. On the other side of the room was series of large windows that were covered by white gathered curtains. The soft fabric easily let in the light of the moon and kept the room from being overly dark even at night. The bedroom was minimally furnished, giving it a spacious feel. There was a writing desk covered in scrolls and pieces of parchment, a messy dresser, and a comfortable seating area. Off to one side of the room was a circular bed, at the foot of which stood a large golden harp. Warren was barely able to toss his crown onto its pillow by the dresser and rip off the loathsome cravat before collapsing onto the bed. He rolled to the center with a groan and closed his eyes, instantly drifting off into slumber.

Not a moment passed before a clanging metallic noise disturbed him. Warren jarred awake and sat up. Grabbing out the small dagger on his belt, he searched the room with his eyes. Warren listened intently for the noise, but all was quiet and there was no sign of movement. He lit a candle and carefully examined his dresser. Everything seemed normal. His work desk was also as he left it. The silhouette of his couch stood, as usual, on the oval rug by the wall. The gathered silk curtains hung motionless in the moonlight against the semicircle of windows encircling the tower. Warren looked about, quieting his own breathing to better hear the noises around him. Warren set down the candle on his desk and leaned against the bookshelf behind him. He was beginning to think he had imagined everything when suddenly, he heard a second rumble coming from what seemed like below him. The noise was louder than before. Looking down, Warren studied the faded oval rug. It was woven together in wide, flat coils. Without a second thought, he flipped back one end of the rug. The floorboards beneath looked no different from anywhere else in his room. Suddenly, a patch of the floorboards trembled. Warren drew back, suddenly cold with fear. There was a loud thud from below, and a puzzle piece of the floorboards sprung open revealing a trap door. The hidden hinges screamed a whiny question as a dark shape emerged from the black hole. An un-manly screech erupted involuntarily from Warren's mouth and he flung himself at the cloaked intruder appearing from the cloud of dust. The villain easily deflected the attack, catching Warren by the wrist, and with one motion plucked the knife from his hand. Warren fell back against the couch.

"Why are you screaming like a little girl?" the man grunted in a voice Warren knew better than his own.

"Salvador! You scared me half to death!" said Warren feeling weak in the knees. "I'm so relieved that you're—" Warren broke off. "Wait—Salvador? What are you doing here? asked Warren, astounded.

"Shh, quiet!" said Salvador nervously, gesturing for Warren to lower his volume. He threw back the hood of his cloak. He was no longer wearing his armor. Salvador's face was alarmed, and his hands trembling. "I needed a place to stash my things." He bit his lip, his eyes darting around Warren's room in the dark. He was very dirty. Beads of sweat ran down his face leaving rusty trails along his cheeks.

"What?" asked Warren.

"You won't tell anyone, and no one will find it here," muttered Salvador feverishly.

"Tell anyone what? What's going on?" Warren demanded.

"No one must find my armor," said Salvador, speaking more to himself than to Warren.

"I'm confused? Why would it be missing?"

Salvador didn't answer. He continued looking about the place with eager eyes until they came to rest upon the wardrobe. He moved toward it, lugging the heavy-looking pack of provisions out of the trapdoor behind him.

"Salvador, please answer me, what's going on?"

With a clank, Salvador dropped the bag on the floor.

"I'm not going," he said irritably.

"What do you mean?"

"I don't care about no stupid prophecy!" His eyes bulged wide open. "That thing had teeth this big!" Salvador spread his arms out as wide as they would go. "The moment I saw it, I said to myself, Salvador, get yourself the hoot out of here!"

"But how did you get *here*?" asked Warren, gesturing to their surroundings.

"I used the secret entry dad told me about," answered Salvador with a shrug.

"You mean to say there is an entrance into the city from outside the dome, and it leads to my bedroom?" Warren felt goose bumps spreading across his arms and down the back of his neck.

"Yup," said Salvador.

"Do you still have the necklace?" asked Warren.

"It's gone," said Salvador.

"Gone?" repeated Warren.

"Oh sorry, I must've lost it while I was *running for my life*!" said Salvador aggressively.

Warren chewed his lip. "What are you going to do now?"

"Simple," said Salvador frankly, "I'm going to hide."

"You can't just not go, everyone's counting on you," said Warren. Salvador was hysterical.

"I just don't see how *I* can help them. And anyway, what were they thinking sending me out on such a suicide mission? It's impossible." His huge shoulders sagged. "I can't do it, *I can't*, I—I don't see how anyone could…" He continued to rant under his breath as he pulled the hood of his cloak back over his head and walked numbly to the door. Standing back, and gently pulling the door ajar, he peered his head out into the stairwell and looked both ways like a fugitive. Then he squeezed himself through the half-opened door and quietly closed it behind him, holding the handle twisted so it wouldn't make a click when it closed. Salvador's heavy footsteps grew fainter as he moved away, heading toward the crossover bridge below that connected Warren's tower to his own.

Warren felt paralyzed. He stared at the pack of provisions. It sat in a lumpy heap in front of the mirror. This precious bag contained the last remaining magical relics of the ancient wizards of the Amethyst era, protected by the people of Sapphire Kingdom for this one vital quest. Warren tentatively moved toward it. He unclipped the buckles and loosened the drawstring with trembling hands. The city would surely perish. The lives of everyone he knew and loved were in danger. The dome would dissolve with the arrival of the next era, or so it was written in the Book of Instruction left behind by the high council of the seven regions. Who knew what the new era would be? Of the few cities that remained, how many still favored the peaceful times of old? It was impossible to tell. The negative energy had grown powerful, taking over the minds of many. Even within the Sapphire Kingdom, traitors and thieves were all about. Survival had become the priority of man, giving honor a new definition. Even Salvador had succumbed to fear, betraying the only hope his people ever had, to briefly spare himself, leaving the destiny of the Sapphire Kingdom in the hands of a stranger, and in so doing had brought disgrace upon his family. He would now have no choice but to live in hiding for the short remainder of the time that was left to them all.

Understanding all this, Warren ripped off his overcoat and flung it on the floor. The room felt sharply colder. He could feel the cool air seeping through his silk undershirt. He reached into the sack and pulled out the helmet Salvador had worn only that morning. It was beautifully crafted with intricate etchings of historic battle scenes. Patterns of glistening light shimmered across its smooth metallic surface, reflecting the dancing flame of the candle melting on the desk and the pale rays of the moon shining through the windows. Warren slowly lifted the helmet and placed it over his head. He felt an abrupt dropping sensation in the pit of his stomach as if he had swallowed a stone. His dinner squirmed around uncomfortably in his belly as he witnessed his reflection in the mirror hung on the dresser door. The helmet was loose. It looked awkward over his slender face. Ignoring the pathetic-looking young man doubling him in the glass, Warren thrust his hand back into the rucksack, and pulled out some silver shin guards. They had wings etched delicately into their tarnished silver surface. He hastily searched through his wardrobe, looking for the most comfortable clothes he could find. Trading the ridiculous pumpkin pants for a pair of regular trousers and pulling on his favorite ankle-high leather boots, he tried not to think too much about what he was doing.

He strapped the shin guards on over his pants. Next he heaved out a sheet of chainmail. Pushing it over his head and shoulders, he struggled with the weight of it. It rebelled against the helmet nearly taking him to the floor. The iron links draped over him like an icy wet blanket, swallowing his slender frame. Warren pulled the gold-rimmed chest plate out of the bag and pulled it over his head, fixing it into position by locking the two clasps on one side. The shoulder plates and armored gloves were next. Clanking awkwardly around the room as he dressed himself, he wondered if it were possible to sneak up on anyone in a suit of armor.

The suit was horridly uncomfortable. Its cold metallic suit was too big, and it swayed and crashed against his body, touching him with icy jabs that were so cold they seemed to burn his flesh even through his shirt. He found it difficult to move beneath the weight of the armor. His knees felt weak from the panic that washed over him in waves of increasing intensity. Warren knelt down to pull the sword out of the bag. His arms shook as he strained to lift it off the floor.

"You've got to be kidding me!" he breathed in disbelief, gritting his teeth as he heaved the heavy sword into the air, with both hands gripping its massive jeweled handle. It required the strength of both arms to wield and all the fibers of his torso to swing it unevenly through the air.

It was said that this unique magical armor may shrink or expand to fit its master if it chooses to accept him, sensing great courage. Warren tried feeling brave, hoping this would happen, but it didn't. There was little time. Struggling to match the tip of the blade with the opening of its case, he sheathed the weapon and strapped it to his side. Warren raked his fingers through the remaining contents of the burlap rucksack. Feeling the map with his fingers, he grabbed the tightly rolled up parchment, and clipped it to his belt next to his dagger. He pulled out a packet of nuts and dried fruit and a small flask of water, which he tucked under his breastplate. Warren left everything else in the bag, taking only what he could carry. Lastly, he picked up his crown from the blue velvet pillow on which it rested. Using his dagger, he pried out the blue sapphire gem from its heart, and slipped the jewel inside his pocket, discarding the silver ring on the floor. Warren pulled the candle out from its holder and turned toward the dark tunnel in the floorboards. As he stepped down the first dusty steps, the flickering light of the candle revealed mossy stone walls, tightly enclosing a winding stairwell. Evidently, he was inside the core pillar of his own spiral staircase. Thick cobwebs embraced his body and clung to his clothes. As he descended down further and further into the black pit, Warren realized he had forgotten to ask Salvador what had happened to his horse.

THE PECULIAR DELUSIONS
OF PATIENT #338

"Ever wonder what's up with that place?" asked Jim, jabbing his thumb in the direction of the creepiest hallway Nella had ever seen. Jim was a notorious insomniac in his late forties who was prone to supernatural hallucinations. He was perched uneasily on the edge of a plastic chair outside an office door. Nella took a seat next to him. She wondered if she too would be here well into her adult life. Nella couldn't help feeling some compassion for Crazy Jim seeing as they were both likely to be nuts; besides, he had a point.

"It does seem odd doesn't it?" she said, looking down the hallway.

Even the staff avoided walking through that portion of the corridor, and it wasn't hard to see why. An eerie pulling sensation grew from the depths of that space from which a cool draft emanated even when all the doors were closed. Something beyond description saturated the atmosphere in that place, and one had to be pretty dense to miss it. She tried to recall if it had been that way the week before. Somehow it seemed like a recent development, although she remembered other places she had lived also having passageways with a similar feel. Sometimes it had been an archway, or a door frame. One time it was a bridge by the park near her foster mother's house that had held this same bizarre quality.

"Some kind of something is over there," said Crazy Jim uneasily, wiggling his fingers erratically. "But what on earth could it be?"

"What do you think it is?" asked Nella.

"Don't know, a vortex maybe?" suggested Crazy Jim. "Or portal to another world?" He nodded seriously making his dreadlocks bounce along his shoulders.

"You think?" asked Nella, respectfully going along with his story.

"Oh sure, it's got to be, unless it's a ghost," he shrugged. "It could be a ghost." Crazy Jim stroked his chin thoughtfully.

An exhausted nurse made her way toward them. Her walk suggested sore feet and uncomfortable shoes.

"I see you've found yourself a new friend, Jim, how wonderful," she said in a falsely affectionate tone. She hunched over him like a mother hen. "It's time for bed now, let me walk you to your room."

Crazy Jim started to protest, "I told you, I can't sleep in my room, there's a giant weevil living in my closet," he stood unsteadily. "Besides, it's still daytime."

"Well, my dear, we both know you won't sleep at night, and I'll be sure to check for weevils," said the nurse sympathetically as she guided him down the hallway in the opposite direction of the strange passageway. They disappeared around the corner leaving Nella to wait for her session.

Nella wondered if this time would be any different than the others. Mentally resolving to act as normal as possible, she sighed and adjusted the pin on her jacket. Its surface was smooth and pleasant to the touch. This one last object was all that remained of her former life before she was brought to this sterile place. She had been passed around to dozens of different doctors who didn't know what to do with her peculiar immunity to their medications. How long could this go on before they gave up on her? She wondered, and what would happen when they did? Her thoughts were interrupted by the opening of the office door. A somber looking man in a blue V-neck sweater stuck his head out. He had a brown mustache that hung down low over his lips, slightly masking the expression of his mouth.

"Hi there, you must be Nella, I'm Dr. Morgan. Step into my office," he said. Only a slight crease in his cheek revealed that he was smiling. Nella studied his back as she followed him into the office. He had the posture of a military man.

"Make yourself comfortable," said Dr. Morgan, with his

nearly invisible mouth. His voice sounded solid, a voice accustomed to assuming power. She took a seat close to the window on a leather sofa and looked out onto the courtyard. Patients were wandering the grounds in their white uniforms below.

"Can you tell me a bit about yourself?" began Dr. Morgan, looking down at her file. "*Patient #338*" read the cover in stamped black letters.

"I have severe schizophrenia, complete with delusions, voices in my head, and daily breaks with reality," said Nella.

"I am well aware of the nature of your condition," said Dr. Morgan calmly, "I was hoping to get to know more about you as a person."

Nella brushed her hair back from her face, tucking it behind her ear. Her hair was a rich brown, with hints of red. It was quite short and cropped asymmetrically on one side.

"What would you like to know?" she inquired.

Dr. Morgan studied her. Nella had a sweet, innocent-looking face. Her complexion was noticeably fair, as though she rarely saw sunlight. She had simple gold studs for earrings. A pin was clipped to the front of her uniform that read, "Boycott Authority."

"Well," began Dr. Morgan, "you look like a serious, modest girl, not the type to wear something like that," he said, pointing to the button. "It is a contradiction of terms."

"Really?" asked Nella, looking down at the shiny object, "Your comment suggests that a person has a limited, pre-determined pattern of behavior from which he cannot stray, when in fact one is free to act in an innumerable variety of ways at any moment."

"Say more," said Dr. Morgan, visibly impressed with her reply. He nodded his head and raised his eyebrows encouragingly.

"As humans, we must have within us every quality that exists in order to have free will," smiled Nella. "So that we may choose to be greedy, or generous, sneaky, or honest." She spoke casually, as though they had spoken many times before. "I am not limited by a personality unless I believe I have one." Nella rose, and walked over to the enormous bookshelf engulfing the back wall of the office. Studying the volumes one at a time, she continued. "For example, if I were to believe that I am a serious modest girl, like you say, then I would have to censor every aspect of my life to appear limited by that concept and stay constantly vigilant that all is modest and serious *looking* about me at all times. That would eliminate, of course, the wearing of insulting pins as well as a large amount of other things that do not support the image of the identity I would want you to accept me as."

Nella pulled a large book from the shelf and glanced up at the doctor questioningly. Dr. Morgan made an open handed gesture that implied the books were at her disposal.

"Anyway," continued Nella, "all that pretending is a lot of work. And what is the payoff? Why, the approval of those who would look at me and say, 'Nella, you are modest and serious, not like those other girls, you are far better than any of them.' If I were in need of such compliments due to a painful lack of confidence in my own intelligence, it would be socially convenient for me to be perceived in this light, as quiet people are commonly stereotyped as more intelligent."

She pushed the book back into its place between the others and it left a bright trail in the dust that had settled on the shelf since it had last been picked up. "In fact, I would take on any label that is likely to produce the kind of flattery that would temporarily relieve my specific feelings of inadequacy. The question is whether or not living in such limitation for a bit of approval is worthwhile? And I have decided it most certainly is not," concluded Nella, scooping up another book.

Dr. Morgan's eyebrows were still in their raised position forming deep creases in his forehead. He cleared his throat.

"Tell me, how would you describe your personality?" he asked.

"Actually, I cannot find any proof that my personality exists outside of my imagination." said Nella, leafing through a small volume of Japanese poetry. "My personality is merely an accumulated series of beliefs, nothing more."

"So you don't have a personality?" asked Dr. Morgan, pressing the cap of his pen to his lips.

"No," replied Nella.

"And do you think I have a personality?" he asked with concern.

"You don't have a personality, Dr. Morgan," said Nella, "it has you."

Dr. Morgan sat back into his chair. He pursed his lips under his whiskers, making him look like a pouting walrus.

"Who would you be without all your ideas of who you are?" she asked.

"I don't know," said Dr. Morgan considering the question.

"And how much of your personality is a facade, a role you forgot you were playing?"

Dr. Morgan laced his fingers together uncomfortably.

"May I borrow this book?" asked Nella, pointing to thick volume titled "Masters of Chess Strategy."

"Certainly," said Dr. Morgan.

Nella returned to her seat, hugging the book into her chest and crossing her arms over it.

"Please describe the hallucinations you commonly experience," said Dr. Morgan, clicking open his pen.

"Well, I have been hearing the sound of clanking metal for a couple of days now," said Nella.

Dr. Morgan began jotting down tidy notes somewhere among the papers in her file.

"Anything else?" he asked.

"Also, I've been hearing worried voices."

"Voices?" asked Dr. Morgan, "What are these voices saying?"

"They are talking about the chosen one."

"And who is the chosen one?"

"I'm not sure, but he was sent on a very important quest which he has already failed," answered Nella.

Dr. Morgan looked down at his writing. Nella watched him with sudden interest. Her blue eyes scanned him inquisitively.

"You were in the military?" she asked.

"Yes," said Dr. Morgan with a smile, still writing. "I was a helicopter pilot."

"Did you go on any rescue missions?"

"Why yes, as a matter of fact I did," he replied. "And I still work in search and rescue when they need an extra pilot."

"How did you wind up working here?" asked Nella.

"You ask a lot of questions," said Dr. Morgan.

"I'm curious is all," said Nella

Noticing a tiny golden hoop piercing one of his ears, she continued. "Did you ever have a motorcycle?" she asked.

"Yes," he said, a faint note of longing in his voice.

"You're pretty hip for a psychiatrist," said Nella.

Dr. Morgan chuckled.

"That's all long over with," he muttered shyly, shuffling around some paperwork.

"Who's the pretty blond woman you think about all the time?" asked Nella.

Dr. Morgan looked up quickly and cleared his throat.

"What are you talking about?" he asked in shock.

"I could see thoughts of her swirling around above your head," said Nella, gesturing to the atmosphere around the doctor. "You doubt she loves you?"

Dr. Morgan was baffled. He was entirely confused by this session. The recent events of his life were indeed moving about his mind, but how could she have known? Dr. Morgan was uncomfortable. He felt a peculiar urge to confide in this patient even though it would be completely unprofessional. There was something so grounding and honest about her presence that it made him want to confess everything. The weight of his unresolved problems wrestled violently around in his chest, dying for expression and overriding his regard for propriety. In an instant, he decided to risk sharing a little about himself in an attempt to win her trust.

"The blond woman is my wife," he began, looking off into the distance as if he were witnessing a remote memory. "She means the world to me. I used to believe that we were destined for each other."

Nella listened intently.

"She began to feel increasingly distant," Dr. Morgan went on, "and although I suspected I was losing her, I never fully believed it. One day, she told me she was leaving me. I was devastated. Life became meaningless to me for a long time. In the end, she decided to stay, but things were never the same between us. I'm not sure what to do now." He concluded.

Dr. Morgan looked at Nella sitting across from him. Her reaction was not what he had expected. Although she was visibly listening with great care, she was not making any sympathetic comments. He wondered if her illness was worse than it appeared, or if his technique for getting through to her was not working. He was suddenly self-conscious. Putting on a professional voice he decided to take a more direct approach.

"May I ask what are you thinking?" he asked.

"I was wondering how long will you tell that painful story before you realize that telling it does not bring you peace."

The smile visibly stiffened on Dr. Morgan's nearly hidden mouth.

"I don't tell it very often," he said.

"Does the sympathy it produces from your audience do anything to heal the hurt in your heart?" asked Nella.

Dr. Morgan was visibly overcome with emotion.

"When will you get so worn out by pain that you will consider a more effective strategy?" continued Nella, gesturing softly with her delicate hands as she spoke. "As much as you want to be angry with her, don't you want to forgive her more?"

"I have forgiven her," said Dr. Morgan, instantly regretting he had uttered those words.

"You obviously haven't if you are still talking about it. That aching story is saying the hurt within you still lives and wants to be healed; that's why it's still hanging around."

Dr. Morgan's face was motionless. "Her questioning our marriage has opened a rift that cannot be healed, it is impossible to forgive that."

"Who suffers when you resent her, even if you have every right to?" asked Nella, looking into his eyes.

Heat rushed to Dr. Morgan's face. He was afraid of blushing like a fool in front of this teenage girl. It took a moment to classify the feeling welling up from the depths of his chest. It finally identified itself as rage, and hit him with a violent force.

"Out of my office at once!" he spoke unevenly, barely containing the anger overwhelming him. "I will not listen to this utter nonsense!"

Rising from her seat, Nella calmly moved to the door and out of the room. When she was gone, Dr. Morgan realized that he was standing. Something wet and salty slipped passed his mouth and splashed onto his notes below, blurring the blue ink as it bloomed into a soggy splotch. He was faintly aware that the root of his upset and humiliation came from the brutal comprehension that she was right about everything.

THE STRANGER

Warren descended the spiraling stairs for what seemed like an eternity, until at last steps leaved out into a path before him. Sweating profusely under the armor and desperate for rest and fresh air, he was nonetheless relieved to be on solid ground once more. The candle had all but burned out. The stub that remained continually spilled hot wax on his hand, where an angry blister had formed. There was a sudden draft, and the flame went out altogether. Having left the matches behind, Warren cursed and trudged on in total darkness, feeling his way along the earthy walls.

His eyes were useless in the darkness, unable to make out even the rough outlines of the tunnel, so his other senses took over. Feeling his way with his hands and listening to the sounds echoing through the space, he pressed forward, intruding on the occasional rat and slipping in the unforeseeable mud puddles. After nearly an hour's progression, he bumped into a wall directly in front of him. His helmet announced the location of the wall with a loud clang. Touching the wall with his fingertips, Warren realized that it was made of wood. He felt around for a handle, and found a metal ring attached to the door. Pulling on the hoop, he cracked the door open. Warren peeked outside. It was still dark. The red desert was desolate. Giving the ring another tug, Warren slipped out into the fresh morning air. The door slammed closed behind him. With a start, Warren turned to look at the place from which he had come just in time to see the wood turning into glass and melding with the rest of the giant dome arching up into the dark sky. A light stencil of letters remained faintly imprinted on the glass. *Seek not the un-findable, lest it findeth thee first*, they read.

Warren shivered and looked about himself. He stood outside the city's dome where no one but Salvador had been in nearly a thousand years. The air was fresh, but dusty. Large rusty boulders were scattered throughout the plain. An endless desert stretched out before him, its surface scarred and dry. Not a single plant was in sight. He wandered away from the entrance. Looking down, Warren could see Salvador's large hurried footprints leading toward the hidden passageway. He tracked them around the dome for a short distance. After that, the tracks led off into the desert. Warren followed them out until they came to an abrupt halt, indicating the point at which Salvador had dismounted from his horse. The earth was heavily trampled in this area with the smeared prints of man, horse and something *else*. The signs of struggle were evident. Although there were hoof prints leading to this location from the direction of the dome, there were none leading away. Warren felt suddenly sick to his stomach. He looked down at his feet, observing the addition of his own tracks to the scene. Warren went about shuffling his feet through the soil below, looking for the necklace. It was nowhere to be found. There was a soft thud somewhere behind him. Warren looked up. A warm breeze tickled the back of his neck, an odd thing on such a chilly night. Sensing motion behind him, Warren slowly turned around. To his utter horror, a massive winged creature stood before him not more than an arms length away. It stared at him with half a dozen yellow eyes the size of saucers. Its enormous head seemed heavy with a mouth-load of the largest, slimiest teeth Warren had ever seen. Apparently, Salvador was not exaggerating when he had described this impressive attribute. Thick, greenish-gray fur covered all four of its towering legs. Warren trembled inside his armor. The creature sucked in a gasp of air and bellowed a deafening roar. A gust of nasty rotten breath hit Warren's face with the force of a small hurricane, and he leaned into it to keep his footing. His head pounded with the sound of the monster's ringing roar and the racing of his own heart. He drew his sword, struggling to keep ahold of it as he stumbled backwards. The creature lurched forward. Warren swerved away from it. The monster snapped its mouth at him, just as the youth twisted out of reach. It caught the rolled up map on Warren's hip with its enormous teeth. The creature chomped at the parchment, biting through it, and swallowing it whole. Glancing down, Warren saw a tiny stub of rolled up parchment bouncing against his belt. Coping with the loss of the map, Warren struggled to keep ahead of the creature pursuing him.

Suddenly, a second massive beast erupted out of the ground behind him a hundred yards away, momentarily distracting the first monster. Dust spewed into the air. The beast used its deadly claws to drag its belly across the earth toward Warren. It opened its ugly mouth, revealing a nest of suction cups. Warren panicked. The creatures charged simultaneously. There was no time to think. Warren dropped his sword and ran for his life. Diving into a small crevice between two giant boulders, he barely managed to escape the claws ripping at the edge of the rocks. The creatures tried desperately to dig him out, but Warren was just out of reach. He wedged himself to the very back of the crevice, trembling from head to toe.

Time wore on. Eventually the monsters settled down, lying in front of the crack waiting for him to come out on his own. The toothy one rested its massive head and multiple eyes directly in front of the entrance, folded up its wings, and curled up for a nap. Warren smelled its ghastly damp breath blowing toward him in putrid rhythmic bursts. In the moonlight he forced down a bit of his dried fruit even though his stomach was in knots. As the hours dragged on, Warren remained wide-awake against his better judgment. His eyes felt gritty but they refused to close. The stars traveled across the sky, and he knew that daylight would soon come.

A small curious-looking creature scampered by his stalkers. It had mossy blue antlers and a long squirmy torso. It moved on agile little paws in a weaving serpentine pattern. Only the light of the moon on its silky blue hide betrayed its stealthy existence. The monster to the left of the cave's entrance narrowed its eyes at the intruder. With the speed of lightning, its powerful jaws snapped open and closed. Warren peered into the darkness. The small creature was nowhere to be found. There was a sucking noise that lasted several long minutes, after which the monster spit out a flat piece of blue hide, apparently belonging to the creature that had been sucked dry of all its fluids. Warren felt a thread of adrenalin unwind through his exhausted limbs.

Finally, the creatures fell asleep and began to snore. Warren carefully stood. He had to get out. No one would ever find him here. He knew his only chance to slip past the dreadful beasts was while they slept. He stepped forward. His armor clanged quietly against the stone. The shock of it made him drop his bag of dried fruit. He froze, cringing, and then stooped to pick it up. The six-eyed creature cracked one of its eyes half open and then quickly closed it, continuing to snore peacefully.

Warren peered out of the cave to check if he had woken the monsters. The monsters lay motionless. He inched out of the cave, his own body resisting the direction he was moving. He crept to the entrance and peeked his head out. There was no way around them. Their great bodies obstructed any path of escape. He would have to jump over the narrowest portion of one of their towering bodies. Tiptoeing outside of his shelter he gingerly lifted one foot off the ground and began stretching it over the neck of the six-eyed monster's head. He reached with his toes as far as they would go. Holding his breath, Warren decided he would hop over its head and make a break for it. He was nearly over when the monster unexpectedly opened all six of its gleaming eyes. Warren looked down to find it staring up at him gleefully.

"Bloomen' Salvador!" Warren whispered. The beast leaped to its feet, lifting Warren off the ground, and onto its head.

Warren soared upwards. He clung to the thick gray fur. The beast snapped its snout sharply into the sky trying to toss Warren into its toothy mouth. Warren tightened his grip on its fur and was sent flipping over onto its back between its wings. The monster shrieked in pain. Warren found his hands full of the greenish mangy fur. It bucked furiously, waking the second monster.

Recoiling with rage, the second creature sunk its coiling claws into the dirt, readying to attack. Hissing a warning, it darted toward the first monster. The beasts collided with a powerful impact. Warren was thrown to the ground. Snarling and roaring, the beasts wrestled around in the dust. Warren was winded. He struggled to breathe. The monsters tore at each other for a moment before the toothy one pinned the other to the ground. Standing on its skull about to sink its teeth in for a final kill, it suddenly looked up at Warren. Slowly, it released its victim and moved in the direction of the boy. The other monster rose and steadily approached as well. They took their time, seeing Warren could not escape. Warren scampered backwards, tripping in the sand. Something bit his hand sharply. Glancing over, he discovered the ancient sword by his side. Blood leaked from his palm, but he grabbed the glinting handle with gratitude. Rising swiftly, Warren raised the blade and took a fighting stance. The monsters circled him. Warren blindly swung the sword in every direction, slicing the air in broad whooshing cuts. They closed in on him. His blade made contact with one of their thick bodies, and one of the beasts snarled a cry of pain. It vengefully swiped at Warren with its claws. Warren fell to his knees. He had failed the quest, and had doomed the entire city in his stupidity. He should never have gone on this journey alone, he thought. The monsters greedily licked the drool off their lips, and slowly opened their mouths. "No!" shouted Warren, pressing back up to standing and blindly swinging the blade. The monsters drew closer.

"Warfuuna-muffuldoff!" erupted a man's voice. Everything became abruptly still. After a moment, Warren opened one of his wincing eyes and looked around nervously. The monsters towered above him, completely paralyzed in their "pre-eat" position; only their yellow eyes moved, their eyeballs following Warren shocked dismay as he cautiously rose to his feet. The monsters were slowly turning a dull gray color. In disbelief, Warren reached out a hand and touched the black snout of the overly toothy winged beast. It was warm and wet. A sudden frustrated exhale issued from the beast's nostrils making Warren jump.

A deep rumbling bark echoed from nearby.

"It's alright Wooffen, settle down boy," said the man's husky voice. "Are you alright in there?" he called in Warren's direction.

Stooping, Warren eased out from under the cover of the hovering monsters, realizing numbly that it was already light. An old, white-bearded man walked toward him. He was a good bit taller than Warren and broader in the shoulders. A strange tattoo could be seen imprinted on his scalp beneath his thinning hair. The pattern snaked down his neck, and disappeared beneath his robes. An odd, goblin-like creature bounced happily at his heels. It had long velvety ears, an elongated torso, and stubby legs. Its short fur was colored in splotches of white brown and black. In all his years Warren had never seen such an animal.

"Hello there," said the stranger. As light as his spirit appeared, there was something burdened about his posture. One of his eyes was blue and the other brown.

"How did you do that?" asked Warren. "How did you freeze the monsters?"

"That's not important now," replied the man, "We need to take care of your wounds."

For the first time Warren noticed that blood was streaming down his breastplate. The metal was torn in three jagged cuts across his chest. He felt dizzy. Glancing behind him he saw the immobile beasts who had just about eaten him only a few moments before. The last thing he saw was the old man rushing toward him with outstretched arms before the world went dark.

OATMEAL

"**I** apologize for the other day," said Dr. Morgan. "It was improper of me to be so rude in asking you to leave."

Nella shrugged forgivingly, and took her former seat on the sofa. They watched each other for a long moment in silence.

"You are not very talkative today," observed Dr. Morgan.

"What is there that can be spoken that is not already known?" sighed Nella quietly, looking down at her hands.

"I see," he said, Dr. Morgan. "Perhaps you are just a little shy?" he offered.

"Perhaps," she replied. "Though to be shy is not an endearing quality, for to be shy is to be afraid."

"Of what?" asked Dr. Morgan.

"Of disapproval."

"There's no harm in being shy or afraid," said Dr. Morgan.

"True, though it can be a painful way to live," replied Nella. "Shy people often find themselves watching their dreams pass them by, all the while doing nothing to claim them as their own." She finished.

"This shyness, does it ever keep you from what you want?"

"Sometimes it does," confessed Nella. "I'm still working out how I came to be this way. I want to understand this shyness within me rather than exterminate it." She turned around in her chair to glance at the bookshelf behind, unable to forget it was there.

"Tell me, would you say you feel as though you fit into society?" asked Dr. Morgan, watching the fidgety girl with uncertainty. Her peculiar answers were difficult to diagnose.

"I have often felt as though I don't belong or fit in socially, but what are the alternatives? I cannot live as others do, focusing so much of their time on the avoidance of and the escape from what they perceive as reality. And that leaves me with only one option, which is to dig deeper into myself, and find peace with, and even love for, the very society my mind is so eager to despise."

"Hum," said Dr. Morgan, putting on his reading glasses and looking down at the notes he had written in her file during their previous session together. Cringing, he scratched out and scribbled over the written words. Catching Nella's clear eyes observing his behavior, he froze and cleared his throat.

"Eh-hem, I hear you are studying martial arts at the recreation center? You are taking both," he glanced at her file lying open on the desk before him, "Aikido and Tai Chi?" He looked at Nella. "Do you feel unsafe in the world?"

"It's not that," began the girl," I just like the philosophy behind those martial arts."

"What about your family life; I understand you were living with your adopted mother?"

"Yes."

"Would you say your family life was a happy one?"

"Well, as I grew up, my illness became increasingly more severe."

"You have not answered my question," said Dr. Morgan.

"I had many wonderful moments."

"You still haven't answered," he said.

Nella was quiet.

"I cannot help you unless you reply," said Dr. Morgan looking helpless.

"James. That's your name isn't it?" asked Nella unexpectedly.

"Yes," said Dr. Morgan, glancing at the nameplate on his desk. It read, *Dr. J. S. Morgan.*

"And your wife's name is Sarah?"

"That information is easy enough to discover, but it concerns me that you have been investigating my personal life."

"I haven't been snooping around, if that's what you mean," answered Nella.

"Then how did you find that out?"

"I could see her name come up in your thoughts."

Dr. Morgan looked doubtful.

"Its easy to see what another person is thinking when he is upset because the same thoughts cycle through repeatedly like a negative mantra," said Nella.

"I am not upset," said Dr. Morgan.

"Yet your thoughts are melancholy," noticed Nella. "In order to stay unhappy, one has to keep thinking the same depressing thoughts over and over again, otherwise their mood would begin to lift, returning to its natural peaceful state, much like a wooden block will float when released after being held under water."

She looked into his eyes. Dr. Morgan's mind was suddenly flooded with vivid shifting images of his wife. The office seemed to sink in the corner by the window, and spin faster and faster, until it whirled about him. Pieces of office furniture leapt about like wild, shape-shifting animals taking their posts on a new set. He felt as if a movie had come alive around him. He closed his eyes.

"Good morning dear," said his wife's voice. It had a brassy piercing tone. His eyes sprung open. Dr. Morgan found himself in bed. Light streamed in through the window. The covers over his body were warm and heavy. In amazement, he watched the events of that very morning unfolding in perfect order for the second time.

"Sarah?" he asked, looking at his wife uneasily. He was having trouble telling which reality was the real one, the one he had just arrived from or the one he had just woken up to.

"Did you have a bad dream?" she asked. "You look pale."

She was already dressed. She had on a pastel flowered dress. "You'd better get a move on, or you'll be late for work," she piped. Her blond hair echoed her every move.

He glanced at the clock. It was 6:30. He was more likely to be early than late.

"What do you want for breakfast, James?" she asked briskly.

"Oatmeal," said Dr. Morgan, sitting up in bed and studying her static face. She laughed suddenly, barely moving her lips.

"Oatmeal again?" she mocked folding her arms across her chest. He reached for her hand and pulled her into an embrace.

"My darling wife, it is my favorite breakfast, you know."

She pulled away playfully, "Yes dear, but I am ever hopeful that it will someday change because it is the most boring breakfast on planet Earth." She bared her teeth at him in a dazzling fake smile before heading in the direction of the kitchen.

Dr. Morgan reached for a pair of pants with a heavy sense of deja-vu. Every morning he savored the few quiet moments he had all to himself. Slipping on a blue collared shirt, he took his time buttoning it. He caught himself wishing there were more buttons, hundreds more. That he could slowly pass his fingers over each of their round, pearly faces for miles. Was this really such a pleasant task, he wondered, or was there a barely detectible dread of going into the kitchen driving this procrastination?

"What nonsense!" he muttered to himself, throwing up his hands in irritation. Sometimes he wondered whether everyone wasn't just as crazy as the patients of Jenson Valley Asylum, including himself.

"What's that?" asked Sarah, suddenly reappearing in the doorway. She didn't wait for a reply. "What's keeping you?" she asked, reaching cool fingers toward his neck. He felt the fabric tighten uncomfortably around his collar as she concluded the buttoning process for him.

"I was just heading over in your direction," he said apologetically, bringing her hands to his lips. They smelled of soapy roses. He felt guilty for he knew not what. Sarah began to leave, and he followed her into the kitchen. Breakfast awaited. James picked up his spoon and eyed the oatmeal apprehensively. It was watery and undercooked as usual. After a spoonful or two, he decided to get underway. As he left the house, Sarah waved goodbye and before loudly slamming the door behind him.

He wondered why he felt a sense of relief pulling out of the driveway away from his beloved wife. His stomach growled hungrily.

Dr. Morgan blinked. He was back in his office. Sinking down in his chair, he puffed out his cheeks and let out a slow breath.

"I like oatmeal too," said Nella.

CROLACKROLITE

Warren opened his eyes. He was lying in a bed in a quaint, cozy room. A painting on the wall beside his bed depicted a young lady warrior looking across the desert. A silver cuff capped her right elbow where she was missing an arm. Warren looked around, studying his new surroundings. The air was warm and held the faint smell of wood smoke. Comfortable wooden furniture was placed thoughtfully within the room. There were millions of things to look at; strands of herbs dangling from hooks, old dusty books and scrolls piled high on the work desk, stones, crystals, bird feathers, and terrariums containing twisted bonsai trees lined the windowsills. A large animal hide very closely resembling that of the very toothy monster Warren faced outside the dome was draped over an armchair. Glancing down at his own torso, Warren discovered bandages wrapped around his chest. His stomach squeezed an impatient request for food. He tried to sit up. Wrenching pain stabbed through his body. Wincing, he slid back down on the bed. He felt a fresh wave of despair sluice over him, and wondered how he had gotten himself into so much trouble so quickly.

The peculiar animal that had accompanied his rescuer the day before was resting by the crackling stove with its white tipped tail tucked into the side of its long body. Its extra skin pooled against the floor in a fat wrinkle. Warren could guess by its relaxed posture that sleeping by the fire was a frequent pastime for the odd creature. Sensing Warren's attention, the animal lifted its head and looked at him with droopy, conscious eyes.

"Meet Wooffen," said the old man, entering the room. "He's a Basset Hound."

"A what?" asked Warren.

"A bas..." hesitated the man, "Oh, I'll explain later."

"Thank you for saving me," said Warren, overcome with questions. "Why did you help me?" he asked.

"Because I could," answered the stranger simply.

"What did you do to those creatures?" asked Warren.

"I put them under a binding spell," explained the old man, taking a seat next to the bed. "They will have fully turned to stone by now."

"A spell? What does that mean? Can you do magic? I thought the last of the ancient magic was lost at the end of the Sapphire Era?" Warren asked.

"I am the descendent of a long line of wizards," replied the stranger, "and I have inherited and sought out many magical texts."

Warren glanced once more at the mountains of books.

"Can you teach me?" he asked breathlessly.

"I will teach you what I can, but we haven't much time."

"How did you get me here? When I fainted, I was still near the dome," asked Warren.

"I carried you."

"You carried me?" asked Warren, looking at the old man in disbelief.

"I used a suspension spell," said the man with a laugh, looking at the boy's bewildered face. "My name is Wendell Odelious Bloomer. Folks know me as The Pebble Maker, and you may call me Bloom." He introduced himself and outstretched his hand. Warren shook it firmly. "I assume you are prince Salvador Theodorin Miramar, the chosen one?" asked Bloom.

"No, I'm Warren."

"But you are the chosen one, aren't you?" hesitated Bloom.

"No, Salvador is the chosen one," said Warren.

"Then why did they send you?"

"They didn't," said Warren.

Bloom raised a bushy eyebrow.

"But Salvador is coming, isn't he?" asked Bloom.

"No," said Warren. Remembering the quest, Warren fought to sit up again. Bloom restrained him gently.

"For now, you must rest," he said.

"But the pillar..." Warren trailed off.

"Our journey will have to wait one more day," said Bloom. "You are in no shape for travel."

"What do you mean *our* journey?" echoed Warren with distrust.

"If you are to succeed, you will need my help."

"How do I know you are not trying to use me for your own agenda?"

"You don't," said Bloom. "However, at the moment you need me more than I need you, seeing as you don't even have a map."

Warren frowned. "The map has been eaten," he said glumly.

"We will have to find a replacement," said Bloom clasping his chin in contemplation and looking off into the distance. "And that may not be as easy as it sounds, since there are only three."

"There are other maps besides the Seer's Map of Diamondell?"

"Yes," said Bloom. "Telenor's Prism of Refraction, of the Colsmith region can be set to work as a map for the pillar. It is no doubt in use at this very moment.

"What is the third?"

Bloom sighed. "I am not sure, although I have my speculations."

Warren looked at Bloom, realizing for the first time how oddly he was dressed. A thick leather harness was strapped across his waist and shoulders over a short rough tunic and leather trousers. Dozens of small pouches hung from the harness engulfing his body. The faded bags bulged with a mysterious content that seemed to be distributed as evenly as possible across his wide, ancient shoulders. A series of sacks was even sewn down the length of his sleeves and the outer seams of his pants. They trailed in dangling lines, pulling the fabric tight with their weight.

"Why do they call you The Pebble Maker?" asked Warren curiously.

Bloom blinked as if startled out of deep contemplation. Absently loosening the drawstring on one of the many pouches, he reached in and brought out a smooth black stone. It's glossy surface was perfectly round, distorting Warren's reflection and making his nose appear large and nasally.

"What is that?" asked Warren, gaping at the polished object.

"Crolackrolite," said Bloom grimly.

Warren looked confused.

"Long ago, I was cursed for my misuse of magic by a powerful wizard, who thought I would learn to wield it more wisely if I had to carry a small burden for each time I used it."

Warren stared at the heavy-looking bags attached to his harness. Bloom dropped the crolackrolite bead back inside the pouch. It made an audible clack as it collided with the contents of the bag.

"And he was right," Bloom concluded.

"Why do you carry them?" asked Warren.

"Each time I use magic a stone is formed that traps a small amount of my life force within it. If even one tiny stone gets more than an arms span away from me, it begins to suck out my life force until it has emptied my body, and absorbed into the stone, leaving me dead."

Warren was enthralled. "Where does it—er, go, the life force, I mean?" asked Warren. "Does it stay in the stone? Is it painful? Did you have to make any of those things when you helped me yesterday? And if you did, will you have to carry them for the rest of your life like the others? And did I hear you correctly when you said you knew a wizard? How old are you exactly? If the crolackrolite contains a part of your life force, does it then prolong your life?"

"Enough questions for now; it will all become clear in due time," said Bloom, handing Warren a goblet filled with a green liquid. A small sundial was attached to the old man's wrist by a leather strap. As Bloom moved, the sundial spun around on its own, always pointing north. Captivated by Bloom's impressive watch, Warren accepted the drink without looking at what he was being handed. When he finally looked at the drink itself, he made a face.

"Ugh, what is this?" he cried. It looked like pond scum mixed with grass and pine needles.

"It will speed your healing," said the old man.

"What's in it?" asked Warren suspiciously.

"All good things," answered Bloom on his way out of the room. Wooffen scampered after him, disappearing into the kitchen.

Warren was fascinated by Bloom's story. He had a million more questions, but his body's need for food couldn't wait. Warren closed his eyes and tentatively brought the glass to his lips for a reluctant sip. The flavor of the drink was surprisingly pleasant and sweet. It tasted fresh, and felt soothing to his stomach. It wasn't long after he had finished the green drink before Warren drifted off into a deep, restful sleep.

THE FIRST LESSON

Day broke with a brilliant pink sunrise spilling over the horizon in a raspberry flood. Warren awoke and lightly touched his wounds. They felt tender, but the pain had noticeably reduced. The cut in his hand was nearly healed. He gingerly rose onto his elbows and was pleased to find that he could sit up without much struggle.

"I can't believe I feel so much stronger already," he said to Bloom who was writing a note at his desk.

"Good morning," said Bloom, looking up from his work desk to acknowledge his guest, his eyes briefly flickering past Warren as if seeing through him. Warren followed his gaze, looking behind himself at the portrait of the lady warrior hanging up on the wall. He was about to ask who she was when Bloom rose and went into the kitchen. The old man soon returned holding a tray with a pot of tea, some pumpkin bread and two ceramic mugs. Setting the tray down on the cluttered desk, he poured the tea and handed one of the mugs to Warren, keeping the other for himself.

Warren took a series of large gulps from his cup. The tea was spicy and sweet.

"When can you start teaching me magic?" he asked.

"Right now," said Bloom, settling back into his armchair. "Because of the nature of my curse, I will not be able to show you how to cast a spell, but I will do my best to explain how it is done."

Warren nodded solemnly.

"Get dressed," said Bloom, downing the rest of his tea, and tossing a stack of clothes onto Warren's bed on his way out of the room.

Warren carefully got out of bed. He slipped on the rough linen tunic he had been given atop of the bandages. "Thanks for lending me these clothes," said Warren, and reached for his armored breastplate. To his surprise, the gashes in the metal were gone and the surface had been seamlessly mended. "You fixed my armor?" Warren called across to the kitchen.

Bloom popped his head into the bedroom. "No. It's self-healing armor," he said, and disappeared back into the kitchen.

Warren looked at the breastplate in awe. Upon close examination, he discovered a tiny new image etched into the shiny metal. The scene depicted a young man, wielding a sword, encircled by two enormous monsters. He slipped inside the armor, deciding to leave the chainmail and clunky silver helmet behind.

Wooffen lay stretched out by the fire. He was a big animal on little legs. Warren struggled with his pants, hopping on one foot and then the other. When at last they were on, he searched around for his shoes and stockings. They were on the floor by the bed. Warren carefully bent over to reach them and quickly discovered how painful it was to move in this way. Grinding his teeth to keep from calling out from pain, he straightened himself and clutched his chest while the ache subsided. Wooffen looked up at him from the floor. His tail thumped against the wood several times before he got to his feet. Wooffen's claws clicked mellifluously on the floorboards as he scuttled toward Warren. Scooping up a shoe in his mouth, Wooffen placed it up on the seat of a chair within Warren's reach and went back for the other one.

"Where did you find this animal?" Warren asked Bloom, who had re-appeared holding a walking stick.

"I brought him here from Earth," said Bloom.

"Earth? Where's that?" asked Warren, wiping shallow puddles of drool from his shoes with an embroidered sock.

"It is a sister planet of our world," said Bloom, "Its size and atmosphere resembles that of our own planet. There are similarities in the inhabiting life forms as well." Bloom looked at Wooffen. "There are also many differences." He sat down on a stool by the fireplace and leaned on his staff; a magnificent violet crystal was set in the wood at the top end. It was transparent even though it was angular and visibly uncut.

It glowed faintly at the center.

"How did you get from here to there?" asked Warren.

"A windore was opened long ago that leads to Earth."

"Isn't that dangerous? Why was it opened?" asked Warren.

"Some say it was to hide a precious treasure," answered Bloom.

"What kind of treasure would require an environment similar to ours for preservation?"

"I intend to find out," said Bloom, "It is an odd thing; while the portal end on Windefera is stationary, the one on earth appears to be moving around. I suspect it may be charmed to a specific object." He was thoughtful. "Or subject," he added quietly.

"You went through more than once?" asked Warren in astonishment.

"Yes, and to my surprise, the second time I went through, I came out in a different location altogether."

"However did you get back?"

A shadow passed over the old man's face. His lips pressed themselves together in an unwillingness to explain. Warren was alarmed by his response.

"And both times you didn't find it?"

Bloom shook his head.

"Yet you are hopeful you may find it still?" asked Warren.

"I have a hunch that it may not be what I at first thought it to be." Warren seemed to want to say something, and Bloom continued in a rush so as not to be interrupted, "What's more, I think it may be time for *it* to come through the windore itself."

It was Warren's turn to raise his eyebrows.

"No, I am not certain," Bloom replied to his silent question. He looked older for a moment. "I only feel the time is *now*. Come, we have a ways to travel yet." He stood, swiftly throwing on a lumpy brown cloak over his chest harness, and shouldered one of two small backpacks, which he had apparently readied and set by the door earlier that morning. He handed the second pack to Warren. Bloom strode out of the room with Wooffen bouncing happily at his heals. Warren pushed his unwilling feet into shoes, and slung the canvas backpack over his shoulder, before rushing out after the old man and his hound.

They set off at a brisk pace, winding along a dried up creek bed that Bloom apparently used as a path. Eventually the trail began to show signs of moisture and plant life. A small trickle of water could be seen weaving along the sand between the scattered oval stones. After a while they came upon a tiny meadow. It was greener than anything Warren had ever seen. It had vibrant-looking grasses and plants growing easily to knee height. Many of the plants had blooms reaching up toward the sun or hanging from the tips of their stems. At the heart of the meadow was a gurgling spring of crystal water. The company stopped for a drink, thirsty after their hike. Bloom produced a glossy ceramic mug, and scooped it full of water before bringing it to his lips. Warren felt exhausted from the short journey, and gratefully sipped the sweet smelling water out of his cupped hands. Standing up and wiping his mouth with his sleeve, he looked about him at the oasis in the middle of the desert. It had apparently been shielded from the red energy by the steep hillside that cradled it.

"Beautiful isn't it?" said Bloom, "Our world used to be this way everywhere." Bloom bent over and picked a small green leaf, holding it up in the light. "There was a time when these peaceful blooming life forms were cherished and revered, but the powers of plants were quickly forgotten when people became dependent on the protection of kings, instead of the ancient wisdom that had belonged to each of them."

Wooffen took his turn to drink, and slurped noisily from the spring.

"Let us discuss that which truly belongs to you, Warren. For there are many things you may believe to be yours that can be taken from you. What is truly yours is that which never leaves you. It is what you carry with you always without the need of pockets. All of your true belongings are invisible, and they are more valuable than anything you could ever buy. You may believe your material possessions are yours, but "mine" is only what you call them now. And when you leave, someone else will call them that, but these possessions will not be his, just as they were never yours. There are seven things all people are equally given: the ability to be happy regardless of circumstances, the freedom of choice in spite of all imposed obligations, prisons, and laws, the experience of love which in itself can never be stolen, forbidden, broken, or destroyed, the inner wisdom that surfaces through all conditioning, the knowledge and skills that come from life's experiences, the desire to do good, and lastly, the bottomless well of creative energetic magic that flows from within."

Warren listened attentively as the old wizard continued. "Few remain who remember that magic is already within us and therefore equally available to all," continued Bloom, "It is the same energy that is keeping you and me alive in this very moment. It emanates from within each person like this spring endlessly exudes fresh water from the ground beneath." He leaned on his staff and continued, "During the amethyst era manipulating magic was far easier, since a very wieldable energy flowed through the very makeup of our planet. But even today, though it is far more difficult, anyone who wishes may learn to use it, although most are unwilling to make the effort."

Warren paid close attention, though he was having trouble standing. His chest ached uncomfortably. A dragon bug landed softly on his exposed arm. Its green body was the size and shape of a pear. It sported a short, scaly tail and tiny, three-pronged claws. Its slender snout pressed cold lips against Warren's skin for a sip of his warm blood. Warren swatted it away. The bug flapped its translucent, pinkish wings, lifting itself easily into the air. It flapped away, only to return again momentarily.

"You will learn to concentrate your energy and expel it in powerful bursts to manifest what you want. This will leave you exhausted at first, but with practice, and the understanding that you are one with all that is, the unlimited power of the Universe will channel through you, helping you create what you desire," continued Bloom, oblivious to Warren's wandering attention.

The dragon bug deviously landed on Warren's shoulder blade. Using its tiny claws, it tore a small hole in his tunic between the armored plates, and began eagerly sucking his blood. Warren felt dizzy.

Stabilizing him with one hand, Bloom spotted the animal attached to Warren's back. He grabbed the dragon bug. It opened its eyes and made a piercing squeak as he pulled its now chubby body off of Warren and threw it into the air. It flapped its wings but was now too heavy to fly. The bug tucked its tail into its body forming a ball to prepare for impact. The green ball plummeted to the ground. It bounced once in the dust before it uncurled itself and scurried away, resentfully glaring over its shoulder. With a few excited barks, Wooffen chased after it.

Bloom knelt and picked a plant from underfoot. He crushed it slightly in his hands and then handed it to Warren so the boy could press it to his bleeding shoulder.

"Plantain makes an excellent bandage for flesh wounds. It draws out toxins such as snake bites and poisonous insect stings from one's skin," said Bloom, momentarily digressing from the lesson.

Warren pressed the cool leaf against his shoulder. He felt less nauseous almost immediately. Bending down, Warren found a similar plant underfoot and picking a leaf studied it intently. He looked around the small oasis.

"What about that plant over here?" Warren pointed to a spectacular purple flower. It was made up of many tiny delicate flowers grouped together forming an elongated purple cluster. It had elegant green leaves protruding out from under its stunning bloom in wide fingerlike arrangements.

"That one is called lupinus formosus," said Bloom, "and it is highly poisonous. If ingested it causes respiratory depression, slowed heartbeat, sleepiness, and convulsions."

Warren was captivated by the magnificent looking plant. "How could anything so beautiful be so poisonous?" he wondered aloud.

"Looks rarely decide the nature of one's character," said Bloom.

Warren suddenly thought of Salvador and a wave of sadness washed over him. He missed his brother. They had never been separated for so long before, and Warren wondered if he would ever see him again.

"Enough botany for now," said Bloom, observing the shift in Warren's posture. "Let us now try some magic."

Warren followed Bloom and Wooffen across the grassy field back in the direction of the spring. The three of them climbed down onto the sandy soil of the riverbed where a small gully had been formed by the gradual erosion of the stream. A thin wisp of water snaked past their feet.

Bloom pulled the ceramic cup from within his robes and placed it on the ground near the stream.

"Fill this cup with water for me," he said.

Warren reached for the cup, but Bloom stopped him with a gesture.

"Without touching it," he added.

Warren stared at the object in front of him, not knowing where to begin.

"Telekinesis is the most basic form of magic," said Bloom. "The art of moving objects with one's mind does not even require so much as an incantation and can be indispensable in action." He took a seat on a large rock and leaned heavily onto his knees. "Go on, move the cup," said Bloom.

"How?" asked Warren.

"Focus on the object, and use your energy to affect it."

Warren locked his eyes on the cup, his body leaned toward it with concentration but nothing happened. He looked uncertainly at Bloom.

"Try again," said Bloom.

Warren reached both of his hands out toward the vessel. His whole body tensed and trembled with effort. The veins stood out on his neck, turning his face the color of beets.

"Remember to keep breathing," reminded Bloom helpfully.

Warren let out a burst of exasperated air.

"I feel stupid," he said.

"Why?" asked Bloom.

"Because energy can't move anything," said Warren, "How can I move a physical object with a non-material substance?"

"Have you ever turned around to discover someone looking at you?" asked Bloom.

Warren considered this question. "Yes," he said. "Many times."

"It was their energy that moved you," said Bloom. "You were affected physically without being touched. The observation of this phenomenon implies that energy has an invisible, yet measurable density, that can, and does, affect the physical world on a regular basis."

Warren sighed.

"Keep at it," said Bloom, making himself comfortable and pulling out a small book from within his robes. Warren couldn't quite make out the title on the tattered cover. Wooffen curled up at his master's feet in preparation for a nap.

The day wore on. Warren spent an hour zapping the cup with invisible blasts of energy and hovering over it until sweat beaded on his blazing forehead and glided across his skin in salty dribbles that vanished into the sand below. He tried mentally imagining the cup weightlessly levitating, but it remained offensively earthbound. Warren strained to project every drop of his will to move it, while the vessel only mocked his efforts, innocuously sparkling in the sunlight. Frustrated beyond belief and miserably tired, Warren sat down in the riverbed feeling utterly defeated.

"Maybe I'm just an ordinary, boring guy who can't do magic," he said, shooting a nasty glance toward Bloom, who ignored the remark, peacefully engulfed by his book. Warren moved his fingers over the thin stream of water trickling by his feet. Propping his head up with one hand, he absentmindedly hovered his fingers over the water, feeling its shallow cooling atmosphere against his palm. The water was beautiful, running over the bare ground. It hurried to an unknown place, softly touching everything it passed. Closing his eyes, Warren imagined what it would be like to be water flowing in a clear swift flood, seamlessly winding past obstacles. A fluid crystal trail, constantly relinquishing its position, unattached to any path or place. Stillness filled his body. He felt the absolute tranquility of a deep lake. He opened his eyes. I am water, he thought. I move as water moves. Warren rested his attention on his hand facing palm downwards above the surface of the glistening stream. Slowly, he began to lift it upwards. A small mound of water formed under the center of his palm. He lifted his hand higher, and the mound grew. Encouraged, Warren shifted onto his knees and raised his hand even further. The mound diminished significantly, splashing back down onto the sand. Warren knelt by the stream once more.

"I am water," he said firmly, moving both hands toward the

flowing liquid. The mound formed obediently beneath his palms, its cool breath exhaling against his fingertips. He drew his hands toward his chest before swiftly projecting them out in the direction of the cup. Water spewed forward, leaping over the cup and raining down on a sleeping Wooffen in an icy torrent.

"AWWOOOO!" howled Wooffen, jumping to his feet. He barked irritably, swearing in his foreign tongue and frantically shaking the vile liquid from his hide.

"He doesn't like getting wet," explained Bloom.

Warren repressed a triumphant grin.

"You can smile, Warren," said Bloom, "I won't hold it against you."

Bloom stood and clapped Warren on the back. "The water likes you, Warren. That is most auspicious." The old man shouldered his backpack once more and set off toward the mountains.

"That's not the direction of home," noticed Warren.

"You're right," said Bloom. "We're not going home."

Warren followed him. "And I believe the Wanderers' Mountains are not that way either," he said.

"Correct again, but before we set a course for the Pillar of Dominance, we will first need a map," said Bloom.

WINDORE

Dr. Morgan opened Nella's file. His colleagues had unanimously agreed that she was beyond help. Dr. Morgan considered everything that had happened during the last few sessions. Something was unusual about this patient, that much was for certain. Her ability to guess what he was thinking as if she could see into his mind and witness memories was positively alarming. Perhaps this was why so many doctors had insisted on handing her over to someone else as quickly as possible.

The phone rang and he answered it mechanically.

"Hello, Dr. Morgan speaking."

"Good morning, my name is Dr. Maverick Elson," said a crackly, masculine voice on the other end. "I'm calling on behalf of a young woman you are currently working with. She's a new patient of yours I believe. Her name is ah, let me see..." There was the sound of shuffling papers. "Nella, her name is Nella Lira Johnson."

"I know of whom you speak," said Dr. Morgan.

"It has come to my attention that she has been institutionalized for quite some time without any visible improvements," said the voice. "It may be time to take more drastic measures. There is a government program that can help girls with her condition with the consent of a physician—"

"Government program?" Dr. Morgan interrupted. "I have never heard of such a program. Nor have I, in nearly twenty years of practice, met another patient with a condition like Nella's. Jensen Valley is among the top leading psychiatric facilities in the country. If she is to improve at all, it will be here."

"We will come to collect her in two days time."

"I won't allow it," said Dr. Morgan angrily. "You do not have the consent of this physician!"

There were dial tones on the other end of the line.

Dr. Morgan slowly put down the receiver. He was deeply unsettled by the call and suspected that Nella was no longer safe at the Asylum. Someone had discovered her unique talents and had the intention of using them for their own gain. Of course the staff at Jensen Valley would only be happy to be rid of her. They would go along with whatever story they were fed as long as the paperwork checked out.

There was a knock on the door.

"Come in," called Dr. Morgan, still troubled by the call.

The door opened and Nella stepped in.

"Good morning," she said, placing a book on his desk. "Thank you for lending this to me."

"You're welcome," said Dr. Morgan distractedly. "Nella, can you tell me more about the voices you've been hearing?"

"Oh sure," she said. "They are louder than ever today. They've been talking about a windore all evening."

"To whom do the voices belong?" asked Dr. Morgan.

"Two men, a younger one named Warren, and an older one named Bloom."

"And what is a windore?" asked Dr. Morgan.

"As far as I can tell it is a portal to another world."

"Should I ask the nurse to up your medication?" asked Dr. Morgan.

"Medications don't help me," said Nella. "Anyway, crazy Jim knows about the windores too. He showed me where one was even before the voices told me about it."

"Jim?" asked Dr. Morgan, "And where might this windore be?"

"It's in the hallway just to the right of your office," said Nella.

Dr. Morgan ran his fingers through his hair anxiously. She was not speaking sanely. Yet he knew that she didn't belong here, and could not remain here much longer.

"I want to get you better so you can go home," said Dr. Morgan.

"But the delusions are getting worse," said Nella. "And I haven't a home to go back to."

Dr. Morgan shifted uncomfortably in his chair. "We will find a way to get you well," he said.

"How?" asked Nella.

Someone rapped on the door. The same tired nurse from before opened the door and wheeled in a metal cart.

"Nella is refusing to eat," she complained to Dr. Morgan. "Perhaps you can convince her of the necessity of this daily practice." She placed a tray of food on the table beside Nella.

"I'm not hungry," said Nella, eyeing the mashed potato paste, canned peaches, and jello.

"Eat your food," said the nurse smoothing a stray wisp of gray hair back into her bun. "There are children starving in the world."

"I don't see how my gluttony helps the starving children," said Nella.

"You see what I have to deal with?" said the nurse to Dr. Morgan, gesturing irritably in Nella's direction. She left the tray beside Nella and wheeled the cart back out of the room muttering to herself.

"Why are you not eating?" asked Dr. Morgan gravely.

"The visions are so strong I can no longer stomach anything," said Nella.

"Visions of what?" asked Dr. Morgan.

"A world ruled by a powerful negative energy for one thousand years, or rather, what's left of it." Nella looked into her hands.

Dr. Morgan was at a loss for words. He sighed helplessly.

"Perhaps you can talk to her," said Nella, abruptly changing the subject.

"Talk to whom?" asked Dr. Morgan.

"Your wife," said Nella, "She is angry with you, and if you don't communicate with her, you will split up over a simple misunderstanding."

"We are not here to discuss my private matters. "

"Alright," agreed Nella. "What would you prefer to talk about?"

"Don't you see? It's not a simple matter!" Dr. Morgan went on, unable to leave the subject that concerned him the most. "Relationships are complicated beyond belief!"

"Or perhaps it is our beliefs that complicate our relationships?" offered Nella.

He glared at her.

"What are you afraid would happen if you were fully honest with her?" asked Nella.

"Its easy for you to escape in the thoughts and problems of others instead of examining your own, Nella. This is no good, no good at all."

"You are right, and even so, what do you fear would happen if you told her the total truth, just as it is for you?"

"She would leave me once and for all, and I would be alone forever."

"Can you know that she would leave you, and do you want her to stay with you even if that's not what *she* wants?"

"No," said Dr. Morgan firmly. "But I'm afraid to lose her!"

"Why?" asked Nella.

"Because I don't know who I am without her."

"You are already living as though you have lost her," said Nella.

Dr. Morgan rubbed his temples.

"And you are using her to hold your own identity together," she went on, "That is a difficult way to live because in order to even feel like yourself, you must do whatever it takes to stay on her good side, meaning you sacrifice your freedom and what you really want each day for her approval."

"Naturally," said Dr. Morgan.

"Furthermore, if you believe she makes you who you are, then you are bound to both love and resent her at the same time," said Nella. "Because you will desperately need her approval to feel like a good person, which will make you manipulate her to get the approval you crave, which will make you disgusted by your own manipulation, which will drive you to resent her for making you into a manipulative person, and you will end up mistrusting the approval she gives you anyway."

"I hate to admit it, but what you just said actually made some bizarre kind of sense," said Dr. Morgan grimly.

"Doesn't needing her approval instead of feeling like a good person from within your own self hurt as much as living with a physical wound that won't heal?" asked Nella. "You have nothing left to lose. In the worst case scenario, you get to find out who you really are, without her shaping your identity."

"What are you, my guru?" said Dr. Morgan with a cringe. "Why are you so philosophical all the time?"

Nella laughed, and fell back against the sofa.

"And another thing," said Dr. Morgan, "I don't like how we have reversed roles here. I am the therapist and you are the patient, not the other way around."

"And with no story of what roles we ought to be pretending to believe in, client, therapist or otherwise, how would it feel to inhabit this moment?" asked Nella.

"With no story, we are equals, and that is frightening," said Dr. Morgan, "and there would also be nothing separating us. The intimacy and un-guardedness of that is even more terrifying and uncomfortable."

"Why do you think that is?" said Nella.

"Because dropping all titles makes the facades become visible and as they fall away they leave me as totally unidentified, and unknown even to myself, it leaves me..." he trailed off.

"Free," said Nella. "And isn't it that freedom what you have worked toward, and run from your whole life? Haven't you been yearning for a break from the stress-creating stories of who you think you are and at the same time terrified of letting them go?" asked Nella, smiling innocently.

"Alright-alright," said Dr. Morgan, waving her away and checking his watch. "We're out of time for tonight."

"See you tomorrow, Dr. Morgan," said Nella, hopping to her feet. She skipped to the door and out of the office.

Dr. Morgan packed up his things to go home. He threw on his jacket and grabbed his briefcase. The copy of "*Strategies of Chess Masters*" Nella had borrowed lay on his desk. He faintly remembered having wanted to read that book some time ago. He tucked it under his arm and switched off the light.

Standing out in the hallway, he felt a slight tug on his clothes. Dr. Morgan turned around to see if anyone was there, but there was not a soul in sight. The sensation persisted. A cool draft wafted from the dim hallway. Dr. Morgan walked toward the dark end of the corridor. The draft seemed to pick up in this area. He knelt down on one knee and pulled the book from under his arm. Without thinking twice, he hurled it through the hallway. It sailed through the air. There was a sudden blast of electric light illuminating the empty corridor and engulfing the object. Dr. Morgan listened for the sound of the book hitting the floor, but it never came. He straightened up and cautiously walked down the hall looking for the bright yellow cover. It was nowhere to be found.

SPARKS

"We have five more days to reach the pillar before it vanishes for another millennium," said Bloom.

They had broken for lunch after a strenuous trek. Bloom dipped a spoon into a small pot above the campfire for a taste of the soup. Wooffen's nose quivered in the direction of the spoon.

Warren poked at the hot coals with a stick. "And we have no idea where it is, no way of getting another map, and are three days behind our competitors for the Dominance, few of whom are likely to be traveling on foot," he said with a note of panic in his voice.

"Everything is not so bad," said Bloom, adding a pinch of spices to the pot from a leather pouch.

"Not so bad?" cried Warren. "We've covered only half the distance we planned to this morning due to my injuries. Even if we were to reach the windore in time, what makes you think the treasure will be there, that we will be able to recognize it, or that it will be any assistance to our quest at all?"

"Time has taught me to trust life's events to unfold as they do," said Bloom. "If we do not yet have the map, it is because we do not need it."

"We must do something!" Warren groaned, grabbing his hair with his hands.

"We are doing all we can with what we have been given," said Bloom.

"You don't understand!" shouted Warren. "All will be lost!"

"Can you know that for a fact?" asked Bloom calmly.

Warren stared at him blankly as the old man continued, "Let

us look at what we know to be true, not in theory, but in reality. At this moment, nothing is lost, you are recovering most excellently, and we are about to have a delicious soup."

Warren snorted. "In a desert filled with horrible wild animals, with a wizard who cannot use magic, and a four-legged troll for a guard!"

Wooffen shot him a resentful glance. Bloom patted his dog on the back.

"Now that you have learned to wield magic yourself, there is hardly a need for my help," he said.

Warren rolled his eyes.

"As for Wooffen," Bloom went on, "his nose is among the best of all the dogs on the entire planet of Earth. I gladly entrust my safety to his impeccable senses."

At these words, Wooffen straightened up, puffed out his chest, and tilted his head upwards showing off his impressive nose. His pose was so self-important that both men cracked up with laughter. Wooffen looked thoroughly insulted.

"Do you think he understands anything we are saying?" asked Warren.

"I doubt it," said Bloom with a smirk.

To which Wooffen rose, burned them with a sad, meaningful glare, and moved to the opposite side of the fire from where they were sitting.

"It's time for your next lesson," said Bloom, "Let us now work with the fire."

Warren looked unhappily at the blazing logs before him.

"Just as with the water, I want you to mold the flames with your mind," said Bloom. "Try to get a sense of this new material, how it moves, what energies fuel or inhibit its form."

Warren tried to focus on the flames, but his attention kept wandering back to the quest. He wasn't even supposed to be here. Whatever happened to 'Salvador the hero' he wondered angrily.

A spark leaped out of the flames and exploded with a loud pop.

"That's it," said Bloom.

"Did I do that?" asked Warren uncertainly.

Bloom shrugged.

"We'll only know for sure if you can do it again."

Warren directed a wave of frustration toward the fire pit, thinking of all he had been through and all he had parted with. A shower of sparks erupted from the ring of stones.

Warren smiled at his success.

"Fire is easier to wield than water."

"Easier to wield, harder to control," replied Bloom. "Water requires a stillness of mind that few can attain, but in the end, that kind of peace is a much more powerful force."

Warren was thoughtful. "What happens if no one finds the pillar?" he asked unexpectedly.

"It's difficult to tell," replied Bloom, "I'm guessing the previous era would repeat, its intensity diminishing over time as it gradually morphs into a new era at its own natural pace. That is why even a prosperous era needs to be re-set in order to be sustained."

"So the red energy would wear off?"

"Certainly," answered Bloom. "After a very, very long time."

"Perhaps it would be better not to meddle with the pillar at all, and allow windifera to set her own energy dominance?" offered Warren.

"There are planets that operate that way," said Bloom.

They both looked at Wooffen, who was busy digging after a rodent, his nose pressed to the dirt. He barked into a small hole he had dug in the ground, his voice muffled by the sand. Wooffen's muzzle was very dirty. Wincing one eye, he inhaled sharply and sneezed, rousing a cloud of dust around him that quickly settled, coating his fur a pastel orange. Warren struggled not to laugh so as not to offend the hound for a second time. Smiling, Bloom divided the soup into three metallic bowls. The company ate in a hungry silence. Only the lapping of Wooffen's long, pink tongue disturbed the otherwise quiet evening. The combination of herbs was like nothing Warren had tasted before, but the flavors somehow reminded him of home. He mentally saw the many faces of the people he loved and imagined what they may be doing. Much to his amazement, Warren discovered that as his bowl emptied, and his hunger was relieved, so too were the feelings of homesickness.

Shadows slowly extended in preparation for the night. The enormous sun hung low in the sky, a freshly minted coin, hot and shimmery. Soon they were on their way again, moving quickly across the evening desert.

SESSION NUMBER 4

Nella took her usual spot on the red leather sofa. Dr. Morgan was at his desk still engrossed in some paperwork.

"Good morning Nella," he said, smiling broadly and tossing the papers aside in a thick stack.

"Good morning indeed," said Nella, observing his mood. "Have you asked Sarah why she chose to stay with you?" she asked curiously.

"It is not appropriate for me to talk with you about my personal life," said Dr. Morgan looking out the window to avoid her gaze. A small cleft formed in his cheek to the right of his mustache.

"I can already see that you have," said Nella with a smile. "What did she say?"

"I know you don't have to ask to find out," said Dr. Morgan, "and that is why I appreciate the question even though I don't intend to answer it."

Nella beamed.

"Those thoughts are your private property, and I will do what I can not to trespass, but if you keep thinking so loudly, I will not be able to help it. Since the only thing louder than sad thoughts are happy ones."

Dr. Morgan helplessly broke into a smile.

"You would have to see it to believe it," he said, guilty with happiness.

"Perhaps you can show me?" suggested Nella.

"Nella!" exclaimed Dr. Morgan. "What am I to do with you?" He grinned sheepishly.

"Close your eyes," said Nella.

Dr. Morgan sighed, but complied, and as he did so, his mind was instantly filled with flashing images of hours past. They flickered before him in a rushing slideshow. Bits of conversations zipped by as his mind raced through the records of his life. The office shifted and swirled around him once more, morphing into the living room of his own house. With a final wobble, the walls snapped into their new shape, supporting the familiar structure of his own house. His life had rewound to the pervious evening. He was sitting on the couch. Its fabric was itchy and uncomfortable even through his clothes. He was wearing his favorite wool sweater. The room was warm and quiet. Sarah slipped in silently, and sat down on the opposite end of the couch, holding a mug of tea in one hand. She picked up the remote control and switched on the television. A buoyant toothpaste advertisement jumped to life across its glassy gray surface, casting erratic bursts of blue light across her face. Sarah caught her husband's gaze.

"What?" she asked defensively.

"Nothing," said Dr. Morgan feeling trapped in the overly warm sweater.

"How was your day?" she inquired in a more pleasant tone.

"Fine," said Dr. Morgan dejectedly.

"So glad to hear that dear," she said, a hard note in her voice. Her words were spoken like a punishment.

"Are you trying to kill me with kindness?" asked Dr. Morgan.

"What is going on with you tonight?" exploded Sarah, roughly setting down her tea to give him a stern look. Hot liquid splashed out onto the coffee table forming a tiny mint lake on the glass.

"I'd better clean that up," she said as she reached for the mug, visibly eager to leave the room.

"Hold on," said Dr. Morgan, catching her at the wrist. "We need to talk."

"I am not one of your patients," shouted Sarah recoiling from his touch. "There's nothing to talk about!" Her small frame shook.

"I'm afraid there is," Said Dr. Morgan sadly, "and it cannot be put off any longer."

He reached for the remote and clicked off the television. With an electronic groan, the animated images imploded off the screen. Dr. Morgan got to his feet.

"Sarah," he said moving toward her to better see into her eyes. "I love you, and I don't need you to stay with me."

Sarah pressed her lips together to keep them from trembling. Tears welled in her blue eyes.

"I have been pretending that I need you too much to let you go, but you are free to leave me and I would be alright if you did," said Dr. Morgan, looking at her tearful face.

"I don't want to do this again," cried Sarah. "I already chose to stay with you." Her breath was irregular with emotion.

"You chose to stay with me at the expense of your own happiness," said Dr. Morgan. "When you live to make me happy, there is no longer room for you in your own life. This is not a sacrifice I ever wanted you to make."

"Are you trying to hurt me on purpose? I'm still here aren't I, what more do you want from me?" pleaded Sarah, her face contorted with pain.

"I'm bringing this up because I don't want you to hurt like this anymore. You deserve to live the life you desire," said Dr. Morgan. He reached out a hand and rested it on her shoulder. "The life of your dreams."

"Are you throwing me out?" asked Sarah in between sobs, "Don't you care about me at all?"

"Loving you makes my existence worthwhile," said Dr. Morgan, landing a kiss on her cheek. "I treasure every moment with you, and would love you just as much even if you left."

She threw her arms around him.

"I don't want to be away from you!" she cried into his sweater. "And yet I feel like a prisoner."

"I can see that you are going through some difficult things," he said returning her passionate embrace. "You don't have to go through it alone."

"I am miserable and I have been blaming you for all of it." She sobbed. "I resent you for not giving me..." she trailed off, "...for not giving me all the things I never asked for," she finished. She laughed through her tears, "That sounds awful, doesn't it?"

He rocked her gently in his arms.

"It sounds honest," he said. He held her close. "What do you want, my darling wife?" he asked.

"I don't know what I want," said Sarah, pulling away to look up at him sadly.

"Then let's find out together," said Dr. Morgan drawing her in again. "What would you fill your life with if you were free? Because Sarah, you are free!" His voice was warm. "I'm here, and I'm not going anywhere. You are safe with me."

Sarah rested her head on his chest.

"I don't believe you," she said.

"Then I'm going to keep telling you until you do. And eventually, when many years have passed and I'm still here just like this, you won't be able to keep from believing me."

"That might work," smiled Sarah, looking up at him. Her eyes brimmed with fresh tears. "I would go dancing more," she said thoughtfully. "And I would tell you how angry I am with you for ignoring me." She lightly hit him through the grey sweater. "And I would get a job so I don't have to be cooped up in this house for so long by myself, and could depend on your money less, and get a dog."

"Well that's a good start," he said. "We will do all of that, and everything else you discover you want."

Sarah began crying softly again.

"What is it?" he asked.

"It's been too long since I let myself love you like this," she answered.

Dr. Morgan blinked and was back in the office. Nella beamed at him.

"Thank you," he said to her, a quiet happiness in his voice. "For helping me talk to her."

"My pleasure," said Nella with a smile.

"Funny how life can go from painful to wonderful in so short a time," said Dr. Morgan thoughtfully.

Nella nodded.

"There is also something I have been wanting to talk with you about," he went on, a wrinkle forming between his eyebrows. "The delusions you've been having may not be what we thought."

"What do you mean?" asked Nella in surprise.

Disturbed voices erupted outside the office walls. Dr. Morgan glanced in the direction of the noise before continuing.

"What I mean to say is that the wind—" he broke off.

Three huge men in black police uniforms burst into the office. Dr. Morgan became noticeably tense. Standing, he moved himself between them and Nella.

"Who let you in here?" he demanded. "You cannot be here."

One of the men brushed Dr. Morgan aside, shoving him hard against the office door.

"She is no longer your concern," said the man, releasing Dr. Morgan, who slid down several feet before regaining his balance. "Nella, you are to come with us," the large man continued. The sleeves of his shirt were tight around his muscular arms, his eyes hidden behind dark glasses.

"Why should I go with you?" asked Nella.

"Because I have the authority to take you away," said the man.

"And what is authority?" said Nella.

The man stared at her through impenetrable dark lenses.

"How did you acquire this power?" inquired Nella.

"It was given to me," he growled.

"But how can you be given something that doesn't exist?" asked Nella. "Since authority is a fictional power that does not exist in reality. It has been made up to give people the illusion of control over others."

"You will do as I say," breathed the man angrily, taking a step toward her and taking ahold of her arm, "or you will get a taste of my authority, and I don't think you're gonna like it."

Nella noticed Dr. Morgan trying to get her attention behind their backs. He waved her toward the door.

"And if I don't do what you say, where does your authority go?

If it is my compliance that grants you this imaginary authority, then it is not your power at all," said Nella, "it is mine!" Turning her wrist, she pulled it out of his grasp where his thumb and fingers overlapped and dove between the three men who lunged at her all at once. Nella felt huge arms press down heavily on her back. She ducked down and away from the attackers, barely managing to escape.

"This way!" shouted Dr. Morgan flinging open the door just long enough for the two of them to pass through before slamming it shut and bolting it closed from the outside. Grabbing her hand and pulling her behind him, he bounded down the hallway at full speed. Nella could hardly keep up with him.

They heard loud bangs exploding inside of the office. Patients peeked their heads out of their rooms to watch the commotion.

"Listen to me, Nella!" Dr. Morgan yelled looking back at her. The white walls zipped by them. Another loud bang issued from the office door and it burst off its hinges spitting splinters of wood across the floor.

"You are not crazy!" cried Dr. Morgan. His eyes shifted their focus to something behind her. A shadow swept across his face. "These people mean you harm," he said.

Nella felt tears drawing from her eyes and she fought hard to resist them. Her throat was choked and her vision blurred. They were almost at the center of the creepy hallway when Dr. Morgan came to a sudden halt. Three dark shapes barreled toward them, closing the distance rapidly. Dr. Morgan clasped Nella's shoulders firmly with both hands.

"But I am crazy," cried Nella. "Why else would I be here?"

"Listen!" rushed Dr. Morgan. "The windore exists! And you must go through it now!" He gently pushed her forward.

"What about you?" hesitated Nella.

"I'll be fine, just go!" he bellowed turning away from her to face the policemen.

"I can't leave you to face them alone," said Nella.

"Just let me save you this one time, alright?" he called over his shoulder rolling up his sleeves. "I want to feel like a righteous psychiatrist for once. Now run!"

Nella ran. The hallway got shorter and shorter. A horrible dead end wall barricaded her passage only thirty feet ahead. She felt sick. Suddenly, her uniform rustled against her skin as if moved by a powerful wind. A blinding light erupted from the atmosphere like a bolt of electricity. Nella heard a shrill rewinding sound surge through the hall. There was a flash of blinding light, and she felt herself sucked forward.

With a shout, Nella fell onto red dirt. She tasted grit. Weakly pushing herself up onto her hands, she looked about. She was outside in a lifeless desert. The air was dusty and dry. Rusty cliffs were scattered across the earth like giant sleeping whales, their dull surfaces gleaming faintly in the evening sun. This strange deserted place sharply reminded Nella of the delusions that had filled her mind for so many years. She collapsed on the ground gasping for breath. Tears streamed down her cheeks.

"There-there," said a deep voice behind her.

She whirled around. A great monstrous beast stood behind her. She screamed and fell backwards onto the rough soil. Her eyes widened in horror, and her heart threatened to leap from her chest. The beast was the size of an enormous tiger. Dark fur covered its giant body in ungroomed shaggy locks. Long whiskers hung from its protruding pink snout. Its powerful back arched upwards behind its large head in a tight knot of muscle.

"No need to be frightened," said the beast with a smile of razor teeth. "I will not harm you." The creature's violet irises contracted and expanded as it looked at her hungrily.

"You can speak?" she whispered in shock.

"Of course I can speak, what a silly thing to ask," it answered stepping closer.

"W-what are you?" stammered Nella.

"My name is Tigorious, I am a Stealthalore Phelenium, and I will be your guide through these dangerous lands," it answered. "I was sent to collect you. We have long been awaiting your return." He bowed gracefully with his front paws.

"You have?" asked Nella cautiously.

"Yes, and now I will take you to his Majesty Prince Coonan Malden, ruler of the city of Augden of the Diamondell Region."

"What is this place?" she asked, gesturing to their surroundings.

"You are on Windiffera, a planet three googles away from the planet Earth," said Tigorious.

Nella stood and absentmindedly brushed herself off.

"So far away from home," she muttered sadly as a fresh swell of tears gushed to her eyes.

"This is your true home," said Tigorious, "and I think you will fancy it in due time."

Nella was quiet. Looking down, she noticed a spot of yellow in the dirt no more than a yard away. In disbelief, she reached over and picked up the chess book she had borrowed from Dr. Morgan.

"How on earth did this get here?" she asked out loud in bewilderment.

"Don't you mean, 'how in Windiffera did this get here?'" asked Tigorious with a smile. Four impressively large fangs glinted from underneath his lips in the fading light.

Nella smiled back weakly.

"Come now, it is a two-day trek to Augden City, so we'd best be on our way." With these words Tigorious turned away from the sun sinking behind the horizon in a glowing bronze orb and set off in a smooth prowl. Nella watched him slink ahead a few paces. She was somehow doubtful he was worthy of her trust. A distant wild sounding howl disturbed the silence of the desert. It was joined by several others.

"Wait up for me," said Nella, breaking into a jog to catch up with Tigorious.

A MEETING OF WANDERERS

"**W**ooffen, stay close. It's not much further," said Bloom, as they trudged on in the total darkness. Wooffen trotted over to his master's side. Every now and then the tops of his velvety ears would lift ever so slightly as he listened for things inaudible to the ears of man. The road was rough and rocky. Warren had already twisted both of his ankles many times, and could feel them swelling uncomfortably inside his shoes. He wondered whether he would be able to walk at all the next day. The wounds on his chest had finally pulled closed but they still stung when he twisted his torso in any direction and threatened to split open once more. Warren hated the loathsome armor that weighed on his body. Its loose, icy touch made him stiff with cold. He could barely stand from exhaustion. It took all his will and concentration to not fall behind his companions, and he limped stiffly after their dark, bobbing forms.

Suddenly, Wooffen whined a quiet warning. They froze, and listened closely.

"What is it Wooffen?" asked Bloom unable to hear the disturbance himself. Wooffen pressed his nose to the ground and crept forward in a crouched position.

"What's going on?" whispered Warren.

Bloom pressed a finger to his lips.

"I thought you said this desert was uninhabitable?" said Warren.

Bloom gave him a stern look.

They continued carefully forward. Before long they were able to make out the muffled sounds of conversation, and could see the dancing shadows of a campfire leaping across the red boulders around a small campsite ahead.

"This could be dangerous," said Bloom. "Be prepared to use magic."

"I'm not prepared to use magic," said Warren weakly.

Bloom stepped forward in the direction of the camp.

"Oh no. We're not going over there, are we?" hissed Warren.

Bloom ignored the question leaving Warren no choice but to follow him.

"Oh well," sighed Warren, hurrying to keep up with the wizard. "So long Wooffen, don't look for me in the morning, I'll likely have been some monster's dinner by then." Warren felt an unpleasant squirming sensation in the pit of his stomach as he headed toward the firelight. It was uncomfortable to think of what might meet him there. They slowly drew closer to the camp, keeping to the shadows. At last, they were just beyond the light ring of the small campfire.

"Intruders!" hissed a deep voice from behind, "Show yourselves or die anonymous!"

Without turning around, Bloom stepped into the light. Warren ran up beside him. His eyes were afraid to look. He glanced reluctantly at the campsite, feeling his eyebrows lift in surprise at what he saw there. A human girl sat near the fire warming her hands. She wore a peculiar white suit and simple shallow slippers of the same color. She looked up. With a gasp, the girl rose to her feet. Warren felt an unraveling sensation in his chest. She reminded him of someone he had seen before. His mind reeled, searching for the memory of when he had seen her before. The girl had an uncommon face that had a loveliness one quickly came to love, and seek out in the rest of the world. It was an attractiveness capable of setting a new standard of beauty. Warren struggled to tear his eyes from her. At that exact moment, Wooffen let out a warning howl. Warren wheeled around in time to see an enormous shaggy cat pouncing onto him from behind.

"Watch out!" cried the girl.

The great cat fell onto Warren throwing him forcefully against a large boulder. A low growl erupted from its throat. Powerful paws pressed heavily on Warren's armored breastplate, and for once he was grateful for his armor. Only inches away from Warren's face, the horrible cat stared at him with unblinking florescent eyes that seemed to suck his will into their terrible depths.

"Spies!" the cat growled furiously, its voice rumbling like a rockslide. "You will pay for trespassing with your lives!" Spitting out these words, the cat wrinkled his snout into a wicked snarl. Four fangs the size of daggers moved in unison toward Warren's neck. Wooffen barked violently at the creature, his whole body shaking with exertion. The dog threw himself at the cat and took a merciless chomp at his hind foot. The cat growled and shook him off angrily, returning his focus to Warren. Warren sensed his concentration faltering. In a flood, he felt his memories leaking out of his grasp into the mind of his attacker. Out of the corner of his eye Warren saw Bloom shifting rhythmically nearby as he prepared to wield magic.

"Bloom, no!" shouted Warren, unsuccessfully trying to pry himself from under the beast in time to stop his friend.

At the sound of that name, a shadow swept across the cat's contorted face. Its lavender irises pulsed violently and it slowly turned its attention to the old man, unevenly closing its dreadful mouth. The wizard met his gaze sternly. He was poised and ready to cast a lethal spell, the palms of his hands glowing brightly in the night. The cat released Warren at once, sending him crashing to the ground.

"The pebble maker?" growled the beast, as they began circling each other. "What brings you to the Wanderer's Desert?"

"I should ask you the same thing," said Bloom coolly.

The cat shot a glance at the girl. He was visibly agitated.

"Take your leave, and I will spare you both just this once," said the cat.

"Come now, there is no need for such hostility," said Bloom.

"I offered you the chance to leave. Do not think I will offer it twice!" hissed the creature. The fur on the ridge of his back rose and stood on end, as he advanced toward Bloom on silent paws. Warren got up and stood beside the old wizard.

"What do you want with the human anyway?" asked Bloom. "We will take her off your hands, surely she is no more than a burden to you."

"Do not play coy with me!" growled the cat.

"Then you leave us no choice but to accompany you to Augden city, for that is where you are heading is it not?"

"Enough!" cried the cat, crouching in preparation for a lethal pounce.

Wooffen leapt in front of Bloom, growling fiercely at the enemy. The giant cat, more than ten times Wooffen's size, only sneered and licked his lips.

"If she is what I think she is, then there will be others after her," said Bloom. "You will need our help keeping her safe."

"I need no one," spat the cat, narrowing a furious glance at the barking hound. Wooffen howled, pawing at the ground in fury.

"Tigorious, I know them," said the girl, moving between him and Wooffen. "Bloom is a friend."

Tigorious growled angrily.

"I have seen them in my dreams." She smiled at the newcomers, and knelt to pet Wooffen on the head. Wooffen melted immediately, wagging his tail and licking her hands.

"Get out at once!" shouted Tigorious.

"Wait, Tigorious," said Nella. "We will need them if we are to leave this place alive, and they will need us. Our names indeed resound in the minds of many beings all headed this direction."

"You can read minds?" asked Warren horrified at the news.

"Nella, you must resist using your powers until it is absolutely necessary," warned Tigorious. "The last of the diamonds have been lost to us, and with nothing to draw from, your sight will diminish with each use."

The girl knelt and picked up a thick log from beside the fire pit. After briefly inspecting its durability, she handed it to Warren.

"Hold this," she said, handing it to him. "Like this," she added, adjusting it in his hands.

He followed the odd instructions unable to take his eyes from her face.

"They will only be in the way. If they refuse to leave, killing them is our only option," said Tigorious advancing toward Bloom.

There was a whizzing sound. From the darkness of the night, an arrow shot through the air and drove itself deep into the log in Warren's arms. The blow forced him to take a step back. A second arrow whizzed past the atmosphere where his head had been only moments before.

"We're under attack!" yelled Bloom.

Dark shapes of men riding huge reptilian beasts oozed from the perimeter of the stones encircling the campsite.

"Get behind me," Bloom commanded to the humans.

"Gators," hissed Tigorious, and lunged onto an approaching reptile rider.

Pulling the log away from his chest, Warren touched the tip of the arrow. It had split clear through the piece of wood, stopping just before it broke the surface of his armor and entered his heart. Aghast, Warren looked about. Arrows filled the air. The green leathery beasts moved quickly across the sand snapping horrible elongated jaws. Tigorious wrestled viciously with one of the beasts. Beside him, Wooffen sank his teeth into the ankle of a masked man. The man yelled in pain and swung his curved sword at the dog. Wooffen barely managed to dodge the blow before the black clad assassin raised his weapon once more. Warren threw his log at the attacker. It missed his head by several inches. Enraged, the man turned toward the boy and charged him, weapon drawn.

"Warren, use the fire!" bellowed Bloom.

Warren reached for the fire with his mind through the confusion. He pushed it in the direction of his attacker. The man dropped his suddenly red-hot sword with a yelp and looked down at his singed gloves long enough for Wooffen to take a chomp at his other ankle and take him to the ground.

Bloom fenced three men with the weapon of a fourth he had taken hostage. One of his foes fell backwards onto one of the reptilians and was dragged shrieking away into the night. Warren sensed motion out of the corner of his eye. He snapped his head in the direction of the movement. An archer was nimbly perched on a boulder just outside the camp. With the speed of lightning he dipped an arrow into a flask at his belt. A thick green substance covered the metallic tip when he pulled it back out. He took aim at Bloom's back. The archer released the arrow.

"Ash!" yelled Warren, shaking with adrenaline, and focusing his attention upon the arrow. The arrow burst into flame as it zipped through the air, dissolving into gray ashes upon impact with Bloom's back.

Warren scanned the battlefield. Nella stood near him. Her eyes were frightened and her hands tightly pressed to her mouth. She watched Warren wide eyed, and unaware that an enormous monster had crept up behind her. It leapt upon her, its oily green skin glinting in the firelight.

"No!" shouted Warren. Flames churned in his chest. He felt a fire rising to his face and hands.

"I am fire," he said firmly, his hands clenching into fists. With a sudden gust of whooshing wind, a wall of flames rose from the ring of stones at the heart of the battle. Everyone looked up in shock. In a twisting spiral the flames shot toward the giant green lizard attacking Nella. The beast shrieked and tore off into the night wearing a dark singe mark where the flames had touched it. Seeing this, the other monsters screeched in horror and fled as well. Warren looked around. Bloom had enlivened several pieces of rope that were quickly binding the ankles of men who had not managed to escape. His troop was safe. Warren fell to his knees in exhaustion. Just before Warren lost consciousness, he was dimly aware of his armor tightening around his body in a metallic embrace.

THE MAP

"**I**s he going to be alright?" asked a sweet feminine voice.

"Yes, he is just unaccustomed to using magic," Bloom's voice answered.

"He is too weak to wield magic for long," said the voice of Tigorious. "His frail body will wear out from using it."

Warren opened his eyes. Several faces were huddled around above him. Among them were the strange beast, and the young woman. Wooffen whined and licked Warren's face. Warren restrained him with one hand and rose to a seated position.

Tigorious rumbled a low growl. Wooffen returned the evil growl.

"Now Wooffen, behave yourself, you are a guest," said Bloom dropping a new bead into his pouch.

Wooffen thumped his tail against the dirt, innocently looking up at his master. Warren glanced at the girl and had trouble looking away.

"The sculpture," he said

"What?" she asked.

"The one in the courtyard," said Warren incoherently. "There is a sculpture in the palace courtyard that reminds me of you..." he trailed off hopelessly, resolving never to speak again.

She smiled pleasantly. There was a deep cut on her forearm and one on her shoulder, leaving a bloody mark around the torn fabric of her uniform.

"My name is Nella."

"I'm Warren," he answered.

"I know," she said.

Tigorious sniffed.

"And so," said Bloom, "We accompany you to Augden City."

The giant cat ground his teeth together flexing the powerful muscles of his jaw, and prowled away to a large flat rock where he pretended to go to asleep.

Nella sat down by the fire. Wooffen was instantly curled up in her lap to receive a petting. He too had several bleeding gashes in his fur. Warren spotted some plantain growing nearby and plucked several leaves, two of which he handed to Nella, and the others he pressed to Wooffen's wounds.

"What should we do with the prisoners?" asked Warren, turning to the three men cloaked in black. They were securely bound together at the waist as well as individually at the wrists and ankles.

"What have you come for?" asked Bloom.

The men were silent, their green eyes reflecting the firelight.

Bloom gestured for Warren to come closer. Using a dry stick, the old wizard wrote two words in the sand.

"This is an incantation for retrieving information," he said to Warren. "Read it to yourself several times, and then pronounce it firmly."

Warren stared at the words.

"Acrilla-mikerdova," he uttered, pronouncing the new words uncertainly. Nothing happened.

"Once more," said Bloom.

"Acrilla-mikerdova!" said Warren, and suddenly, a thin golden haze began to pull from the heads of the three prisoners.

"That's not half bad," said Bloom.

The haze formed a transparent cloud above each man. Simultaneously, the clouds were filled with moving images as the memories of each Gator rider played back from his recent past. One of the clouds depicted a man parting with a dark-haired crying woman. In the memory the man held her, letting go of her hands slowly as he moved away. She dissolved into silent tears.

The second Gator had images of his last meal. All that was visible was a bowl of soup, and his hand scooping up the liquid with a spoon and bringing it toward the direction where his mouth would be. Every third spoonful was given to a young boy sitting across the table from him with his chin propped up on his hands.

The third cloud was filled with images of a vast army and a general giving fierce silent orders. There were blurry impressions of rushed action, and some kind of large reptiles.

With a wave of his hand, Bloom made the ropes go slack. In an instant the men were on their feet and sprinting into the night. Bloom slipped his hand into his pocket. The new crolackrolite bead made a soft clack as it crashed into the others.

"Why did you let them go? Won't they be back with others?" asked Warren.

"They will track us no matter what. Let the return of these men speak as our living messages of peace to discourage future violence." Bloom looked out at the desert beyond. "We will take turns watching over the camp for a few hours, seeing as we cannot go on without rest. I will take the first watch, and Warren, you will take the second."

Warren nodded, and unrolled his sleeping gear.

"Nella, you may use my blanket tonight," said Warren. "I will sleep with Wooffen for warmth."

Wooffen looked unhappy to leave Nella's side.

"Thank you," said Nella.

With a yawn, Wooffen limped over to Warren and laid down next to him.

It was difficult to sleep on the cold desert floor even next to the fire. Warren felt restless. He wanted to leave this place. It seemed that he had barely closed his eyes when Bloom woke him for his turn to keep watch. Rising stiffly, Warren moved to the lookout position and sat down on a large rock. It was striking how cold the desert was at night. Tiny crystals of frost lined the perimeter of the pebbles beneath his feet. His armor fit more comfortably than ever before, and for a while he entertained himself by exploring his new range of motion. The armored gloves had opened up in the palms, leaving two perfect circles of bare skin. Warren marveled at this development. He could hear Bloom getting comfortable, and Wooffen snoring lightly. Warren's eyes wanted to close, but he willed them to stay open. Looking at the same desert setting made it difficult to remain alert. Was there some movement he had missed while he had blinked? Had those shadows always been there? How did Bloom make everything look so easy? Warren was at his wits end when he heard light footsteps behind him. Turning around he saw Nella approaching.

"What's the matter?" asked Warren. "Can't you sleep?"

"No," said Nella. "I have jet-lag."

"What?" said Warren.

"That's what they call it back home when you travel and need to adjust to a new time zone."

"You can travel through time?" asked Warren.

"No, but when we fly..."

"You can fly?" asked Warren, finally awake with astonishment.

"Well no, not really," Nella struggled to explain. "We fly inside great metal birds called airplanes."

"That sounds incredible," said Warren, thoroughly impressed. "So where are you from anyway?"

"Earth," said Nella.

"Really? That's where Wooffen's from," said Warren. Warren's eyes got bigger all of a sudden. "Wait a minute. You're from Earth?" he asked.

"Yes."

"When did you get here?"

"Earlier this evening," answered Nella. "I came through the windore and was met by Tigorious on the other end. He said the people of Windifera have been awaiting my return."

"But that means..." Warren trailed off.

"What?" asked Nella.

"You're the treasure!"

Nella looked confused.

"The treasure that was hidden on Earth, it's you!" whispered Warren. "No wonder so many are after you. Maybe you were better off on Earth."

"They were after me there too," said Nella glumly.

He looked at her as if for the first time. Nella blushed slightly.

"You look so much like the seer," said Warren, "you know, the sculpture I've been telling you about?"

Nella nodded.

"Only, she had much longer hair," finished Warren. He looked away from her, suddenly feeling awkward. He wanted so much for Nella to have long hair like the sculpture. Closing his eyes he could almost see it, golden-brown and shining, slightly wavy, silky, beautiful hair falling down her shoulders.

"Warren!" cried Nella.

Warren opened his eyes and looked at her.

"Oh no!" he exclaimed, "I'm so sorry."

Nella's hair was growing rapidly longer.

"I can make it stop—I think," said Warren doubtfully.

Meanwhile the thick brown locks were still lengthening quickly. Now they passed her shoulders. Now they were down to the middle of her back. They extruded longer and longer, streaming down in wavy rivers.

"Warren! Do something!" said Nella in shock.

"Stop hair!" commanded Warren.

But these words had no effect. The locks were forming a small pile behind Nella on the stone she was seated on. She looked up wide-eyed at Warren, when her hair abruptly came to a stop on its own. Nella ran her fingers through her newly grown hair. It was thick and shiny in the moonlight. She was serious for a moment, and then, looking at Warren's distraught face she broke into a burst of musical laughter. Relieved by her reaction, Warren also smiled, releasing the breath he'd been holding.

"I'm sorry," he said.

"That's o.k." she smiled. "I could always cut it off."

"And I could always grow it out again!" laughed Warren.

She punched his arm.

"Hey! What was that for?" asked Warren indignantly, pretending to be hurt.

"You make enough noise to rouse the dead," hissed a stern deep voice from behind them.

Warren turned around to find Tigorious glaring furiously at him.

"I was just—" began Warren.

"I relinquish you of your duties, Nella I will take over from here," growled Tigorious.

"But I—" protested Warren.

"Just go," said Tigorious, his eyes irradiating Warren with a powerful loathing.

Once again, Warren got the sense that his thoughts and memories were transparent to the creature's violet eyes. With a last glance at Nella, Warren turned in the direction of the fireside where Wooffen and Bloom were happily dozing.

Warren was upset, and he couldn't understand why. He lay down and tried to sleep, but remained helplessly awake. No more than an hour later the company was packing up camp and readying for the road. Nella had only one possession, an odd yellow book. Upon seeing how attached she was to it, Warren offered to carry it for her in his pack so it would not occupy her hands while she walked, and she gratefully obliged. Tigorious, (accompanied by a resentful Wooffen) had managed to hunt down a few rodents for their breakfast, and Bloom had produced several handfuls of dried fruits and nuts for the humans.

"I love what you've done with your hair," said Bloom handing Nella her breakfast.

"Thank you," said Nella with a grin. "Actually, Warren did this to me." She ran her fingers through the river of golden-brown hair trailing behind her. It fell down past the backs of her knees.

"Excellent work, my boy," said Bloom cheerfully.

"Well I tried to stop it," said Warren defensively, "but it refused to obey.

"Did you really want it to stop?" asked Bloom.

Warren blushed deeply and looked down at his feet.

"It is your heart's desire that drives your magic, not your will. When you learn to hear the innermost wants of your soul, your magic will effortlessly comply with your commands," explained Bloom, winding a white whisker around his index finger in an attempt to hide a smile.

It was still dark when the five of them set off across the desert in silence, only occasionally exchanging glances. Tigorious prowled ahead, while Wooffen guarded them from behind. With tense nerves and cautious footsteps they treaded across the vast plains. The sun began to rise, and with it came the heat. Without so much as a drop of water between them, they quickened their pace in hopes of reaching the shelter of the old forest by midday. Before long, the heat waves radiating off the sand had turned the desert into an endless shimmering phantasm. Hot wind grazed against their faces in roasting torrents. After several strenuous hours, Wooffen let out a high-pitched whine. Bloom stopped immediately.

"Tigorious, we must rest," Bloom called ahead to the cat.

Tigorious doubled back.

"We haven't got time," he hissed.

"Wooffen's intuition is never wrong," said Bloom. "He seems to think rest is more urgent. And he does have a point; if we are attacked in our current state of fatigue we will hardly manage an escape."

Tigorious growled with impatience. "I will see if we are being followed," he grumbled, and wandered off a little ways behind them.

"It's okay," said Nella patting Wooffen's head gently, while the dog watched Tigorious retreat with a look of utmost indignation.

Bloom and Warren took off their packs and sat next to Nella and Wooffen. Warren was exasperated. He ran his fingers through his gritty hair.

"Go ahead," said Bloom observing his mood, "tell me what troubles you."

"My people are counting on me!" exploded Warren. "We are wasting precious time, Bloom. What are we doing here?" he demanded.

"We are assuring Nella her safety," answered Bloom.

"She is safe with Tigorious."

"Is she?" asked Bloom.

"This is hopeless," said Warren on the brink of angry tears. "We're never going to find the pillar." He stood with frustration.

"There's still a chance—" began Bloom.

"We don't have a map!" Warren cut him off, "The Wanderers' Mountains are vast, we don't even know where to seek it!"

"I know where it is," said Nella quietly.

They looked at her simultaneously.

Nella picked up a dry twig. She drew a jagged line in the sand. "These are the seven peaks of the Wanders' Mountains. The location you seek is here, on the north side of the caldera." She drew an x at the top of the southernmost slope. The tip of the last mountain she drew was flat instead of pointed like the others.

Warren gaped at her unable to speak. Bloom contemplated the image as if memorizing it.

"I've been seeing this location in my dreams for as long as I can remember," said Nella in response to Warren's bewildered gaze.

Suddenly, a set of thick heavy paws jumped onto the sand before them, destroying the drawing.

"Enough resting," growled Tigorious. "The knights of the Gator Region are not far behind, we must hurry."

Warren and Bloom shouldered their packs once more, and the company pressed on at twice the previous speed. They had not covered more than a couple of miles when Wooffen began showing signs of distress. In the distance they saw a line of trees. With great relief they hastened their footsteps, but the forest did not appear to be getting any closer. In dismay, the travelers realized how much further away the trees really were and the full complexity of their predicament began to sink in. They were exposed to the enemy from every direction with nothing to hide behind in case of an ambush. It was highly possible that the Gators had allowed them to get ahead in order to run them into a trap. The panic level was rising in Warren's chest. He kept glancing in Nella's direction. She was evidently unaccustomed to such intense exercise, and was gradually falling behind.

In the distance behind them a dust cloud appeared on the horizon. The thundering of heavy feet could be heard in the sizzling silence. Glancing over his shoulder, Warren could see the cloud gaining on them. Rusty-colored reptilian shapes were bounding toward them through the dust. There were gator riders like the night before, and alongside them were huge scaly monsters running on thick muscular legs with scores of men on their backs strapped into green leather harnesses.

"Run!" spat Tigorious, and they fled.

"Come on Nella!" yelled Warren, upon seeing her struggle to keep up. The forest ahead was still a considerable distance away. There was no guarantee that Gators were not waiting for them inside the trees. Warren understood that something had to be done, but what could he do? He had barely mastered the elements of water and fire, neither of which were available in the current environment. Warren pushed ahead beside Bloom.

"There's nothing here for me to use against them," panted Warren.   "Sand," huffed Bloom. "There's lots of sand."

An arrow whizzed by Warren's ear.

"Sand?" panicked Warren.

"Think, what does sand do?" urged Bloom.

"It—" began Warren, "it, spreads, and sifts."

"Good," said Bloom, "what else?"

"It blows in the wind, it trails, and exaggerates temperatures," said Warren numbly trying to answer the question in spite of the earth quaking with the thunderous footsteps of the giant reptiles behind him.

"What else does it do?" asked Bloom without slowing his pace.

Warren thought about the endless desert surrounding them. There was a scream. Warren looked behind to see Nella on the ground, a ferocious lizard only yards away.

"It engulfs!" said Warren, projecting his energy into the desert floor behind Nella. With the help of the adrenalin pumping through his veins, his energy moved from his hands in a concentrated flood. As the monster advanced, it began to sink into the sand, fiercely thrashing and roaring as it fell through up to its neck. The men attached to its harness unstrapped themselves as fast as they could, but many were too late, and were sucked into the sand along with the massive body of the creature. Warren rushed to help Nella to her feet. More beasts advanced toward them.

"Take my hand," said Warren, reaching toward her. Together they ran for the forest while arrows whooshed past their heads. Tigorious, Bloom, and Wooffen were already among the trees.

"Hurry!" yelled Bloom.

As Warren and Nella closed the final distance to the edge of the forest, their attackers abruptly terminated their pursuit. Warren and Nella rushed into the shade of the twisted trees.

"That's weird," said Warren, out of breath and still holding Nella's hand, "Why aren't they following us?"

Tigorious glared at him, and Warren released Nella's hand. It was nearly dark in the woods, even at midday. Gray moss hung densely from the dry and crumpled trees.

"They're just going to give up? Just like that? Does anyone else find that weird?" mused Warren. Bloom looked troubled.

"Quiet," said Tigorious sternly. He turned away from the blindingly bright desert just outside the trees. "Follow me," he growled.

The company trailed after him as he moved deeper into the forest. The further they moved into its spindly depths, the more convinced Warren became that they were heading in the direction of danger. As they moved onward, small rodents with long furless paws and snarly thin faces peered at the travelers over the fallen trunks of trees and dusty boulders. Growling occasionally, they crept beside the travelers, keeping to the shadows like spies. More and more of them gathered around, until the forest itself seemed to be made of liquid shadows. Bloom found a large dry branch, and began collecting long hanging strands of moss as he walked. He tightly wound the grey moss onto one end of the stick.

As darkness began to fall, and the evening mist stretched its damp fingertips out across the forest floor, the rodents finally began closing in. Closer and closer they drew, until one leapt onto Warren's ankle, gripping his pant leg with its claws. In an instant, thousands of the rat-like creatures followed suit, landing on the travelers in great numbers. Warren struggled to throw them off. There was a crackling noise behind him. The sound was muffled by the hairy bodies of the creatures obstructing Warren's face and ears. He felt a pair of teeth sink sharply into his arm. Suddenly, the forest was drenched in light. The rats screamed in a chorus of piercing voices, and drew back. Bloom wordlessly clipped a small piece of flint back onto his belt, and lifted up the torch in his hands, lighting the way. Wooffen barked at the terrible creatures, chasing the last of them into the brush. Tigorious glanced at Nella. Once he was certain that she was in one piece, he continued on through the forest. Warren pressed a hand over the place on his arm where the rat had bitten him. Red blood pooled in the cracks between fingers. He could remain silent no longer.

"Where are you taking us?" he demanded.

Tigorious wheeled around to face him as if he had been ready and waiting for such an address.

"I'm taking Nella to Augden City where she will dwell as the honored guest of Prince Conan Malden. As for the two of you, you were never invited to come on this journey, and you are not welcome in the city of Augden."

Warren was outraged. "What does the prince want with her?" he asked bravely holding the cat's purple gaze.

"Diamondellians are the descendants of the Great Seers of the Diamond Age. Augden City is Nella's true home. We have long awaited the day of her return," snarled Tigorious. The cat looked at the dark woods, noticing that the rodents were beginning to creep out from the shadows once more. He growled angrily into the night and the creatures briefly drew back.

"I think she had better come with us," said Warren, looking over at Nella who stood beside Tigorious. "Nella what do you say?"

Nella tried to speak but Tigorious cut her off.

"You think she is safer with you on your deadly quest?" he growled. "Do you even know who he is?" he asked, indicating to Bloom.

Warren glanced at the old wizard. Bloom held his gaze, but remained silent.

"You know much less than you think, and you are a fool to trust the pebble maker," snarled the cat. "With you, Nella would be in danger at every step. There are many foes who seek to use her gifts for their own gain."

"And how do I know you are not one of those foes?" shouted Warren, forgetting about holding the bite on his arm and letting the blood now soak his shirt.

"If I sought to destroy you, you would have been dead long ago," said Tigorious through clenched teeth. He moved his face close enough to Warren for the boy to feel the heat of the cat's breath on his neck. Tigorious ejected his blue claws out of his paws for a moment and then he relaxed once more.

"We will break camp here for the night, and continue on in the morning," said the cat. "Wooffen and I are going to hunt down some dinner." And with those words he disappeared into the brush followed shortly thereafter by a grumpy, hungry Wooffen, who, by his genetic makeup was unable to resist a good hunt.

Warren turned to Bloom.

"What did he mean?" he demanded.

Bloom sighed heavily. Nella looked at the old wizard with concern.

"Please," began Bloom, "understand, I never wanted to keep you in the dark, I was going to tell you…" he trailed off. "I was just waiting for the right moment—"

"Who are you?" shouted Warren, throwing his pack to the ground.

Bloom shook his head. "After all this time, it still isn't easy…"

"Tell me now!" said Warren with deadly resolve.

"I'm the one…" said Bloom, gesturing around himself, "who did *this*." He swallowed hard.

"What?" asked Warren.

"I'm the one!" repeated Bloom. "Don't you see? I am responsible for the Red Era!"

"No!" cried Warren. "Tell me this is untrue!" He took a step back. Nella was silent. Her hands were trembling.

"You?" breathed Warren, "you are the evil wizard!"

"I am he," said Bloom with a bitter smile.

"But of course, how could I not have seen it? That's why you know magic, that's why you were cursed, because you are HIM!"

"Yes."

"You deserve…" Warren's voice broke off. He was overwhelmed with the knowledge that his friend and mentor was the greatest enemy their world had ever known. Angry tears were forming in his eyes. "You deserve to die!"

"No, I don't deserve it," answered Bloom, and it was apparent that he was not being defensive, "not yet."

"You traitor!" shouted Warren, "how could you? You ruined everything."

"I did," said Bloom. He looked steadily at the youth.

"I trusted you!"

"For that I am more grateful than you know," said the old wizard.

Nella touched Warren's shoulder. He looked at her.

"He is not the same man," she said.

Warren glared at Bloom.

"That does not redeem him."

Bloom took off his backpack and knelt to open it. Pulling out a pan, he began preparing the ingredients for a soup.

"We can't stay here," Warren said to Nella.

"I do not blame you for mistrusting me, yet tonight, there is nowhere for you to go. I assure you your safety. Tomorrow, you may go your own way if you wish."

Nella began clearing a space for the fire on the forest floor. Bloom wandered around the campsite foraging for herbs and mushrooms to make a wild edible soup. Warren stormed angrily away to find water. He made sure to stay within earshot of the campsite to keep an eye on Nella, and make lots of noise to keep the rodents at bay. When he returned, Nella had built a small pile of thin twigs and was trying to light it with what remained of Bloom's torch.

"Let me help you," said Warren, and with a moment's concentration, he burst the pile into lively flames. There was rustling in the brush as the rodents scurried away from the light.

Nella beamed at him.

"That's surprisingly easier when I'm upset," Warren sighed. He sat down by the fire.

"I'm moved by your concern," she said, "and I want you to know that I am at peace with whatever happens tomorrow."

Warren looked unconvinced.

"Thank you for showing me the map," said Warren.

"You're welcome," said Nella, pulling out her yellow book and opening it to a bookmarked page.

"I just want to know one thing, though," said Warren. Nella looked up. "Why did you trust me with that information, and not um," he paused to pour some water into a pan, "someone else?" he finished.

"Because you risked everything to save what you love," she answered.

"Thanks, I guess," said Warren. He drove two sturdy Y-shaped sticks into the ground on either side of the fire pit, and placed a long iron rod across them from which he hung a pan. The flames were now cheerfully consuming a large dry branch.

"So what did you mean when you said *my people*?" asked Nella, studying a page in her book. "Are you some kind of a prince or something?"

"Um, yeah. I am, sort of," mumbled Warren awkwardly. Looking at her in the firelight, her hair and eyes shining alongside the flames, he was suddenly aware of how her face had grown on him, and how much he did not want to let her go. She caught his gaze, and they both turned away nervously.

Soon, Bloom returned from his scavenging with a cloth full of fresh edibles. He was respectfully unintrusive, focusing on the task at hand. Before long a fragrant soup was well on its way, with thimbleberries for dessert. Tigorious and Wooffen reappeared from the forest with round bellies.

"Did you enjoy your dinner?" asked Nella, pulling a small white feather from the corner of Wooffen's mouth. Wooffen wagged his tail happily and plopped down next to Warren, placing his head on the boy's knee. Warren petted Wooffen's enormous velvet ears. At a distance, Tigorious trampled around in a circle trying to get comfortable for the night. Observing this, Warren and Nella shared a quiet giggle. Tigorious glanced suspiciously at them over his shoulder, but they managed to straighten their faces in time for his sharp eyes to miss their mischief.

Bloom poured the soup into several bowls and handed them out. Wooffen's nostrils twitched in the direction of the soup. The three humans ate hungrily. When Bloom was half way done with his soup, he placed his bowl on the ground for the hound, who rocked himself up into a seated position to lap at the tasty liquid. Warren watched the old wizard feeding the ever-hungry hound and, try as he might, he couldn't fight his feelings softening for the old man. Who knew what he had been through in the years he had lived? Perhaps he had suffered more than anyone from his own actions. Still, Warren could not imagine ever trusting him again. His feelings toward Bloom were forever changed, and he missed the bond he had had with the old wizard only a short while back. Losing that connection was the biggest betrayal of all. Just when he'd thought he had found a true friend, someone he could really look up to and count on, the friendship was so brutally severed.

Beds were soon readied and Nella bid Warren and the others good night. Wooffen curled up beside her, and Bloom stretched out on his mat a short distance away. Warren had the first watch that evening, and it was a good thing too, because he felt wide awake. Lost in his own world, he couldn't help thinking of the things he had learned and what would happen the next day when they reached Augden City. He could not decide what to do with the situation at hand. Warren was certain Nella was winding her way deep into a dangerous web. He did not know how to save her, or even if she wanted his rescuing, but how could he let her blindly follow Tigorious into some horrible trap? Warren was certain there were pieces of the story the giant cat was leaving out. Bloom had reveled himself as untrustworthy, and could not be counted on for help, yet Warren knew he could not do this alone.

At last, after the moon had risen and traveled a good distance across the sky, Warren nudged the old wizard awake.

"Tomorrow, we steal her from that witless brute."

"He is more clever than you think," whispered a sleepy Bloom. "What he says of the Diamond City is true. They have indeed long awaited her return."

"There's no way I am leaving her in his evil paws."

"Then tomorrow, we must act at our first opportunity," said Bloom.

"Yes," agreed Warren, "and we shall."

WOOFFEN'S CURSE

Warren awoke at first light. Bloom was still asleep. Warren yawned and took a sip of water from his flask. It was a very quiet morning. Slowly, he sat up and looked around the camp. Bloom awoke with a start.

"Where's Nella?" he asked.

"Off with Tigorious and Wooffen?" suggested Warren.

The two of them looked uneasily at each other, instinctively listening closer to the sounds of the forest.

"Pack your things," said Bloom. They hastily collected their belongings and stuffed them into their packs. Warren felt apprehension building in the pit of his stomach as he blindly shoved his bedding into its case. Suddenly, Wooffen appeared out of the bushes. The hound tore toward them with a frightened howl. Yelping, Wooffen circled them, nipping at their ankles. He tried hard to make them follow him back the way he had come.

"What is it Wooffen?" asked Warren, getting down on one knee.

Wooffen whimpered a pitiful cry, impatient with Warren's attempts to settle him. The hound began walking in an odd manner, widening his stance until his belly nearly dragged on the ground, imitating a stealthy prowl. He growled and swiped at the dirt with his paw. Then, quickly jumping around in the opposite direction, he perked up the tops of his long ears as far up as they would go and lengthened his back. Stretching out his neck and tail, he began trotting about in a dainty fashion. Wooffen abruptly began acting catlike once more. He pounced onto an imaginary victim, snarling and wrestling wildly in the dirt.

Finally, he froze and looked up questioningly at Warren and Bloom. He stared hopefully at one face and then the other.

"I think he's trying to tell us something," said Warren.

Wooffen let out a defeated whine, and sat with a thud in the dirt.

Bloom sighed heavily. Crouching down, he patted the dog's head affectionately.

"I had hoped it would never come to this, and I ask you to forgive me, my friend, for what I am about to do," he said.

Wooffen looked up at him apprehensively. Bloom reached out, briskly brushing his hand over Wooffen's unmoving form. He closed his hand. Tiny light rays emanated from between his fingers.

"Darrza rechyedoom!" Bloom muttered the incantation. He slowly opened his fingers to reveal a large crolackrolite stone the size of a walnut. For a moment, its flawless black surface reflected their three gawking faces before Bloom silently stuffed it into one of his many pouches.

Wooffen immediately howled a series of reprimanding barks at Bloom's newest sacrifice.

"Wooffen," said Bloom calmly, "use your words."

"ARRRG! WOOF! WWOOF! W-W-WOOFFEN!" bellowed the dog. Wooffen paused, shocked at the sound of his own voice. His eyes widened in disbelief.

"That's it!" encouraged Bloom. "Now tell us what happened to Nella."

"GERRR! AWOOOO! W-WOOFFEN ANGRRRY!" barked Wooffen, snorting and clawing the dirt.

"Wooffen," said Warren firmly, "We need you to calm down."

"WOOF! WOOFFEN KNEW! ARRREWWW! AH-WOO-WOO-WOO!" howled Wooffen.

"What happened? Where's Nella and Tigorious?" asked Warren.

"FFFRROOF! HARRRG! TIGORRR-IOUS! GERRR! WOOFFEN DISLIKE!

"Wooffen!" said Warren.

"TIGORIOUS TAKE NELLA ON LONG WALK—

GERR—FAR AWAY—WOOF! HE POUNCE ON NELLA WITH OTHER HUNTERS—GRRR! THEY TIE UP!" Pretending that his short legs were suddenly bound by invisible ropes, Wooffen toppled onto one side of his long body and struggled dramatically in the sand. "THEY TAKE NELLA AWAY—AWOOOO!" He lifted his head in a final howl and collapsed in a heap.

Warren looked at Bloom. His jaw was set. The two of them stood at the same time.

"Wooffen," said Bloom, "after them!"

Without another word, Wooffen pressed his nose to the ground and with a quick sniff leaped into the forest at full speed. Throwing on their packs, Warren and Bloom charged after him.

They pressed on late into the night. Worried and weary they stumbled in the dark over mossy rocks and the tangled roots of trees. Long after the moon had risen, they came upon a large clearing. From the edge of the forest they looked across the wide open field at the far end of which towered an ominous dark fortress built into the side of a steep cliff and surrounded by a huge city. Even at this distance they could distinctly hear the roar of waterfalls. Warren took a step further, meaning to go on, but Bloom restrained him.

"We must rest before we go on."

"She could be dead by then!" cried Warren brushing him off.

"The fortress is heavily guarded, we must not only regain our strength, but devise a plan for how we are to break in as well as escape," said Bloom.

Warren took a step back, he knew Bloom was right but he could not rest while knowing Nella was in danger. "Can't we just improvise?" said Warren.

"You must remember that there is more at stake here than just our lives," reminded Bloom.

"WOOF—WOOFEN WILL GUARRRD!" barked the dog.

"Wooffen, you don't need to yell!" said Warren.

"WO—WOOF! I-I don't?" said Wooffen in surprise.

"We go at first light," said Warren irritably, turning back to the forest.

They broke camp. Forcing down a few bites of food, Warren collapsed next to Bloom, who was already asleep. Wooffen remained awake, sniffing the air, listening intently to the sounds of the forest.

AUGDEN CITY

Tigorious slowed his pace. Nella lifted her head from his back, wearily taking in her surroundings. The soldiers who had assisted in her capture were not far behind. They wore red uniforms and wielded sparkling glass spears. Tigorious and his captive were the first to arrive at the glossy gates behind which towered a vast cityscape. Shrouded in darkness the odd structures gleamed in the moonlight. Two guards also armed with spears bowed low to the giant cat.

"Welcome Tigorious," said one of them. "Shall we alert his Majesty Prince Coonan Malden of your arrival?"

"Yes," said Tigorious. "Tell him I have brought him the Seer."

A look of awe passed across the guard's face and he glanced at his companion to see his reaction. The other guard hastily closed his mouth, which had fallen open at the news.

"So it is true?" said the first guard, his brows knitting together in nervous disbelief.

The soldiers carefully cut Nella free from the harness on the cat's back. The ropes slacked at once and the men helped her to her feet. She nearly collapsed, but the soldiers supported her on either side. Her wrists were still bound. The ropes had burned visible red welts into her pale skin. Tigorious shot her a sideways glance. She looked at him, searching his eyes. His violet irises enlarged and shrank more fiercely than usual.

"Why is the seer bound?" asked one of the guards.

"She refused to come willingly," explained Tigorious. "She does not yet understand why she is here. I will let the prince explain," said the cat looking away from the girl. Nella's hands were untied by the nervous guards. Tigorious peered into the forest behind them where the trees stood as a wall of jagged teeth on the horizon. "Send soldiers into the forest," he said darkly. "We saw a group of rebels on our way here. There are two of them, an old man and his student. Kill them on sight, they are more dangerous than they appear."

"We will do as you instruct," said one of the guards with a bow.

Nella felt a sinking sensation in the pit of her stomach. She swallowed hard. Her throat was dry, and tasted of metal. The men wordlessly opened the gates and the cat and his hostage stepped into the city.

A crystalline coach was waiting, drawn by two creatures Nella had never seen before. They reminded her of the snow leopards she had once seen in a zoo on Earth, only these creatures were larger and hairier with gold spots instead of black ones on their lustrous white coats. They looked at Nella with green eyes, and flicked the tips of their tails. Nella was lifted up to the coach by one pair of hands and pulled inside by another.

"To the fortress," grunted Tigorious, leaping into the carriage as the cabin jerked into motion. Nella tried to recall if she had seen a driver or any reins on the creatures pulling the carriage, but as far as she could tell the creatures pulled it of their own accord.

The carriage raced past vacant streets. Several times Nella caught glimpses of sinister-looking creatures prowling in the shadows and alleyways. Somewhere in the distance they heard a woman scream. A cold chill ran down Nella's spine.

The carriage came to a sudden stop. Nella was drawn out by force and walked towards a towering glass fortress. The fortress was comprised of clusters of sharply pointed towers that glowed from within. The glass itself appeared to be the source of the light, radiating from the inside.

Stepping through the large double doors into the great hall, Nella was blinded by a million brilliant refractions as though she were moving within an enormous chandelier. The countless polished and faceted surfaces of glass refracted narrow beams of light in every possible direction, creating a magnificent luminance in the spacious hall.

At the back of the great hall was a sparkling throne. A man

was sprawled across it. He was visibly older than Nella, perhaps in his late thirties. Dark haired, and pale, his green eyes were deep set and underscored by heavy shadows. The rim of his iron crown was cut into several jagged points, two of which trailed downwards, covering his temples. He smiled upon seeing who Tigorious led toward him.

The giant cat nudged Nella forward, and prowled beside her as she moved across the sparkling floor, her dusty white shoes thudding softly on the glass. Nella felt increasingly more ill as she approached the man on the throne. He seemed to radiate a poisonous energy.

"Welcome to the city of Augden," he said, as Nella walked towards him. The great hall faintly echoed his every word. "Isn't it beautiful?"

"It is," answered Nella, glancing up once more at the magnificent hanging clusters of crystalline jewels adorning the ceiling. Apart from the uncomfortable presence of the dark haired man, Nella felt a strange familiarity with the fortress.

"Tell me, has it changed much in the four thousand years you have been away?"

"I'm not sure I understand what you mean," said Nella looking at the man.

"Come now, don't tell me you have forgotten your own history? Do you even have the gift? Or are you not who they say? Tigorious, who is this you have brought me?" he demanded.

Tigorious moved gracefully forward avoiding Nella's eyes. Nella remembered her friends and felt a silent sob sting painfully in her throat and tears brimming in her eyes.

"Your Majesty," said Tigorious bowing low, "she is the one who has

been hidden. I saw her come through the windore myself."

"A windore you say?" The man looked awestruck. "That is impressive indeed." He sat up in his chair and addressed Nella once more. "Allow me to introduce myself. I am Prince Coonan Malden, ruler of the city of Augden, and your very own great-great-great-great-great nephew," he finished, "four hundred and thirty six times removed. And what do you go by these days?"

"Just Nella."

"Well *just* Nella, while you are here, you are free to do as you like," continued Prince Coonan Malden, "That is, as long as I like what you do." He winked. "So don't get any ideas," he finished darkly, readjusting his crown.

Nella was starting to feel very unwell indeed. The room appeared to be fluctuating in brightness and spinning slightly as she strained to keep from fainting. She felt weak and forced herself to remain standing even though her legs trembled and her hands shook.

"I assume you must be tired from your journey," said Prince Coonan Malden. You may have your old room back. It is up that way," he pointed to a wide cascading stairway to his left. "In the North tower."

Nella turned toward the sparkling stairway.

"There is one more thing I need from you before I let you retire to your chambers," said the prince leaning forward on his throne. "Tell me the location of the Pillar of Dominance."

Nella was silent. She knew with every fiber of her being that it would be a mistake to tell him.

"You know where it is, don't you?

Nella met his gaze.

"Yes, I can see that you do," he said. "You will tell me, in the end. The only question is, how much will you suffer before you do?" He clapped his hands twice. "Guards, take her to the Brute."

"No, not the Brute!" said Tigorious, taking a step forward and looking suddenly lost. The guards looked at each other in shock.

"Never question me," snapped Coonan Malden. "Or you will be next!"

"But she is only a child, surely torture is—"

"Enough!" cried the outraged Prince. "Take her away."

The guards hesitated.

"DO IT NOW!" shouted the Prince losing his self-control altogether.

Nella looked into the fearful eyes of Tigorious as strong hands grabbed hold of her from both sides. Nella was led from the room by half a dozen guards. On her way out she heard fragments of continued conversation.

"Tigorious," asked the prince, "have you taken care of the wizard and his pupil?"

"I have, your majesty," answered the deep rolling voice of the giant cat.

"Good," said Prince Coonan Malden.

Nella allowed the tears to flow from her eyes. Her feet were unable to support her weight, and the guards dragged her down a long corridor followed by a dark stairwell and then into the bowels of a dungeon. There, among the many iron hooks, blades, chains, and assorted torture devices loomed the silhouette of a large man in front of a glowing fire pit.

"Leave us," he said without turning around. He pulled a red-hot stake from the coals.

The guards hastily rushed from the dungeon leaving Nella to stand alone.

CAPTURED

"Wa-Warren! Wo-wo-wake up!" said Wooffen nudging the boy with his nose.

"What is it Wooffen?" asked Warren rubbing his eyes.

"Th-there's something out therrre," whispered Wooffen, trembling from head to toe.

"What?" asked Warren, "Where?" He sat up and searched the darkness for signs of movement. Somewhere up above a branch snapped. By the sound of it, the creature who broke it was heavy.

"There it is again!" whined Wooffen, crouching to the ground until his ears dragged in the dirt.

"Don't be such a scaredy-dog," said Warren, feeling weak with fear himself.

Bloom snorted in his sleep. Warren found a small pebble and tossed it at Bloom's sleeping back. The old wizard instantly startled awake.

"No, not the launch bed..." he mumbled sleepily, and looked over at the others. The old man sat up. There was another snapping sound and Warren put his finger to his lips, slowly reaching for the hilt of his sword. A silent shadow crossed over the moon, making its light momentarily flicker in and out. Wooffen pressed himself down flat against the forest floor and squeezed his eyes shut.

"What was that?" asked Warren.

Bloom threw off his blanket and stood examining the dark sky. "I don't know, but it can fly," he said.

"Get down!" yelled Warren as the shadow circled back. They dropped on their stomachs as a giant shadow passed overhead. Wooffen crept under the nearest tree and pressed himself into its trunk, nervously glancing upwards. As the predator flapped away, Wooffen whimpered a trembling note.

"Birds? He's afraid of birds?" Warren asked Bloom.

"Warren," said Bloom still lying flat against the ground, "It's time for you to learn the magic of air."

"What, *now*?" asked Warren, propping himself up on his elbows. "Couldn't you have taught me this sooner? Why am I always learning this stuff when my life is in danger?"

"I prefer a more hands-on approach to teaching," explained Bloom with a shrug.

"I'll be lucky to still have hands when you're through teaching me," replied Warren.

Bloom ignored the snide remark. The moon was briefly blocked out once more.

"There are many applications for the use of air," began Bloom, "The most important thing when working with air is—" but he was unable to finish his sentence, for it was at this very moment that a ring of soldiers charged at them from the line of trees. They were dressed in the red uniforms of the Augden City army. After quickly rising, Warren rushed to help Bloom to his feet. The two of them stood with their backs to each other, Wooffen between them. Thirty men formed a tight ring around the wizard and his apprentice, pointing sparkling spears at their bare throats.

"What do we have here?" sneered their leader. His robes were closer fitting and more complex than the others, showing off his rank. "Rebels!" he snorted at Bloom. "I admit, there are more of you roaming these woods than I expected, but you are fools if you think you stand a chance!"

"WOOF-WOOFFEN PROTECT MASTERRRR!" howled Wooffen. Bloom settled him by holding a hand over his back. His palm did not radiate light, and he did not make any stones, but Warren knew that Bloom was using some kind of subtle magic.

"What a curious creature," said the sergeant, eyeing Wooffen with a greedy gaze. "But what *is* it?"

"Clear your mind and stay prepared," Bloom muttered under his breath in Warren's direction. The sergeant snapped his attention on the old wizard.

"What are you whispering?" he demanded suspiciously.

"I am describing to my young student how to wield the element of air," answered Bloom.

"How to *wield* it?" mocked the man in feigned interest. "Pray, do tell. I'm sure we'd all love to learn this unlikely bit of wizardry."

"Air requires great skill because it must be used in conjunction with other elements," replied Bloom. "It helps to use an incantation to manipulate it, for without one, there is simply not much to work with when it comes to this evasive element." He slowly reached his hand down to unclip an oval-shaped flint rock hanging from his belt by a chain. Sensing Bloom's discreet movement out of the corner of his eye, Warren slowly tilted his head to one side, enabling him to glance down at the flint rock. Understanding instantly what Bloom had in mind, he waited for the signal.

"Are you some kind of hocus-pocus expert?" mocked the sergeant, unable to come up with a better insult. He was not a born leader, and it was painfully obvious. He tried hard to win the respect of his soldiers, and in doing so, only continued to lose esteem in their eyes.

"I am an expert, it is true," responded Bloom.

"And what is this so-called *magical* phrase?" inquired the sergeant contemptuously.

"The incantation for molding air is, *vozdor*," concluded Bloom. As he spoke the word, a gentle breeze blew the sergeant's dark hair back from his forehead.

"Ooooh, now that really terrifies me!" joked the sergeant. His men laughed uneasily. "No, not air! Please don't hurt me with air!" the sergeant made a helpless quivering motion with his hands as if shielding himself. His soldiers rolled with laughter. It was unclear whom they were laughing at. Bloom's confidence was unwavering. He looked on, alert yet unalarmed, allowing events to unfold as they would, his every word and action incontestably proving him powerful and worthy of respect.

The sergeant looked away from the wizard, unable to hold his gaze. He was starting to hate the old man for a reason his consciousness refused to reveal.

"Kill them both, leave the velvet goblin to amuse the prince," he commanded, pointing his spear at Wooffen. The atmosphere grew tense. The soldiers hesitated to attack, instinctively sensing an unknown danger associated with the group of misfits. The sergeant noticed nothing, wrapped up in his own appearance, he was blind to the true nature of the situation.

"Well? What are you waiting for? Do as I say!" he commanded, the conviction faltering in his voice. Fearful of losing control of his men, he barreled on with his orders, ignoring the building sense of unease growing in the pit of his own stomach.

The soldiers moved forward, and as they did so, Bloom pressed a shred of fabric against the flint with his thumb and struck the rock with a steel dowel. Instantly, a flea of a spark ignited, and nestled its way into the cloth. It glowed bright orange. Bloom outstretched his hand toward the guards.

"Vozdor!" shouted Warren, projecting his energy at the tiny speck of light. A ball of fire whooshed into life, and flew at the soldiers, forcing them to duck beneath it.

"They're wizards! Seize them at once!" ordered the sergeant, not willing to take on the challenge himself. "I order you to do as I say!" he shouted over the commotion.

"In the right hands, the gentlest element is the most powerful," smiled Bloom, striking another spark. Warren uttered the incantation again, projecting a rush of energy to ignite the second spark. It didn't take long for Warren to discover that he could roughly shape the flames. Bloom spun around, shedding sparks at the attackers behind him. Warren multiplied the sparks, making them rain down in crackling downpours that were followed by angry bursts of fire.

A dark shape circled up above, dropping ever lower on silent wings. Warren sensed that it posed a threat, but was unable to look away from the battle scene before him. Suddenly, a giant bird dove at Warren from the sky. Its ashen grey feathers were nearly invisible in the dark. The predator opened its long beak and screeched a piercing cry. It swooped down just about grazing Warren with its glossy curved talons. The soldiers dove out of its way. Wooffen crawled between Warren's feet and ducked to the ground. Bloom struck a spark in the direction of the passing bird and Warren blew it into a raging surge of flames. Flapping away, the bird caught fire. In a loud, ripping whoosh, its body was engulfed by orange and gold flames. The fire did not appear to harm it in any way. It circled back toward them, its eyes glowing embers on a living torch.

"Oops," said Bloom. A swell of soldiers charged him, and Bloom blocked the jabs of their spears with his staff. They came at the old man without mercy, forcing him away from his student.

Wooffen trembled against Warren's boot. The firebird dove toward the boy for the second time. Everyone scattered in a ring around him. Dropping down to the ground, Warren pressed his body over Wooffen to protect him from the incoming flames. The phoenix was right over them. Warren could see its glowing shadow singeing the yellow grass around him. In shock, he felt the talons of the giant bird scrape against the back of his armor, and he felt himself being yanked up into the air. Woofen slid from his arms as the phoenix tore Warren from the ground and took him into the navy sky.

Warren soared upwards, each flap of the firebird's wings taking him higher and higher. Warren's sword slipped from his belt and landed with a clunk beside a horrified Bloom. The guards quickly bound the wizard's wrists, concluding the old man's capture. Warren looked down in despair, unable to rescue Bloom and Wooffen from the grasp of their foes. All the while, the firebird gained altitude. The flames engulfing its body tore and raged in the wind. Within seconds the ground below looked like a quilt of tiny pastures. The threat of being dropped escalated every second. The air around them became icy cold. Gliding on crackling fiery wings the creature moved in the direction of the fortress. Warren had the sinking suspicion that he had been kidnapped.

Waterfalls could be heard gushing throughout the glass city below. The bird flew toward the tallest tower of the massive fortress. As they approached, the phoenix tossed its prisoner onto the tower's balcony. Warren fell onto the cold glass floor and looked about. He was at the top of a mighty tower.

"Get up," said a familiar rumbling voice behind him.

Warren wheeled around, "You!" he said, furiously glancing up at Tigorious.

"Shhh!" hissed the cat.

"Where is she?" demanded Warren, fearlessly advancing on the cat.

"Warren, shut up!" growled the cat, "I need your help saving Nella."

"Saving her from the trouble you put her in no doubt!" said Warren maliciously.

"You don't understand. She is the rightful ruler of Augden City, and the only one who can put an end to the rule of Coonan Malden. She is destined to restore the city to the glory of legend. She is the very last of her kind, our only remaining chance."

"I've heard all that before," said Warren. "Legends mean nothing to me, and glory means even less."

"You don't understand," snarled Tigorious. "She's not just *a* seer, she's *the* Seer."

Warren paled. "What do you mean?" he asked.

"She is the *one who has been hidden*."

"No, she is just a girl," said Warren stubbornly.

"She is the most powerful seer that has ever been born!" said Tigorious angrily, frustrated with Warren's ignorance.

"So you are using her for her sight to get to the Pillar?" shouted Warren, still in shock from the news and defensive over having failed to figure this out for himself.

"Must I explain everything?" growled Tigorious. "The diamonds have been lost to us. The Era of the Seers is over forever. Coonan Malden has forged a new stone, he wishes to place it on the Pillar and rule the rest of the world as he rules Augden City. We must not let that happen," finished Tigorious staring intensely at Warren's face. His irises pulsed.

"Where is she?" Warren repeated his question.

"In the dungeon."

"What do you mean?" exclaimed Warren.

"I had hoped that with her arrival, the people would rise up and take back the city, but I fear they will not even get the chance because the prince has never had the intention of letting Nella live past the point she is useful to him."

A light went on in one of the peaked towers below. Tigorious crouched down and ducked inside the room adjacent to the balcony on which they stood. Warren followed suit, and found himself inside a beautiful room. It looked to be the dwelling place of a young girl, obviously a princess. Stuffed toys lay neatly on a bed of dusty silk sheets. Pink fabric was draped elegantly from the ceiling. A white lacy dress was laid out on the bed.

"The rebels plan their attack today at noon in the great hall. You are to fight alongside us."

"You left Bloom and Wooffen to die, and you dare ask me for my help?" snapped Warren angrily.

"Odelious? He is too hesitant to use magic because of his curse," answered Tigorious. "He would have been useless to us anyway."

Warren boiled at that last remark.

Tigorious paced the room. "If we should fail to overthrow the prince and take over the fortress, Nella will die." He looked at Warren. "I'm the one helping you," he said, "you want her to live and would have broke into the fortress anyway, only to be slain for your own stupidity."

"What about Nella?" asked Warren.

"We rescue her once the battle is won."

"I have not come to fight your battle," said Warren.

"Your presence here leaves you no alternative but to pick a side and fight," said the cat. "You must stay here until I return. The fortress is swarming with guards; if you are found elsewhere, you will be tortured and killed," he warned. With those words, Tigorious leaped to the door. "I will collect you when the hour is ripe," he growled over his shoulder. The door slammed shut behind him. Warren rushed to the door and tried the handle. It was locked. He banged his fist on the oak. "Open the door!" There was not reply. Warren stepped back and kicked the door with all his might, but it barely trembled in response.

"I've got to get out of here," said Warren to himself. Warren searched the room with his eyes. He moved to the balcony. First, he looked up at the sky where angry storm clouds were gathering in the night and then down at the three-hundred-foot drop. One third of the way down the tower, off to one side was a large, half-opened window. Warren knew that getting to that window was his only chance of escape. Cold wind rushed at them in an icy gust. He stepped back numbly. Turning to the bed, he once again looked at the white dress lying on the pink bedding. Although the room appeared to be that of a young girl, the dress was sewn in a larger size. It looked like it would fit a grown woman. Without a second thought Warren grabbed the dress and stuffed it under his breastplate. He managed to cram it in, and found that fit securely without much discomfort. Next, Warren pulled the sheet out from under the many blankets. He testing the strength of the ancient fabric with a firm tug, it seemed to hold. Warren moved to the linen closet. Hurriedly opening the drawers, he was pleased to find it well stocked. He pulled out handfuls of ancient, moth-eaten sheets. Dumping them onto the floor, he began tying them together at the ends forming a long knotted rope. Warren worked quickly until he ran out of sheets. He then secured one end of the rope around the bedpost and hurled the rest off the balcony. The cable whipped around in the wind and fell several feet below the window. Warren gave the line a firm jerk. It held fast. With a final glance around the room, he gripped the knotted cable and stepped over the balcony. Blustery streams of frigid air beat against Warren's face making his eyes water. Chewing on his bottom lip, he slid down several feet until he could reach the glass sidewall of the tower with his feet. The thick walls of the tower were built from layered sheets of solid glass. Pressing his shoes against its smooth surface, Warren slowly moved one hand below the other steadily lowering himself.

There was a rumble in the sky up above. Warren's knuckles had turned white and his body trembled with effort and concentration. A large drop of rain landed on the back of his hand. Warren glanced at it in alarm. There was a scooting noise above and he felt himself sharply drop down several yards as the bed skidded across the bedroom floor and out onto the ledge above. The sheet slipped through Warren's hands until, to his great relief, they came upon a knot, and he came to a stop. Warren's heart pounded in his ears, drowning out the first rolls of thunder. Drops of rain fell around him in ever growing numbers, quickly beginning to run down the glass wall of the tower. Warren struggled to keep his footing on its now slippery surface. One of his shoes slipped off and fell for several seconds before impacting silently with the ground below and lying still as a tiny dark speck on the ground. Warren swallowed hard. His hands were getting tired of supporting his bodyweight. To his horror, the sound of tearing fabric issued from the bedroom above. Cautiously, he tried to pull himself up the line. There was another ripping noise. Warren felt the line jerk forcefully in his hands. Sheets of rain pounded down upon him. Lightning flashed near by and was echoed soon after by the deafening applause of thunder. Wiping the water from his face with his shoulder and glancing upwards, Warren could see the bed lodged against the side of the balcony.

Looking down, Warren saw the window several yards below him to one side. In desperation Warren gathered his wits about him and pressed powerfully off the wall with his legs. He swung himself around the tower in one frantic swing. There was a loud shredding noise as the line finally gave out. It was followed by the explosive grinding sound of wood breaking through glass. Warren was hurled forward, and just as the wrist guard on his forearm made contact with the windowpane, which instantly shattered sending him through the broken glass, his fingers released the line of sheets, which ripped from his hands and went whooshing down past him like a giant dead serpent followed by a billowing bed.

Warren leapt to his feet. Wind howled past the broken window behind him. Glass shards covered the floor. A few streaks of blood formed along Warren's cheek. He was inside what appeared to be a greenhouse encasing the long spiral staircase of the tower. Unusual plants bloomed about him in deep, clear containers. The air was filled with their mixed aromas. Warren looked nervously around for guards. His eyes came to rest upon a terrified-looking gardener with a whistle in his mouth. The man inhaled a trembling breath and puffed out his pale cheeks. In an instant Warren had covered the distance between himself and the gardener. The whistle gave a choked squeak as Warren grabbed the man by the throat, plucked the whistle out of his mouth with his other hand, and squeezed the air out of the man's inflated cheeks.

"I have come for the princess," said Warren. "Where is the dungeon?"

The gardener fainted, and Warren caught his limp body, slowing the man's rapid journey to the floor. Quietly stepping over the unconscious gardener, Warren slipped out of the greenhouse and quietly descended the stairs.

THE BRUTE

"**W**hy do they call you the Brute?" asked Nella through gritted teeth, as the man drew another line on her forearm with the red hot metal spike. A blistering burn trailed behind the object alongside the other fresh burns that paralleled the one he was making. Nella pressed her lips together and inhaled sharply through her nose, coping with the pain as best as she could.

"I will ask the questions," said the Brute, and shoved the spike back into the flames. His face and hands were heavily scared. When he turned away from her, his profile was ragged and lumpy. He had striking blue eyes of a very light shade. They radiated an uncanny intensity. These were not the washed out, watery eyes of a drunk, they were like two electric portals to another realm.

The Brute unstrapped the leather buckles that attached Nella's ankles to her chair, and began tying a rough rope around her chained hands. The giant man looped the opposite end of the rope to the pegs of a large wooden pinwheel. As he cranked the handle of the pinwheel, the rope tightened, suspending Nella by her wrists. Next, the Brute walked over to a shelf of whips. He took his time picking one out and came to stand behind her.

"Tell me the location of the Pillar, and your suffering will end."

"It's kind of you to want to end my suffering," said Nella, "but I prefer to be tortured to telling the prince where it is."

The Brute drew his thick arm back and landed his first blow. Nella felt a sharp stinging sensation across her back. She closed her eyes. The man continued striking her with the whip for some time before he paused. Nella felt blood running down her back. The Brute came around to face her. His face was unshaven and grimy with soot.

"I am puzzled," he said. His teeth were yellow and broken with neglect. "Few men are able to take so much pain and you don't even yell. Tell me, what is your secret? How do you take it?"

"What is my pain compared to yours?" replied Nella.

He was visibly taken aback by her words. His brow rumpled with complex emotions and his mouth fell open slightly.

"Even while torturing me," continued Nella, "you show me more mercy than you show yourself."

The man's face hardened and he raised his weapon to land what appeared to be a final killing blow. Nella looked away to spare herself the anticipation of the strike, but it never landed. Slowly, she opened her eyes, only to find the guard on his knees before her. Tears streamed down his face.

"Can I ever redeem myself from the horrid things I've done?" he cried, hiding his face in his hands.

"What would it take for you to have your own forgiveness?" asked Nella.

"I would have to un-do every single hurtful thing I have ever done," he said. His voice trembled as he spoke. "Find every person I—" he trailed off. "I don't know where to begin, it seems impossible." Large tears continued to fall down his scarred cheeks.

"What would be less difficult," asked Nella, "to ask forgiveness from every person you've ever hurt, or to continue on like you have been doing?"

He hung his head.

"I'm a terrible person, who would forgive me?" he whispered bitterly.

"I forgive you," said the girl. "Who is to say others are less kind than I?"

"It is too late!" shouted the man. "It cannot be undone!"

"Every moment is a new beginning," said Nella. "What is stopping you from choosing to live differently in this moment?"

"Nothing is stopping me, but what is the point? In this forsaken world filled with corruption, hatred, and lies? What does it matter how I live?" said the Brute, his shoulders sagged, the muscles of his arms flexing in anguish.

"It matters to you," said Nella. "It brings you to tears, the way you have been living."

Fighting back a fresh onset of emotions, the giant man pulled on the wheel, lowering Nella to the ground. She collapsed on the floor before him rubbing her bruised wrists together beneath the coarse rope.

"You have been doing your worst, daring someone, *anyone* to confront you, to stop you, and no one has, thus proving to you that there is no morality in this world," Nella continued, rising with difficulty. "But you have forgotten about the wisdom within *yourself* that sees all you do with un-judging eyes, and waits with infinite patience for you to look within and hear its ceaseless plea to *stop*. You cannot hide from that, not in the deepest dungeon, for it sees through your own eyes, and is the very essence of who you are!"

"My hands feel no pain, and my heart cares not for the foolishness of kindness!" spat the Brute, shaking with each word.

"Yet your hostile actions have made you desperately unhappy, isn't that evidence enough of the peace-loving nature of your being?" she paused, "Why are you so convinced that it is all so wretched anyway?"

"I am not blind! I can see how it is!"

"Perhaps it is this very conviction that masks an otherwise beautiful world as the unfair, lonely place you describe."

"But I don't know *how* to do good!" he screamed in despair.

"There are many different voices that fill ones mind," replied Nella. "Most of them are quite loud and persistently contesting for attention. One of them is a victim eternally bemoaning his fate. One of them is a thief, looking out for his own gain. One of them is a critic splitting the world into right and wrong, condemning or idolizing all he sees. One is a dreamer, always longing for what could be or might have been. One of them is an assassin on the hunt for someone to blame and punish to hide from the shame of his own shortcomings. But there is another. The one, which is so often overridden because it is soft spoken and does not try to compete with the others. Let it direct your actions, and you will find a goodness living through you, that will fulfill you like nothing else in this world or any other."

"I have never heard that one voice you speak of," said the guard.

"Then you have never listened," answered Nella. "Be still and you will hear it, it is as unfailing as the rising of the sun."

They looked at each other for a long moment.

"I was once the head priest of a monastery," he said, "until the day I lost my family and my faith in all that is good."

Nella held his gaze without faltering.

"You are not afraid of me?" asked the guard.

"No," said Nella.

"How can that be?" he asked, "I do not believe in anything good, and am therefore capable of the most atrocious things."

"You do not need to believe in good for it to prevail," answered Nella. "Neither is believing in good what keeps one from harming others. In fact, believing in good and bad inspires many violent actions and has led to most of the wars that scar our histories. For we become what we condemn the moment we are consumed by the desire to be right." She faced him, looking into his unusual eyes. "I do not believe in good and bad," said Nella, "only in good, since all that I thought was bad turned out to be an illusion."

"You are mistaken, for if ever there was a bad person, I am he," said the Brute, forcibly jabbing a thumb at his own chest. His face was red with tears and anger.

"We spend our lives looking for someone to see the good in us that we dare not see in ourselves, but only secretly suspect, trying to prove to others that we are bad, unworthy, unkind, and all the while wordlessly daring them to see through the facade. I have searched my own mind, meeting every thought with love, until there was nothing left to fear, and nothing left that wasn't welcome. I have seen through my own façade, and that is why I can see through yours. No, I am not afraid, for I know you as I know myself."

"And what is my facade?" asked the guard.

"You are pretending to be the unfeeling brute you've never been, and I am not fooled."

"But I am an unfeeling brute!" cried the man, "How else would

I have been able to do all those terrible things?"

"Given what you believed, did you think you had any other choice?"

"No."

"*Do* you have a choice?"

"Yes!" said the man weakly, his face and hands trembling.

"So you have been confused. If you had known then what you are finding out now, would you have done any of those things?"

The man was silent. He reached for the rope binding Nella's wrists, and began to untie it.

"I hear that voice you spoke of," he said.

"You do?" asked Nella.

"Yeah. It says to clean and dress the wounds I made across your back."

INSIDE THE FORTRESS

Warren felt the cool touch of glass beneath the foot that was now missing a shoe as he crept down the stairs. Finally, he reached the mouth of the stairwell and peeked out into the great hall. The glistening room was in disarray, swarming with guards and soldiers. The crystal ceiling sparkled high above. Groups of servants pushed heavy-looking carts full of weaponry from the armory towards the main entrance for unloading and then back. The carts had big wheels and were skirted with a dense red fabric that did not quite reach the floor. Hunching over, Warren quickly lifted the skirt of one of the passing carts and dove under it. The cart continued moving, and Warren crept below the pleated red cloth at an uncomfortably slow and irregular pace. Suddenly, the cart came to a dead stop. Cringing, Warren quickly grabbed onto the wood panels inside the cart to keep from crashing into it.

"A rebel has broken into the fortress and is after the princess!" yelled the gruff voice of a guard who had obviously found the gardener in the greenhouse.

"Find him!" ordered an officer in an authoritative voice. There was much commotion as the men scattered in every direction to seek out the intruder. Warren chewed his lip, feeling even more vulnerable in his hiding place. The cart began moving once more. They had almost made it out of the hall when the cart abruptly stopped once again. Not anticipating the change in pace, Warren fell forward and bumped his head on the inside of the cart with a loud thud. He rubbed his forehead, wreathing in silent pain.

"Do you hear that?" asked the servant pushing the cart. "My cart is making a funny sound again. I told you to check the wheels! But no, nobody listens to old Granure! What for? He is just a useless old man.

Forty years of servitude and this is what I get?"

Warren could see Granure's shoes coming around the side of the cart.

"Come on Granure, you know we respect you and do the best we can," replied one of his companions.

"Yeah stop being so grumpy all the time," muttered a third servant. "Clean my wheels, load my cart, do this, do that! We all work just as hard here, and, some day, we will be old like you, and do you think we will complain?"

"Certainly, once you know how it feels," snorted Granure, "and when I lift this cloth and find that you did not do your work, the amount I will complain about it will age you four years in the next hour, so that you may learn how it feels all the sooner."

Warren peered out from under the drape. On the opposite side of where Granure was standing was the shallow entrance of a narrow hallway. Warren rolled out from beneath the cart and down the hallway, quickly disappearing into its shadows.

"My word! These gears look like they haven't been greased since the beginning of the Sapphire Era!" complained Granure, his voice growing fainter as Warren moved further down the hall.

It appeared as though the passageway was newly constructed. While the rest of the fortress had an aged, ancient feel, this part appeared new and was built entirely of murky, olive-green glass. The style of this peculiar addition seemed to impose rudely on the noble structures surrounding it. Up ahead, Warren made out the entrance of a doorless chamber. Inside the small room the walls seamlessly melted into the floor giving the space a hollowed out feeling. The room had no windows and yet appeared to harbor an odd source of light. Upon approach, Warren could see that the chamber contained a single piece of furniture. A stone pillar stood at the heart of the gloomy room, and on that pillar rested a square, grey stone. Warren stepped inside the doorway, and suddenly felt ill. He took another step closer to the stone, trying to figure out what it was. The very presence of the object was unbearable. It was difficult to approach it through the powerful negative energy it radiated. An array of acid orange and red colors sparkled out of the grey stone, casting bright refractions across the ceiling. "Prince Coonan Malden's stone," whispered Warren. He dared not take another step toward it, for it was getting increasingly difficult for him to breathe. The power of the stone seemed to both paralyze his body, and drain him of his strength at the same time. All he wanted was to be away from the thing. It made sense why a guard was not required to protect it. Warren was not certain that a person could even get close enough to the stone to touch it without dying from its poisonous energy. He backed away, feeling immensely better with each step he took.

Several workers' cloaks hung on a peg outside the strange chamber. In dire need of a disguise, Warren quickly pulled on the cloak moved back down the narrow passageway toward the great hall. Once he reached the far end, he looked around, and slipped discreetly out of the narrow hallway and into the main corridor. Several watchmen stood nearby, but they were facing away looking in the opposite direction. Keeping to the shadows, Warren slinked past the huddled watchmen. He tiptoed behind them as they jabbered about what they had seen.

"I don't even know *what* is going on!" said a guard. "Are we looking for a rebel, or what?"

"They say he has a velvet goblin for a pet," chimed in another.

"I swear this place is getting weirder every day. What am I supposed to say when my wife asks me how my day was?"

"Tell'er the truth. Tell'er you was chasin' a blood thirsty rebel with a demon for a pet, who had wings dangling from either side of his head."

"How is she going to believe a thing like that? I don't even believe it, and it happened to me!" cried the first guard.

Warren quickly moved away from the group of guards behind him. He was quite pleased with himself for managing his way past them when suddenly, one of the men spotted him.

"Hey you!" cried the guard from behind. "Back to the armory! You've no business here, this is the soldier's dining area!" His voice was stern.

Warren slowed his pace, his rigid posture betraying his unease. He dared not turn around.

"What is your division number? Get back to the armory at once!" continued the guard.

Warren hesitated for a second before making a break for it. He flew down the hallway.

"Stop!" yelled the guard. "Seize him!" The three men lunged after Warren simultaneously.

Warren ran blindly through the fortress. The guards rushed after him. Warren found himself in a large dining area. He upturned chairs and hurled them behind himself, creating obstacles for his pursuers. A whistle was blown. With a glance behind, Warren found that the number of armed men after him had tripled.

"Fire!" yelled Warren, momentarily blinding his attackers with a burst of sparks. A table caught fire, and quickly turned into a blaze in the dining area. Warren glanced behind at his pursuers, and suddenly came to an abrupt halt, sensing an obstacle in front of him. He turned his attention back to the path ahead just in time to skid to a stop before being impaled on the sparkling spears of the guards who had come from the opposite direction in order to corner him. He whirled around. In an instant the guards chasing him had caught up. They pointed their gleaming spears at his throat. Warren lifted his hands in surrender.

"Filthy rebel," said one of the three guards from before. "You will pay dearly for this intrusion." Warren's limbs were bound at the wrists and ankles by the guards. "Take him down," said the guard.

"Where are you taking me? To the dungeon?" asked Warren hopefully.

His question was ignored

"Should we find out what he's after?" asked one of the men.

"We'll leave the questioning for the Brute," said the guard. "He is always so compelling when it comes to extracting information." He gestured for the others to take Warren away.

Warren was escorted from the dining area and down a long stairway. As they descended, the air around them became increasingly more damp. The guards thumped down the steps for what seemed like an eternity. Warren began to panic. His plans of saving Nella were not going well. Suddenly, Warren stepped down into water. The splashing sound made by his feet extinguished his last hopes. The foot missing a shoe ached with the icy cold of the water. They had arrived at a great underground river. The water was dark as it rushed by in a glossy rough sheet. The roof of the cave hung low over the river. Warren was shoved into a small rowboat. Two guards climbed into the boat after him and pushed off from shore. The other men retreated back up the stairway.

The current carried the rowboat effortlessly down the river. One of the two guards accompanying Warren used the oars to correct the direction of the small vessel, while the other watched their new prisoner with contempt. They passed numerous prison cells on either side. The small barred chambers were submerged in water. Warren couldn't tell if the cells had occupants or not. The whole place seemed abandoned and had a haunted feel. They pulled up next to a dark cell. One guard grabbed ahold of the shiny metal bars to keep the boat steady while the other unlocked the gate. He opened it a crack.

"Ready?" said the first guard.

"Yup," replied the second. He unsheathed his dagger, and taking a handful of Warren's tunic, sliced through the boy's bonds, first at his ankles, then at his wrists. The first guard opened the door a bit wider and Warren was hurled from the boat into the prison cell.

During the split second Warren was in the air he managed to inhale deeply and the next instant the icy water engulfed him, rushing at his face in a gushing, green blur. His armor pulled him down into its stirring depths. Warren reached his toes down in hopes of finding a floor to press off of, but the river appeared to be truly bottomless. The boy struggled to move toward the surface, wrestling against the current of the river. He pushed his arms and legs through the water forcing his body upwards. The air in his lungs fought to get out. It choked in his throat urging him to breath. In a final push, Warren broke the surface and gasped for air. He grabbed the bars and looked out at the disappearing rowboat and the dark vacant water before him. The current tugged at his clothes. The water level appeared to be rising. His head was almost pressed against the roof of the dungeon. If ever there was an awful place to be trapped, this was it, thought Warren. He trembled with hypothermia and adrenalin and closed his eyes. Warren had no idea how he would ever get out of this horrid place.

There was a splashing sound behind him. Warren's eyes snapped open. He was not alone in the cell! Warren looked nervously behind him unable to locate the maker of the noise. Fear lurched though him.

"Who's there? Reveal yourself!" commanded Warren.

A large shape swam from the shadows.

"Stay back!" cried Warren.

"Warren?" said a masculine voice.

Warren recognized it right away.

"Salvador?" cried Warren. He threw himself at his brother. The two embraced like long lost children, nearly drowning each other.

"What are you doing here?" asked Warren in disbelief. "If not for these dreadful circumstances, I would be dearly glad to see you."

"At last I have found you!" said Salvador. "It was horrible. It was all so horrible," he cried.

"You came to save me?" choked out Warren, overcome with emotion himself.

"Of course!" said Salvador. "When I heard you were missing, and the entire royal staff was unable to find you, I was so crushed that I went after you. As you can see I didn't make it very far."

"Salvador! You're so stupid, you shouldn't have left the protection of the dome."

"Oh you're one to talk!" said Salvador, struggling to contain his emotions. "Even if I was killed before I found you, it would be better than doing nothing and just letting you die out there on your own in some horrible, unknown way."

Warren splashed water on his face to wash away his tears. The two of them fought back tears.

"I missed you too," said Warren. "I was afraid I'd never see you again."

"I know! It's the saddest thing I've ever had to deal with!" said Salvador, pulling one of two small hand shovels out from the clay ceiling above and handing it Warren.

"What's this?" asked Warren, stiffly taking the shovel from his brother with a puzzled expression.

"This is for you to dig," said Salvador grimly.

"What?" asked Warren.

Salvador proceeded to scrape a large scoop of mud from the ceiling and throw it down into the water.

"The water level rises every time it floods," he explained through chattering teeth. "If we don't dig out the roof of the cave, next time, there will be nothing for us to breathe.

"How often does it flood?" asked Warren.

"It's always different," said Salvador. "Anywhere from once, to three times a day."

Warren whistled.

"That's not even the worst part, if we miss even a day, no—even an hour of digging during a flood, we're dead meat."

Warren followed Salvador's example. It was more difficult than he expected, having no leverage to press off of in the water. They scraped mud from the ceiling and for a while and Salvador explained how he had been captured. The guards of Dimondell had caught him stealing a yam from their campsite near the Wanderers' Desert. Abruptly, Salvador stopped speaking.

"What is it?" asked Warren in alarm.

"Oh no," said Salvador. "The flood's over!"

Indeed, the water level was dropping rapidly. Salvador stabbed his shovel into the mud in the ceiling and indicated for Warren to do the same. Warren managed to jab his shovel into the clay ceiling next to Salvador's before the water sucked them both downward. The water level plummeted. Down and down the boys fell with the draining river.

"How far down does this thing go down?" yelled Warren, fighting the current as it swirled them around in a whirlpool.

"You'll see," shouted Salvador back to him from the other side of the cell. Finally, the water pressed them hard against the jail bars as the last of it rushed past them and the boy's reached the floor of the cell. The remaining water rushed past their knees and into the damp, empty corridor. Long, thin jail bars glistened high above. Warren's heart pounded in his chest like it was trying to break out. He struggled to stand. Salvador collapsed next to him and did not try to get up.

"How long have you been here?" asked Warren, breathing heavily and leaning on the bars.

"A few days," panted Salvador.

Warren took in the wild state his brother was in. His clothes were shredded into dirty rags and his blond hair was gritty enough to be standing on end.

"So how are we going to get out of here?" asked Warren.

"Get out?" Salvador snorted. "Forget about it, I'm just happy I don't have to die alone."

There were footsteps outside the cell. Warren grew tense.

"Relax," said Salvador, "It's just the food man. You should see this guy. At first I was frightened to eat anything he gave me for fear it would be poisoned." The guard approached with heavy footsteps. "Then I got so hungry I decided to chance it, but this was no piping hot bowl of porridge from the royal table…" rattled on Salvador.

"Hold on," whispered Warren, "There's someone with him."

Indeed, upon listening closer they could make out a second set of footsteps, so light they were nearly inaudible. The boys pressed their faces between the bars for a better look. From the depths of the empty riverbed emerged first the shape of a massive man, and then the tiny feminine form of a young woman in a light colored uniform. They conversed quietly as they moved forward. Warren sucked in a breath.

"That's Nella!" he whispered breathlessly to his brother, before opening his mouth to yell her name. "Ne—!" Warren managed to squawk only the first syllable before Salvador pressed a large hand firmly across Warren's mouth.

"What are you doing?" hissed Salvador. "You're going to get us killed!"

Warren struggled against his brother, falling backward onto the wet sandy floor. They wrestled, each one determined to win. Warren's heart raced with the desire to explain everything, but there was no time. Although he was no match for his brother's strength, the upset he felt gave him an energy that for once evened out the odds. They squabbled in the mud.

Nella and the guard slowly passed them until their shapes were absorbed by the darkness at the other end of the tunnel. Warren was furious. He wrenched his face away from his brother's hand for a split second.

"Nella!" he yelled, projecting one of his hands toward his brother's chest. Salvador was blasted against the bars of the cell in a sea of sparks. He looked utterly aghast. Warren stood and tried to brush himself off, but the mud and sand was clinging to his wet clothes.

"How did you do that?" asked Salvador.

"Magic," said Warren.

"Magic?" mouthed Salvador, stunned mute.

They heard footsteps. Nella ran up to the gate, the giant guard at her side. Her eyes grew big as she saw who was behind the bars.

"Warren? What are you doing here?" she asked.

"I came to rescue you," said Warren.

Salvador elbowed him in the ribs.

"Um, This is my twin brother Salvador," muttered Warren.

Salvador took a bow.

"And what is he doing here?" asked Nella.

"He came to rescue me," explained Warren with a slight cringe.

"You didn't tell me you were here to rescue a damsel," snickered Salvador.

"You never asked," responded Warren curtly.

Salvador grinned.

"You're hurt!" cried Warren seeing the bloody slashes in Nella's clothes and the burns on her arms.

"I'm fine, really," said Nella.

"Who did this to you?" asked Warren in horror.

"I'm afraid I did," said the burly man by her side.

Warren gaped at him. Nella looked kindly at the man.

"This is Tolvin Toliver," said Nella. "He's a priest."

"And he's the guy you recruited to help us escape?" said Salvador hysterically. "I'll take my chances with the next flood!"

At that precise moment, a loud crashing noise thundered from the depths of the dark hallway.

"The dam has been re-opened!" Tolvin said urgently. "We have to get out of here!" He looked down the tunnel nervously. "There isn't time!" he cried as a mountain of water charged down the hallway in an angry stampede. Tolvin crammed a large key in the lock and wrenched the door open. Warren and Salvador pulled Nella into the cell. Tolvin was barely able to leap inside and slam the gate closed before the gushing flood blasted past the jail bars, spraying and crashing with a wild force. The water level in the cell began to rapidly rise once more.

"Swim!" commanded Tolvin.

Swirling currents stirred them about the cell as if in a soup. The four of them worked to keep their heads above water, pushing ever upwards through the rising waters. After several minutes of battling the current just to stay afloat, Warren grew weary and wondered how Nella was holding up. Upon spotting her in the dim chamber, he noticed Salvador was already at her side helping her stay afloat. Warren felt a stab of jealousy twist uncomfortably in his chest, and decided to keep a distance from them.

Finally, the rushing waters ceased to rise. The roof of the cave was considerably closer than it had been earlier. Their heads were pressed right up against the roof of the cell. Salvador pulled his shovel out of the ceiling.

"Who builds an underwater prison anyway?" he asked, sinking slightly with the weight of his own question.

"They didn't build it, they just didn't fix it when the dam began flooding the dungeon," said Tolvin.

"Why didn't they fix it?" asked Warren.

"They didn't need to, since the desire to live was driving the prisoners to maintain the functionality of the facility," explained Tolvin.

"That is the most depressing thing I have ever heard," said Salvador.

"What about the bars?" asked Nella.

"What about them?" asked Tolvin in surprise.

"Do you need to repair them?"

"No," said the man.

"Don't you need to lengthen them? Or keep them from rusting?"

"No, they were always long and perfect like that." He shrugged.

Warren looked at the bars. Even in the dark they gleamed a bright lustrous silver without a trace of rust or tarnish.

"Discovering the bars is what prompted Prince Coonan Malden to build a prison down here in the first place. All we had to do was forge gates which was a nasty job because the bars are forged from unbreakable steel. We were all surprised to see how long they extended when the prisoners began digging them out."

"They were really built to last," mused Salvador.

Warren looked at Salvador, then at Nella, and sighed.

"There must be some reason they are here," said Nella. She glanced upwards. "And look at that," she said pointing to the ceiling. "There is steam coming off the clay up there."

"So?" said Salvador.

"The water is cold," replied Nella. "The formation of steam requires heat. What do you suppose might be a heat source down here?" Nella looked thoughtful. She began touching the walls.

"What are you doing?" asked Salvador.

After a brief examination of the walls, Nella swam back and grabbed Warren's shovel. She began digging at the back of the cell.

"It's no use, that particular wall is like a solid rock," said Salvador. "Don't think I haven't tried that.

"It's the warmest," explained Nella.

Warren grabbed his brothers shovel swam over to help her. She smiled at him and moved over slightly so they could both dig in the same spot. They heard a loud splashing noise as Salvador came to join them. The mud was hard to dig. They took turns using the small shovels. Together, the three of them made quick progress, and before long, a deep chunk of the wall had been carved out. As they dug, the mud became more and more dry, until it became a solid sheet of compacted stone.

"Move aside," said Tolvin joining the group.

The three of them made way for the guard. He took the shovel from Warren and struck the hard wall with all his might. When he pulled the instrument away, a hole appeared at water level. It sucked water into itself as if there were a vacuum on the other side. A dim orange light flickered into the flooded cell from the gap in the wall. They treaded water in silence.

"What do you think is back there?" asked Warren.

"I don't know," answered Nella, "But I'm pretty sure the bars are part of a gigantic, long-forgotten cage."

"Seeing as we are already inside the cage, maybe digging toward whatever is at its center is a bad idea?" suggested Salvador.

"If there was a secret cage underneath your castle wouldn't you want to know what was in it?" asked Nella.

"Whatever it is, it's probably dead by now," said Warren.

"If it's dead, then why does it still radiate heat?" Tolvin pointed out.

Warren was stumped.

"This could be dangerous, Nella," he said.

"Has any part of this journey not been dangerous?" asked the girl. "Besides, taking a few risks to save something that has been imprisoned for so long that no one is left who remembers it even exists is a just cause."

They turned their attention back to the hole in the wall. Tolvin gave the wall another strike. A large piece of the thick, cemented clay chipped off and fell into the glowing abyss on the other side. The guard struck the wall again and again, forming a large opening just above water level. Heat radiated from the opening. Warren peered over the edge. His eyes ached as they readjusted to light. Before him was a deep chamber with a blurry glowing core at its center. It had the shape of a giant bowl. Even if the steel cage had once been square, the accumulated mud and debris had slowly piled up in the corners until it had swallowed most of the room and hardened into a crust as hard as stone. The walls appeared bone dry, as though an unknown heat source had dried them out. Warren felt himself being sucked downwards by the water. He realized with alarm that the flood was over. He grabbed on to the wall but before he could speak, Nella jumped through the hole and began sliding down the steep sloping sides of the cavern.

"Nella, stop!" yelled Warren, throwing himself after her.

Salvador pulled himself up through the hole behind him, pausing only to help Tolvin. "Take my hand!" called Salvador from the hole in the wall, but it was too late. Tolvin was taken down with the water as it plummeted to the prison floor.

Warren stumbled down deeper into the dusty cavern after Nella. The temperature grew warmer as he moved toward its center. Within several seconds Warren found himself breaking a heavy sweat.

"Nella, hold on!" he called ahead. She slowed her stride. As Warren approached her, he noticed a giant grey heap at the bottom of the slope. "What do you imagine that is?" he asked.

She looked at him without speaking, complex emotions fluttering across her face.

"What is it?" asked Warren.

"Its presence overwhelms me with sorrow," she said.

Salvador slid to a halt beside them.

"We lost Tolvin," he panted, placing his hands on his hips.

Warren and Nella exchanged a worried glance.

"He'll be fine," continued Salvador. His eyes fell upon the object at the heart of the room. "Look at the size of that thing!" he exclaimed, taking a giant step toward it.

"Do you think Tolvin is alright?" Nella asked.

"Sure," said Salvador distractedly.

Nella looked behind her at their entry point.

"He'll be alright," said Warren. "The prisoners go through that every day," he pointed out.

The three of them advanced toward the shape. The temperature intensified as they drew closer. Salvador was the first to reach it.

"Come look!" he said, "it's an odd-looking statue!" he yelled. "You can see the scales and everything!"

"Just don't—" broke off Warren.

"And it's hot to the touch!" shouted Salvador.

Nella and Warren ran to Salvador's side. A colossal stone lizard towered above them. Although time had visibly aged the stone, the amount of detail remained striking. Powerful wings were folded against the creature's massive back. It lay, with eyes closed, in a solid mountainous heap partially sunken into the floor. The ground beneath it glowed faintly orange.

"Salvador, don't mess with it," said Warren.

"You were right, little brother, it's as dead as an over-baked brick," said Salvador with a smile, and gave the hind quarters of the massive statue a loud slap.

Nella sighed quietly. Warren looked at her questioningly.

"I feel so much sadness here," she whispered.

Salvador remained oblivious.

"Incredible!" he said, putting his foot against the side of the sculpture to tie his shoe, "I can't get over how lifelike it is!"

"Salvador," began Warren, "I think you should…" he trailed off.

There was a deep rumble within the statue. Frowning, Salvador pressed his ear to its side. The three of them froze and looked at the sculpture in shock. A crack had formed in the stone above Salvador's head. For a moment, all was deathly quiet. Then another cracking noise split the silence, sending fractures cascading down the side of the creature's body. A piece of hard dry stone chipped off the statue and fell to the ground revealing a spot of silvery black skin beneath.

"Run!" shouted Warren.

Salvador took a step back in shock. The mountain before him began to splinter all over revealing a living dragon within. Its muscles flexed and stretched. Charcoal, armor-like scales covered its wrestling body, and two rows of spikes ran down its nose and the length of its back. Pieces of hardened clay rained down like roof shingles, revealing a glowing orange underbelly. One of its wings was scarred and torn at the edge.

Warren grabbed his brother's arm, and yanked him up the slope. Salvador stumbled as he was directed, tripping after Warren and Nella. Warren shoved him up the hill, all the while knowing there was nowhere to run. The creature bellowed a raspy cry, and charged after the humans. The slope was becoming too steep to climb, and Warren found himself backed up against it with his friends. Nella and Salvador stood behind him, ready for action, but able to do nothing. The dragon moved closer until it was eye to eye with Warren. Its narrow orange irises peered unblinkingly into his own. It wrinkled its horrible snout. A wisp of smoke issued from its nostrils. Warren swallowed hard, mentally preparing to be grilled and eaten.

"Guessstsss?" hissed the dragon breaking into a fanged grin.

"W-what?" breathed Warren, feeling the front of his clothes getting painfully hot in the presence of the creature and feeling oddly grateful to be soaking wet.

"I apologize for the ssstate of thisss den, I wasss imprissssoned for sssso long." The dragon rolled its eyes as if to convey the immeasurable length of time it had been here. Flames licked out of its mouth as it spoke.

"Uh, it's okay," mumbled Warren stiffly.

"How did you end up here?" he asked.

"Long ago, I wassss defeated in a great battle, and my cage was brought here to guard a sssecret tresssure hidden beneath the glasssss fortresss."

"What's this treasure?" asked Salvador.

"I don't know, it'ssss a ssssecret," replied the dragon.

Salvador looked around much more attentively than before.

"I'm thrilled to have sssome company," said the dragon, stretching its wings and fighting back a yawn. "I have had no one to ssspeak to in agesss." It smacked its lips like a sleepy child. "Itssss lucky I have sssseveral persssonalitiesss of my own," it added.

Not sure he wanted to find out what that last statement meant, Warren decided to keep the conversation as light as possible.

"I am Warren," he said, "and this is Nella and Salvador." He gestured to his companions. "We are prisoners as well. We stumbled upon your chamber by accident."

"Pleasssssed to meet you," said the dragon. "My name isss Montour Densstur Sssanothonssstir."

"That is a very noble name," said Nella.

"You like it?" said the dragon with delight, "My oldissst sssisissster picked it out when I wasssss jusssst a pup." His deep voice rumbled like a grumpy volcano. "Yessss, thossssse were the dayssss…" he trailed off, a whimsical look in his eye. "I wasss ssso cute, sssssmall human children would assssk their parentsss if they could keep me assss a pet!" he exclaimed, his forked red tongue hanging out the side of his mouth.

He bulged his orange eyeballs at them playfully, and then, as if suddenly remembering where he was, he looked past them at the dusty clay walls of the cell. "But now there isss only thissss ssssmelly old dungeon for me." A puff of smoke erupted from his nostrils and curled upward in a vanishing gray spiral.

"We will find a way out of here," said Nella.
Warren looked tense.

"That would be sssspectacular," said the dragon. "But if we don't, I may regrettably have to eat all three of you quite ssssoon." The dragon's face twitched and hardened, taking on a very different expression.

"No, no," said Warren, "we will find a way out for sure." He tried to sound convincing.

"I don't see how we are going to get through the prison bars," said Salvador studying their entry point in the steep wall high above, "if they are made of unbreakable steel."

Warren glared at him. "Unbreakable by fire and water, but entirely destructible by magic, the very substance from which unbreakable steel is forged." He looked at the dragon. "Eh-heh, I will try to dissolve them." He projected his hands forward, concentrating his attention on the bars.

"Magic!" hissed the dragon, its lips twitching spastically into a nasty snarl, "It wasss a magic wielder who imprissssoned me!" His glowing underbelly grew brighter, turning more yellow than orange. The heat level rose sharply in the cavern.

Losing his focus, and turning nervously to the upset dragon, Warren searched for a way to soothe the creature. He lifted his hands, and projected a gentle energy through his palms, as he had seen Bloom do. For the first time, the heart of his hands began to glow faintly. He was immensely uplifted by the experience of his own light tugging softly through his arms and wrists as if lured out by an unseen magnet.

"I am not like the one who imprisoned you," said Warren, " for I will use what little magic I have to help you *escape* this prison."

The dragon's underbelly dimmed, and the light in the dungeon softened. Warren's clothes felt stiff and dry like paper near an open fire. His tried to wrap his head around the task at hand. Warren estimated that the cage was roughly three stories tall and over a hundred feet wide. Closing his eyes and reaching out his hands, Warren mentally felt around for a more precise sense of the space. He could feel the cage extending through the built up clay walls and into the outer cells of the other prisoners. In his mind, the bars seemed to glow a faint reddish light.

"How's it going?" whispered Salvador.

Warren opened his eyes. "Shhh," he said to his brother, "I need to concentrate." He closed his eyes once more.

Salvador shifted his weight from one foot to the other, peering sideways at the dragon. The dragon snapped its eyes onto him, and with brooding narrow pupils stared at the blond youth. Salvador tugged on Warren's sleeve.

"It's looking at me," he whispered. "I think it's planning to eat me first."

Warren exhaled in frustration and scowled at his twin.

"What?" shrugged Salvador.

Warren shrugged his twin off his sleeve, and returned his focus to the bars of the cage. All was quiet for several tense minutes. Warren sensed the cage was made out of a rough and hasty energy. The young wizard let his own calm energy flow out from within his core and infuse the giant cage. He imagined the bars collapsing in his mind and willed them to return into the nothing from which they were foraged. Warren reached for his innermost sense of freedom and focused on that feeling with every fiber of his being.

"Look!" said Nella, as the visible portion of the bars up above began turning to inky red smoke to waft away.

"Incredible!" said Salvador.

The dragon moaned a chilling cry. It searched the ceiling with its eyes in disbelief. Spreading its wings and standing at full height, the dragon moved around spastically, moaning and shifting its weight from one foot to the other. It was obviously overwhelmed. The dragon arched its back and flicked its scaly tail, looking up at the hole in the wall where the three humans had entered. Nella smiled, tears streaming down her cheeks, watching the creature experience its freedom. Warren and Salvador laughed, overjoyed by the scene taking place before them.

Speechless, the dragon lowered its chest to the ground allowing Warren and the others to climb onto its back. Nella seated herself behind Warren, and placed her arms around his mid section. Salvador climbed up behind her. The dragon flapped its leathery wings and leapt eagerly into the air. They rose up and up, until their elevation paralleled the opening Tolvin had chiseled so high up in the wall.

"Hold on!" shouted Warren.

The dragon lurched toward the opening even though it was obviously too small, and they smashed through the wall and plummeted downwards through the narrow cylindrical column of the jail cell dug out by prisoners of the past. The dragon's wings smashed though the clay walls on the way down, destroying the cell. The dragon pulled up just before impacting with the floor and effortlessly turned up the dry riverbed. Below them, the passage way was filled with soaking wet prisoners pouring from their cells and charging down the hall. Tolvin was in their lead, showing the prisoners the way out. A swarm of guards came at the captives from the opposite direction. But the inmates were fearless, prepared to die rather than be caged again. Uplifted by their sudden freedom, and the vanishing of the bars, they yelled as they threw themselves into battle, armed only with the desire to live free. Many of them glanced up as the dragon swept over them, alarmed or delighted by the sight. The dragon hit the guards with a single, but powerful blast of fire before leaving the dungeons to flap over the long stairway in the direction of the main hall.

"I mean, I assumed he could probly do that, but I never thought it would just be like, *BLEH*," muttered Salvador to Nella, sticking out his tongue to imitate the dragons fire.

They whooshed up the stairs and through the narrow hallways of the crystal fortress, leaving a trail of destruction as they smashed forward. The dragon was barely able to fit inside the translucent hallways without shattering the walls. The passageways were a blur in Warren's eyes. He clung to the back of the dragon, ducking from bits of exploding glass around him, and tried hard to orient himself within the massive building. He knew it would not be long before they were discovered. The dragon reared up onto its hindquarters and burst through the next set of doors.

ESCAPE FROM AUGDEN CITY

"**W**hat's this you've brought me?" asked Prince Coonan Malden. His face was turned away, but his posture and tone was visibly displeased.

The guards shoved a hooded man to his knees before him.

"We found him just outside the city, your Majesty," said a guard, and threw back the hood.

The prince smiled, and the guards took a step back from the man. Bloom looked up at the prince, and then at the guard who held his staff.

"It seems," said the prince, "Tigorious has not been as thorough as he claims." There was a threatening note in his voice. Wooffen barked from nearby, a thick loop of rope around his neck. The soldier that held the rope yanked Wooffen back.

"Surrender the Seer and the young wizard and I will leave you be," said Bloom.

"Odelious," continued the prince. "What a rare opportunity. I have heard many impressive things..." he trailed off. "Bring me the crolackrolite," commanded the prince abruptly to his guards.

The guards did not dare approach the wizard. Bloom shifted his weight as he conjured a spell. The many reflective surfaces of the great hall reflected the light pouring from the old man's hands. "Razarvarr!" he uttered. Immediately, the guards around him were blasted ten feet away as if by a powerful invisible explosion. A set of new guards rushed toward him. A single, pea-sized crolackrolite bead fell from Bloom's palm and rolled away from its master across the glassy floor. Bloom glanced at it in horror. He reached after it desperately as pain contorted his ancient face. He tried to rise from his knees. A dozen guards surrounded him, pointing their gleaming spears at his throat. One of them picked up the bead and hesitantly brought it to the prince. Wooffen barked a helpless cry behind his master. Bloom gritted his teeth to keep from calling out, and fell forward onto his hands. With every step the guard took, Bloom's pain seemed to double. The wizard appeared to be ageing rapidly as the stone moved away from him. Struggling to breathe, he collapsed, looking wearily up at the prince with a trembling, continually shriveling face.

Barking, Wooffen squirmed and pulled wildly on his leash but was held back.

"Perhaps luck is on my side today," smiled the prince, looking at the shiny black marble in his palm. "This mishap has worked out in my favor after all. Now that I have a stone that contains the life force energy of the most powerful wizard who ever lived, I can finally wield the power I have always deserved." He brought the bead to his eye for a closer look, and his lips curled into a grin.

Tigorious bounded into the hall.

"Traitor!" screamed the prince at the sight of him. "What am I to do with you?" He dropped his voice to a half whisper, still fingering the crolackrolite bead, and sat back in his throne. "Perhaps it is time to remind the people what becomes of traitors within this kingdom."

"You are the only traitor this kingdom has ever known," snarled Tigorious, taking a defensive stance.

"Guards!" yelled the prince, "Seize him at once!"

At that moment, approximately one third of the guards threw off their red cloaks revealing shining silver robes beneath.

"Join the rebellion or die," commanded Tigorious to the remaining guards who advanced toward them, some intent on fulfilling their orders, while others hesitantly joined the silver clad soldiers. With a clang, the blades of the guards and rebels collided in ferocious battle.

The prince laughed and sat back in his throne enjoying the display. A messenger nervously approached him and bent down to whisper something in his ear.

"What?" shouted the prince, leaping to his feet. "She's escaped?"

he hollered. Upon overhearing these words, many of the warriors looked up at the messenger in mid action.

"The young wizard has stolen her your Majesty!" shrieked the messenger.

"Find them! Take them to the Brute!" spat the prince.

"But the Brute has turned against us!" shouted the terrified youth.

"Then throw him in the dungeon to drown for his betrayal!"

"The dungeon is no more!" choked the messenger.

"What do you mean?" asked the prince in an icy tone.

"It has vanished into thin air!" cried the young man.

A look of stunned disbelief swept across the pale face of Prince Coonan Malden.

"Then kill them! Kill all of them!" commanded the prince. But no one was looking at him, for the aghast, and open-mouthed faces of his spectators were now turned away from him and looking toward the back wall. Prince Coonan Malden followed their gaze, and his mouth too fell open, for there, shimmering through several thick sheets of glass was the giant black shape of a monster that rapidly grew larger as it advanced, quickly smashing through the walls toward them. There was a whooshing sound like a violent gust of wind moving through a chimney, and suddenly, a large portion of the back wall of the fortress melted into a hot orange liquid. Sheets of glass seemed to tear at the seams as they dissolved into a molten mass around the newly formed entrance. A black dragon with three riders astride its back bounded through the hole with a crash and landed inside the crystalline hall, forcing the guards and rebels to dive out of the way. White ring fractures spread across the floor beneath the monster's heavy feet. Wooffen yanked hard on his leash one last time, and the rope slipped from the hands of the soldier holding it. The dog bounded towards his master.

"Bloom!" shouted Warren. He leaped from the dragon's back and rushed to the old man's side. Wooffen skidded to a halt beside the boy and whined a high-pitched note.

Behind them, Salvador helped Nella dismount from the dragon. The guards bowed low before her. The movement of red and silver robes swept across the hall like ripples of water.

"Kill the Gator!" yelled one of the silver clad men, pointing his sword at Prince Coonan Malden.

"Gator?" asked Nella. "The prince is a Gator?"

Salvador shrugged.

"For Princess Nella!" shouted another man drawing his weapon and starting up the battle again. Blades collided in an explosion of metallic clangs.

Warren was at a loss at seeing the condition Bloom was in. Barely alive, Bloom struggled to lift his trembling head and suck in a raspy breath.

"He has a stone!" he breathed.

Warren glanced at the prince in alarm. The prince was giving orders from his throne on the other end of the hall.

"Stay with Bloom," said Warren to Salvador and Wooffen. "And protect Nella," he looked up at the sneering Coonan Malden. "I'll get the stone."

Salvador nodded, and hastily pulled the rope from the Wooffen's neck. As the first guard lunged at Salvador, he wrenched the weapon from the man's hand and instantly used the sword to deflect the next attack. As more guards closed in around him, Salvador masterfully swung the sword, fighting off the guards with perfect form. One of the men tried to stab the blond youth. Salvador deflected the attack, throwing the man back against the others so hard that the first and second row of fighters behind him clamored to the ground. The surrounding soldiers fell back upon seeing the first example of Salvador's strength and skill, hesitating to endanger themselves again.

"Here, take this!" shouted Salvador handing Warren the sword.

"What about you?" asked Warren.

"I can find another," said Salvador, stealing a curved blade right from the belt of a rebel next to him. The man looked at Salvador in alarm, and then back down at his empty belt, before Salvador shoved him backwards and he was swallowed up into the mill of battle.

Warren dove through the mob towards the prince. The guards grabbed him, but Warren wrestled free and charged towards the Prince.

"Give me the stone!" shouted Warren.

The Prince clutched Bloom's stone in his fist. "Its mine now!" he said with a manic grin, shoving the object into the pocket of his robes and drawing his golden sword.

Warren charged forward, and his simple sword met the golden blade of the prince with a loud clang. After only a few strikes it was apparent that the boy was no match for the swordsmanship of Prince Coonan Malden. Warren immediately found himself blocking instead of striking, but he bravely held his ground, refusing to be pushed back into the milling soldiers and rebels behind him. The Princes' blows came down harder and harder. Coonan Malden swiped his weapon towards Warren's midsection, and the boy jumped back, barely avoiding the tip of the shining sword. The Prince advanced, seeing an opportunity. He jabbed maliciously at Warren, aiming to slay him where he stood. Warren struggled to avoid the blade.

On the other side of the hall, the dragon narrowed its eyes at Bloom. "Wizzzard!" spat the dragon, hungrily eyeing the shriveled old man. Its hot breath gushed out in bright sputters of flame, "I hate thissss one mossst of all!" it hissed, its rumbling voice climaxing unstably on the last syllables. The once friendly creature was transformed, its face contorted with hatred.

"I think it was Bloom," Nella said to Salvador, who was busy fencing some off some soldiers, "Bloom put him here."

"What makes you think—" broke off Salvador.

"For one thousssand yearsss, I lay rotting in that cage!" screamed the dragon as it advanced still further toward its victims, its whole body tense with wrath.

"Dragon," said Nella, fearlessly standing before the towering creature. "Revenge cannot erase the pain you have been through."

"I will not forgive, and I cannot forget!" hissed the dragon, his underbelly glowing neon orange. "He musssssst pay!"

"You think he has not paid?" asked Nella. "And what will taking his life give you? Will it end your suffering?"

There was a whooshing as the dragon opened its mouth. Nella's eyes widened, and she inhaled sharply in alarm.

Locked in in combat, Warren looked up in time to see a torrent of flames erupting from the dragon's mouth in an angry blaze aiming at his friends. He saw Salvador pull Nella behind a large shield in front of Bloom and Woofen. Warren knew for certain that the shield would not keep them safe for long. It was at this exact moment that Warren felt the cold blade of Prince Coonan Malden's sword upon his neck. The Prince reached into his pocket and drew out the crolackrolite stone. He held the tiny black sphere in his fingers mockingly while pressing the blade of his sword to Warren's throat.

"I want you to know before you die," spat the Prince, "that all I needed to complete my plan was a stone from the Pebble Maker, and that it was your foolish and predictable actions that made it possible for me to acquire it."

In desperation, Warren focused his attention on the stone in Coonan Malden's hand. The prince made a puzzled face, as the fingers of his own hand slowly began opening against their will. Warren strained for the stone with his mind. Trembling with effort, the prince fought to keep his fingers around the stone, but it was no use. The crolackrolite sphere pulled itself free of Coonan Malden's fingers and shot strait into Warren's open hand. The boy closed his fingers securely around the stone, and feeling the energy of victory surge powerfully through him, blasted the Prince away with a burst of magic. Warren rushed to aid his friends.

"I cannot let him live with what he hassss done!" roared the dragon

"And how will you live with what you will have done to him?"

Upon hearing these words from the legendary Princess Nella, two nearby fighters from opposing sides paused their battle. A stray swing of a spiked club came flying at one of their heads. Instinctively, the other man lifted his shield and deflected it, saving his enemy's life. Changed by this remarkable event they moved to Salvador's side forming a quarter circle around Nella, wordlessly choosing to protect rather than to destroy. They aimed their strikes to detour their opponents instead of kill them. The two soldiers were soon joined by other guards and rebels who filled in the gaps, forming a ring around their princess. Their silver and red robes were mismatched, but the intentions of the warriors were aligned.

"The wizard mussst die!" the dragon growled, wrinkling its horrible snout and inhaling deeply. As Warren raced towards the old wizard, the old man began growing rapidly younger. Adrenaline surging through his veins, Warren projected his defensive and angry feelings in a powerful stream of fire. The dragon met the challenge with ease. The two rivers of fire met in the middle in a molten gush.

"Warren, no!" cried Bloom, his voice frail and cracking. Warren's attention snapped down at his friend in time to see the old wizard's face contorted with emotion. The look in Bloom's eyes extinguished Warren's anger instantly. Quickly tucking the crolackrolite stone in the old wizard's hand, Warren turned once more to face the dragon.

"Dragon!" he said. "By wizard's hand you were imprisoned, by wizard's hand you are set free! Go your own way."

The dragon breathed an even more powerful torrent of flames toward the boy. Warren projected a gentle energy toward the attack and the flames were splashed away with a small burst of water. The two elements hissed as they merged. The falling droplets of water thudded against the floor in a brief spell of indoor rain that steamed upon impact with the hot glass. Warren positioned himself between the dragon and his friends. He wasn't sure how long he could hold the dragon at bay.

The dragon inhaled deeply, drawing in a chest full of air.

"Warren, do something!" shouted Salvador, helping a barely conscious Bloom to his feet.

"I don't know what to do!" Warren yelled back. He felt overwhelmed, trembling with frantic energy, and yet unable to take action. The pressure building within him was tearing him apart. The handful of spells he had learned were useless in the current situation. The men fighting to protect them were being swarmed by greater numbers of soldiers. All around them, the rebels hacked at the guards of Augden City. Feeling lost, Warren looked up at the giant dragon towering above. Its underbelly glowed white hot, and its eyes blind with rage. There was a tiny pause in the dragon's breath as it turned from an inhale to an exhale. And that was when it happened. Warren felt a mass of wild energy ripping from his chest, like a dam breaking through its threshold and spilling forth in an unstoppable flood. In an electric bolt Warren's powers surged through him leaving all four of his limbs buzzing.

There was a flash of brilliant light and the dragon began to shrink. Its emerging fiery breath, coiling in ribbons of orange and red, diminished alongside its body. Smaller and smaller it grew, alarmed at its own transformation. Shrinking rapidly, the dragon fell through the air like a stone. Impulsively, Warren reached out and caught it. It landed in his glowing hands like a heavy piece of fruit. Roughly the size of a pear, the dragon abruptly stopped diminishing in size and looked up at Warren with large, adorable eyes. It breathed a tiny stream of flames, burning Warren's fingers.

"Ouch!" cried Warren, drawing back his hands.

Denied its perch, the dragon flapped its wings and caught itself in mid air. It took off through the giant tunnel of destruction it had made on its way in and slipped out of the first broken window it could find above the heads of battling men.

"I wish I had thought of that myself," sighed Bloom behind Warren.

Warren turned around, relieved to see Bloom standing beside him alive, if not entirely well. They were in the middle of the hall, surrounded by over three hundred men. Wooffen wouldn't leave his master's side. Salvador fought beside the rebels and guards protecting Nella, but the soldiers were breaking through.

"Teach me the suspension spell!" cried Warren.

"Suspension?" whispered Bloom, with the calm of a man who had reckoned with death far too many times to fear its eager clutches. "Well, let me see…"

"Guys, do you want to hurry it up a bit?" asked Salvador hysterically. He swung a sword at the six men who were charging him. Their blades collided with a scraping clash. Salvador used one foot to press hard against the multi-layered crossing weapons, shoving the men backwards in a tripping heap.

Nella was stricken with a silent sorrow. She stood beside Warren and Bloom looking over the battle with a growing conviction writing itself on her delicate face.

"Suspension may be attained in many different ways," said Bloom.

"Which is the easiest?" cried Warren.

"The easiest is the most unreliable," answered Bloom.

"So give me the second easiest then!" rushed Warren.

"The second is too advanced, perhaps I should be the one to—" began Bloom.

"No," Warren cut him off. "I will do it, teach it to me now!"

"The easiest?" confirmed Bloom.

Warren jerked his chin in a firm nod.

"Choose a subject, imagine it weightless, and then utter the words, leversaura awen almenaura," said Bloom, the wrinkles deepening on his brow.

"Leversaura, awen almenaura!" shouted Warren. There was a cascade of yells in the great hall as a wave of fighters surged through the battleground as if tossed up by an invisible hand and then clamored to the ground.

"You have to choose a *specific subject* first," said Bloom, "and hold onto it in your mind, otherwise you have no control over what will happen."

"Got it," said Warren.

"Also, this is a very draining spell. You risk losing your hold if you try to maintain it for too long."

Warren struggled to focus what was left of his energy into his hands. He felt weak in the knees.

"Warren! Get us out of here!" yelled Salvador, blocking strike after strike. The circle around them had been broken. Soldiers shoved past their opponents toward Nella.

"Seize the Princess!" shouted Prince Coonan Malden.

The soldiers hesitated, their alliance wavering.

"Do it now!" shouted the Prince furiously.

Men lunged at the girl.

"Leversaura, awen almenaura!" commanded Warren, concentrating on Nella. With a scream, she shot upwards. Nella grabbed

Warren's hand, clinging to him as an anchor, and with a jolt, he went soaring up with her. They whooshed unstably upward, turning the heads of the soldiers below. Warren fought to keep hold of Nella's hand. Below them, Salvador was overwhelmed by fighters. Warren ground his teeth, focusing with all his might. Self-levitation was even trickier than he had expected. He kept forgetting to include himself in the spell. He and Nella hung loosely in the air, dropping abruptly every few feet when Warren lost his focus. The crystalline chandeliers above poked down at them like daggers.

"No, no, no," said Bloom. "Not like that—like this!" He raked his fingers sharply through the air. "LEVERSAURA, AWEN, ALMENAURA!" he uttered. Warren and Nella immediately stopped bobbing up and down, suspended effortlessly in the spell. The old wizard dropped his new beads into his pocket.

"Bloom!" shouted Warren, reaching down. He clasped forearms arms with the old man and pulled him up into the atmosphere beside Nella and himself. Bloom tumbled into the air, weightless and unburdened by the crolackrolite beads. The old man smiled slightly, savoring the long forgotten sensation.

Salvador dodged the group of assaulting fighters closing in on him and ran for his life. Wooffen darted ahead of him weaving between the legs of rebels and soldiers. Catching up to the dog, Salvador grabbed Wooffen around the waist and tossed the Basset Hound high into the sky.

"AWOOOOOOOOO!" howled Wooffen as he sailed through the air.

Warren used a swimming motion to reach the dog, grabbing his canine friend's hind paw just as Wooffen started on his way down. Suddenly floating, Wooffen whined, scampering his stubby legs uselessly around in the atmosphere and turning himself in a somersault. Salvador took a powerful leap upward and Warren grabbed his brother's arms, heaving Salvador into the levitating spell along with the others. The soldiers below followed the floating company in rivers of red and silver.

Unstable in the atmosphere, Nella flipped upside-down, her long hair dangling to the floor. A soldier grabbed her flowing golden-brown locks. Nella cried out as he yanked her hair toward him pulling her down. Warren pushed off of Salvador and drew his dagger. Upon reaching Nella's side he used one swift movement to cut through her hair well above the soldier's head. It grew back immediately to the same exact length. Warren pushed Nella's ankle and righted her.

"Hold on to me!" he directed, his nerves at their maximum stress capacity. Nella clasped his arm firmly. Warren swung her around him to propel her toward the shattered walls leading out, sacrificing his own momentum and speed to ensure her escape. She flew toward the opening quite fast at first, and then slower, and slower, gradually dropping out of the atmosphere. Warren sunk slightly and he knew the magic would not last much longer, at any moment it could dispel. Nella was only halfway to the doors. The soldiers stabbed up at her with their spears. Warren glanced back at Salvador and the others. Only Bloom was enjoying himself. Wooffen had his tail tucked between his legs and appeared to be terrified. Unaccustomed to the lack of gravity, the dog spread out his paws until the webbing was stretched tight between his toes, as he searched for something to push off from. Salvador swam in powerful yet ineffective bursts toward his twin.

Below them, Tigorious charged ahead, overtaking Nella. Falling out of the spell, the girl landed onto the giant shaggy back of the cat as he barreled past the guards. Nella put her arms around his neck.

Panicking, Warren collided with Salvador and Bloom. Pushing his friends forward, he allowed himself to be shoved backwards still deeper inside the great hall. Salvador and Bloom were propelled forward as they descended toward the floor. They landed in a spot free of fighters and ran ahead, chasing after Nella. On his way out, Bloom grabbed his staff from the soldier who had taken it from him, wrenching it from the man's hands with a dignified scowl. The man dared not challenge the wizard.

Wooffen was still floating slightly and his claws scratched the glass floor in quick repeated scrapes as he struggled to ground himself.

Warren found himself hopelessly falling from the air. He stepped on the head of one man, the shoulder of the man next to him, and the back of a bent over rebel as he propelled himself forward with the last of the spell and fell out of the air back to the ground. Still floating slightly, his feet felt useless and untrustworthy, as if they couldn't quite push off the ground. In spite of fatigue, Warren commanded his legs to comply. Soldiers clamored after him in a noisy rush. Warren could see no escape.

"We need to find a way to slow the soldiers down," he yelled to Bloom who was several yards ahead of him.

The old wizard glanced behind, looking positively exhausted. "Good idea," he said, and mumbled a complex incantation, tightly closing his fist around yet another crolackrolite bead.

It became suddenly quiet. Warren looked over his shoulder. The clamoring mob of soldiers and rebels appeared to be moving in slow motion behind them.

"Awesome," said Salvador, as they charged ahead quickly putting distance between themselves and the other fighters.

"Wooffen, grab my shoe!" said Warren, recognizing his shoe on the grass where it fell from the tower. Wooffen snatched it up in his mouth.

"That way," said Bloom, pointing to the alleyway down which Nella and Tigorious had gone. Wooffen and Salvador went first. Warren rushed after them. With a nervous glance over his shoulders, Bloom followed. They dashed across the glass cobblestone path. Up ahead at the far end of the tunnel, they heard the rush of water. From the shadows, a dark shape leaped out in front of them.

"Where do you think you're going?" hissed Tigorious. His powerful shoulders rolled with muscles. As the cat advanced, the group slowly backed away. Warren moved himself between Tigorious and the others. Nella was trapped behind the giant cat, unable to reach her friends.

"Grrrr!" growled Wooffen, with the shoe still stuffed in his mouth.

"Tigorious," said Warren, "she cannot stay here."

"She must!" growled the cat, "It is our only chance to win back the city!"

"Not this time," said Nella.

"You must lead the rebellion!" spat Tigorious.

"Let us go," said Nella.

"I cannot!" growled the giant cat.

"Tigorious, mind your manners before I make a rug out of you," said a gruff voice from deep inside the tunnel. A giant man stepped from the shadows. He lit a torch.

"Tolven!" cried Nella.

In the light of the fire, the floor of the tunnel glistened with an odd reflective liquid.

"Follow me," said Tolvin, waving to the others as they filed past Tigorious.

"No!" roared Tigorious leaping after them.

Tolvin touched his torch to the ground and a wall of flames rose up between them and the cat of Diamondell.

Tolvin directed the group to the far end of the tunnel where a small dock swayed and bobbed in the rushing waters. A rowboat was tied to the dock and the company clamored inside it.

"Come with us," said Nella to Tolvin from inside the boat.

The giant man was somber. "Not yet," he said, untying the rope and tossing the loop to Salvador who caught it and reeled it in. The rowboat was quickly pulled into the rapids of the wild river.

Wooffen darted around the boat with a growing panic.

"Settle down boy," said Bloom. The old wizard kept looking back over his shoulder at the glass fortress.

"Why do you keep looking back there?" asked Warren.

"When you slow down time, it always compensates by speeding up again."

Just as he spoke these words, the boat seemed to gain momentum. The whitewater rapids that were far away were suddenly right beneath them. The falls ahead came into view, their roar growing louder each second.

There was a blast behind the boat, and the water splashed up in an icy fountain beside the boat. Warren glanced behind. The soldiers were moving at double speed in a chaotic blur along the fortress walls. Archers were perched on the bridges, and cannons had been arranged in mere seconds.

"Row!" yelled Warren, throwing Salvador an oar.

"Oh no, oh no!" whimpered Wooffen.

The falls were coming up ahead.

"Wooffen, you can talk?" asked Nella, looking at the Basset Hound in shock.

Arrows zipped though the air.

"Stay low!" cried Warren.

Wooffen darted around the small boat. He whined anxiously. Nella moved to restrain him. Without warning, the hound leapt from the boat and into the wild rushing waters.

"Wooffen!" cried Bloom, and dove in after him.

Nella was next, followed by Salvador. Left alone in the boat, Warren shook his head, and followed suit, throwing himself over the edge. He fell deep into the rusty, churning rapids. The icy water forced the air from his lungs. Warren fought against the powerful current, pushing his way up to the surface. He burst out above the water, gasping for air. The bridge was far behind. Ahead he could see Nella's head bobbing in the rapids. Salvador was beside her. He was able to locate Wooffen's paddling form as well, but Bloom was nowhere to be found. With a shock, Warren realized that not only was the old wizard weakened by recent events, but that he also had weights attached to his clothes, and so he may not have been able to fight his way up for air.

"Where's Bloom?" he called across the water. Salvador and Nella began searching the water as well, calling the wizard's name, but he was out of sight. Warren felt a sense of panic rising in his chest. The noise of the waterfall roared up ahead. The current quickened, pulling them quickly forward. Wooffen tried paddling back toward them, against the rushing water, but was still being pulled downriver by the powerful current. Salvador swam toward him, grabbing the dog with one arm, and Nella's hand under the other. Salvador pushed himself through the water to shore.

Suddenly, Warren hit an object with his leg. He dove down. Bloom's lifeless body floated beneath him in the water. Warren pushed himself to the surface.

"Salvador!" he yelled. "He's here!" Salvador heaved Nella and

Wooffen out of the river, and plunged back in the swirling waters, heading in Warren's direction. Nella collapsed on the sandy shore, too weak to stand. Wooffen rushed to the river's edge, barking and searching for his master.

Warren struggled to keep his place in the current. He grabbed ahold of Bloom's wrist and tried to pull him upwards, but the old man was too heavy, as he was laden with hundreds of crolackrolite stones. Salvador swam toward him with powerful strokes.

"Down here!" said Warren, as he dove under. Warren got underneath Bloom and shoved his body upwards. Salvador wrapped an arm around the old wizard's chest and pulled him to the surface. The boys swam to shore, pulling Bloom's limp body between them. They hauled him onto the sand. Salvador touched his wrist. "He has no pulse," he said. The wizard was turning purple. His mouth hung open, and his eyes were closed. Wooffen darted around whining anxiously.

"Lay him on his side!" commanded Warren. Salvador helped his brother push Bloom onto his right shoulder. Warren hit the wizard's back with the palm of his hand.

"Come on, breathe!" he muttered. He kept hitting the middle of Bloom's back.

"Bloom!" cried Nella.

"Breathe!" shouted Salvador, "Come on!" Warren hit Bloom on the back again. Suddenly, Bloom coughed. "That's it!" said Warren, still tapping his back with his palm. The old man spewed water, the life returning to his body. Salvador sat back in relief. Wooffen licked his master's hand.

"He's going be okay," said Warren, still kneeling beside the wizard. Salvador helped Bloom up into a seated position. The old wizard sucked in slow raspy breaths, looking at the rushing river.

"Thank you," wheezed Bloom.

Warren sank to the ground with relief, letting his knees fall onto the muddy riverbank. Nella shivered with cold beside him. The three teenagers sat close beside the old wizard, grateful for his every labored breath. Little by little Bloom was recovering. The atmosphere in the company was somber. Warren heard a chewing noise behind him.

"Wooffen, what are you doing?" he asked, glancing over his shoulder.

Wooffen looked up with a guilty expression. He had been gnawing on the leather shoe.

"Just a little nibble?" asked Wooffen through a full mouth.

"No!" cried Warren. "I need that! The quest depends on it."

"Pweh!" said Wooffen, spitting out the soaking wet shoe. "You're rrright, I'm sorry, I don't know-ow wo-what came over me." He hung his head in shame.

"Eh!" said Warren, picking up the shoe with two fingers. It was soaking wet and covered in drool and teeth marks. "You slobbered all over it."

"Well, carrrrying it made my mouth wo-water," said Wooffen.

"We must still travel on before we break camp for the night," said Bloom, attempting to rise. Seeing the old wizard struggling to stand the boys scooped Bloom up on either side and the company moved once again into the shelter of the forest. They worked their way uphill along an abandoned path. The group made slow progress but trudged along in spite of fatigue. At last, sensing that Bloom could not walk a single step further, Warren found a more or less comfortable resting place and together with Salvador set the old man down. Bloom did not protest.

Nella took a seat by the recovering Bloom. She was silent. In the distance, the glass city sparkled like a cluster of crystals. The expression on Nella's face was lost. Warren came over to sit beside her.

"So you're *the* Seer," he said, remembering what Tigorious had said.

"I guess," said Nella sadly.

"What is it?" asked Warren, sensing something serious on her mind.

"I'm losing the sight," whispered Nella.

Warren looked confused.

"I can feel my powers lessening each day," she admitted. "My abilities were much stronger on Earth, and they have gradually been fading since I got here. Maybe I'm not the seer."

Warren looked over at the city.

"I'm pretty certain you are, and we will find out how to get your sight back. But if you're not…" he paused and looked at her wet face as she blew a droplet of water from her nose. "There's nothing wrong with not being the chosen one," he said. "It doesn't make a person any less capable of great things."

"I wasn't the chosen one either," confessed Bloom. "I was a beggar for most of my youth, stealing food in order to survive. If it wasn't for the kindness of my teacher, who pulled me off the street and gave me a place to live, I would have never discovered magic at all."

"I actually *was* the chosen one, and so I can't relate," said Salvador, opting out of the conversation to go find some firewood.

"But how can I help the people who need me without my powers?" asked Nella.

"We will find a way to help them," said Warren. "For now, we must defend the pillar from our ill-willed opponents." Nella shivered. The back of her long-sleeved, previously white shirt was streaked with blood. Suddenly, Warren remembered the dress.

"Hold on," he said, "I have something for you." Warren pulled out the garment from underneath his breastplate. It was mostly wet. He smoothed the wrinkles and handed it to Nella.

"I found this in the fortress," he said, handing her the wet dress.

Nella didn't seem to mind the condition it was in. She touched the fabric and her eyes widened.

"This reminds me of something," she said absently.

"A vision?"

"No, it is a memory!" exclaimed Nella. "I remember my mother sewing this dress for me."

"You do?" asked Warren in astonishment.

"Yes," said Nella. "I was just a small child, but I remember her hands working with this exact fabric. She said it would help me remember all that I would forget. I didn't believe her at the time."

Warren smiled.

"Where did you say you found this?" asked Nella, unfolding the dress.

"In the tallest tower of the fortress," answered Warren.

"That used to be my chamber!" cried Nella. "Prince Coonan Malden told me so himself."

"I felt like it belonged to you when I saw it," said Warren.

Bloom looked at the cloth in Nella's hands. She showed him the beautiful dress. Its smooth surface shone brightly in the light.

"Ah, an ancient treasure," said Bloom, smiling kindly. "And very timely indeed," he added, taking in her condition. "Those wounds of yours need to be addressed. Press some plantain leaves across your back under your new garments," he instructed.

Nella wandered away until she found a discreet area where she could change.

Having lost all of their supplies, Bloom and the twins found whatever they could to put a makeshift camp together. Salvador wandered around gathering dry branches, while Bloom showed Warren a new plant with bulbous roots, which Warren proceeded to dig up for their meal. After they had gathered enough, Warren washed the roots in a nearby stream. Exhausted, Wooffen lay uselessly in the dirt. When Salvador finished gathering firewood, he went to work forming a circle of boulders forming a fire pit. He set the firewood he had found inside the circle of stones, leaning the sticks against each other in a conical shape. Warren sat down next to his brother. He looked at the dry twigs. Warren cleared his mind and focused his thoughts. He projected the intention of flames, and within a moment, sparks erupted from the air above the pile of brush.

"Vozdor!" said Warren firmly, and a stream of air enlivened the sparks into a vibrant fire.

Salvador rubbed his chin with his hand.

Bloom speared the tubers on a long stick and placed them over the flames studying Salvador.

"Do you want to try?" Bloom asked Salvador.

"Naw, that magic stuff is not for me," replied Salvador, folding his arms. "Do you think they will see the smoke?" he asked, changing the subject.

"It doesn't matter. They know exactly where we are," answered Bloom. "Many of the people of Augden still have a portion of the powerful sight they once possessed. No doubt we are being watched at this very moment."

At these words, Wooffen perked his ears and huffed a quiet bark.

"Perhaps we should get to someplace safer?" asked Salvador.

"We are no longer safe anywhere," replied Bloom.

"Is Nella really the last of the ancients then?" asked Warren.

"Princess Nella was foretold to be the most powerful seer this world has ever known," said Bloom. "I assume that is why she was hidden on earth. It was the only way to keep her safe from the forces that sought to destroy her due to the threat her abilities posed to their plots of dominance." Bloom placed another branch of tubers over the fire before he continued, "She was hidden so long ago that her name had become no more than a children's fable. It was impossible to know whether she ever existed at all, or if she would truly someday return."

"That's another thing I don't understand," said Warren, "how is it possible that she remembers her mother even though the woman lived four thousand years ago?"

"When one travels through a Windore, he moves unevenly through the time-space continuum," answered Bloom. "During her journey to Earth as a small child, she must have leaped a few thousand years ahead in time, and possibly a few more when she returned. Even if the destination is clear, which is extremely rare, one never knows *when* one will arrive at the desired location after passing through a windore."

"You said you've traveled through one of those things yourself?" asked Warren. "How did you manage get back into the same time?"

"I didn't," said Bloom. "Even though my journey to Earth took no longer than a day, I arrived back home seventy years after I had left, and that was too late... much too late..." He trailed off, suddenly somber, no longer in the mood for talking.

"Too late for waht?" Warren asked.

But Bloom remained silent, staring deep into the orange flames. Warren felt bad for pressing the subject.

"I wonder what's keeping Nel—" Salvador broke off, just as Nella emerged from the forest path. Her wavy, exceptionally long hair fell down in rich brown spirals. The dress fit perfectly, and suited both her complexion and slender figure, and the silver fabric highlighting both the brightness of her eyes, and the healthy glow of her cheeks. The long fitted sleeves ended in a narrow sliver of lace at her wrists. Nella wore a necklace set with a single black pearl, and matching shell earrings. The earrings were each carved into a series of elegant spirals.

"I found the jewelry inside one of the pockets," said Nella, reaching up to touch her earrings. "They were my mother's."

Wooffen trotted up to her wagging his tail and barking happily, forgetting speech altogether.

"You look splendid, my dear," said Bloom with a smile.

"Um, yeah," said Warren. "You ah, look... good." He blushed scarlet and hastily returned to tending the fire which had suddenly become a wild blaze.

They ate the strange sweet roots with vigorous appetites. Only Wooffen remained unsatisfied and looked around for something else.

"What are these things?" asked Nella, hungrily swallowing a sizable bite. "They remind me of potatoes."

"They are called Helianthus Tubers. They will give us energy for the road ahead," said Bloom. With those words he looked up across the vista. Warren followed his gaze. In the distance, seven colossal peaks rose steeply into the sky.

"The Wanderers' Mountains," said Nella, observing the direction of the company's attention.

"Why are they called that?" asked Salvador.

"Many souls were lost there seeking the Map of Inquisition," answered Bloom pensively. "Some of them wander there still."

Wooffen growled, and Bloom patted his back soothingly.

"The Map of Inquisition?" asked Warren, slipping a hand in his pocket to find the blue sapphire gem from his crown. He absentmindedly pulled it out. Its weight and size were oddly comforting in the chill of the coming night.

"It is a scroll that contains an incantation of immense power," said Bloom with a sigh. "Powerful enough to grant any single desire of its announcer. It was written by Delominar the Great, a master spellmaker of the Amethyst Era. Like all his works, Delominar created the scroll to be indestructible. Frightened by what may come lest it fell into the wrong hands, he tried to destroy it but was unsuccessful. He kept it hidden, but in time, word of the scroll began to spread in spite of his efforts to conceal it. The map was then stolen by a famous piratess, Miss Maddy Alamore. In her day, her beauty was second to none; neither was the speed of her reflexes or the cleverness of her plots. She outwitted the old Wizard, and took the scroll intending to use it to resurrect her lost love. As it turned out, her love was not dead, but he was simply using her to get the scroll for himself. Once he had the scroll, he sold it for an unthinkable sum to a Lord. The Lord had been cheated out of an inheritance by his older brother. Bent on revenge, he wanted to use the scroll to travel back through time, turn the tables, and cheat his brother before he himself would be cheated. From there, the scroll was confiscated by Prince Theodore Annannok, of the Colsmith region, who planned to use it to prolong his life in order to win the next Dominance. That was when Miss Maddy Alamore stole the scroll for the second time and hid it somewhere in the midst of the Wondrous Mountains, as they were then called. And there it remains still. Maddy mysteriously vanished and was never seen or heard from again. Many men have lost their minds seeking the Map of Inquisition," Bloom finished. He looked more tired than usual. Wooffen whined at his master and Bloom began stroking the dog's head absentmindedly once more.

Salvador stared at the gem in Warren's hand, his eyes glued to the blue stone sparkling in the firelight.

"All that for one wish?" asked Warren. "Hardly seems worthwhile."

Bloom's expression was hard to read. They hadn't noticed how darkness had crept up upon them. As tiredness made itself more and more known, they made preparations for the night, piling leaves and pine needles around the fire pit for their beds.

"I will take the first watch," said Salvador, "and keep the fire burning."

No one protested the offer. Warren took off his armor, and got as comfortable as he could on the lumpy ground. His clothes were still damp on his backside, so he slept facing away from the fire to dry them.

Salvador made himself comfortable on top of a large red boulder at the edge of the camp. For a long while he sat quietly mulling over some unknown thoughts. At the end of his shift, Salvador approached his twin. The dark haired youth was fast asleep. Nella awoke at the sound of Salvador's cautious footsteps. Salvador stood over Warren for a moment before he knelt beside his brother and gingerly reached a hand into his pocket. Warren awoke. Salvador pushed him firmly on the back as if he were shaking him awake.

"Get up, it's your turn," he said casually. Warren yawned and sat up. Salvador moved away to the other side of the fire and lay down. Warren reluctantly rose and took his position at the lookout point.

Salvador lay abnormally still by the fire pit. Nella looked at his frozen form. She had seen what Salvador had tried to do.

BATTLE IN THE CLEARING

An hour before dawn, after putting out the fire, and gathering their few belongings, Nella indicated the direction they were to take, and the group set off on the final leg of their journey. They formed a single file line along the same narrow path leading toward the Wanderers' Mountains. Wooffen was at the rear.

"Ooooh-woo, the rat on the bone, and the bone in the bog, and the boowggg dooow-wo-wn in the valley oooohwo-wo-wooo!" Wooffen sang. Using a knife, Salvador cut off a small piece of fabric from his tunic and ripped it in half. He scowled as he stuffed the woven fibers into his ears.

Warren snickered behind him.

"It really is a curse," he said to Nella, who smiled back, enjoying Wooffen's silly song.

"I never thought I'd hear anything like it," she said.

Bloom joined in, whistling the backup tune for the singing Basset Hound. The wizard had a deep, clear sounding whistle and was a master of vibrato. Warren and Nella exchanged surprised glances at this new musical accompaniment.

They were crossing through a large clearing. Salvador had moved ahead, determined to escape the music. The dusty trees stood motionless, reaching out their yellowing pine needles. Thin clumps of grass rustled underfoot as they passed.

Suddenly, there was a yelp up ahead. Wooffen and Bloom cut off their tune in mid-song.

Warren rushed forward. "Salvador?" he called. Up ahead, his brother was swinging upside-down from a branch, high above, suspended by one foot. A loop of thick rope was tight around his ankle. A dozen guards dressed in dark red uniforms stepped forward from the brush holding a net. They threw it over Warren. He wrestled inside it. Looking around through the squares formed by ropes that contained him, he saw an entire army of men encircling the clearing. Warren looked at the countless soldiers in red uniforms spilling from the trees and he had a sinking feeling in his chest.

Bloom looked down, his hood low over his eyes. Six guards approached him, but he blasted them away in one smooth motion. Three crolackrolite stones fell from his palms and landed at his feet. He did not bother to pick them up.

"Bind the wizard, and bring me the girl!" commanded the familiar voice of Prince Coonan Malden. The Prince rode forward from the line of trees astride a black stallion. He wore a suit of ruby studded armor. The iron plates rippled with his every motion. Twelve more soldiers threw themselves at Bloom. They seemed to simultaneously trip in midair, and began floating upwards. Up, and up they went, soaring into the sky, finally coming to land amidst the uppermost branches of the giant trees surrounding the clearing. The men clung to the pine trees looking down through the sparsely growing branches with worried faces.

Bloom waved his hand through the air and Salvador's rope untied itself from his foot and then leaped from the tree toward a group of soldiers, binding ten men at the waist. The soldiers exhaled an audible whooshing breath as it wound around them. Bloom stood firmly in the middle of the battlefield whispering incantations. Warren's net sprung off of him and stretched out over his head like a spider web. Salvador fell onto it, bouncing off its taught surface like a trampoline. Salvador used the momentum of the rebound to leap into a standing position right before a nervous-looking soldier. The net threw itself on the soldiers pouring from the forest behind him. The soldier charged Salvador with his weapon drawn. Salvador stepped out of the way of the blade. As the man jabbed his sword past him, Salvador grabbed his wrist, disarming him and sending him staggering into the forest. Salvador met the next slew of oncoming attackers with readiness. The army men glanced at each other nervously, before running from Salvador. He chased them across the field.

"Kill the girl, I already know where the pillar is!" commanded Prince Coonan Malden, waving his golden sword. "All I want is the wizard!"

Scores of soldiers poured from the trees in squadrons.

Warren cast a burst of sparks at a group of men encircling Nella. They stepped back, and he dove to her side, hitting them with a second burst of energy that pushed them away once more. They quickly recovered and advanced again. Wooffen stood beside Nella, fearlessly protecting her the best he could.

A giant monster leapt from the trees and charged toward Bloom. It had matted reddish fur that covered its rusty hide in wiry patches. It stormed toward him with its hideous, drooling mouth hanging open. Its long purple tongue lolled to one side, dripping slime as it advanced. The wizard pulled a stone wall up from the ground before him to take the impact. The creature collided with the stone with a terrible force, shattering the block. It shook its massive head and scampered around the obstacle trying to get at the wizard. Bloom did not budge from where he stood. Crolackrolite stones poured from his palms as he cast spell after spell with reckless abandon. He redirected the creature's attention by lighting the end of his staff. The purple crystal began to glow brightly, mesmerizing the orange eyes of the beast. Red energy poured from the creature's eyes into the stone. The monster visibly began reducing in size. Its hide was rapidly changing color as well. Soon the animal took the form of a common boar and ran away into the woods with a squeal. The crystal on Bloom's staff now glowed bright red. Bloom discarded the staff. As his fingers let go of the wood, the light went out of the stone turning it a dull brown. The army advanced, filling the valley with red uniforms.

"Get a stone from him!" shouted Prince Coonan Malden to his soldiers, but no one could get anywhere near the wizard. Bloom shot coils of fire through the battlefield, forcing them back. He clasped the medallion hanging on his neck with one hand and whispered to it, facing it up toward the sky. It seemed to grow suddenly darker. A roll of thunder crackled above. Glancing up, Warren saw grayish purple clouds accumulating rapidly over the battlefield. As the soldiers advanced, lightning sporadically crashed into the field in long electric bolts trailing from the sky. Men shouted and dove away from the flashing bolts. Hard lumpy globs of enchanted hail pelted select soldiers and many of them had to retreat to the shelter of the trees.

Salvador fought his way over to Nella and Warren. Their attackers were backing down, their numbers dwindling. Warren blasted them back again and again, weary but relentless.

The battlefield was chaotic. Faced with the wild magic of a repressed wizard finally set loose, many men were visibly consumed by terror. They ran in their cowardice, infecting others with their fear.

"Retreat!" shouted a general, and the army pulled back.

"Fight, you fools!" counter commanded the prince, but his men refused to listen, disappearing in great numbers inside the forest.

"Must I do everything myself?" hissed Prince Coonan Malden as the last of his men retreated. He dismounted and strode angrily toward Nella. Salvador and Warren stood in front of the girl, shielding the Seer with their own bodies.

The prince was pelted with a personalized hailstorm just for him. The apple-sized globs of ice struck his helmet with a racing force making his armor ring and vibrate. He yelled furiously at the phenomenon as the hailstorm ceased and six bolts of lightning hit the ground around him in a ring. Prince Coonan Malden froze, his eyes still locked on Nella. The wind was picking up. The prince took one step forward, and a tiny tornado shot down from the clouds above sucking him up into the air and spinning him in tight circles several yards above ground. Prince Coonan Malden grabbed onto the limb of a tree, ripping himself from the tornado. When it let go of him, he leaped to the ground and ran for his horse. Quickly mounting, he galloped from the valley with the twister chasing after him into the forest.

Up above, the sky immediately cleared, reminding Warren that it was still early in the day. It was suddenly quiet and peaceful in the valley once more. Warren, Nella, and Salvador rushed to Bloom's side. The old wizard was waist deep in a mountain of crolackrolite. The black beads spilled out around him in every direction. He looked unwell. His hands were raw and bloodied from the stones that had ripped through his palms; some had been the size of lemons. The sleeves of his cloak were stained red. Wooffen circled his master whimpering with worry. Warren, Salvador, and Nella watched the old wizard in dismay, their own injuries forgotten for the moment.

"Warren," said Bloom, and the young man approached, trying hard not to disturb the beads that spilled across the ground. "You must go on without me," said Bloom when Warren was close. The boy started to protest, but Bloom silenced him with a gesture. "I will be here when you return. I assure you, I will be safe.

"We will not leave you," said Warren.

"I'm afraid you have no choice."

"We will find a way," said Warren, "we will each carry a little."

The old man shook his head. "All that I want is for things to be set right. It is my heart's desire." Tears formed in his ancient eyes. "Set it right, Warren." Bloom drew the boy in for an embrace.

Warren pulled away and looked at the old wizard helplessly.

"We'll come back for you," he said, swallowing hard.

Bloom smiled sadly and nodded.

"Now hurry," he said, to Warren and the others behind him. "There will be more coming for you. You've fought bravely, but the greatest battle is still ahead."

"But Bloom—" began Nella.

"You must waste no time, go now!" Bloom urged, and waved them on.

The three reluctantly turned up the path. They leaned into the hill, silently moving ahead, avoiding each other's eyes. Wooffen refused to leave his master's side. "Go with them," said Bloom.

Wooffen whined.

"I said go with them!" commanded Bloom. Wooffen twitched, but did not budge. He stared up at his master.

Nella looked over her shoulder, tears streaming down her face.

"Go with them, Wooffen," said Bloom. "Go!"

Finally, the Basset Hound bounded toward the three humans. When he caught up to them, he paused and looked back.

"Masterrr?" he whimpered sorrowfully.

"I'll be fine," called Bloom from behind them. They moved onward, soon summiting a small hill. The path turned downward once more, and Bloom was quickly lost from their line of sight.

The group walked on in silence. Wooffen's tail dragged in the sand, and his nose trailed barely above ground level. A rodent scurried across his path and Wooffen didn't so much as look up, even though everyone knew he could smell a rat a mile away. The trail wound into a small gully and gradually began to climb the base of the steep mountains ahead. The atmosphere within the group was grim. They trudged on late into the afternoon. When Nella and Wooffen began falling behind, the twins decided to break for a short rest. Salvador sat down on the path and leaned back against the side of the mountain. Warren picked some nearby berries that Bloom had taught him were edible. Wooffen and Nella were not far behind. Upon their arrival, the dog looked back down the path they had come from.

"It's alright Wooffen," said Nella, "We'll meet up with him on our way back."

Wooffen thumped his tail halfheartedly against the ground.

"I miss him too," said Nella.

"This will take forever!" exclaimed Warren in frustration, looking down at the small handful of berries he had managed to gather. "At this rate, we'll starve." Impatiently, he swooshed his free hand through the air in a raking motion, and the patch of thimbleberries before him produced a series of popping sounds, as the berries detached from their stems and sailed into his cupped hands. Warren offered his edible treasure to Nella and his brother.

"I can't see the point of learning magic," snorted Salvador, who was in an awful mood, "It takes so long to master, you'll only be good at it as an old man."

"That's just your ego talking," said Warren defensively.

"My ego?" asked Salvador.

"Yes," replied his brother. "You want everything to be fast and easy, but generally, anything worth having is worth working for."

"I don't have an ego," said Salvador.

"Have you ever had your feelings hurt?" asked Nella.

"My feelings are being hurt right now," replied Salvador.

"Then I'm pretty sure you have an ego," said Nella.

Salvador rolled his eyes.

Nella continued, "When I first heard about feelings as a child, I imagined them to be little organs in my body that registered an unpleasant feeling of suffering when others said hurtful things to me." She nibbled the pink berries from Warren's hands. "I realized after a while that these so called *feelings* were actually not a part of my physical body at all, but rather an entirely imagined source of mental pain, nothing more than my ego defending itself against a perceived threat. Yet we say, *you hurt my feelings* as if we had been physically damaged, and expect others to apologize and feel ashamed for hurting us in this cruel way."

Salvador looked confused.

"You may even feel the pain of hurt feelings physically, but that pain is imagined."

"So what am I to say now when I feel insulted? You're hurting my ego?"

"That would be more accurate," said Nella with a shrug. "And the statement, *my ego is hurting,* would be more accurate still, since others cannot hurt our thoughts because thoughts are immaterial things."

"So what is an ego anyway?" asked Salvador.

Nella sighed. "The ego is a critical survival mechanism, that although fairly negative, is absolutely necessary," she said. "It is the voice in your head that never stops chattering, it is the part of you that knows only self-interest. The part of you that is vain, greedy, and selfish. When you see a beggar and you have the urge to help him, it is your ego that tells you it is his own fault and you are wasting your money," Nella explained, as they rose and began moving up the trail once more.

"So it's my ego that makes me miserable?" asked Salvador.

"Yes, and it is your ego that resents having an ego," said Nella. "In truth, the only voice that poses a threat to the ego's reign is the voice of your conscience. That is why, sensing the steady quiet power of the conscience, the ego tries desperately to shut it up, to snuff it out. The ego will even try make you to do something self-destructive or immoral on purpose, in an attempt to kill the conscience, thereby leaving its own hold over you unchecked. It is true, the more destructive things we do the quieter our conscience grows, its voice becoming wounded and shallow. At times like this, the ego will gloat over its triumph. '*What's that, conscience?*' it will ask, '*No one cares what you say, so shut up!*' But the ego knows that the conscience cannot truly be killed, and may rise up once more if allowed to recover. The conscience is resilient, and powerful beyond belief. It alone can stand up to the ego, if the desire to do good should arise, and it usually does the moment the ego lets down its guard. But the ego is clever, sometimes it poses as the conscience itself. At these times, we feel tortured by shame and guilt and may be fooled into believing our moral compass is an enemy. But the true voice of the conscience brings with it only relief."

"Well, how am I supposed to tell when my ego is talking or when its uh, really me?" asked Salvador.

"Your ego will often use the words 'we' or 'you' instead of 'I' to refer to itself." expounded Nella. "For example, the thought "I am hungry," is a simple want arising from your brain's computation of your body's need for fuel. On the other hand, the thought, "We shouldn't have an enormous appetite because it makes us look a greedy hog," is a thought produced by your ego in an attempt to appear a certain way in front of others to get the approval on which it thrives."

"How is my mind able to clearly tell those two voices apart, and yet still believe that both of them are my own?" asked Salvador.

"Your ego knows it is not you, but the only way it can live is if it can get you to believe that it is, since it exists in your mind only. That is why it masks its stealthy existence by using the joining word, 'we' to speak its wants as if they were your own without your detection. There is also a part of you that knowingly ignores this peculiar mind invasion because you have become attached to the identity created by your ego, however false it may be. After all, what would be left of you without your stories of who you are? In the end, your ego is not an enemy and its purpose is to serve you, but somehow, many of us have come to serve *it* instead."

Salvador looked worn out. He shook his head to clear his thinking.

"You're giving me a headache. How do you know all this stuff anyway?" he asked.

"I spent many years in a mental institution sincerely believing I was insane. During that time I listened attentively to the many voices inhabiting my head," answered Nella.

"I've never met anyone like you and I think you are a very strange person," said Salvador. "Bonkers, is the word that comes to mind. Are you sure they weren't right about you?"

"Salvador!" said Warren.

"I'm just saying," laughed Salvador, "it isn't normal."

Nella laughed also.

"I'm laughing at you, not with you," explained Salvador.

"I'm laughing at me too," said Nella. "I'm laughing at me *with you.*"

They were gaining altitude. Soon the sky had turned dark blue, and the evening rolled out its carpet of dew. It grew colder. They pressed on into the night. Finally reaching a portion of the path wide enough to build a small fire and sleep, they busied themselves gathering wood and seeking out what bits of food they could forage. Salvador picked up a piece of wood and began shaving it with a pocketknife. He carved it for a while, shaping it into a rough comb. Once it was complete, he handed the flat, five-pronged object to Nella with a smile.

"This is for you," he said. Nella returned the smile, and pulled her hair free from the large bun at the back of her head. It spilled down behind her. She proceeded to methodically comb the long locks, totally absorbed in the task. Nella was so beautiful, seated on her small boulder, grooming herself by the fire, that Warren and Salvador had trouble both looking, and not looking at her. Finally, Salvador pulled his brother aside.

"Lets go find some more firewood," he said loudly, even though they had already gathered plenty. He dragged Warren down the path after him. As soon as they were out of earshot, Salvador stopped short and pulled his brother around to face him.

"How do you know she is not using you to put her own stone on the pillar?" he whispered.

"She doesn't even have a stone!" cried Warren.

"Shhh!" hissed Salvador. "You are in love with her and therefore you are blind to her tricks."

"You're the one flirting with her to no end!" said Warren.

"I am just trying to discover her plots," said Salvador.

"No, you're not! You're in love with her yourself!" snorted Warren. "I hear you sighing and see you looking at her with longing."

"How dare you? What, you think I am so stupid? *Oh Salvador is blind, he is so dumb he misses everything*? Well I'll have you know, I'm as sharp as the blade of a sword! I'm only pretending to miss stuff, but I'm on to her and she is up to no good. I just know it, little brother!"

"Stop calling me that!"

"All I'm saying is you don't know what's on her mind. It could be anything!"

"Salvador, stop," said Warren.

"She plans to come between us."

"I don't see how that would help her."

"Just keep your wits about you. That's all I ask," said Salvador, handing Warren a dry log, and picking one up for himself, as they headed back to camp.

Nella had woven her hair into two thick braids hanging down on either side of her head. The braids draped down her back and were bound at the ends with the thin stems of dry grasses. The ties sported tiny weeping wheat ears and contrasted against the color of her hair. Salvador placed his log on the fire. Nella rose.

"Warren, may I talk with you for a moment?" she asked.

"Certainly," said Warren, and he followed her up the path in the opposite direction he had gone with Salvador. Warren glanced over his shoulder at his brother. Salvador mouthed the words, "*I told you so*," behind him. Wooffen lay by the fire curled up in a ball at his feet.

Warren followed Nella up the trail until they came around the bend. She paused, and leaned her back against the cliff, looking out at the purple desert below.

"What did you want to talk about?" asked Warren.

She chewed her lip. "I'm worried about Salvador," she said, glancing up at the night sky. "There's something he's not telling us."

Warren sighed heavily.

"If I had my sight like before, I could see what it is exactly. I have been using up my powers little by little, and I want to save as much as possible of what is left just in case there will be a time of need later. Something tells me such a time may come. It is difficult to be so blind, and it is tempting to use it now," she said, studying his face, "but I know it is best not to."

"What is it you suspect him of?" asked Warren.

"I'm not certain what it is he is planning I just wanted to let you know that I noticed..." she trailed off.

"Noticed what?" asked Warren.

She hesitated. "Some strange behaviors."

"Such as?" prompted Warren.

"Well, he stares at your sapphire gem a lot. Sometimes I wonder whether he's not still determined to be the hero of this quest after all."

"Surely you don't think..."

"No, he would never betray you," she interrupted. "Knowingly," she added as an afterthought.

They headed back to camp. Warren looked at the girl in silver walking beside him, and wondered what the future held for this delicate creature. How would she make it through what they were about to face? He did not know if he could protect her.

Nella caught his gaze and smiled at him reassuringly, as if catching the drift of his thoughts. When they arrived, Salvador was roasting an acorn on a stick. It was charred and smoldering.

"Dinner is almost ready," he said.

Nella returned to her rock but Warren remained standing. The three of them stared into the flames, each pretending to not watch the others. The air was tense. Somewhere in the forest a tree creaked. Wooffen instantly startled awake and perked his ears, listening to the night.

"I will take the first watch," said Salvador.

"Again?" asked Nella.

Salvador shot her a dirty glance. "Well, I can hardly leave it to you, seeing as you wouldn't hurt a fly even if our lives depended on it."

"I will be the first," said Warren, secretly dreading the task.

"Warren, you're in no shape to be the lookout either. I can see your eyes closing from here," exclaimed Salvador. "I, on the other hand, feel wide awake." He sniffed the acorn and made a face.

Warren looked helplessly at Nella.

"Alright," he said, suppressing a yawn. "Wake me on my turn." With these words, he halfheartedly pushed some leaves toward the fireside with one foot, and collapsed on top of them. Within several minutes Warren was fast asleep. Nella lay across the fire from him with Wooffen curled up next to her. She fidgeted every now and again to let Salvador know she was still awake, but her movements gradually grew less and less frequent. Salvador sat a little way off, leaning his back against the trunk of a thick, withered tree and waited for her to fall asleep.

PHANTOM IN THE WOODS

Salvador glanced in the direction of the crackling fire and held his breath to better hear the sounds made by his companions. Warren moaned quietly from exhaustion, but was obviously fast asleep. It had been nearly an hour since either Nella or Wooffen had stirred. Salvador quietly rose. He crept to Warren's side. Slowly, he pulled open Warren's pocket and snaked his hand inside. His fingers closed around a weighty, faceted object that was cool to the touch. Gingerly drawing it out, Salvador gaped at the magnificent gem winking in the firelight. The blue jewel Warren had pried from his crown rested in the center of Salvador's palm. It sparkled seductively, drawing Salvador's gaze into its dazzling depths. Uplifted by his success Salvador smiled to himself. He pulled out his handkerchief preparing to wrap up the jewel and hide it away, when he heard a faint echo of his name reverberating through the forest.

"*Salvador…*" said a sweet woman's voice. "*Salvador the hero…*"

Salvador clutched the jewel, and looked wildly around. There was no one in sight.

"Who's there?" whispered Salvador, his heart racing in his chest. He searched the darkness with his eyes. A misty white shape materialized and moved through the trees. It vanished, but soon reappeared much closer to the campsite.

"*Salvador…*" sighed the voice. "*Come to me…*"

The ghostly shape of a woman drifted toward him from the forest.

"Who are you?" asked Salvador, unconsciously taking a step toward her.

The beautiful woman made no reply. She swirled around him,

her boots barely touching the ground as she studied him. She wore a fitted corset over a flowing blue dress. A long dagger hung from her waist belt, and a gleaming white stone floated weightlessly around her neck on an ethereal chain. The top of the stone was encased in silver. Her whole figure gave off a soft luminous light. Salvador grew lightheaded, enchanted by her perfume.

"You're Miss Maddy Alamore the piratess, aren't you?" he asked breathlessly.

"*So handsome…*" She touched his cheek with a translucent hand, making a chill run down Salvador's spine. "*You are a brave and honest man, worthy of the map,*" said the woman.

"The Map of Inquisition?" asked Salvador. "You know where it is?"

"*I am the one who hid it,*" confessed Maddy Alamore. "*Come, Salvador the brave, I will lead you to the Map of Inquisition, and anything you wish will become a reality.*"

Salvador glanced back at his friends sleeping beside the fire.

"*We shall return before they wake,*" whispered Maddy Alamore. "*Your friends will praise you for the map, for it alone can help them win the Dominance.*"

She drifted swiftly toward the trees, her hair and dress trailing behind her in a cloudy haze that blurred and disappeared at the edges. Salvador followed her. They wove a confusing trail through the dark forest. Ducking under branches and pushing through curtains of grey-green moss, they trekked further and further off the beaten path. In time, Salvador grew worried that they had been gone so long.

"How much further?" he asked.

The piratess turned around to look at him, her face aglow with other-worldly beauty.

"*It's just beyond those trees,*" she whispered. "*If we hurry, we can get back before your friends awake.*"

WARREN'S LIFE

Warren awoke with a start. He instantly knew something was wrong. It was almost light and he had not yet been woken for his turn to keep watch. Warren sat up. His body was stiff from sleeping in the same position for many hours on the hard ground. The fire had long gone out.

"Salvador?" asked Warren, looking around the camp. There was no sign of his brother. Wooffen lifted his head and yawned.

"Salvador's missing," said Warren. Wooffen licked Nella's face and gently pawed her arm. The girl awoke and softly pushed the dog away.

"Wooffen, stop it," she laughed sleepily. Nella sat up. Upon seeing Warren's posture, her face grew serious. "What is it?" she asked. She looked around. "Where's Salvador?"

"I don't know," said Warren, picking up Salvador's handkerchief, "but I have the feeling he is in some kind of trouble." Warren let Wooffen sniff the lacy handkerchief. "Can you help me find him?" he asked.

Without a word, Wooffen pressed his nose to the ground and quickly found Salvador's trail. Wooffen moved a little way down the side of the hill and away from the main path. He looked back over his shoulder at the two humans.

Warren and Nella exchanged glances. In the light of the new day they could see that the direction Wooffen was aimed looked like something from a frightening story. The dead, craggy trees were covered in spider webs and moss. They leaned in sickly archways forming a maze of irregular naturally-occurring corridors. The forest floor was whited out in a low-hanging mist.

"Come on," said Nella, following Wooffen's lead.

Warren went after her, a growing sense of apprehension building in his chest.

They made their way deeper into the labyrinth until Warren had lost all sense of direction. He could no longer identify which way they had come from. Several times he noticed strange words etched into the sides of boulders, and he wondered if these were messages of warning. Abruptly Wooffen came to a halt. Warren and Nella caught up to him, and then passed him by. They were several strides ahead when Wooffen let out a quiet whimper. Warren turned around.

"What is it Wooffen?" he asked.

"Woof-Wooffen not go on," said the dog.

"Why not?" asked Warren, a puzzled look on his face.

"This place not for Wooffens."

"What do you mean?" asked Nella.

"This land marrrked not good."

"Wooffen, we must find my brother," said Warren. But coax as they might, nothing they said could convince Wooffen to take a single step further. He seemed to sense an invisible boundary which he would not dare cross.

"What are we going to do?" asked Warren. "We can't just leave him here."

"I will stay with him," said Nella.

"I think we should stay together," said Warren. "What if something happens to you? Besides, I don't know how I will ever find you again."

"I'm afraid we are entirely out of options," replied Nella.

Warren was at a loss. He searched the misty forest apprehensively.

"Just yell for me if you need help," he instructed, all the while knowing that the fog would mute the sound, preventing it from carrying very far. "Don't leave this spot. I'll be back as soon as I can," he said.

Warren reluctantly moved away into the forest. Within several minutes, he was alone, having left Nella and Wooffen behind. Warren had no idea how to track his brother without Wooffen's help. A sense of despair wound itself ever deeper into his chest, stabbing at his heart in painful jabs. He was pretty sure he had made the wrong choice in going on alone. Certain as he was that he was lost, Warren moved on nonetheless. Dry branches scraped against him as he pushed on. A shape appeared in the fog up ahead. Warren paused, uncertain whether it posed a threat. It moved closer, taking the shape of a middle-aged man. He wore flowing pale robes and a rectangular shoulder bag. A narrow brimmed hat gave him the look of an explorer. The length of his beard betrayed the amount of time he had spent in these woods before he died. Warren drew his dagger.

"Don't come any closer," he said.

The ghost laughed in a raspy coughing burst, and drifted through the dagger, whooshing straight through Warren's body and coming out the other side behind him.

Warren backed away. He felt a brief spell of cold wash over him and his breath momentarily froze in his lungs as the man passed through him.

"I know where he is," said the ghost.

"Who?" asked Warren.

"The one you seek," said the ghost with a grin. "He is your brother, is he not? I could take you to him," the man looked Warren over, "for a price."

"Take anything you want," said Warren. "You can have my magic armor. It is worth more than a chest full of gold."

"There is only one thing you have that I want," said the explorer, a greedy look in his eyes.

"And what is that?" asked Warren.

"Your life," said the ghost.

"I can't give you my life!" cried Warren.

"I will only take a little," said the man, swirling around in the fog.

"No," said Warren, "you cannot have that."

"Then I cannot help you," answered the ghost. "All I can tell you is that you are going the wrong way." He vanished without a trace.

Warren looked around himself. An eerie quiet consumed the

forest, making the atmosphere feel dense and uncomfortable. Suddenly, somewhere in the distance Warren heard the muffled cry of a living man. Though faint, it was unmistakably the voice of his brother. The sound echoed so that it was impossible to know from where it had come.

"SALVADOR!" Shouted Warren.

There was no reply.

"Alright!" Warren said firmly. "I agree to give you my life."

"Then we have a deal," said the ghostly man, instantly reappearing beside him. "Follow me." The explorer drifted ahead, his beard trailing in the breeze. Warren followed. They moved through the arching corridors, weaving an unidentified path. At length, the ghost man stopped.

"Its time for my first payment," he said.

"Go ahead and take it then," said Warren.

"You must will it to me," replied the ghost, drawing closer to Warren. "It cannot be taken but must be willingly given."

Warren could feel the cold radiating off his unlikely guide. He tried to find a way to feel some compassion for this man in order to pass him a portion of his life force. It was difficult for Warren to see past the man's vile, greedy face. Looking at the ghost, Warren saw his worn, threadbare clothes, and dirty, mud-soaked shoes. Who knew what fate he had suffered? A thin wisp of golden light leaked from Warren's mouth, leaving his body with his breath. The ghost hungrily breathed it in, sucking it from the atmosphere. He looked less transparent than before. Warren, on the other hand, felt a slight numbness settle over him. As though he didn't care as much about anything.

"Let's go on," said Warren.

The ghost regretfully continued onward, but it wasn't long before he stopped again.

"Give me more," he said.

"We haven't gone but five minutes," argued Warren.

"We had a deal!" exploded the ghost impatiently. "Do you want to find him or not?"

"Alright," said Warren. He reached for the now familiar sensation, and again, the golden light poured out of his mouth. This time the ghost inhaled it as if he were trying to pull out a little more than Warren was willing to give. Warren closed his mouth. The explorer seemed even more material than before. There was another cry from deep within the forest. Unmistakably Salvador's voice, it was much fainter than before.

"You have been leading me astray!" shouted Warren in outrage. He turned to run in the direction he thought may have been the source of the echoing sound, but the ghost grabbed Warren by the wrist.

Warren looked back at him in alarm. The explorer's grip was strong. Warren looked at his own hand, and realized that it had a slight transparent quality. He had given the ghost more than half of his life force. The explorer grinned.

"Now that your will is my own, you will give me the rest!" he said. He opened his mouth, and inhaled deeply, his yellow teeth bared like a wild animal and his face distorted into a mass of angular wrinkles. The golden light poured in a rush from Warren's own mouth against his ability to stop it. He willed himself to remember what he was seeking, all the while feeling himself losing touch with what was important to him. Perhaps Salvador did not need his help after all. Let the next era be what it will. Was there a girl in silver waiting somewhere, or was that only a dream? Why hold on to this physical form when there is nothing worth living for anyway? His thoughts overwhelmed him. Somewhere in the back of his mind, filtering faintly through as though from the end of a long dark tunnel Warren remembered Salvador. His brother. His twin. He needed help. Salvador was in danger. Warren looked weakly behind the explorer. On a giant boulder towering behind him two words were etched into the stone. "*Neflehfate-youlaw*" they read.

"Neflehfate-youlaw!" whispered Warren, his knees buckling.

The explorer's eyes widened in horror. Releasing Warren at once, he let the boy sink to the ground.

"No!" shouted the ghost, shielding his face with his hands. "NO!" There was a burst of light and a magnetic sounding pulse. The explorer's chest jerked violently upwards, and he was gone.

Warren turned in the direction he thought he had last heard Salvador's voice. He tried to rise, but tripped, and fell face first in the mud. He did not have the strength to stand.

"Salvador," he tried to shout, but only a whisper came out. He stared blankly ahead. "I'm coming," said Warren, his eyes tearing with the despair of his own futility. He gritted his teeth, and pushed himself up onto his elbows. Dragging himself to the nearest tree, Warren grabbed the slender trunk, and forced his way to a standing position. He pooled his strength into a single step forward. Catching himself just before falling once more, Warren put out his other foot, taking a second step. He lumbered his way through the forest, each stride promising to be his last.

WOLF

Salvador stood at the bank of a shallow stream. The milky grey water bubbled up in a small geyser and poured downhill, disappearing back under the ground several yards away. White steam rolled off the surface of the warm water bubbling up from the spring.

Salvador doubled over and let out another yell, dropping the carved stone ladle from his hand. It slipped through his loose fingers and hit the forest floor with a thud. A drop of the grey water ran down Salvador's chin.

Ghosts rushed to the spring from every direction, their trailing pale bodies moving straight through the trees without needing to weave around them. They screamed their excitement in hollow voices, their eyes enlarged with anticipation.

Miss Maddy Alamore circled Salvador as he struggled to breathe. She looked at the ghosts who gathered around them like fog.

"Where is Olimphious?" she asked of the gathering.

A frail-looking boy no older than seven moved forward from the crowd to answer her. His transparent body was smaller than the rest, and he floated several feet above the ground to compensate for his lack of height. His small feet dangled downward as if he had forgotten what they were for.

"Olimphious was forced to cross over!" he whispered.

"What?" breathed Maddy Alamore.

"I saw it myself," said the boy. "It was so terrible." He began to cry.

"Who dared speak the forbidden words?"

"He knows the incantation and he comes this way!" cried the boy.

"We must stop him!" commanded Maddy Alamore to the gathered ghosts.

There was a murmur among them. None of them wanted to go.

"Go or I'll cross you over myself!" she shouted.

One by one, the ghosts slipped away, pouring thickly into the forest behind her.

Salvador crashed onto the ground without putting his hands out to break his fall. His face hit the dirt with a heavy thump. Salvador did not flinch at the impact. Staring blankly ahead, his eyes remained wide open. A milky white haze had glazed over Salvador's blue irises, making his eyes look grey. Dirt clung to his cold, sweating cheek as he lay, barely breathing on the forest floor.

Maddy Alamore circled him. She drew close to Salvador's face, hovering over him.

"*Wolf Baron, return to the world of the living*!" she chanted. "*Return and bring forth your ways unforgiving. Take this here body for your own, and return Wolf Baron, to flesh and to bone!*"

Salvador rolled over onto his back. His muscles tensed and his back arched off the ground in a spastic fit. His pupils enlarged and turned a reflective green. A growl issued from his mouth in a voice that was not his own. The deep rumbling sound made the ghosts gathered around him draw back.

"Maddy!" snarled the Wolf Baron's voice through Salvador's mouth, "You let me be dead for too long!" Salvador's hands clenched into angry fists as Wolf Baron rose to standing.

"It's not every day I find a body suitable to host you, your grace," justified Maddy Alamore, bowing before the Baron.

"Where is the wizard who killed me?" demanded Wolf Baron, his lips pulling back form his teeth like a wild animal.

"He is long dead," said Maddy Alamore.

"You know he's not a mortal man!" shouted Wolf Baron viciously, barely managing to contain his wrath. The spit flew from his mouth in foamy specks.

"It has been over six hundred years, my lord," answered Maddy Alamore calmly, intent on bending him to her own will.

"I will erase his kin!" howled Wolf Baron, throwing back his arms, and arching his back, his hands clenched into fists.

The ghosts by the spring looked alarmed, but Maddy Alamore only smiled.

"All in due time, at present there is another matter to attend to."

The Wolf Baron's eyes looked hungrily out of Salvador's face.

"It is the end of the red millennium. The Pillar has appeared but the dominance has not yet been set!" Maddy explained.

Wolf Baron's eyes grew suddenly alert.

"Where is it?"

"It is not far."

"Have you the stone of the dead?" asked Wolf Baron.

"I have kept it safe, awaiting your return," said Maddy Alamore, fingering the stone on her necklace.

Wolf Baron smiled darkly upon seeing the familiar object floating around her neck.

"You have done well," he said moving his fingers through the immaterial stone as if through a cloud.

Miss Maddy Alamore touched the stone with a ghostly hand and cast down her eyes in a perfect performance of modesty, while silently reminding him why he needed her.

"Only a material being can place the stone," said the Wolf Baron.

"But only a ghost can handle the stone of the dead," said Maddy.

"We shall rule the new era together!" smiled the Wolf Baron.

There was a muffled cry from the forest.

Maddy Alamore and Wolf Baron jerked their attention to the direction of the noise.

Warren stumbled weakly toward them through the trees. Ghosts swirled around him in a thick ring.

"Neflehfate-youlaw!" shouted Warren.

Several screams were heard, and three ghosts were yanked upward before their screams were abruptly cut off and they vanished without a trace.

"Only you can stop him," said Maddy Alamore to Wolf Baron.

Wolf Baron tensed, his shoulders rising up to protect his thick neck.

Warren barreled unstably forward. "Salvador!" he cried upon seeing his brother. Only several paces away, Warren suddenly paused. Something alarmed him about his twin's face. "Salvador?" he asked.

Wolf Baron leapt at Warren in a way unnatural for a man. Powerfully projecting off the ground with his legs, he pushed forward with his arms extended out. He shoved Warren to the ground, his face distorted with anger. Warren looked into his eyes. They were the reflective eyes of a carnivore. Warren blasted him away with a quick burst of magic.

Wolf Baron flew backwards and dug his fingers into dirt to regain his balance. When he looked up, his eyes looked blue for a split second before the pupils changed back into inky green mirrors surrounded by a ring of milky grey.

"What have they done to you?" asked Warren, trembling uncontrollably as he backed away.

Rising from all fours, Wolf Baron prepared for a second offence. "You should have stayed away, your cowardice would have saved you. Now, Wizard scum, it is too late to run, for I will hunt you down no matter where you hide."

Warren drew his dagger.

The Wolf Baron sneered.

"If you kill me I will haunt you into insanity. I will be waiting to face you when you die, and die you shall!" With these words he leapt upon Warren again.

Warren threw the dagger away from himself so as to eliminate the chance of harming his brother's body. They wrestled in the dirt. The ghosts clasped Warren's arms and legs with icy fingers making it difficult for him to fight back. Warren felt as though he were moving in slow motion. The Wolf Baron reached for the dagger above Warren's head. Warren gripped his wrist and strained to keep Salvador's hand away from the weapon. Wolf Baron punched him in the jaw. Warren responded by kneeing his opponent in the stomach. Wolf Baron hunched over, and as he did so Warren noticed a ghost trail of movement following his brother's body. It was the shape of another man.

"Salvador!" shouted Warren, "I know you're in there!"

"Your brother is gone!" snarled Wolf Baron. But even as he said those words, his voice faltered momentarily revealing the sound of Salvador's clear baritone.

"That's it," cried Warren, "fight it!

"Enough, finish him!" commanded Maddy Alamore.

Wolf Baron wound up for a final punch. Warren shoved him in the chest with both feet. He fell backwards against a stump and moved to quickly rise. Warren blasted him against it once more. He crashed into it. The stump splintered and exploded behind him.

"Neflehfate-youlaw!" rushed Warren, as the ghost trail briefly separated from Salvador's body.

There was a deep angry cry, and the ghostly shape of a very hairy, hunched over man with mangy grey hair was jerked upwards and then vanished above them. Ghosts shrieked in horror and scattered from the spring, tearing off through the woods.

Salvador opened his eyes. "We did it," he said, and lost consciousness.

"NOOOO!" screamed Maddy Alamore.

"Stay back!" commanded Warren rising and then falling to one knee once more.

Maddy looked wide-eyed and angry.

"Come any closer and I'll cross you over," threatened Warren.

Maddy Alamore changed her tactics immediately.

"If you cross me over, how will you ever find the map?"

"I don't need it," said Warren.

"You could have all that your heart desires."

"All that my heart desires is for you to leave us alone!"

Maddy looked aghast. There was a pop, and Maddy Alamore vanished from the air. Salvador was coming to. Warren gripped his forearm and helped him up.

"I got you," said Warren pulling his brother's heavy arm over his shoulders. They limped from the clearing.

"Am I leaning on you, or are you leaning on me?" asked

Salvador.

"Shut up," said Warren. He looked about, having lost all sense of direction.

"How do we get out of here?" asked Salvador.

"I don't know," replied Warren. He thought of Nella alone in the forest, and suddenly he heard her voice.

"*This way*," whispered Nella's voice.

"Did you hear that?" asked Warren.

"Hear what?" asked Salvador.

"Come on," said Warren, pulling his brother in the direction the whisper had come from. Faster and faster the twins moved through the forest, feeling less burdened the further they moved from the spring. At last, up ahead Warren heard a familiar bark and spotted a shimmer of Nella's silver dress. Wooffen went berserk. He attacked Salvador, barking and licking his face.

"You were worried about me?" asked Salvador.

"AWOO-WOO-WOO-WOO-WOO-WOO!" barked Wooffen.

Warren embraced Nella. "I'm so glad I found you again," he said. "Thanks for guiding us back."

Nella beamed at him. "Glad to help. I'm just relieved you're alright," she sighed, holding him tightly. She rested her head on his shoulder.

"Am I missing something?" asked Salvador, looking at the two of them.

Warren laughed, pulling out of the embrace. He was embarrassed, but unable to let go of Nella's hands.

"Shall we go then?" asked Salvador after a long pause. "Don't we have a pillar to defend or a dominance to win or something?"

"Which way, Nella?" asked Warren, working hard to repress a reappearing grin.

Nella looked up toward the seven peaks towering into the sky. The one nearest them was flattened at the top.

"It's not far," she said.

The company set off once more, this time keeping off the path, and winding their way up higher and higher through the wilderness.

THE SACRIFICE

After several hours of steady climbing, Warren began to hear a dull roar. It was a sound unlike anything he had heard before. This was not the rushing thunder of waterfalls, nor the howling of a powerful wind. Wooffen propped up the tops of his long ears, nervously listening to the foreign sound. His tail hung low to the ground as he moved alongside his cluster of humans, taking care to make as little noise as possible. Salvador impatiently strode ahead. Nella and Warren hurried to keep up with Salvador.

The roar steadily grew louder as the company moved on. The sun was just about overhead when they began to see the light of day through the trees up ahead. Breaking through the final line of trees, they abruptly discovered the source of the noise, as the blare of battle finally hit them with its full volume. Here, the clang of steel, shouts of man, and roaring of beasts were almost deafening. The ground sloped steeply downward before them. Looking out, they saw the caldera spread out below, scooping out the top of the mountain in a giant bowl shape.

The valley before them was a raging battlefield. Four colors of robes milled together as soldiers from four different regions battled for the Dominance. Besides the military men, there were knights, thieves, beggars, rebels, and monks, altogether comprising thousands of men. Countless monsters and reptiles were scattered throughout their midst, inflicting damage with frenzied eagerness. It was unclear whose side the beasts were on. At the far end of the field was a tiny cave in the side of the mountain.

Warren felt his heart rate escalate. "That's where we need to get to," he said, pointing at the tiny black spot on the opposite side of the caldera from where they stood.

Wooffen let out a whimper.

Salvador allowed his jaw to fall open as he witnessed the brutal scene taking place before him.

"I can get you through that," said Nella quietly.

"Through that?" asked Salvador in disbelief, pointing to the chaos before them.

Nella nodded. "Follow me," she said, striding forward.

Exchanging a nervous glance, the brothers went after her moving to either side of the girl with Wooffen creeping unhappily at their ankles.

"This is suicide," said Salvador, trying hard to discourage the girl as they drew closer to the danger zone.

"Trust me," said Nella, "I can get you across." She reached out a hand and quickly caught the handle of a dagger flying toward Salvador's face. She cast the weapon aside. A drop of blood appeared on the bridge of Salvador's nose where the blade had grazed his skin. He touched his face with his index finger and looked back at his hand, watching the red blood sink into the groove of his fingernail. Salvador's face twitched in a spasm and his eyes briefly rolled back into his head. For a second, Warren was worried that Salvador would faint, but his brother managed to recover.

"Didn't you say your abilities were leaving you?" asked Salvador.

"I may have enough left to do this one last thing," answered Nella.

"You *may?*" gulped Salvador, his voice cutting off in mid-sentence.

"Warren, duck," said Nella.

Warren crouched down.

"Lower!" shouted Nella.

Warren collapsed his knees and elbows, flattening himself to the ground and tilting his head to one side, making his ear flush with the red dirt. A large round shield with razor edges zipped low through the air, hurling over Warren's body and scraping the back of his armor making it ring and vibrate.

"Holy smokes!" screamed Salvador, grabbing his hair. "There's got to be another way!"

"There is no other way," said Warren, rising from the ground. Dirt clung to his cheek, and he brushed it away with the back of his hand.

"Guys, we gotta go back," begged Salvador, stepping over an unconscious soldier.

"Pick up that sword," Nella instructed him.

Salvador knelt over the soldier, trying hard not to look at his immobile face, and took the sword from his loose hands. The soldier moaned quietly and was still once more.

They had entered the first line of fighters. Wooffen darted forward. A thick man in turquoise robes swung a double-edged ax at the hound and Salvador stepped forward deflecting the strike. Salvador hooked the blade of the ax with the hilt of his sword and yanked upward disarming the robed man. Salvador then clasped the iron shaft of the ax and tossed it, handle first, over to Warren.

"This is *not* my first choice of weaponry!" exclaimed Warren, catching the heavy ax in mid air and swinging it unevenly toward a row of fighters who jumped back and out of the way of the blade.

Nella moved deeper into the war zone. She seemed to slip in-between the battle itself, always in the right spot at the right time to stay perfectly unharmed.

With the chilling sounds of horns, two more armies poured into the valley from the left, Prince Coonan Malden at their lead. Over six hundred Gators and Diamondellians armed with spears, curved blades, and reptiles spilled down into the battlefield, mixing with the other fighters in a fresh wave of combat, their red and black robes mixing swiftly with the other colors in a bloody surge.

"Still alive, still alive, still alive," muttered Salvador, placing a boot against the ax wielder's chest and shoving him back. The man grabbed Salvador's foot, and fell backwards, yanking off Salvador's shoe. Salvador glanced down and wiggled the toes on his freshly bare foot. "Still alive, still alive, still alive," he chanted.

Wooffen pounced onto the ax wielder and wrestled his pant leg to contribute to Salvador's effective attack before bounding after his humans once more.

"Warren, overhead," said Nella, her tone steady and disciplined.

Warren glanced up. A winged monster was barreling down toward him. It had a dry, wrinkly-looking hide that was entirely devoid of fur. Its grey wings had claws at the ends with broken, hooked talons. The creature's head was small for its body, but it had a wide mouth and throat as though it were made for swallowing its prey whole. The hindquarters of the creature were underdeveloped, indicating a preference for flight. Warren pressed hard off the ground intending to leap up and hit the beast with a burst of sparks to discourage it from coming any closer. Instead, he shot upward well over thirty feet. Warren yelled until his lungs ran out of air. He briefly paused in mid air eye to eye with the creature. There was a faint buzzing below. Warren glanced down. The wings etched into the outer sides of his shin guards had popped out and were flapping at a tremendous rate, keeping him up in the air. Warren began losing altitude. The winged shin guards were apparently good for leaping, but not for flying. The monster lurched after Warren as he sank downward, returning to the battlefield. Warren desperately sent up a whorl of sparks, interrupting the monster's path of attack. He was surprised how willingly the magic poured from his hands. The creature temporarily pulled back. Warren landed hard on the ground beside Nella, touching one hand down to the ground to regain stability. His feet left a pair of deep prints on the rusty desert floor.

"Don't tell me you could have done that this whole time," said Salvador with a scowl, as he swung a spiked club at a new group of soldiers. "And don't forget that those shin guards really belong to me." Salvador fought with the effortless expertise of a natural hero, while glancing eagerly over at Warren's new toy. "If we survive, I'll be wanting them back," he concluded, shoving past his attackers to face a swordsman brandishing double-edged curved blades in each hand.

A tall man lifted a hammer high over Nella's head. Warren made an effort to reach her, but he was too far away to cover the distance in time. Wooffen gnawed at the attacker's ankle while Nella grabbed the man's arm just below the elbow, and pushed him backward in a diagonal motion. He lost his balance and tripped, releasing the hammer and tumbling to the ground.

"Where did you learn to do that?" asked Warren, looking up at the monster circling back around for another attack. Nella shrugged. Warren shrugged back, and leaped upward at the monster once more. The wings buzzed at his ankles holding him up in the air. He swung the ax around himself and released it aiming it at the monster's neck. It flew over the creature's shoulder, right beside its nasty head, and fell down into the battlefield, landing directly at the feet of Prince Coonan Malden himself. The iron handle of the ax was still glowing gold with Warren's magic.

"Oops," said Warren, starting to sink to the ground once more. He shot sparks out toward the monster, but this time the beast was unafraid, and snapped its jaws at Warren as they plummeted downwards together.

Prince Coonan Malden looked up at the flashes of fire erupting in the sky not far from where he stood. He grabbed the handle of the ax and yanked it angrily from the dirt. A silver box was welded to the back of his iron glove on the hand that now wielded the ax.

Warren landed with a thud, rousing a cloud of red dust, and placed his forearm before his face bracing himself for the monster's wide mouth of teeth. Instantly, a milky white shield extended itself out of his wrist guards and sealed around Warren in a perfect sphere. The monster rubbed its teeth against the shield as if over an impenetrable balloon, its fangs squeaking across the surface of the shield. The force field around Warren molded with the impact of the monster's attack, but did not break.

Salvador rolled his eyes at his brother. "That would have been useful like a million times!" he exclaimed. Having already gone through over a dozen different weapons, Salvador had somehow managed to find himself a pitchfork and was currently using it to trap the blades of four different swordsmen. He twisted the pitchfork and the fighters were forced to relinquish their blades. Salvador swapped his pitchfork for a regular sword and took a few practice strikes.

Warren rose, momentarily dissolving the shield, and strained to project a surge of energy toward the creature who was still intent on destroying him. The beast was strong enough to resist Warren's attempts to force it back. Digging its claws into the ground, it pulled itself toward the young wizard right through the spell. Wooffen barked fearlessly up at it.

"Salvador, on your right," called Nella.

Salvador wheeled around with a theatrical growl. Several soldiers jumped back and out of his reach. Salvador smiled to himself, his expression quickly sobering as he saw what was behind them. As the soldiers moved aside, they revealed a huntsman not more than three yards away, aiming a crossbow at Salvador's chest. Salvador had no shield.

"Warren!" yelled Salvador, as the huntsman released the arrow.

Glancing over, Warren instantly took in the situation. The thick arrow sped through the air. In a strong burst of magic, Warren shoved the creature attacking him in between Salvador and the huntsman. The creature skidded across the dirt and the arrow buried itself deep into its flesh just below the shoulder blade.

"Arooowar!" cried the creature, collapsing on the ground.

Warren ran around the thrashing creature.

"Are you happy now?" he demanded of the huntsman.

"It's nothing personal," shrugged the huntsman, lowering his weapon awkwardly, "it's a war."

"That's a lame excuse," said Salvador.

Blue blood oozed heavily from the creature's side around the injury. The arrow was buried deep, all the way to the black feathers that lined the end of the shaft in symmetrical rows. Warren quickly pulled it from the creature's hide. Wooffen circled at his feet, watching his back while the young man worked.

"Arrrrrooooo!" whimpered the creature, jerking with the sudden pain.

"I know it hurts, and I'm sorry," said Warren, "but to be fair, you were trying to kill me." He placed a hand over the wound and projected a gentle energy. The wound began to swiftly heal, pulling together and regenerating the flesh. Fully recovered, the creature leaped to its feet. It brought its head level with Warren's. For a moment, Warren was worried he would be attacked once more, but instead the creature turned away, fixing its orange eyes on the huntsman, who was backing away slowly.

"The best way to defeat an enemy is to make him your friend," quoted Nella.

"Says who?" asked Salvador, fencing with a couple of swordsmen.

"Abraham Lincoln," answered Nella.

"Who's that?" asked Salvador.

"Oh never mind!" cried the girl.

Warren moved back in the direction of his companions. Picking up a long, gem-studded blade from the ground and holding the sword with his right hand, Warren left his other hand free to wield magic. His armor accommodated this decision. In a metallic rippling motion, the metal glove pulled back from Warren's left hand, leaving it open to move freely. The palm of his exposed hand was glowing with a blinding light. Warren rejoined his friends.

"What did I miss?" he asked.

"Can't talk—" panted Salvador, "fighting to—" he ducked and dove out of the way of a knight on a horse, "stay alive—" finished Salvador, slicing through the straps of the saddle as the rider passed. The knight began to slide to one side of the horse as he rode away.

A large man in a yellow robe lifted his blade above Nella. Both Warren and Salvador simultaneously leapt forward to defend her, their blades colliding with the attacker at the same instant. Together, the twins pushed past him.

Nella, Warren, Salvador, and Wooffen were steadily making their way through the battlefield. All around them warriors were engaged in fierce combat. In a moment of safety, Warren swiftly unclasped his wrist guards and slipped them onto Nella's forearms. The armor was loose on her wrists.

"What about you?" asked the girl.

"I'll be fine," said Warren. He heard a loud clang. Looking around, he saw Prince Coonan Malden hacking his way toward them, a manic look in his green eyes. Six Gators followed close behind him.

Warren glanced nervously at the others. "We've got to get to the cave," he said.

"A gambit," offered Nella.

"What?" asked Warren.

"It's a chess strategy I read about where you sacrifice a piece to get ahead."

"Who do you plan on sacrificing?" inquired Salvador.

"It's me he wants," said Nella.

"Never, no! I don't like this plan!" said Warren.

"You need to get to the pillar," argued Nella. "I have the wrist guards, just go with me on this!" She stepped forward. Warren noticed that the wrist guards had already molded to her forearms.

"Nella I—" began Warren, but it was too late. Prince Coonan Malden and his gang of gator riders had reached them. Three of the green-clad fighters were astride giant reptiles. The beasts twisted around and snapped their elongated snouts. The Prince jeered at Warren, Salvador, and Nella, his face ugly with hatred.

"I challenge you to a duel for the throne of Augden City!" shouted Nella.

"I accept," said Prince Coonan Malden calmly, locking his eyes on the girl.

"She's out of her freakin' mind," groaned Salvador, covering his mouth with his hand and staring at Nella with bulging eyes.

Warren felt sick.

Prince Coonan Malden smiled. "I'm going to enjoy this," he sneered, testing the blade of the ax with his finger. A drop of blood appeared where his skin had touched the razor edge. "I think I'll kill you slowly, so I may savor my final victory over this land." He took a few practice strikes with the ax. "Soon, very soon, the Diamondell region, along with the rest of the world, will belong uncontestably to me."

"Over my dead body," said Nella.

"Agreed," smiled the Prince, and lunged at the girl with the ax high over his head.

"Nella!" shouted Warren. Wooffen went berserk at his feet, barking so hard he was foaming at the mouth.

The three Gators formed a ring around the girl and Prince

Coonan Malden. The next instant, half a dozen soldiers clad in red aggressively attacked Warren and Salvador, keeping them from rescuing Nella from the duel. The twins struggled to fight them back. Warren glanced at Nella in horror, unable to help her. Wooffen chomped at the legs and ankles of the red-clad soldiers.

Nella shifted the position of her feet. Taking only two steps she somehow managed to end up right beside the prince. His ax landed on empty air. Nella's shoulder was right against the prince leaving him no opportunity to harm her. The prince twisted toward her, swinging the blade around his body, trying to get at her, but she moved with him, staying well out of the way of his weapon. The prince leapt away from Nella and swung at her again. Nella simply stepped off the line of the blade. The ax kept landing on empty air. Prince Coonan Malden was getting frustrated. He swung at her in faster, less accurate blows.

"Why won't you die?" he growled through clenched teeth. When the ax was over his head, Nella moved in and grabbed his arm at the elbow. She pushed his outstretched arm down to her hips and then took a step backward, spinning the prince around her body and throwing him face down to the ground. She pinned his arm firmly to the dirt.

"Had enough?" she asked. "Do you surrender?"

The prince pulled a dagger from his belt with his free hand. As the dagger came around, Nella leaped up and away from the blade. The prince quickly pressed himself up from the ground. He switched the dagger into his right hand. The second he drew back the knife, Nella moved in and pushed his arm across his body. Pulling on his arm, the girl swung Prince Coonan Malden around herself in a spiral motion. Continually taking his balance and forcing him to comply Nella once again pinned the prince to the ground, only this time in a more painful position. She held his arm twisted behind his back and locked in a position where she could easily break it if he struggled. She plucked the dagger from his hand and placed the blade on his neck.

"I win," she said.

The prince snapped his fingers. At once, the three Gators turned toward Nella.

"When will you learn? You cannot win, not with me," whispered

Prince Coonan Malden, leaving Nella to face the replies as he made a mad dash for the cave entrance.

Nella leapt up and put her forearm in front of her face. The reptiles attacked her at the same time, their teeth squeaking against the shimmering milky surface of the shield.

Warren's eyes were glued to Nella. Salvador ran past him in the direction of the cave.

"Salvador, catch!" shouted Warren, reaching into his pocket to throw him the gem. Suddenly, he felt his stomach drop and a wave of panic wash over him. He felt faint. His head swam. The sapphire was not there. He desperately felt around his clothes. "I don't have it," he whispered to Wooffen. The dog let out a whine. Warren could barely breathe. He felt numb, empty, and stupid. The noise of battle was suddenly muted and far away. He patted down his body through his clothes. Finally, Warren located a round weighty object in his pocket on the opposite side of his trousers. Relief swept over him. How could he have forgotten which side it was in? Warren was about to pull the stone from his pocket and toss it to his brother when Salvador was unexpectedly overtaken by a group of soldiers in yellow uniforms. Wooffen let out a bark. Warren looked up.

At the cave entrance, five men were locked in fierce battle. The crowns on their heads indicated they were the rulers of their regions. The finely crafted armor that covered their bodies differed greatly from one man to the next. There was a man in a suit of black armor obviously from the Colsmith region fighting a man in yellow armor that appeared to be made out of wood. They wrestled on the ground, their armies filling the valley around them trying to keep the others at bay. A man in a suit of turquoise, jewel-studded armor fenced a man in brown, slinky plates that moved with him like water. His crown was built into his helmet. The rulers kept each other back just enough to prevent any one of them from getting to the cave. When one of them got ahead, the others fell on him. They were visibly tired, having been fighting for hours. Several of them were wounded. For a brief moment, the path to the cave was suddenly clear before Warren, Salvador saw this.

"Guard the pillar, I'll be right there to place the stone!" shouted

Salvador as the hoard of soldiers fell on him. Unsure what Salvador meant, Warren reached his energy out and pulled the soldiers from his twin. The men flew backwards with an unexpected force. Again, Warren was surprised how easily the magic was coaxed from his hands. He felt powerful, as if he had a great source of magic within him, and he mused at this strange sensation. The soldiers recovered quickly and came at Salvador once more.

Warren glanced back at Nella. She was safe beneath the shield. She locked eyes with him for a second.

"Go!" he heard Nella's voice in his head, "now!"

Red and green clad soldiers charged toward Warren from both sides obstructing his path. He pressed off the ground and pushed forward in a powerful leap. The shin guards did not fail him, and the wings popped out once more, propelling him right over the soldiers. Craning their necks at Warren's unexpected maneuver, the men bumped into each other as they struggled to change directions. Warren landed hard just ahead of the royal knights battling each other for the pillar. He stumbled forward, scampering into the mouth of the cave. The rulers instantly abandoned their fighting and raced after him, pushing ahead of one another.

"No!" screamed Coonan Malden, rushing for the cave entrance as well. He opened the silver box affixed to the back of his glove, exposing the square stone from the fortress. The knights around him instantly fell to their knees, several of them fainting from exposure to the cube. Prince Coonan Malden dove after Warren.

Looking up from the battle taking place before him, Salvador saw his brother dive into the cave, followed by Prince Coonan Malden, and the other rulers, and scores of soldiers and rebels. The men poured into the gap as if sucked into a funnel. Salvador felt a terrible burst of panic twist painfully through his entire body. He was acutely conscious of the small weighted object resting in his pocket.

Warren plunged into the darkness, blinking fast to help his eyes adjust to the dark. It was cold in the cave, and the floor sloped sharply downwards. Warren rushed forward, the sounds of boots echoing loudly behind him. He did not know how he would hold them off. Wooffen was at his heels watching him with building anxiety. The dog had no trouble seeing in the dark. The cave opened into a small chamber with a short sandstone pillar at its center. There was a steep ledge where the ground broke off and sank deep into the darkness to one side of the pillar. A narrow beam of white light fell onto the center of the crumbling column forming a perfect circle. Warren was almost surprised to have suddenly found it. He reached inside his pocket. Feeling the stone with his fingers, he wondered why the faceted sapphire felt so smooth and heavy. He pulled it out and opened his fingers to find a large crolackrolite stone resting in his palm, its reflective surface unmistakable even in the dim light.

"AWOOOOOOO—" howled Wooffen at the sight of it, his voice torn and ragged, ripping forth in a burst of raw emotion. Warren felt his stomach drop. He swallowed hard, looking at the dark sphere in his hand, understanding in an instant what Bloom had done. Bloom had sacrificed himself, dying a horrible death to provide Warren with this stone that would give him great power and assist in his quest. This stone now contained the life force of the greatest wizard that ever lived. As Warren stood before the pillar, he was flooded with memories of the old Wizard. He saw him stooping to pick a plant in the little valley near his hut to teach Warren about wild plants, and glancing up from his book while Warren had struggled to wield the element of water for the first time. He saw Bloom sharing his last bit of soup with Wooffen, and smiling, leaning on his walking stick, looking back to check on the company behind him. Lastly, Warren saw the old wizard's hooded, and determined pose as he fearlessly battled the army in the clearing.

Prince Coonan Malden, followed by the other rulers and soldiers rushed into the cave behind Warren. They seemed to be moving in slow motion as they lunged at him.

Warren reached out his hand, and without hesitation, placed the crolackrolite stone under the beam of light. For a moment, nothing happened. Beneath the circle of light, the stone glowed dark green at its center. Suddenly, there was an explosion of brilliant green light and a wave of powerful energy hit Warren in the chest. He flew through the air backwards and landed on the cold sand several yards away. Wooffen fell beside him with a thud. The other men were also taken down from the blow. Everything went dark. Unable to see, Warren pressed himself up, and hastily felt around for the stone on the now disintegrating pillar. His fingers found the warm object and he snatched it up before rushing from the cave past the soldiers who were scrambling around in the dark. At the cave entrance, he looked out at the valley.

The green energy rushed out from where he stood, engulfing the lifeless soil and healing the wounded world. Giant trees sprouted and rose into the sky before his very eyes towering hundreds of feet above, their branches blooming and fruiting instantly. Ferns, grasses, and flowers burst from the ground covering every inch of soil with lush, vibrant plant life. The battle in the valley ceased, as everyone looked about at their changing environment in awe, realizing all at once that the dominance had been determined. A flock of multi-colored birds flew over the valley, each singing its own chiming song. As the green energy spread out and passed over the monstrous creatures in the battlefield, they transformed into smaller, nobler animals with glossy fur hides and elongated snouts. They ran into the new forest, disappearing into the thick brush. Springs burst out from beneath the dark soil, casting forth clear streams of water that rushed down the mountainsides and spilled over cliff ledges, forming small gurgling waterfalls. Pink fish splashed in the crystal waters. They flipped up out of the streams and dove back in, their scales sparkling in the sun. The sky paled, changing from orange, to pink, to bright blue. The crisp clouds above became so white they seemed to have a slight greenish tint to their contours. Warren breathed in the air. It was so fresh that it almost tasted sweet and it held an aroma reminiscent of watermelon. The world spreading out before him was like nothing he had ever seen or heard about in all the loveliest of fairytales. He knew that this would be an abundant era, the first of its kind in all of history. He leapt in the air.

"Hooray!" he shouted. "We did it!" Cries of joy erupted from the valley below. Nella and Salvador ran toward him. The Kings and soldiers came up behind him in the cave.

"It's over!" said Warren over his shoulder, and tore from the cave toward his friends. Wooffen raced ahead. Warren ran through the grass, a fresh breeze blowing in his face. Nella sailed into his arms. He swung her around. They laughed and cried at the same time. Salvador picked them both up in his arms, whooping and squeezing them with his powerful arms. Wooffen circled his friends.

"What did you place on that pillar?" demanded Salvador, setting Warren and Nella down and gesturing to the atmosphere questioningly.

"This," said Warren, pulling out the crolackrolite stone for all to see.

"Oh Bloom!" cried Nella, falling against Warren for a second tearful embrace. Warren held her close.

"I only wonder what became of my sapphire?" he wondered aloud. "I can't imagine where I may have lost it."

"I have it," said Salvador producing it from his own pocket. The gem sparkled in his open palm, reflecting the color of the sky. "I took it for safe keeping," he explained with a half shrug in response to the look of shock on his brother's face.

"Oh Salvador you shouldn't have done that—" began Warren.

"What's it matter now? Everything worked out," laughed Salvador.

Wooffen hung his head. "Woof-Wooffen misses master," he howled, squeezing his eyes shut. His voice was hoarse with sadness. Salvador picked him up, and kissed his nose, for which he received a big lick. All about them soldiers gathered their arms and retreated, many were smiling, unable to repress the elation of the exquisite new world surrounding them, even though they had lost the dominance. Prince Coonan Malden kicked at the fresh grass in an angry tantrum as he tripped from the mouth of the cave.

"No!" he shouted falling to his knees and ripping at the plant life underfoot with his bare hands. The silver box that contained his stone was collapsing in on itself. He tore it from his hand and threw it to the ground as it began smoldering and crumbled into a fine black powder. "No-no-no-no-no!" he shouted. A wounded soldier from his clan lay near him recovering from battle. Overcome with frustration, the prince hit the soldier with his fist.

"Beating a subordinate is no longer legal in the Diamondell

region," said Nella approaching him.

"Says who?" asked the prince.

"Say I, Princess Nella, the rightful ruler of Augden City."

The prince was aghast. He leaped to his feet and kicked the injured soldier.

"Get up!" he shouted. With difficulty, the man rose. Other soldiers slowly gathered around the scene.

"Seize her at once!" commanded the prince, pointing to the girl.

"Princess Nella, I am at your service," said the wounded soldier, bowing slightly and holding a hand over a bloody wound in his side.

"As are we," said the others beside him. "What should we do with the traitor?" asked the first, looking eagerly at the prince, and rubbing his fist in the palm of his other hand.

"Don't hurt him," said Nella. The soldier looked at her questioningly. "He is already in more pain than you can imagine," she explained. "Take him to the fortress," directed Nella, "the prince is going to need lots of rest and therapy."

They bound Prince Coonan Malden's hands and pulled his babbling highness away down the freshly overgrown path.

"What are you doing?" barked the prince as they departed. "Release me at once! I order you to comply!" His ranting was soon lost in the distance.

With a grin, Salvador watched him disappear. Looking about, Salvador discovered his missing boot lying in the grass a short distance away. He cheerfully moved to retrieve it.

Warren looked at Nella. Her cheeks were flushed.

"What's next for you?" he asked somewhat reluctantly.

"I suppose I have a kingdom to reclaim," she sighed.

"Tigorious will be thrilled," said Warren with a sigh. Salvador soon rejoined them and together, they headed across the valley. Soldiers bowed low to Nella and followed her at a respectful distance, uncertain how to address their new ruler. Nella seemed entirely at ease with her new role, unafraid of the daunting task ahead of her. Commanding attention came naturally to the forgotten princess, and she strode forward with confidence behind Salvador as the four of them moved down the same path by which they had arrived. Wooffen would not leave her side.

They took the direction of Augend City, silently agreeing to visit Bloom's final resting place before splitting up. They hiked all day, breaking camp in the late evening. Soldiers followed them into the clearing, bearing pots and pans, flint, and firewood. It wasn't long before a delicious-smelling vegetable stew was brewing and a wild green salad was prepared. By the time the soldiers began serving up the food, the noisy rumbling of Wooffen's stomach was the subject of much joking. Nella and her friends were served in fine glass dishes.

"How I have missed being waited on," sighed Salvador, accepting a large bowl of stew. Warren and Nella laughed. Wooffen blew on his stew, impatiently, trying to cool it. A few of the soldiers plucked varying lengths of nearby reeds, and holding them together in their hands, began playing a soft harmonious tune.

It was the first night of the new era, and the atmosphere was filled with exhilaration. Sitting there around the fire among his friends, Warren could not keep from smiling. Giant moths, drawn to the firelight, fluttered through the air on dusty, carpet-patterned wings. Never having seen such graceful night bugs before, Warren lifted up his hand and one of them landed for a brief rest on his fingertips. Roughly the size of a small dinner plate, the moth warmed itself by the fire. It fluttered its wings ever so slightly, like a blossom swaying in the breeze. When it took off once more into the night, the moth left silver trails on Warren's skin that shone orange in the dancing light of the fire. Warren knew he would never forget this evening, and he watched the events unfold around him as if already viewing a distant memory, half unwilling to believe that any of it was real.

The following morning, they came into the clearing where they had parted with Bloom. It was difficult to identify the exact location of the former battlefield, for the landscape had undergone a colossal transformation. All signs of war had been overgrown by plants and washed away by a gracefully meandering stream that wove down the gentle slope. Warren realized with a jolt that the very men who had ambushed them, now walked beside them as their friends. A little way down, the stream split into two around a small island at the heart of the valley where Bloom had last stood. A mighty tree grew firmly from the center of the island. Its weeping branches were covered in glossy heart-shaped leaves and plump mulberries. Salvador jumped over the stream onto the island. The others were close behind him. Nella picked a few of the dark purple berries and nibbled them from her cupped hand.

"They taste as sweet as Bloom was kind," she said.

"No, they taste sweeter," said Salvador, licking his purple stained fingers and helping himself to a second giant handful of mulberries.

Warren knelt by the water. Reaching a hand into the clear rushing liquid, he pulled out a perfectly round white stone. Looking around, he discovered the stream was full of them. They varied in size but not in color.

"We should build him a monument," said Salvador.

"This world is his monument," answered Warren thoughtfully. Nella knelt beside him. He showed her the stone.

"I think we should leave them all here," she whispered. Warren nodded, and slipped the stone back into the stream.

Wooffen laid his head in Warren's lap. His droopy brown eyes spoke louder than words.

"Wooffen, it's time to go home," said Warren.

The company moved onward once more, leaving the small valley behind. As he walked away, Warren was filled with a quiet sense of gratitude. He looked back one last time at the little island. The mulberry tree was shrouded in golden sunlight, and Warren knew then, that he had fulfilled Bloom's last request.

No more than an hour later, they came to the edge of the great river. Up ahead, Augden City sparkled in the mist of waterfalls and morning dew. Nella smiled. A stable master awaited them with several horses by the water's edge.

"The time has come to part ways," said Warren regretfully, "The people of the Sapphire Kingdom await our return."

"I understand your urgency," said Nella. "Please take two of these horses to speed your journey home." Warren gratefully accepted the reins she handed him.

"Although I no longer have the sight, I can foresee us meeting again in the near future," said Nella.

"I look forward to many more adventures with you," said Warren.

"As do I," said Nella.

"Wooffen, come here boy," said Salvador, gesturing toward himself, but the hound was glued to Nella's side.

"Boff-Wooffen stay!" said the dog, firmly placing his rump on the ground at Nella's feet. Salvador spread his hands in bewilderment.

"Wooffen, I'll build you a small castle next to my own, I'll take you hunting every day!" pleaded Salvador. But Wooffen's mind was made up.

Warren knelt to the Basset Hound, and petted the top of his head.

"Wooffen, I thank you for your brave accompaniment on this difficult quest," said Warren. "Know that you are always welcome in the Sapphire Kingdom, and that all my brother promises is true." Wooffen thumped his tail on the grass. Warren and Salvador mounted their steeds, and with a final farewell wave, they struck out on a course for home.

RETURN OF THE TWIN PRINCES

As Warren's horse plodded along, bobbing its head and leaving U-shaped impressions in the dirt, Warren could not shake the feeling that he had left something behind. He felt a strange mix of feelings that kept him looking back over his shoulder. So many times he had looked back, in fact, that Salvador had asked if he thought they were being followed. Even now Warren felt the urge to glance behind, but he resisted, not wanting to explain to his brother the complex feelings that overwhelmed him.

"…and I'll say to him, Dad, who's unqualified to rule now, huh?" said Salvador, his chin jutting forward with over-expression, "and he'll want to take it all back, but nooooo! It will be too late! And everyone will see he was wrong about me, you know?"

Warren grunted an indeterminate response, worn out by Salvador's ceaseless chatter.

"Yeah, I showed em' all what Salvador was made of. It's ridiculous, there's just no denying I have proven myself ten times over what's required of a hero—" Salvador broke off suddenly. "Warren, we made it! We're home!" he cried.

It was true. Warren looked up to find that they had left the last of the forest trees behind them and had entered a large field. Up ahead, in the center of the vast green valley, the sandstone towers of the Sapphire Kingdom reached into the open sky. The protective dome had dissolved without a trace. Warren felt his heart stop in his chest. He looked over at Salvador and mirrored the grin outstretched across his twin's face. Nothing felt as good as seeing his home transformed into this lush, prosperous land. The joy of the moment overriding his worries,

Warren flew forward beside his brother toward the castle. Up ahead, an old man pushing a loaded vegetable cart along the overgrown road caught sight of them. "They're back!" he shouted at the top of his lungs. His cart tipped over, its contents spilling across the ancient cobbles. The old man didn't stop to right it. Running toward the gates, he pulled his cap from his head, and waved to the guards pacing atop the castle walls.

One of the pacing guards put his hand to his forehead, shielding the sunlight to see better into the distance. His knees buckled. He quickly rushed over to his neighbor and pointed into the distance. The second man pulled out a spyglass, and put it to his eye. In a burst of movement, the other soldiers ran about, scampering to spread the word. A bell was rung, and was soon followed by several others. Before long, the ringing of bells filled the air with a nostalgic, echoing music. Trumpets blared announcing the return of the two princes.

Warren and Salvador advanced into the city, slowing their horses to a walk. They saw two giant stone monsters just outside of city limits. The statues were crouched over an invisible victim forming a rough archway. Enormous wooden doors had been set underneath them, marking the new entrance to the Sapphire Kingdom. As they drew near, the doors opened, and townspeople flooded out toward them from the street beyond. The two princes rode through the gates and into the city, accompanied by the relentless cheering of the villagers. Flower petals filled the air like confetti. The streets were engulfed with cheering people. Words of praise were directed at the princes' in overlapping streams of gratitude. The twins waved and nodded, smiling at their people as they passed. At last, the main doors of the castle came into view. The boys dismounted just as the great wooden doors flew open, and the queen rushed out toward her children. She embraced them both at the same time, and held them as though she would never let go again. The King was not far behind her. He pried each of his sons away from her grasp just long enough to get in a quick squeeze for himself. He held Warren out at arm's length studying the changes in his face. The King shook his head marveling at his youngest son's posture and confident gaze. The armor on the young prince fit him like a glove, and shone so brightly, it seemed to be glowing instead of simply reflecting the light of the sun.

What's more, Warren's chest was covered in tiny etchings depicting a knight who looked just like him in countless scenes of epic battles. The King had Warren lift his arms and turn around so that he could study the etchings in proper sequence. Warren laughed, and did as the King indicated, turning slowly about so his father could examine the images.

"It seems we underestimated you," said the King. "Perhaps you were the chosen one after all?" His grey brows knitted together in contemplation forming wrinkles of dismay on his forehead. "Forgive me, my son, if I misjudged you all this time."

Warren could feel Salvador tuning in and listening intently behind him.

"We are all the chosen ones," replied Warren. "The world is ready and always waiting for us to take action."

Salvador put his arm around his brother.

"Let it wait no longer!" he told him. "To the chosen ones!" cried Salvador, punching his massive fist in the air.

"To the chosen ones, to the chosen ones!" chanted the villagers in unison, gathering around them in the main square. Warren felt his eyes get watery. It seemed to him, at that moment, that his body was not meant to endure such violent episodes of happiness, and that he may not manage to survive it. Yet death had never been less frightening to him. He squeezed his mother's hand, smiling through his tears at his family, having no choice but to endure the joy he felt, even if it killed him. Moment after moment, he was surprised to find himself still standing.

The celebrations lasted all throughout the night. There was feasting outdoors beneath the starry sky, blazing fireworks, mountainous cakes, song-writing, and so much dancing that by morning the cobblestones in the ancient streets had sunk several inches deeper into the soil. So well compacted were the stones, in fact, that not a single road within the Sapphire Kingdom would need repair for the next one hundred years.

ON THE ROAD AGAIN

In the morning, Warren asked the King to meet him in the council room. While he paced the diamond patterned carpet waiting for his father, Warren held the crolackrolite bead in his hand and thought about what he could do to ensure its safety for the next thousand years. The stone felt cool and heavy within his fingers. He regretted letting it go, and regressing back to his own limited powers, but he knew it was the right thing to do. In time, his own abilities would grow stronger, and although they were hard to earn, those skills would truly belong to him. He understood that unlike the stone, his own powers could never be lost or taken away.

The King arrived, and together, Warren and his father placed the magical stone inside the glass case alongside the Seers Map of Diamondell. It rested peacefully in the center of a silk green pillow to one side of the ancient map.

"It is a powerful object," said the King. "It will require special protection from those who will undoubtedly seek it."

"I will learn a protection spell," said Warren, "and I will apply it to this case."

"Where will you find such a spell?" asked his father.

"In one of Bloom's books," replied Warren.

"It must be done as soon as possible," said his father.

Warren nodded and started towards the door.

"Hold on," said his father. "There is something else. I have been wanting to give you this for some time, and now seems like the appropriate moment."

Warren turned to face his father once more. The King reached inside the glass case and pulled out a small wooden box.

"This is an ancient treasure that belonged to our ancestor, Aleafia Goodlin Miramar. I want you to have it." Opening the box, the King pulled out a broach set with a glowing orange ember. A thin halo of flame engulfed the object keeping it aglow. The delicate purple-tipped flame wavered in the air revealing that the ember was actually burning. The broach even radiated warmth, yet the fire did not burn the King's hands. Warren's father pinned the broach to the front of his son's tunic, right over the young man's heart. "May the courage you have found never burn out," he said, briefly resting his palm over the broach.

Warren smiled at the King, and touched the ember in awe. It reacted to his touch by flickering at the point of connection. The ember was pleasantly warm to the touch and lovely to behold.

"Come, you have yet to see what breakfast looks like in the Green Era," laughed the King, urging Warren towards the exit. Together they left the room and made their way downstairs for breakfast.

In the dining hall, bowls of fresh fruits and berries were set out on the table that Warren had never seen before. There were spiraling baked sweets with bright colored creams, hot steaming teas, and puddings, and crumbles, and other abundant foods that had yet to be tasted.

"I can get used to this," sighed the King, taking a seat beside the Queen, enjoying the new bounty of foods.

Salvador was restless.

"Who can eat breakfast on a morning such as this?" he asked, putting down his silver spoon. Unable to be contained within the castle walls for long, Salvador and Warren went to explore the changes in the city and enjoy a couple of apple tarts at the market.

The Sapphire City was transformed. The once scarce and weak plants that grew feebly throughout the city had experienced a massive growth spurt. Their vigorous branches were now dense with vibrant leaves, and heavy with apples, plums, cherries, figs and clusters of rosy grapes. Although it had only been several days since the Dominance had been re-determined, the produce stands at the market were more plentiful than ever before, and the small wooden tables bowed under the piles of delicious foods. As the boys strode through the town, villagers smiled at them wherever they looked.

Warren was not yet accustomed to the freshness of the atmosphere and he inhaled a lungful of the fragrant air, savoring its aroma. A little boy trailing his mother through the busy street dropped his apple. Warren knelt down and picked up the fruit. After brushing it off and handed it back to the boy and smiled. The little boy took it shyly, hiding behind his mother. The woman beamed at Warren before continuing on her way.

Salvador brooded.

"What is it?" inquired Warren after several long minutes of silence.

"You help people," Salvador exhaled noisily, "I want to help people too!" He looked wildly around. "Like that woman over there," he said, pointing to an old lady struggling with a heavy basket of vegetables. Warren watched Salvador jog eagerly up to her.

"Let me help you with those," said Salvador, snatching the basket from the old lady's hands.

"Get away!" shrieked the woman.

"I'm *trying* to be *helpful!*" growled Salvador through clenched teeth.

"I don't want your help!" she snapped.

"Fine!" yelled Salvador, throwing the basket on the ground with all his might. Vegetables smashed into the dirt. Tomatoes bounced and rolled away, like fugitives escaping for their lives. Under the alarmed stares of civilians, Salvador turned away from the raving woman and walked toward Warren, being sure to step on every tomato in his path. Warren struggled to keep from laughing. Despite his efforts a pig-like snort managed to escape his control.

"What?" asked Salvador defensively.

"Nothing," said Warren with an unperturbed look. He approached the upset woman who was gathering up what remained of the scattered vegetables.

"Allow me," said Warren, respectfully bowing his head and

gesturing to the produce. He projected both hands toward one of the crushed tomatoes. His palms began to glow faintly as he strained with all his might to correct the damaged vegetable. Warren's face gradually turned a purplish color as he trembled over it. Finally, the flattened tomato began to slowly inflate, the cuts and scratches glowing before seamlessly healing. When at last it regained its prior shape, Warren heaved a labored breath and leaned against the frame of the nearby bakery stand.

"I'm still perfecting my technique," he said to the woman. Looking at all the other crushed produce, Warren sighed, and reached into his pocket. He handed the old woman a handful of coins.

"My brother is practicing helpfulness," he said. "I appreciate your willingness to help him learn to do it better." The woman gratefully accepted the coins, and knelt to pick up the tomato Warren had mended. When she touched it, it radiated tiny golden light rays and sparkled brilliantly. She placed it lovingly in her basket on top of the others she had salvaged.

The two brothers continued through the market. Salvador's mood had noticeably soured. He was no longer overly appreciative of the villagers' attention though they continued to smile at him. The twins were passing the city jail when, suddenly, Salvador leaped behind one of the many columns guarding the front of the noble old building.

"What are you doing?" asked Warren, stopping in the street.

"There's trouble at ten o'clock," whispered Salvador.

"What are you talking about?" asked Warren looking about the market place. A blond girl waved at him and doubled her pace toward them, a huge smile on her face. Salvador yanked Warren into the shadows beside him.

"Lets just hid until she goes away."

"She's already seen us," said Warren.

Salvador closed his eyes and took a deep breath. He stepped out into the light.

"What's your plan?" whispered Warren.

"I'm going to choose the weak way in hopes it will undermine my attractiveness," muttered Salvador, placing a hand over his mouth in phony thoughtfulness to disguise their conversation.

The girl had already made it over to them. Warren noticed right away that she was very pretty. She had silky blond hair, brown eyes, and an adorable button nose. She was dressed in a fitted, pink dress with a low neckline and a puffy skirt. Lots of white lace spilled out of her sleeves and at the hem of her skirt.

"Salvador!" she shouted, her voice shrill like an un-tuned violin.

Salvador squinted one eye, as if he were trying to mute the sound. She rushed at him full speed ahead with her lips puckered and her arms outstretched. Salvador put out both of his hands to stop her from running into him. She paused.

"Hold on," he said, struggling to figure out what to do. "Don't come any closer, I'm, err, really ill. I don't want you to get what I have."

"I'll take whatever you've got!" she said eagerly.

"I'm not sure you understand, it's really bad, and very contagious," explained Salvador, holding his breath and flexing his neck muscles to make himself change color.

"I don't care!" she shrieked, a manic love-torn look in her eyes.

"It disfigures your face," said Salvador with a slight cough in her direction.

She took a step back.

"I read your letter every day, all day long, while you were gone." She pulled out several pieces of tattered gray paper from her bodice. "It was the only thing that kept me going." She looked tenderly at the pages and began to read. "*Your auburn eyes like autumn leaves bestow my soul with love,*" she paused to compose herself, tears welling in her enormous eyes, her chin trembling with feeling, "*and like the dance of twirling fall my heart flies with this—dove,*" she wept the last word, dissolving in a sea of emotions.

Salvador threw Warren a nasty look. Warren looked away, biting his lower lip.

"It's—so—beautiful!" cried the girl, her bottom lip trembling as she threw her head back and sobbed up at the sky.

"I'm afraid we can never be together, my illness is far too incurable," said Salvador, with a sad shrug and a sigh.

There was no comforting the girl. She wept hysterically into her embroidered handkerchief. Salvador looked at Warren and gestured for advice on what to do with her. Warren spread his hands and shook his head indicating he had no idea.

"I have to go," said Salvador turning back to the girl with a pained expression.

"When can—I see—you again?" asked the young woman between sobs.

"I don't know, I'll um…" Salvador snapped his fingers, "I'll write you a letter," he said.

She smiled ardently.

Warren's shoulders fell.

Salvador grabbed his brother's arm and took off toward the castle as fast as walking could be without turning into running. Warren struggled to keep up. As soon as they were inside the main square, and Salvador was sure they were not being followed, he relaxed.

"Women," he said with a grin. "Who understands them?"

Warren was deep in thought. He looked at the sculpture of the Seer in the center of the square.

Salvador watched him for a moment. "How about you, little brother, any ladies on your mind?"

Warren sighed. "Sometimes I wonder how Nella fairs with the new order of Augden City."

"I knew it," said Salvador with a sly grin. "Having trouble forgetting her, are you?"

Warren looked in the direction of the Diamondell region. In the distance, out past the green fields, a young forest stood at the base of the Monsonett Mountains.

"She's all I can think about," he confessed.

Salvador gripped his shoulders. "Then you must go to her," he said. "I will take care of the Kingdom in your absence. Don't you worry, little brother, I've got your back."

"Thanks," said Warren.

"I'll even help you pack," said Salvador. He turned to the nearest stand where a husky man was selling cabbages and root vegetables.

"A cabbage for his Royal Highness?" he asked.

"We'll take three." Said Salvador, slapping down several gold coins. "And those giant carrots as well."

Warren looked uneasy.

"Well, what are you waiting for?" asked Salvador. "Go!"

Warren rushed to the stables, his heart pounding in his ears. He fed and watered his horse, Moonlight, rushing to make the necessary preparations for his departure. It seemed to him that Moonlight could sense the importance of this journey. Without complaint, the horse allowed him to pick up each of his hooves to check the condition of the horseshoes. Warren pulled his saddle from the wall and placed it over Moonlight's glossy back. The horse sniffed the air with its giant pink nostrils, impatient with excitement.

"Where do you think you're going?" asked a woman's voice behind Warren. Warren turned around to find the Queen dragging Salvador by the ear behind her. The King was at her side with his arms folded across his chest. Warren frowned.

"I thought you had my back?" he asked Salvador.

Salvador winced. "They cornered me!" he said. "Not even a genius could answer the questions they fired at me." He held a rucksack bulging with food in his arms.

"The cabbages gave him away," said the King.

"Mom, Dad, I have to do this," said Warren, adjusting the saddle, and fastening the buckles.

"But what about the ceremony?" asked the Queen.

"You'll have to celebrate without me."

"Warren, don't you dare get on that horse!" said the Queen. She burned the King with a reproachful glare.

"But he needs to go and find a protection spell for the crolackrolite," the King said to her.

The queen glared at him.

The King cleared his throat. "I'm afraid your mother is right, this is no time to leave. You are the future ruler of this city, and as such, you must show the people your commitment to their city."

Salvador looked aghast.

"I understand why you wish me to stay, and yet I am still inclined to go," said Warren.

The King's eyebrows lifted as far up on his forehead as they would go.

"Father, one thing I have learned on my journey," continued Warren, attaching the rucksack Salvador handed him to the saddle and pulling the straps tight, "is to trust myself and do what I know is right. I cannot explain why I need to go, I only feel that it cannot wait."

"Let me at least find you an escort," said the Queen.

"There is no need," said Warren, pulling himself up into the saddle.

"You don't know what could be out there in the new world," she said.

"And I can't wait to find out."

The Queen looked worried.

"I'll be back before you know it," said Warren, and he urged his horse forward. Moonlight burst into flight beneath him, excited to be free as never before, and they raced away from the castle.

THE UNEXPECTED VISITOR

Warren journeyed late into the night. The ground below, once lifeless was now bursting with juicy blades of grass and wildflowers. Plant life seemed to press up from the soil with vigorous buoyant energy. Moonlight had difficulty resisting the tasty grasses, and eyed them with hungry enthusiasm even though Warren had stopped to let him graze several times. Moonlight strode through the forest that newly carpeted the base of the Monsonet Mountains. Even in the dark, birds hooted and chirped their night songs. The stars above illuminated the path ahead, and ferns brushed softly against Warren as he and Moonlight made their way toward Augden City. Warren wondered what he would say to Nella. The feelings that moved within his chest were difficult to put into words. He was horrified at the thought that he would be unable to explain why he had come. Perhaps he was a fool for even taking such a chance.

Not far up ahead, Warren found a rushing stream, and he followed the meandering current until he found himself before Bloom's wooden hut. Warren dismounted, feeling stiff from the ride, and tied his horse to the base of a slender tree where Moonlight could both drink from the stream and snack on some grass while he rested. Warren went to the house. The door was unlocked, and he let himself in. Everything was just as he remembered it. He lit a lamp with one of the red-tipped fire sticks Bloom had kept around the house. Warren couldn't help feeling as though he were trespassing in the quiet room even though he knew he was there to find a way to protect Bloom's own magic from falling into the wrong hands. A worn patch on the rug before the wood stove marked the spot where Wooffen had slept. The chainmail and helmet Warren had left behind only days ago still rested on the bed. He touched the helmet and examined his fingertips. Not a trace of dust had settled on the gleaming object, and yet it felt like so long ago he had placed it there. Warren moved to the pile of books on the desk. There was a note on the table. Warren picked it up and held it to the light.

"*To whomever it may concern,*" it read, "*I leave all my books, scrolls, and other magical texts to Warren Aleafious Mirrimar. The rest of my belongings and property I do hereby entrust to the care of Amelliea Leonora Bravenheart.*"

Warren read it again. Had Bloom known he would not return all along? And who was Amelliea Leonora Bravenheart, he wondered? His horse whinnied outside. Warren glanced up through the window at his restless stallion. Moonlight was anxious to get underway once more, unwilling to let their journey end so quickly.

Warren set Bloom's note back down on the desk. Turning his head to one side, he began to read the titles on the bindings of the thick books stacked in crooked leaning towers on the desk.

"*Self-help Spells of Ennandale*" he read on the weathered cover of a green volume. "*47 Transformational Incantations*" boasted the title of the next book. "*Everyday Magic for the Hopelessly Helpless and the Haplessly Selfless*" spelled the next cover. There were dozens more. Some were about warfare and defense, while others were about gardening with enchanted vegetables, or building magical contraptions.

Finally, Warren's eyes came to rest upon a large, fabric bound, hard cover book. It was purple in color, and heavily worn on the corners. "*Advanced Protective and Restorative spells, by Delominar the Great*" read the flaking golden letters. Warren liked the look of this book right away. Flipping through the dusty, crackling pages, he discovered that it was handwritten. The looped, cursive letters shimmered gold and silver as the pages turned. Warren tucked it under his arm, and blew out the lamp. On his way out, he grabbed the chainmail and helmet from the bed.

Once outside, he stuffed his treasures into his knapsack and untied his horse. Leading Moonlight back toward the trail he felt relieved to be traveling once more. Warren did not look over his shoulder at the little hut shrinking into the background so as to keep at bay the sad thoughts that threatened to overtake him.

They plodded on for many more miles through the dark forest. Warren noticed a distinct absence of fear. It surprised him, to feel so unafraid in this unknown place, and he wondered if it was the nature of the new world, or his own readiness to face whatever came that brought him this new sense of peace. The moon rose and traveled across the sky.

At last, sensing a relentless tiredness settling into his limbs, Warren broke camp for the night. He sighed, noting the plentiful pack of food, pots, pans, and utensils. It seemed the only thing he lacked was an appetite. Preparing his bedding, and tying up Moonlight so that the horse would not overeat during the night, Warren lay awake looking at the sky for a long while. Was he being foolish, he wondered? Perhaps turning back was the wisest thing to do, but he did not want to risk losing Nella's friendship. Lost amidst his wonderings, Warren felt a gentle sinking sensation spread gradually across his body as he drifted off to sleep.

He dreamed he saw an outline of a girl through the trees. He instantly knew who it was and his eyes anxiously sought her face. He saw her through the trees. Warren sat up. Nella stood with her back to him, a vague outline against the dark forest. He was surprised and delighted by her presence. She glanced over her shoulder, and laughed, running barefoot through the brush, her white dress trailing in the night air. Her laughter echoed softly like chimes inside a great chamber. Warren rose from his bed and followed her. She was just out of sight, around the next bend. He pressed on, between trees and over grassy mounds where wispy pools of fog lingered low forming shallow ghostly lakes. Finally catching up to her, Warren reached for her hand. His fingers slipped through hers as through she were a ghost. He looked up at her in alarm.

"Nella, why are you so pale?" he asked, looking into her transparent eyes.

"Because I am only a memory," she replied. "I am your memory of me, that is all that's left."

"How can this be?" asked Warren, trying hard to understand.

"The distance is too great," she replied. "Your memory of me fades a little each day."

"I will find you, no matter where you are."

"I am nowhere you can go, time has separated us forever."

"Am I to never hold you?" asked Warren. "I want only to be with you."

"Then you must find a way back to our time," she whispered sadly.

"How?" asked Warren. He felt himself being suddenly sucked backwards away from where she stood as if by a powerful wind. Nella looked frightened, she reached out to him. "How?" cried Warren again, shouting over a shrill rewinding sound that pierced the air about them. He tried desperately to grab hold of her hand, but it was no use, he was hurled backwards by a compelling invisible force. The forest before him instantly smeared into a single streaked tunnel of blinding light.

Warren awoke with a start. It was daylight. He lay on his back in his sleeping gear. Moonlight chomped at the grass near his head. He had eaten a perfect ring around the tree he had been tied to, and was reaching for a clump of juicy grass just out of his reach. Extending his lips toward it, and leaning hard against his reins, Moonlight strained for the tasty nibble.

Warren wiped the cold sweat from his forehead with the back of his hand, and pushed himself up into a half-seated position.

"I see you have had breakfast without me," he said to his horse, trying to shake the lingering apprehension that remained from his dream. Warren took a sip of water from his flask, and reached for his boots. Pulling out the stockings he had stuffed inside them the night before, he noticed that one was heavier than the other, and had a weighty bulge near the toe end. Dangling the heavy stocking before his nose, Warren examined the lump. A small hole had been chewed in the knitted fabric, clearly indicating the entry point of the intruder. A patch or brownish-grey fur could be seen rising and falling ever so slightly through the hole, and a quiet snoring issued from within the garment. Warren began to gently peel back the stretchy fabric, rolling it up one fold at a time. A whiskery black nose appeared, followed by the large eyes of a sleepy rodent. The creature yawned, revealing a tiny pink tongue, and buckteeth. He seemed awfully comfortable in Warren's hands, repositioning himself to continue napping. Warren grinned at the creature, finally forgetting his unsettling dream, and nestled the rodent-filled stocking onto a large patch of soft grass beside his pillow. He pulled on his other stocking, stuffed his feet into the boots, and proceeded to pack up the small campsite. Before he mounted his horse, Warren placed a bag of mixed nuts beside the sleeping rodent.

By mid-day Warren could hear the distinct roar of waterfalls. It wasn't long before he saw a light through the trees up ahead and at length emerged into a clearing beyond the edge of the forest. The great river rushed before him. It was more turquoise than he remembered. Silver fish splashed at the water's edge. Although he had been here only days before, Warren had difficulty believing that he was in the same place. Where were the lurking dangers hiding behind the dry and twisted tangles of trees? The atmosphere was now so different. The perfumes of flowers and songs of birds hung sweetly in the air, effortless and unending. The trees themselves had changed, blossoming and fruiting abundantly. Warren reached up and plucked a ripe apricot from a branch above. Biting into it, he marveled at the flavor, unable to relate it to anything else he had ever tasted. He urged Moonlight on toward the bridges of Augden City. Workers were busy in the fields tending the city gardens. As he passed, citizens smiled and bowed to him in gratitude. Each time this happened, Warren felt a squeezing sensation in his chest that nearly brought tears to his eyes. He saw the un-burdened postures and attitudes of the people, and he felt a joy for them that ached painfully and would not abate. He felt shy, and humbled, and confident too as he rode across the crystalline bridges and through the glass cobbled streets. He was glad and honored to have played a part in their new found freedom. The glass blowers of Augden city were still repairing the damage done by the dragon. Warren felt a twinge of guilt as he passed them hard at work in the streets. The fortress itself was mostly restored, and it appeared even more magnificent than before. The thick clusters of sparking spiked towers rose high into the blue sky before him. Warren dismounted and handed his horse over to the stable master who lured his tired horse away with oats and fresh carrots. Warren looked up at the arching fortress entrance.

A flutter of twirling movement caught Warren's attention. To one side of the double doors, two dragon bugs landed on the rim of a small fountain. One of them, obviously female, was pale yellow in color and had an elongated snout with protruding pink lips. The other was charcoal black, and had an orange glowing underbelly. The black one tenderly wrapped its tail around its mate and the yellow bug responded in kind.

Warren broke into a smile, recognizing the dragon he had shrunk, and nodded to the guards standing on either side of the entrance. The men respectfully opened the glistening double doors for Warren, and he stepped inside the great fortress.

At once, Wooffen bounded toward him from across the crystalline hall. "Wo-wo-Worren!" he barked, hopping up against the boy, his tail twirling in rapid circles. Warren knelt and affectionately petted the Basset Hound.

"Wooffen, how have you been?" asked Warren taking one of his paws in his hands.

"Wo-Wooffen loves Nella," said the dog, giving Warren a sloppy lick. Warren rubbed the drool from the side of his face with his sleeve and looked up. Nella rose from her throne at the other end of the shimmering hall. It was a different looking thrown than the one Warren remembered. This one was smoother, and lighter looking. Warren could see Nella smiling from afar. He felt the air grow suddenly still inside his lungs as she approached. She was dressed in a freshly sewn gown. The dress was fitted at the top, with long, lacy sleeves that scooped off her shoulders. A billowing skirt arched out from her waistline and fell down to the floor in weightless cascades of gathered fabric. Various shades of shimmering grey silk trailed behind her. As she walked, glass slippers clicked quietly against the floor. They could be seen winking from beneath the front tiers of her long silver skirt. A portion of her hair was braided across her forehead hugging the base of a short crystalline crown encircling her head. The rest of her locks fell down her back in a wavy auburn river. In this lavish dress, surrounded by the sparking refractions of the crystal fortress, she fit the part of a queen perfectly. She beamed at Warren.

"So you are young, triumphant, and beautiful, is there anything left for you to desire?" asked Warren rising to meet her.

"The pursuit of desire can never yield lasting satisfaction," replied Nella. "For one may quench his thirst, but will always become thirsty once more."

"Your answer only inspires more questions," said Warren. "Tell me what, then, is truly satisfying in this world?"

"To know that all is well, and to see a dear friend," she said, moving forward for an embrace.

Warren felt a long row of silky buttons trailing down her back beneath his fingers.

"I have so much to tell you," she said, pulling back. Her eyes shone brightly. "It turns out, I have a squirrelitorium!"

"I can't wait to see it," said Warren, still holding her and looking deep into her blue eyes. Wooffen jumped around them barking happily.

"Squirrrrrrels! Ooooh! Woof-Wooffen like!"

"The squirrelitorium contains all the rarest squirrels in the world," explained Nella.

"Awwoo!" howled Wooffen, "Black ones, and rrrred ones, brrrown ones, wo-wo-white ones, and even grrrrey ones…"

Warren laughed.

"Oh, but you must be tired," said Nella, realizing her guest had journeyed for several days to get there. She moved away.

"No, I am not tired in the least," replied Warren, taking her hand to keep her near him. He noticed a thin silver bracelet on her wrist. The patterns stamped into the metal were complex, as if concealing some kind of ancient coded message.

"This bracelet was found within a chest buried deep inside the dragon's cage. It was discovered when I gave the orders to permanently dismantle the dungeon area."

"Do you think it is the secret treasure the dragon was guarding?" asked Warren.

"I am not entirely certain what it is. Its energy, although unknown, is not negative. I feel it has some important role to play in the formation of the new world."

Warren looked into her eyes.

"You have a question?" inquired Nella.

"I have come to ask you…"

"Yes?" she asked. He held her hand. Her palm radiated warmth.

"I've come to ask—" he began again, breaking off for the second time, distracted by the sound of commotion outside the entrance of the main hall. Wooffen growled. Warren and Nella both turned their attention to the carved glass doors just as they burst open and a haggard, dirty man stumbled into the room followed by several disgruntled guards. The man had a watery, grey mustache that hung down over his lips. He was dressed in a most peculiar way. He wore a grimy, long-sleeved tunic buttoned down the front, loose uncomfortable-looking slacks, and shallow glossy shoes. An angular striped ribbon dangled limply around his neck.

"Your majesty, we tried to stop him—" began one of the guards. Nella silenced him with a gesture, focusing her attention on the newcomer.

"Nella," breathed the man through cracked lips. His silver hair was cut short, in a style uncommon within the seven regions. He stumbled forward, falling on his hands and knees before her. "Earth is in danger," he breathed, his voice hoarse and raspy. He looked up in desperation. "I had nowhere else to turn."

Nella bent down toward him. "Dr. Morgan?" she asked.

Valya Boutenko is a writer, filmmaker, ceramicist, accordionist, gardener, and seamstress. She resides in Ashland, Oregon. Valya enjoys writing books, traveling, and planting apple trees.